Flight to Freedom

D.J. Wilson

"A bold, brave, and u...
complexities of abuse. ...
astute insight that of...
and women, D.J. Wilson creates a powerhouse novel. *Flight to Freedom* shoul...

PRESS®
Medallion Press, Inc.
Printed in USA

Flight to Freedom

D.J. Wilson

7-08
16-

DEDICATION:

To my cousin, Marsha Tharp—A true survivor.

Published 2008 by Medallion Press, Inc.

The MEDALLION PRESS LOGO
is a registered tradmark of Medallion Press, Inc.

Copyright © 2008 by D.J. Wilson
Cover Illustration by Adam Mock
Book design by James Tampa

Typeset in Baskerville
Printed in the United States of America

ISBN#978-193383637-9

10 9 8 7 6 5 4 3 2 1
First Edition

ACKNOWLEDGEMENTS:

Thanks to Vickie King and Marge Smith who have been with me during the writing of each of my books to-date. They are always there to advise and drag me through the rough spots on my exciting journey.

As always, special thanks to Richard, my husband of thirty-two years. Speaking of exciting journeys, I'm looking forward to the next thirty-two years.

Chapter 1

I KILLED MY HUSBAND, A TOWN HERO, AND THEN CALLED THE police and turned myself in.

Two hours later, without a fuss and with handcuffs painfully securing my arms behind me, a policeman led me from my bedroom. I looked back only for a second.

"He's dead as a doornail," I said to the officer and spit on Harland Jeffers's bloody body.

With my head held high, I allowed myself to be escorted to a squad car outside my house. A house that had been more of a prison than the cell I was headed for.

Cameras flashed. Voices, male and female, called to me as police officers cleared a path through the feverish hodgepodge of media clamoring for my attention.

One familiar voice stood out over the noise. "Why did you kill Harland?" Patricia Simpson called from her porch next door.

Because he needed killing. And I, Montana Inez Parsons-Jeffers did just that.

"Tell us how you're feeling." Someone shoved a microphone

in my face.

I pushed it aside.

On top of the world.

"Could we have a statement, Mrs. Jeffers?" the reporter from Channel 12 asked.

I had plenty to say, but not to them. They would never understand what activated the survival juices inside me and caused me to finally, after a lifetime of abuse, put an end to it.

But I understood, and now it was over. Nothing that lay ahead could be as bad as what I'd left behind.

That's how I intended to start out when I wrote a book about my life. Since that was the exact moment my life began, it seemed appropriate.

Even though my next stop was a dismal jail cell, I felt a freedom in my heart that had never been there before. A kind of euphoria that floated me to my new home and numbed my mind against what my hands had done.

I'd shot Harland with the same gun he'd threatened me with so many times I'd lost count. Each time I fired a .38 caliber shell into his hard, muscle-bound body, I giggled like a child listening to balloons pop.

With each blast, my smile widened. I'd wanted Harland to know how happy I was to be putting an end to his reign of terror and to be moving to the next phase of my life while he rotted in his grave. When the third bullet entered somewhere in the vicinity of his cold, dark heart, he gave up. His eyes fluttered shut, and he died. Not until then did I let my smile die, too.

If people knew what my life was like, they would surmise

that the last beating he'd given me had scrambled my brain. But it wasn't the last smack. Or even the one before that. It was a culmination of years of pain, bruises, broken bones, and emotional torture.

It was like the old train that used to go over Cascade Mountain behind our house. Its big black engine would pick up speed, dark gray smoke blowing back, thick at first, then disappearing into nothing. It would go faster and faster, wrapping its way around the mountain until it was out of sight. I used to pretend it forgot to go around the bend and would fly off the side of the mountain and plunge into the valley below.

That's what it was like for me. I just kept picking up steam, faster and faster until I flew off the side of the mountain. I didn't plunge to the valley below, though. I was soaring like an eagle. Gliding and feeling the wind under my wings. If I spent the rest of my life behind locked doors, no one could take that feeling from me.

I looked skyward and said aloud, "I'm free."

The process of being booked into the county jail was lengthy. Had I been in my right mind, it would have been humiliating, demeaning, and utterly devastating. But those emotions, Harland had ripped from my soul many years ago.

For so long, I'd walked in a minefield known as Harland Jeffers and geared my every move to keep him from exploding. Regrettably, I never mastered that dance. There always seemed to be new land mines to navigate, and I wouldn't find them until my husband had beaten me senseless.

So, feeling shame like a normal person when being booked for murder wasn't part of my emotional repertoire. Panic, terror, the pain of broken bones, and the taste of my own blood were so prevalent in my world they struck me incapable of embarrassment.

Shortly before noon the next morning, I shuffled my shackled feet into a noisy courtroom for my arraignment. My brain said this was a bad thing, but the word evoked a gala celebration like the coronation of a queen. *Arraignment. My* arraignment. Although my addled brain entertained such silly thoughts, my heart knew the truth. At the end of my new journey one of two things awaited me—a lifetime behind bars or court-ordered death. I was ready for either.

"Mrs. Jeffers?" The judge spoke in a stern tone that told me he'd unsuccessfully been trying to get my attention.

"Yes, sir."

"You are brought before this court today charged with first-degree murder of your husband, Harland Allen Jeffers."

"Yes, sir. I killed him."

Spectators whispered behind me. Their buzzing swirled around me like bees in a hive.

"Order." The judge slammed his gavel down one loud time. I jumped. The courtroom went silent. "Mrs. Jeffers, do you have an attorney present?"

I shook my head.

"State your answers aloud, please." He pointed to the stenographer. "Mrs. Jackson must write what you say. Shaking your head doesn't work." He gave me a tight-lipped smile.

I started to nod in agreement, but caught myself. "No, sir. I don't need an attorney. I've already signed a confession."

"I have that paper right here, Mrs. Jeffers, but you need representation to help you through the legal steps. I'm going to postpone this until you've had benefit of counsel. The court will appoint one for you." He shuffled through a file. "You'll be held without bail. Your attorney will be in touch with you. Dismissed." Again he banged his gavel.

I was led through a side door by a guard whose hand was locked around my upper arm. My usual gait was wide strides and swinging arms, but handcuffs and shackles made it difficult to move. I stumbled and another guard grabbed my other arm, lifting me upright. Pain shot through my shoulder. I bit my lower lip and refused to cry out. Years of practice made that possible. Crying only made Harland angrier, more vicious.

"Take your punishment like a man." Harland's voice echoed in my head.

Not until the guard removed my cuffs, closed the cell door, and disappeared down the hallway did I rub my aching arm. Gently, I shoved the neck of my orange jail uniform aside to look at my shoulder. Just as I suspected, an ugly purple bruise colored a large area of my collarbone and upper arm. A vivid reminder of Harland slamming my body into the corner of the dresser.

I tried not to think about the final minutes before I'd shot Harland to death, but the pain brought it flooding back.

"You lousy bitch." Harland's punch to my stomach had doubled me over and dropped me to the floor. He towered above me, spewing the mantra I'd heard over and over again during the past ten years.

"I own you. You do what I say, when I say, and never," he grabbed my arm and yanked me to my feet, "never question me about anything." He put his nose on mine. "Do you understand, you worthless piece of shit?"

"Yes, sir," I replied the way I knew I'd better.

"You know you're not allowed in my private drawer. That's why it's locked all the time, because you can't mind your own business."

It would serve no purpose to make up an excuse why I'd broken into the top drawer of our dresser. I'd made the grievous mistake of allowing the adrenaline pounding through my body to drown out any sounds or thoughts other than finding the evidence I needed. I hadn't heard him pull into the driveway or enter the back door.

It wasn't until he'd gathered a hank of my hair in his fist and twisted me to face him that I even knew he was there. It was too late for a defense. Like Harland had always said, I would have to take my punishment like a man.

The clanging of the jail cell snatched me back to the present. The guard swung the door open and motioned with a jerk of her head.

"Let's go, Jeffers."

Out of habit, I adjusted the neck of my uniform to make sure my bruises were hidden. My usual wardrobe consisted of high collars and turtlenecks. Except in a few rare cases, Harland didn't hit my face. He concentrated his trademarks to areas of my body that could be hidden by clothes. I often wondered how he could be so out of control, yet precise at the same time.

The guard led me to a room with cold, gray block walls, a long metal table, and a few chairs scattered around it. A light hung suspended from the ceiling. It reminded me of a scene from so many black and white films of long ago, where the room would be dark except for a light just like the one hanging over me. In the movies, it was under that light the murderer would be forced to confess. That wouldn't be necessary for me. I'd already told everyone I'd killed Harland. Except when I talked to God and asked him to forgive my sins, I didn't apologize to anyone for what I'd done. I never would.

I was left alone in the quiet room, wondering why I'd been brought there. I didn't like all the quiet. It gave the voices in my head too much time to ramble on about things I never wanted to think about again.

"He's dead," I whispered. "It's over. Please be quiet." I closed my eyes. "He'll never hurt me again."

The door opened, and I jerked my gaze to it. My heart lodged in my throat.

"My God, what are you doing here?" I stood up.

"Stay in your seat," the guard said.

I sat back down, but my gaze never left the well-dressed man who'd entered and placed his briefcase on the table.

"If you need anything, I'll be out here, Mr. Kane." The guard stepped out and closed the door.

"How are you doing, Montana?" Phillip Kane's question confused me even more than his presence.

"How should I be doing? Is there a handbook somewhere that tells me how to be at this moment?" I hadn't meant to be sarcastic, but it came out that way.

"I guess that was a stupid question."

"Are you my court-appointed lawyer?" Even as the words left my mouth, I knew he wasn't. He was a tax attorney who practiced over one hundred miles away in Camden. What was he doing here?

"No, there was a write-up in the morning paper about you. I saw it and had to come see how much of what happened was my fault." His words took me by surprise.

I half expected him to smile. Surely it was a joke. But he didn't.

"How could any of this be your fault?" I asked.

"Well, I did encourage you to do whatever it took to get free. So, when I read the news, I thought you had done the ultimate to get away from him." He touched my folded hands. "I've made calls to some of the best defense attorneys in the state. I'm here to help."

"There isn't any help for me. I killed him, and I've confessed. Sounds like the case is closed to me. And I'm okay with that." I forced a smile.

"Well, I'm not. I should have done more when you came to talk to me. Even though you told me you were asking for advice for a friend, I saw the desperation in your eyes. I knew it was you. I should have done something to help you get away from him, but I didn't." He shook his head. "I truthfully don't even remember what I said to you that day. I'm sure it was the little speech I tend to give all women who approach me for advice about getting away from an abusive husband. 'You deserve better. Get away from him. Do whatever it takes to get free.'"

He stared at me. There it was. The compassion I'd seen the first time I heard him talking before a group of ladies about raising money for a battered women's shelter in our town. The same compassion I'd seen the day I waited for him to emerge from a church where he had made his plea to another group of women. He had invited me to sit in his car while we talked. He had a kindness in his gaze that let others know he truly understood.

On that day, his "little speech," as he called it, had done nothing to encourage me to kill Harland, as he suggested. But his empathy gave me the courage to start the tedious journey of getting away. It wasn't his fault I'd screwed up my flight to freedom and had killed the man who tried to stop me.

"There is nothing either of us can do to change what happened, but I can get the best criminal attorney to make things go as easily as possible for you," Mr. Kane said.

"According to the judge, I must have someone to walk me

through the steps of pleading guilty. You can do that."

"No, I can't. I'm a tax attorney."

"What does that have to do with it? I would think that if you are a lawyer, you're a lawyer."

"You need someone who knows the ins and outs of this kind of law. I know from personal experience what happens to a woman who defends herself against a monster and goes to prison with no one ever knowing the horrendous torture she'd suffered. Or her story about protecting herself and her son. No one understood that it actually came down to one thing for you—staying alive."

I'd heard the heartrending story of his mother killing his father. Phillip Kane had been only six years old. That was the basis of his plea for funds to build a shelter for women like his mother. Women like me. So we'd have a place to turn when the one who professed to love us also promised to kill us.

"My mother didn't have anyone to stand up for her. The court appointed a total fool who couldn't be bothered. She was sentenced to life, which for her turned out to be six years. Not because she was paroled, but because she died in a jail cell from the loneliness of missing her little boy." Mr. Kane spoke with a catch in this throat.

"What could anyone have done for her?" To me it was pretty cut-and-dried—you commit murder, you pay the price.

"The court needed to hear the extenuating circumstances that drove Mom to kill my father. Had I been older and able to protect her, I would have killed him myself. He deserved to die. My mother didn't." He cleared his throat. "She should have been advised to plead self-defense and given the chance to tell her story. Had a jury heard the way she suffered, I believe they would have let her go or, at the very least, seen she was rehabilitated to get her self-confidence back. My father had made her feel she wasn't worth saving so, in the end, she gave up on herself and on life."

"You truly do understand, don't you?"

"Yes, I do. I couldn't help my mom, but I can get someone to help you."

"It sounds to me like you know exactly what needs to be done. I have a feeling you've researched this thoroughly, and you know what you would have done to defend your mother." Our gazes locked. "Since you and the judge say I need help, then I'll believe you, but I'm only taking it because you say so, Mr. Kane, and only if it comes from you."

He couldn't be much of a poker player because I read his thoughts so easily. I knew the moment his mind relented. His eyes smiled, and he said, "Okay, I'll do it, but only if you call me Phillip."

Later that afternoon, I returned to my cell. Weary from hours of answering Phillip's questions, I was sick to my stomach from some of the things I was forced to remember. By the time our session was over, he appeared as tired as I was. He left with a promise to come back the next day and to pick up where we'd left off. That was somewhere around the time I was relating how my good-for-nothing brother died at the hands of an enraged husband.

There on the hard cot, lying on top of a scratchy wool blanket and a pillow that smelled of disinfected old sweat, I couldn't think of any part of my younger life without remembering how cruel my older brother, Joe, had always been.

Through the years, while I searched for something to occupy my idle hands and stave off insanity, I'd tried many times to write the story of my life. I'd start with something like—I, Montana Inez Parsons, was born on May 14, 1946, in Franklin, North Carolina, on a farm passed on to my mama by her father, John Joshua Whitmore. God rest their souls.

All my life, I'd been told that when I was born, Mama stared at the mountain laurel bush that tapped gently against her bedroom window. She stared so hard she went into a trance and didn't come out until a wrinkled and bluish-red baby girl came into the world, butt first, not screaming, just cooing cat-like meows.

It seemed my entrance into this hard world set the tone for the rest of my life. I quietly backed into everything. Never seeing the whole picture until I turned around. Then always too late.

Now at age thirty-one, I was making my first headlong jump, and I was doing it with a loud commotion.

I rose from my cot and went to the cell bars. Funny, but now that I thought about it, that was as far as I'd ever gotten with writing my life story, because Joe's face would materialize and bring with it things I didn't want to recall.

Allowing the slightest thought of Joe to enter my mind caused my stomach to lurch. My raw nerves ached, and bile inched its way into my throat. He'd definitely been the first to teach me the meaning of the word *cruel*.

I remember one particular morning when I was eight. The rooster crowed its signal for all the members of the Parsons' household to rise.

I had been the first to the breakfast table and the last to be served. Nothing new there.

"I found Ally deader than a doornail this morning," my

older brother, Joe, announced without a thread of remorse in his teenage, cracking voice.

My fork stopped mid-shovel between my plate and my trembling lips. "What happened to her?" I asked. "She was fine when I fed her last evening." Tears blurred Joe's smirking face.

"How should I know, Idget?" He was happy to be the bearer of this bad news about my pet goat. "When I went into the barn to milk the cows, she was layin' there on her side, tongue hanging out like this." He made what he thought was a humorous attempt at imitating the dead goat and then continued. "I kicked her in the butt. But she didn't move a hair. Deader than a doornail, she is."

My mind refused to believe it. A calendar hung on the back of the kitchen door that led to the basement. It had been a Christmas present from the owner of Bryson's Feed Store, and Mom had tacked it to the door with a nail. My young mind surmised that was a doornail, and it was truly dead. Ally was my dearest, actually my only, friend. Now she was dead. Deader than a doornail.

The pain of what that meant hammered through my shaking body. Sadness weighted my shoulders, and I couldn't stand up.

My two younger brothers, Casey and Don, joined Joe in a round of uproarious laughter.

"That's enough, boys," Ma said.

"May I be excused?" I watched my tears drop onto my scrambled eggs.

"Yes, dear." Ma hugged my shoulder. "You can go start digging a hole for Ally. She can't lie out there all day until you get home from school." Removing my plate from the table, she shoveled the remaining scraps into the pigs' slop pail. "I can't do it because I have tomatoes rotting on the vine. Casey, you go help your sister."

As if the cruelty of losing my best friend wasn't enough, I'd also have to dig her grave and put her into the cold, dark hole. But I knew the rules. If we wanted a pet, we had to take care of it from its beginning to its end. I sailed out the screen door and into the backyard away from the laughter of the other Parsons kids.

Again, the reality of how cruel life can be came four years later when my mother died. To this day, I don't know why she died. My twelve-year-old mind could only understand that my mother had coughed until she was dead. We put her into a cold, dark hole not far from Ally's grave.

I thought those were the most miserable times of my life—when Ally died and then when Mom died. Later, when Joe did unspeakable things to me, everything else paled by comparison.

Should I have told Phillip the deep, dark secret about Joe? How could I? Just thinking about it caused me to shake violently and the pain of a full-blown migraine disabled me. I'd long ago decided the instant, painful reaction was my body's way of protecting me from a complete mental breakdown.

No, I'd told Phillip all I could about my brother. I'd truthfully answered all his questions. Surely that would be enough.

"Do you have any family I need to contact for you?" Phillip asked.

"No, my mother and father died when I was very young. I haven't seen my two younger brothers since they were taken away when our older brother was killed. That's all the family I had, and they're all gone."

"How was your brother killed?" Phillip's voice was soft and laced with more kindness than I'd ever heard from a man.

"We were living on what was left of the family farm. Two

years after Mom died, Joe married Sue Ellen Masters. She was four months pregnant at the time. They had a beautiful little girl, Constance."

I had to stop speaking for a moment. I could still smell the sweetness of Johnson's Baby Powder and hear the coos of a baby girl soft and warm in my arms. So many years ago, yet still so vivid in my mind. Longing painfully banded my heart.

"I miss her." I hadn't meant to say that out loud.

"I'm sure your niece was very special to you." Phillip brought me back just before my welling tears could spill over.

I rubbed the heel of my hands into my eyes to wipe the waterworks away.

"I know you're tired," Phillip said. "Why don't you tell me about your brother's death and then we'll call it a day?"

"Sure." I cleared away the knot of dread in my throat. "We had a couple of cows and horses on the farm. Dr. Hauser, the local vet, had made several trips for different reasons to the farm. Each time his wife came with him."

I rose and walked to the barred window that overlooked a parking lot several stories below. The people who milled around on the street were free to go where they wanted to. I'd never be able to do that again. I expected regret to finally find its way into my heart, but it didn't. That kind of freedom didn't matter. Never feeling Harland's fist fly into my body ever again was all that mattered to me.

"Montana?" Phillip stood next to me. "Do you want to wait until tomorrow to finish this?"

I looked up at him. "No. I'll tell you about it. It was well known around town that Dr. Hauser's wife liked men. Every time she came to the farm, she would prance around Joe like a bitch in heat. He ate it up. While Dr. Hauser went to the pasture to treat the animals, his wife and Joe would disappear into the barn.

"I would stay in the house with Sue Ellen. She'd sit in the rocker and hide her face in her baby's blanket, nestled next to Constance's cheek. Sue Ellen would cry softly the whole time Joe and the vet's wife were in the barn. I would watch from the kitchen window, holding my breath and hoping Dr. Hauser wouldn't come back to his car before they'd emerged from the barn.

"About the fourth time this happened, their luck ran out. As they came out of the barn, giggling, flushed, and straightening their clothes, Dr. Hauser was waiting for them. He reached into his doctor's bag and pulled out a gun.

"Mrs. Hauser took a step in her husband's direction, and he shot her." I stopped and turned away from Phillip. I didn't want to see his reaction to what I had to say next.

"I was so disappointed. So angry. The doctor killed his beautiful wife and left my brother unscathed. I wanted him dead, too. As if he'd heard my thoughts, Dr. Hauser shot Joe in the stomach. He went down and flopped around like a chicken with its head cut off." I shuddered.

Phillip moved behind me and put his arms on my shoulders. "I'm sure that was hard to witness."

"No, it wasn't. Joe was evil and caused pain and suffering with every fiber of his body. I was glad when he took his last breath."

I spun to face Phillip. "Do you think I'm evil for feeling that way?"

"Of course not. I'm sure you were feeling the injustice done to your sister-in-law. Her husband was unfaithful right under her nose. That was a terrible thing for him to do."

Phillip's words jarred me like a slap. I had never felt the unfairness for Sue Ellen. My thoughts were only for myself and the wrong Joe had done to me. I shook my head to dispel all the ugliness.

"I'm really tired. Maybe we should stop for today," I said.

"Okay. I want to know every facet of your life, Montana. Even if you think it isn't important, I want to know it. All the information I gather will fit together like a jigsaw puzzle and help me get to the heart of the real Montana."

That night, as I lay in my cell, wishing for sleep but finding none, I thought about the fact Phillip wanted to know the real Montana. How could I be of help to him when even I didn't know myself? I was a thirty-one-year-old woman who shot her forty-three-year-old husband three times. I wasn't sure I wanted to know the person inside me who could do that and feel nothing but happiness that he was dead.

When sleep finally came, it brought night terrors I hadn't experienced in years. The imaginary goblins hiding in dark cracks of my dreams melded with facts of real life, forming a kaleidoscope of good, bad, and evil. I was left with the harrowing task of sorting it all out.

Distorted features of Joe's tortured face towered above me. I squeezed my eyes shut. My throat ached with a scream that wouldn't come out. When I looked again, Joe's eyes glared at me through small slits of a death mask.

I pushed him away, but he started to cry. I looked at my hands and found I was holding a baby. Its squeal pierced a part of my heart that had been dead for many years. Someone tried to pull the baby from me. I held her tight.

"Don't take her away," I cried. I clutched the baby to my

chest and looked down, expecting to see Constance's sweet, pink face. But it wasn't Constance. The baby was snatched from my arms.

I screamed, "Berryanne."

In a heartbeat, she was gone.

Chapter 2

Soft crying woke me, and I quickly realized it was my own. I shifted to my side. As the cot's springs creaked in my jail cell, tears rolled onto my pillow. I couldn't control the physical things Harland Jeffers had done to me on a daily basis, but until the past two weeks, I had been able to close out the thoughts that tortured my mind. And that included not thinking or dreaming about Berryanne. Now everything had changed, and I couldn't keep the bad dreams away.

I sat up and rolled my head to ease the stiffness from my neck and shoulders. My new sleeping arrangements were a far cry from the four-hundred-thread-count sheets and heavenly pillow-topped mattress of the bedroom I'd shared with my husband for ten years. The cold, damp floor sent chills from my bare feet to my knees. My legs ached.

I missed the feel of the lush carpet I'd normally felt when I got out of bed, but not enough to wish I was back there. Not enough to want to undo anything I'd done. I could easily face being stripped of the comforts of my old life, if it meant never having to suffer at the hands of Harland Jeffers again.

A shiver shook through me. *Damn.* Why did I only concentrate on the physical abuse he had administered? Harland's worst form of cruelty came in the way he'd manipulated my mind. Early in our relationship, I'd told Harland things I thought my husband should know about me. All I'd done was spoon-feed him ammunition he'd later spit back at me to destroy my soul.

Sunlight inched its way through the high windows across the hall from my jail cell. Sounds of guards and other inmates stirring were growing with each passing minute. It was time to rise and discover what the new day held.

Phillip had said he'd be in as early as he could, but I wasn't sure exactly when that would be. I went through the motions of dressing and fixing my hair. Shortly after I ate breakfast, I met Phillip in the same conference room we'd been in the day before.

"How'd it go last night? Did you get any sleep?" he asked.

"More than I expected to get." I didn't know whether I should tell him about the dreams I'd had. Was it important he know about that part of my life? That was a stupid thought. Of course he had to know about Berryanne, since she was the real reason I'd killed Harland.

"I obtained the file from when you were in foster care. I've only had a chance to glance through it." Phillip took a seat across the table from me and flipped open a folder.

Someone knocked, and as the door opened, the hinges squeaked. The guard I knew only as Sorensen brought in two cups of coffee. She set them on the table and left.

I picked up the hot brew and sipped it.

"Why don't you tell me about being turned over to child services?"

I took another drink while trying to decide where to start. "After my brother was killed, the sheriff came and arrested Dr. Hauser. The child welfare people took me and my two younger brothers to separate foster homes. Sue Ellen and Constance, my brother's wife and daughter, were still at the farm. That was the last time I saw them. They were just gone like someone had taken a big eraser and rubbed them out of my life. To this day I don't know what happened to any of them."

"I'm sorry," he said.

From his soft, sincere tone, I knew he truly was.

"Tell me what happened to you after that."

"I was taken to the home of Joyce and Dirk Spade." I stopped and waited to see if Phillip would recognize the names. He continued to scribble notes on a yellow legal pad, but never showed any sign that the name Spade jarred him in any way.

After a few quiet moments, he looked up. Instead of being freaked out a murderer sat staring at him, he smiled. "It's okay. Take all the time you need." His voice echoed the warmth I saw in his gaze.

I nodded. "I'm fine. The Spade's had a huge two-story house with five bedrooms. They already had two foster babies and another girl. Her name was Vesta, and she was sixteen, just a year older than me."

"Did you two become friends?"

"She's still my best friend."

"Good. We'll need character witnesses. Tell me about your relationship."

I wasn't sure what he meant. "Like what?"

"Just start at the beginning."

"Vesta and I became quick friends. We'd go to school, come home, do chores and our homework. As long as we did what we were told and stayed out of her way, Joyce didn't pay much attention to us. She let us know early on that we were there to help with the housework, and the state paid her to let us live in her house. Right from the beginning, we knew without being told that showing love and affection wasn't part of the deal."

"So you and Vesta formed a bond." Phillip leaned back in his seat and stretched his long legs out onto another chair.

"Vesta and I loved each other. We were like sisters, and I looked up to her. She was older, worldlier, and made me feel she could protect me. I don't know if I would have survived the three years I spent in the Spade's home had it not been for Vesta."

"What was so special about her?" Phillip asked.

"Everything. Her stories made me believe she'd experienced so much more in her life than I would have ever dreamed possible. There was an abandoned barn at the back of the Spade's property. Vesta and I made it our hideaway. She would talk for hours about her parents and two sisters. Vesta's stories of living in a grand home with servants fascinated me. Her parents had loved her more than life itself, but they had been ripped from her by a freight train when she was ten. All killed, leaving her a ward of the state. That was how she'd ended up with the Spades. I'd loved the tales of her playing in hidden passages in the mansion her father had built with money he'd made with wise investments."

"So, you envied her," he stated.

I nodded.

"Did you ever wonder, if she came from such a prestigious place, why she hadn't been provided for by her parents' estate?" Phillip's question was valid.

"I was too young to even think about something like that. I believed she'd had the kind of life I could only experience through her words."

Phillip dropped his feet to the floor and turned to face me. "I assume you came to realize there was something wrong with the picture your friend painted. How long did you go on believing her stories?"

"Not long. We'd had a friend in school whose uncle had been arrested for messing around with her. It was the first time I'd heard the word *incest* or had any idea what it meant. That evening, as we made our trek to the barn, Vesta turned to me and asked if I'd ever had sex with one of my relatives. She asked in the same tone she might have used to ask if I'd tried the new Folger's coffee."

I stopped talking because I couldn't tell Phillip Vesta's question had made me want to scream, "No, never." But I couldn't say it way back then, nor could I say it aloud to Phillip. Quickly, I passed over my reaction to her question and concentrated on telling him about Vesta instead of about me.

"I can still remember what Vesta said about the girl in our class and her perverted uncle. 'For Christ's sake, Mary must be crazy to allow something like that to go on. I'd have just said no.'

"At the time, my thought was that Vesta, forever the one in control, would have done just that. She never would have allowed anyone to touch her in any way unless she wanted it. She would have said no and fought for what she knew was her right. She would have killed anyone who tried to force her. At the time, I'd ached to be that kind of person."

"Something happen to change your way of thinking?" Phillip loosened his tie and unbuttoned the neck of his pale blue shirt.

His self-assurance radiated around him. I absorbed as much of it as I could and then continued. "I discovered Vesta's tales were just that. They were stories loaded with so much crap only an idiot like me would have believed them. I didn't blame her for making up stories about a beautiful home and wonderful parents. The truth was she didn't know who her father was, and she lived with a drug-addicted mother and whatever boyfriend her mother happened to be with at the time."

A large lump clogged my throat. I drank the rest of my strong, cold coffee. Its bitterness stung my tongue in the same way I knew my next words would.

"One evening, Vesta and I started to the barn. Dirk Spade called her to go back to help Joyce with something. She told me to go on, and she'd catch up as soon as she finished."

I couldn't recount aloud to Phillip the things that happened next, but I couldn't stop them from playing vividly through my mind. I tried to rub the images away with the heels of my hands. It did no good. My mind was determined to drag me back to that day so long ago.

While I waited in the barn for Vesta, I'd settled onto the old rug we used on the dirt floor. I'd pulled matches from their hiding place and lit a kerosene lantern we'd found hanging on a nail when we first started going there.

When the door opened, I didn't even look up because I was sure it was Vesta. It was Dirk. He closed the distance between us and pulled me to him so quickly I didn't have time to get away. Even still, in the darkness behind my closed eyes, I could smell the vile mixture of whiskey and cigarettes as his wet, open mouth closed over mine. My mind raced to figure out what Vesta would do to stop what was happening. I managed to kick out, aiming for his groin, but I missed and connected with his thigh. That only made him angry. He slapped me.

My vision swam. I may have lost consciousness because when I came to my senses he was on top of me. I felt him shove himself inside me. Rising to look at my face, he grabbed my shoulders and then shook me, banging my head against the hard ground.

"You ain't a virgin. You're nothing but a whore." He spit in my face. I gagged. I didn't even know what all those names meant, but if they were bad enough, maybe he would leave me alone. But he didn't. He just continued to thrust his heavy body between my legs. Pounding into me until the pain threatened to tear me in half. When he'd grunted his last sound, he rolled off me, and I exhaled the pent-up breath I'd been holding.

"You're a lot more fun than that slut Vesta. You got fight. I like that. She never does anything but lie there and whimper. I get that much from my old lady. I got a feisty piece of ass now. I'm gonna like having you here."

Dirk couldn't steal my innocence, that had already been done, but he did knock my hero off her pedestal and broke my spirit in a different way.

I didn't hear anything else Dirk said. My mind was trying to wrap around the fact that Vesta hadn't fought Dirk. What happened to the friend I'd admired so much? The girl I thought could handle the world. The girl who would never put up with the things I had.

With Dirk's few bitter words, Vesta had been reduced to my level. Although we had remained friends, I would never think of her as my hero again.

Suddenly I realized I'd stopped talking and had been reliving everything in my head. Phillip was waiting patiently for me to continue.

"Sorry. Guess I lapsed into a dark hole," I said to Phillip.

He nodded as if he really understood. "What did Dirk Spade do?"

"He raped Vesta." Why had I said that? Why hadn't I told him what he needed to know? I was confused, and by the look on Phillip's face, he was, too.

"What about you?" he asked. "Did he do the same to you?" Phillip's dark brown eyes flashed with anger, yet they also reflected deep compassion.

"Yes, he raped me, too." As the words sliced through my heart with the same force it had when I was living through it, I buried my face in my arms and began to sob.

Phillip rounded the table and took a seat next to me. Gently he rubbed my back. He didn't push for more; he just let me cry it out. When I felt I could look at him again without crumbling into a pile of humiliation, I raised my head and met his gaze.

I was shocked to look into eyes that showed honest-to-God caring for another human being. Had I truly sensed it, or was I so starved for it that I imagined it?

"I'm so sorry that happened to you." He pulled a handkerchief from his pocket and held it against my nose. "Blow," he said.

I did.

"Can I get you something to drink?" His kindness helped calm me.

I shook my head. "I guess we'd better get through all this. When will I have to go back to court?"

"We have until next week to get everything together. Then we'll have to enter a plea."

"Do you still believe I shouldn't enter a guilty plea and just take the punishment?"

He smiled. "More than ever."

"Thanks."

"Okay, back to Vesta. Where does she live?" Phillip reached across the table and pulled his notepad to him.

"She lives in Carter with her husband and three kids."

"How can I find her? I'll want to talk to her."

"She owns her own beauty salon—*Vesta's* on Delray Street."

"It'll be good to have a character witness who's known you a long time." Phillip jotted notes. "So you two have stayed in touch all these years?"

"Yes, but we don't hang out together. Harland didn't like her, and he'd get very angry when I met her for lunch or anything like that."

I ran my fingers through my hair. The goose egg caused by my head being slammed against the car door had disappeared. The painful memory hadn't.

"Most times, I'd call her from a pay phone while I was at the grocery store or pharmacy. I hadn't seen her in person for years until two weeks ago."

"Where did you see her then?"

"Shortly after Harland left for work, she knocked on my back door. She'd been waiting at the end of the block for him to leave."

"Had she ever done that before?"

"No, she usually waited for me to contact her."

"What was so important for her to come that day?"

"You."

His gaze snapped to me. "Me? How's that?"

"She'd been following the work you were doing to build a battered women's shelter. You were going to be talking at the Ladies' Aide Society, and she wanted me to go and see what you had to say."

"Well, you've already told me you were at that meeting. Did Harland know you went?"

"I didn't think he did, but when I got home that afternoon,

he was waiting in the garage. On the way to see you, I stopped at Kmart to buy shampoo so I would have an excuse for being out of the house.

"I could tell by the look on his face that something was wrong, but I smiled and pulled my shopping bag from the passenger's side of the car." As I told Phillip my story, it was as if I was reliving it.

"Where have you been?" Harland asked. The garage door closed, trapping lingering exhaust fumes. The odor and fear made my stomach pitch.

I'd barely stood when his hand locked around my throat and slammed the back of my head against the car door. Shards of painful light exploded behind my eyelids.

"I needed shampoo." I forced the words past my constricted throat. I couldn't breathe.

He let go of me and snatched the bag from my hand. After fishing out the receipt and looking at it, he shoved it against my nose.

"The time on this receipt says you were there over three hours ago. Where have you been since then?"

Terror and pain froze my brain. "I just went for a ride, that's all."

Again, my head connected with hard metal.

"Why do you always make me hurt you? Do you like it? All you have to do is tell me the truth, and everything would be fine. But you can't do that, can you?"

"What do you want me to say?" I struggled to stay conscious.

"Tell me all about the bitches you listened to whine about their husbands mistreating them. Isn't it sad? *Boo hoo hoo.* Were they all as pathetic as you? Does each of them make their husbands so mad they have no choice but to knock some sense into their heads?" Harland released me and walked into the house.

He had a strange ritual of abuse. He would verbally shatter my world in any room in the house, but physical violence was confined to our bedroom. If he brought blood or damaged a wall with my head, it was hidden in his torture chamber. The rest of the house was the perfect reflection of a happily married couple.

Although he'd started his tirade in the garage, it ended too quickly. I rubbed the knot growing from the back of my head. When I touched my throat, I could feel heat from my skin already bruising. I couldn't concentrate on the pain. I had to stay strong for the next round that was sure to come.

Once inside the house, I went to the kitchen to start our evening meal. I could hear Harland slamming drawers and doors at the back of the house. He was working himself into a frenzy that would only be smothered by hurting me, followed by violent sex.

I was peeling potatoes when he shouted, "Montana, get in here."

I gripped the handle of the paring knife and wondered if it would make enough of a slice into Harland's chest to cut his heart out. Even if it would, at that moment, I didn't think I had it in me to end his miserable existence.

Funny, but two weeks later, I did just that. And the man I'd gone to hear talk to other abused women was listening to my story, trying to learn why I'd killed my husband.

As I was telling my story, Phillip had been taking page after page of notes. I couldn't imagine how the things I told him would do any good, but he was adamant about getting my story told for the sake of other women, his mother, and for me. I didn't understand, but I'd agreed to tell him everything he wanted to know.

"You came to see me again the very next day." His eyebrows

furrowed, expression grim. "Weren't you afraid he'd find out?"

"Terrified. But I needed your advice." That wasn't exactly the truth. "I wanted to hear you say one more time it was okay to leave him. That I wasn't the pond scum Harland had always insisted I was. I needed to hear you say that whatever the consequences, I was worth it."

"That afternoon you were waiting for me in the parking lot of the church where I'd been speaking to another group of potential supporters. I've tried to think back on every second, on every word. But I can't remember much more than the desperation in your eyes. How had he found out you'd come to see me the first time? How could you chance being caught a second time? The very next day." As if he feared I could still be in danger, panic corded Phillip's voice.

I laid my hand on his arm. "I don't have to be afraid anymore. Remember?" I felt I needed to reassure him. "Knowing he can never hurt me again is all that matters. I'm prepared for whatever comes after that."

"Sorry. Sometimes I feel the pain you've suffered because I witnessed it through a child's eyes." Phillip cleared sadness from this throat. "Tell me why you took such a big chance coming to see me that second time."

"The night before, when Harland called me into the bedroom, I went. My heart was beating ninety miles an hour, and it mixed with the ringing in my ears from the banging my head had taken. I don't remember a blow-by-blow description of what Harland did next, because his first blow was to my stomach. I couldn't breathe. As I'd learned to do long ago, I let my mind go numb. I don't know how long I was out of it, but when I came to, I was naked and tied spread-eagled on our bed."

The conference room of the county jail appeared to be getting smaller. The air was stale, and my stomach lurched. A wave of humiliation swept over me. I closed my eyes and prayed it would all go away.

Phillip didn't let it. "Go ahead. It's going to be okay. Finish your story," he urged.

I stood and slowly walked around the long table. I'd made two circles when Phillip grabbed my wrist. Instinctively, I pulled away, but then realized he only wanted me to sit by him. I did, but I couldn't look him in the eye.

"Beating me always seemed to arouse Harland. While I was tied there, he raped me."

"Is that when you decided you needed to talk to me in person?" Phillip asked.

"Not right then. It was when I awoke the next morning. Harland was gone. I was still tied to the bed and out of my mind with terror."

"How did you get free?" Phillip sounded almost as frantic as I had felt when I awoke that morning.

"A strange series of events occurred that day. One of Vesta's regulars was getting her hair done. She told Vesta she'd seen me at the meeting where you were talking, and she figured I was there to possibly invest some of Harland's money since he was always so willing to help in causes like that."

"I've done some background searches on him and found he used some of the money he inherited when his mother passed away to build a children's wing at the hospital," Phillip said.

"Yeah, in the eyes of the community, he was such a benevolent soul. Very few knew the truth."

Phillip nodded. "How'd you get free? Surely you didn't stay there until Jeffers came home, did you?"

"No. Vesta's patron told her she had run into Harland that

afternoon and commended him for investing in the new women's shelter. The woman had told him she saw me there. Vesta started calling the house, and when I didn't answer, she came over. When she looked through a crack in the bedroom curtains and saw me on the bed, she called my name. I told her Harland wasn't there. She picked the lock to the back door, came in, and untied me."

"She picked the lock?" Phillip asked.

I couldn't help but smile and nod. "Yes. Just one of the many talents Vesta possessed."

He smiled, too. "What happened next?"

"I told her I wanted to talk to you, but I couldn't move my car. Harland did all kinds of things like marking tires, checking mileage, different things so he would know if I'd gone somewhere. So, she took me to the church. She went inside and found out when you were expected to come out."

"God, Montana, I know you told me you were asking those questions for a friend, but I knew it was you who was in trouble. I should have done something right then."

"I believe in fate, Phillip. Things turn out the way they're supposed to. I could have asked you to help me, but I chose to distance myself from the truth by pretending I was after information for a friend. I wanted you to tell me step by step what I should do to walk away and never look back. It wasn't your place to do that. It was my decision to make and then to do it."

"But you didn't make a move then. It was two weeks later. What happened?"

"Harland would have never let me simply walk away. I made the decision to gather all the funds I could without him knowing, and then take on a new identity like they do when they place someone in the witness protection program. I had no one to answer to. I was just going to disappear."

"How far did you get with your plan?"

"I couldn't do anything without Harland knowing every move I made, so Vesta did most of the footwork for me. She helped me find a man on Forty-Seventh Street who gave me a fake driver's license and birth certificate. She sold off some of my jewelry, good silverware, a few things Harland wouldn't miss, and then she got a safe-deposit box at the bank and hid the money there."

Phillip closed his eyes and leaned back in his chair. "Did you use the license for any reason?"

"No, I have it all squirreled away in the safe-deposit box. Waiting until I had a flawless plan and somehow found the guts to run."

"Good. Using fake identification is against the law," Phillip said.

My unexpected laugh appeared to surprise him. Hell, it surprised me, too. Definitely a foreign sound coming from me.

"Was that funny?" Phillip smiled.

"I was wondering what they could do to me. Put me in jail?" I laughed again, but stopped abruptly. "I didn't mean to disrespect the system. It's nervous energy trying to find a way to escape."

"I didn't find it disrespectful. I found your laughter very pleasant. Hopefully, we can find a way for you to laugh more often." His eyes twinkled like he'd uncovered a secret.

I had discovered one, too. Some men were capable of kindness.

Phillip glanced at his watch. "Our time is almost up for today. They'll be coming soon to take you back to your cell." He cringed like the words *your cell* tasted bitter on his tongue.

"The second time you came to see me, what did Harland do when he found you had gotten loose from the bondage?"

"He never knew." I sat a little taller and answered Phillip's quizzical look. "Vesta tied me back up, and I waited for Harland. At lunchtime, he came home and set me free. He was still angry about the day before when I'd gone to hear you talk. I think he was afraid I'd told someone and that would put an end to his meticulous reputation." Suddenly, I began to feel ill. I pressed one hand on my stomach.

"If I'd told anyone," I said to Phillip, "he would have killed me. I thought I'd taken my last breath so many times, I'd lost count." My stomach began to roll, and nausea swept through me. I took deep breaths and finally the uneasiness passed.

Phillip touched my hand. "We've done enough for today. I have a lot of work to do this afternoon. You go on back to . . . your room and think about the things we discussed today. Try to remember any other details that might be important to your case."

"What's being done about a funeral for Harland?" I asked.

"They're doing an autopsy first. I'm not sure when they will bury him." Phillip tapped on the door, signaling the guard we were through. "Do you want me to see what I can do so you can attend his funeral?"

The thought hadn't occurred to me. I only wanted to know when they would put his sorry carcass into a dark hole, but I didn't say that to Phillip. "No, thank you. If I saw him all laid out in his casket, I might feel remorse. My survival will come from remembering only what the last few minutes of his life were like. The hatred he had for me, the pain he inflicted, and the look in his eyes when he knew I had won the final battle."

Later that night darkness closed in around my jail cell. It amazed me how much I'd come to think of the cold, stark niche as the safest haven I'd known since my mother died. With four kids and a farm to take care of, she ran it all with an iron hand, but I knew she loved me.

Being her only daughter, sometimes I received special treatment. Later I learned that my brother Joe resented the bond my mother and I had. He'd been a terror and treated me badly, but not until the day of my mother's funeral did I find out how deep his loathing for me truly was.

Joe was seventeen and had worked the farm along side Mom since he was ten. We had no other family, so it was a natural assumption that Joe would continue working the farm, and my two younger brothers would help Joe work the fields after school. The responsibility of cleaning the house, laundry, and cooking would be my job.

The last of the mourners had left us four Parsons children alone in our big farmhouse. The kitchen was clean, and all I wanted to do was go to my room and cry my heart out. I couldn't bear the thought my mother was dead and buried only a few feet from my pet goat that had died a few years before.

I was curled into a fetal position, holding on to my body for dear life. Downstairs, I heard Joe tell my brothers to go milk the two cows. A few minutes later, my door squeaked open, and I turned to find Joe standing by my bed. The sour look on his face was like none I'd seen before. I instinctively grabbed the neck of my nightgown, making sure it was closed.

To this day, the things that happened next were so much of a blur I couldn't retell them if my life depended on it. I just remembered my hands being pinned above my head. As my gown was shoved upward, humiliation hammered my mind. My panties were pulled all the way down and over my ankles. Joe stuffed my underwear into my mouth. After that, there was so much pain in the pit of my stomach I forced myself to black out.

I awoke with a quilt thrown over me. I clicked on the bedside lamp. My gown was still up and my panties on the floor. When I reached for them, my wrists ached. They were covered with purple bruises representing each of Joe's five fingers.

As I crawled out of bed, pain ripped through me. I swiped at tears flooding down my cheeks. *Don't cry. Don't cry*, I told myself. I dressed in my everyday clothes, got back under the covers, and left the light on. I continued to sleep with a light on until a few years after Harland and I were married and he refused to allow it. By that time, I wanted to be in the dark so I wouldn't have to look at the face of the monster sleeping next to me.

During the two years following my mother's death, the light stayed on each night. Unfortunately, it didn't keep Joe away from me. Nothing did. I wished him dead. Like my goat. Like Mom.

But he continued to live while I continued to die a little more every day. After each encounter with the evil being I couldn't even classify as human, I prayed he'd drop dead. I even thought of ways to help that happen. As Joe would button his pants and glare at me through crazed eyes, I'd imagine horrible deaths for him. And when he swore he'd kill me if I told anyone what we had just done, I dreamed of ways of killing him deader than a doornail.

But I didn't. I would just step into a corner of the hayloft and throw up my dinner and continued to heave until I was sure I was rid of all the evil Joe had put inside me. That was my usual response to the twice-weekly event that started the day Mom was buried and continued until Joe married Sue Ellen Masters, the day after I turned fourteen. Even though he left me alone after that, I continued to want to kill him.

Thankfully, and like a blessing from heaven, Dr. Hauser did it for me. I thought it was an answer to every prayer I'd ever had. Little did I know it was only a prelude to the hideous life that awaited me.

When Joe died, so did the chance anyone would ever know what he'd done to me. Even though Phillip kept insisting I tell him everything about my life that was a part I would never tell anyone. Even Vesta didn't know, and I intended to keep it that way.

Phillip made it easy to talk to him. To let the demons in my heart pour out and not feel degraded. He even made me believe I was not the flawed individual I'd always believed I was. I'd been able to tell him everything except what my brother Joe had done. They were unthinkable things, and they were a part of me that no one would ever hear spoken.

The next morning, I was escorted back to the conference room. Expecting to find Phillip waiting, I was startled when I saw a thin woman, with stringy blond hair. She rose and rushed at me. I took a step back and bumped into Sorensen.

"Go ahead and have a seat," the guard said. "Your attorney will be right back."

I moved around the blond woman and sat but never let my gaze stray from her vaguely familiar face. She sat next to me.

"Don't you recognize me, Montana?"

She'd aged and not in a good way. Her voice had lost its girlish tone, but yes, I knew who she was.

"Sue Ellen," I said.

She nodded rapidly and threw her arms around me. "I had to come, Montana. I'm so sorry things have turned out this way for you."

I was at a loss for words. "How . . . how did you find me?"

"Mr. Kane found me. He came to my house yesterday and told me what happened. He said it was important for everyone to know the real Montana. I told him I couldn't have asked for a better sister-in-law." Sue Ellen sucked in a ragged breath. "I've always loved you, Montana. I've missed you so much."

Dumbstruck, I stared at the woman who hadn't been more than a child the last time I saw her. Yes, I had loved her, too, but for reasons she would never suspect. She had taken my place in Joe's screwed-up mind. Sue Ellen was the reason he'd left me alone. I owed a lot to her, but I could never tell her why.

As if she read my mind, my ex-sister-in-law leaned close to me. "I told Mr. Kane," she said.

Panic gripped my throat. What had she told Phillip? She didn't know my darkest secret. She couldn't know. "What did you tell him?" I barely squeaked out the words, and as I waited, my heart quit beating.

"Joe bragged about the things he did to you. He'd threaten me that if I didn't do the weird things he wanted, he'd go to your bed. To help you with your defense, I told Mr. Kane about you and Joe."

Chapter 3

"OH MY GOD, SUE ELLEN, YOU DID WHAT?" I JUMPED TO my feet, sending the chair scraping across the jail's conference room floor. The sound grated against my tender nerve endings causing me to shiver. "How could you tell Phillip what Joe did to me? You had no right. I never wanted anyone to know," I screamed at Sue Ellen. "*You* weren't supposed to know."

She stared at me with a horror-stricken expression—face pale, her usual blue eyes dark with fear, her lips trembling.

"I'm sorry," she cried. "I thought I was helping. I'm so sorry."

I knew she was. Sue Ellen would never deliberately hurt me, but in that moment, as my mind painfully spiraled with the reality that the most horrific moments of my life were now public knowledge, I couldn't comfort her. I couldn't reach out to her and tell her I forgave her.

How could I? I couldn't forgive myself for allowing those things to happen. I'd told myself that I was young and weak. I couldn't keep Joe from hurting me. But what was my excuse now? I was thirty-one years old. Joe had been dead for years.

Yet there I stood, hurting to my bones, feeling my heart crumble slowly, agonizing over every painful second, and knowing Joe had reached out from the grave and raped me again.

By then, Sue Ellen was crying so hard, I thought she might throw up. I wanted to join her, but mortification blanketed me, stealing my ability to move, breathe, or think. I wanted to be dead and never have to look another person in the face.

Listening to Sue Ellen sob, pain and misery swirled in the pit of my stomach. When it subsided, sorrow took its place; but for Sue Ellen, not for me. Every ounce of her remorse resounded in her weeping, and I longed to comfort her. To absorb it from her. After all, it was for me she was mourning.

I pulled her to her feet and into my arms. "It's okay, Sue Ellen," I whispered against her ear. "It's not your fault. None of it is your fault." I held her tightly. She continued to cry, and I automatically sank into my caretaker mode. Although self-appointed, taking care of others had been my lot in life, especially with Vesta and Harland.

Since she was older, I thought Vesta would protect me. But, once I'd come to realize she wasn't as strong as her fabricated life led me to believe, I'd made it my job to protect her in every way I could. I'd do my chores and help Vesta with hers to keep Joyce Spade from beating her. By trying to protect her from Dirk, I usually ended up being the object of his repeated sexual abuse.

With Harland, I thought I'd finally found someone who would shield me from life's injustices. I was wrong again. I ended up taking care of him in every way possible. Not out of desire or duty, but for survival.

Now again, when I wanted so much to simply receive my punishment for killing Harland and to be responsible for no one but myself, the most personal and hurtful part of my life had been ripped from my heart and put on display for all the world to see. Yet, instead of anyone soothing my hurt, I was consoling the person who had told my secret. I felt bad for *her*. I wanted to stop her tears and make her feel better.

"Come on, Sue Ellen." I guided her back to a chair. "It's all going to be all right. Dry your eyes."

She sniffed a couple of times and swiped away her tears. "Will you ever be able to forgive me?" she asked.

My head pounded. My shoulders slumped. "Of course. Just stop crying." I pushed a stray piece of her dirty-blond hair behind her ear. Some sparkle returned to her sad eyes.

"Where have you been all these years?" I asked.

"The government took over your family's land because of back taxes. Constance and I moved to Raleigh with my cousin Kate. You remember her?"

I nodded.

"I went to secretarial school and then to work for an insurance company. I've been there for fifteen years." Her smile quavered.

"That's wonderful. I'm proud for you. And Constance, where is she?"

"She lives in Raleigh, too. She has two little boys, and they are the sweetest things."

"I can't believe that precious little girl I used to hold has two babies of her own." I'd loved my niece very much and often wondered where she was. I closed my eyes and could almost smell her sweetness and feel her in my arms.

"Montana." Sue Ellen touched my arms, which I had unconsciously folded across my chest.

"I've told Constance all about you. As soon as we find out what's going to happen to you, she wants to come see you."

41

"It's probably best if she doesn't come. Both of you need to forget you ever knew me. I'll either be here forever or . . ." I started to say *or I'll be put to death*, but the horrified look in my dear sister-in-law's eyes stopped me. "I don't want her to see me behind bars."

"But I want you to meet Constance," Sue Ellen said. "She looks just like you. She has your dark hair, trim figure, and her eyes twinkle with a light of hope just like yours used to. But your eyes have changed, Montana. They've seen so much sadness, the light has gone out." She choked back a sob. "Oh, dear, I'm so sorry things have turned out this way. Maybe I should have tried to keep you with me instead of allowing them to take you to foster care."

"You were too young. They wouldn't have allowed you to do that. You can't blame yourself."

"Mr. Kane said you have no kids of your own," Sue Ellen said. "Is that because of the things Joe done to you?" Her voice faded.

Her question cut deep. "No, it wasn't anything Joe did."

I knew I'd have to tell Phillip all about the reason Harland and I never had any children, because it was an important part of my life. But right then, I didn't want to volunteer the information to Sue Ellen.

"I shouldn't have asked that," she said, "but it was the first thought that came to my mind when Mr. Kane said you'd never had any of your own."

"No, we never had any." My inability to have children was part of the reason Harland hated me.

"You would have made a wonderful mother." Sue Ellen's warm smile brought me back from the cold thoughts.

"I think I would have, too, but I wasn't given the chance to find out."

The door of the conference room opened, and Phillip Kane stepped in. My gaze snapped in his direction and then back to my lap. Humiliation returned with a vengeance. I closed my eyes.

"Sorry I'm late."

I couldn't look at him. He sat, putting me in the middle between him and Sue Ellen.

"Were you surprised to see your sister-in-law?"

I didn't move.

"I shouldn't have told you about Joe," Sue Ellen said to Phillip.

He quickly analyzed the situation and took my hand. "Listen to me. I want to know *everything* about you. Good, bad, ornery, or just plain rotten." He forced my chin up.

I opened my eyes and met his stern, but gentle stare. "I've seen and heard a lot in my life. Nothing you tell me will shock me. I want to know every detail. I need to be able to put it all together and form my best argument to keep you from spending the rest of your life in prison. Or worse."

A shiver climbed my spine. I knew my punishment was a fact I'd have to face, and I was ready for it, but once in a while, the reality of what that could mean made me shudder.

"Montana, I've taken your case for two reasons: to help you get the least time possible and to do for you what should have been done for my mother. I don't want to fail, but to succeed, I need your help." He smiled, and I tried hard to return it.

"We are in this together. Agreed?" he asked.

I nodded.

"Say it aloud for me."

"We are in this together." I smiled, too.

"Montana and I have a lot of work to do." Phillip stood and

so did Sue Ellen.

"I know." She leaned down to hug me. "Constance and I will be back to see you as soon as they'll let us."

I squeezed her hard. "Thank you."

"I love you, Montana."

I nodded and only managed a weak "I love you, too."

After she left, Phillip and I settled around the table.

"What is the next thing I need to know about you? Don't leave anything out. It's all important in the big picture." Phillip pulled his notepad from his briefcase and readied his pen.

"I guess I need to tell you about Berryanne." I was surprised how sweet her name sounded. "That's the first time I've spoken her name aloud in at least fifteen years."

"I'm not sure who that is, but maybe you need to say it more often," Phillip said. "I can't believe how your eyes danced."

I felt my lips curve at the sides.

"It's good to see you smile."

Quickly, I wiped away any sign of happiness. This wasn't the time or the place. I had more dreadful moments to sort through, none of which contained anything to make me warm and fuzzy.

"Who's Berryanne?" Phillip stared at me expectantly.

"She was my baby girl."

"I didn't realize you and Harland had a child."

"We didn't." I instinctively rubbed my stomach, which fifteen years ago had been swollen with my precious daughter.

Phillip flipped through my foster care folder. "I don't see anything in here about you having a baby."

"You wouldn't. It was a big secret." I swallowed hard. "I . . . got pregnant by Dirk Spade sometime during the first three months I lived in his house." I waited for Phillip's expression to turn hard with disgust, but it didn't. He actually seemed understanding.

"That must have been a tough time. How old were you?"

"It was a few weeks short of my sixteenth birthday when I told Vesta I had skipped my period. Being raised on a farm, I knew enough about the facts of life to know I was pregnant. I was terrified. I didn't know what I was supposed to do or who to tell. How could I tell Joyce I was carrying her husband's baby? The welfare lady only came periodically, but I was never left alone with her. I was afraid if I told Dirk he'd kill me to hide his secret."

"Who did you tell?" Phillip asked.

"Vesta and I didn't tell anyone. I'm not sure what we thought. Maybe that if we ignored it, it would just go away. I knew it was wishful thinking." While I told Phillip the story of the only baby I would ever have, it all played like a bad movie in my mind.

As close as I could figure, I was in my fifth month. Joyce called me into the kitchen and told me to take a seat at the table. I couldn't imagine what I'd done wrong, but I felt I was in deep trouble for something.

"My guess is that you're about five months along." She glared daggers at me.

I splayed my fingers over my protruding tummy.

"Surely you're not stupid enough to think I wouldn't know you're pregnant and who the father is." Her voice was hard and angry.

I just shook my head.

"Here's how things are going to go: Now that you're sixteen, you can legally drop out of school, and you'll do just that. You'll have the baby right here, delivered by a midwife, and the whelp will be put up for adoption. Until then, you will be housebound, and no one is to know you are having my husband's bastard child. Is that understood?"

"I can't give my baby away." I'd already felt its movement inside me and knew I'd love my child forever.

Joyce slammed her fists against the tabletop and pushed to her feet so hard her chair tipped over. My heart hammered painfully against my chest. Tears blurred my eyes.

"This is not a debate. You will do as I say, or there'll be hell to pay!" she screamed.

My paralyzed body had no response. All I could think about was that none of the hell I'd been through so far would compare to giving my baby away, but fear kept me from voicing that thought.

"The midwife will be here in a few minutes to check you out." Joyce leaned closer. "I want you to do as you're told and keep your mouth shut."

She didn't wait for me to say anything. She stormed out of the room, leaving me to wonder if I should wait there, or run as if my life depended on it.

Dirk came through the back door followed by a heavyset woman dressed in a white uniform pantsuit. Her gaze was soft and her smile warm. Some of my fear and panic dissolved until I looked at Dirk's hideous smirk. My hands shook violently. My stomach tumbled. I thought I might be sick.

"It's okay, honey," the woman said. She moved next to me, wrapped her hand around my elbow, and helped me to my feet. "Come on back here with me." She led me to my bedroom. When we got to the door, she turned to Dirk, who had been following us.

"You go find something else to occupy your filthy mind."

The woman spoke in a commanding voice. She crossed her arms, and I took refuge behind her, all the while holding my breath, waiting for Dirk to verbally or physically assault her.

He did neither. When I heard him turn and stomp down the hall, I stole a peek around the large woman. Dirk's retreat was rapid. His hands swung fisted at this side. When the woman left, I was sure there'd be hell to pay, but for the moment I loved that Dirk was apparently afraid of someone. I almost snickered.

The woman turned to me. "He better not hear you laughing at him." She chuckled and guided me inside my bedroom. "My name is Ina. I'm a midwife, and I'll be taking care of you until after your baby is born."

"Taking care of me? Do I get to go live with you?" I prayed it would be true.

"No, I'm afraid not. I'll come by here to check on you once a month for the next couple of months, then every week until you deliver. Let's you and I talk for a while. Do you have any questions?"

I was with Sue Ellen when she went into labor with Constance. I knew she was in a lot of pain, but other than that, I didn't have a clue what giving birth was all about. "I don't guess I do." I shook my head. "Well, maybe one. Can you make them let me keep my baby? I don't want to give it away."

Ina rubbed the back of her hand along my cheek. "No, honey, I can't do that. I work for the adoption agency that will place your baby in the arms of a family who will love and take good care of it. They will give it the kind of life you can't, especially at your young age. Don't you want that for your baby? I would, if I were in your place." Her gentle tone made me feel she was right. I wanted my child to have so much more than I ever had.

Ina examined me and declared I was evidently from good stock and would be able to deliver my baby with no problems. That night, when I told Vesta, she said that one of her mom's boyfriends was a cowboy and that was how he talked about the cows on the ranch. They came from good stock, too.

"Great," I told Vesta, "not only are you comparing me to a cow, but I'm going to be as big as one by the time I deliver this baby."

"You sure are, Montana. Moooove on over." Vesta flipped the covers high in the air and climbed into the bed we'd shared at the Spades.

Long after she'd gone to sleep that night, I lay awake trying to come to terms with the fact that I would carry a baby inside me for four more months and then I would bring it into the world only to have it taken away. Mulling over Ina's words, I had to agree my little boy or girl wouldn't have much of a life with me. Its only hope was for me to let a loving family adopt him or her. Reluctantly, I settled into that way of thinking and longed to have it all over and done with. Time crept by. No matter how hard I tried not to think about the little being growing, kicking, moving, and turning inside me, my love for it multiplied with each passing day.

The next month, when Ina came to see me, she brought me two maternity dresses. My other clothes had grown uncomfortably tight, and I always self-consciously tried to stand behind anything that would hide my tummy. The things Ina brought me were oversized and covered my expanding stomach. I felt grown-up in my mommy-to-be clothes. I spent much of my time pretending I was married and my husband was off protecting foreign shores. As a dutiful wife, I awaited his return.

My vivid imagination was what got me through the long

months of my pregnancy. That, and my friend, Vesta. She constantly did things to make me laugh. The laughter was like medicinal salve rubbed on terrible sores. It soothed and even healed, but the scars were always there.

Three weeks short of my due date, I awoke with a start. A sticky wetness soaked my nightgown and the mattress beneath me. I reached for Vesta. She was wet, too. I shook her.

"Wake up, there's something wrong with—" Before I could finish, a pain sliced through my stomach. I screamed. Vesta flew off the bed and flipped on the light.

"Oh . . . my . . . God," she cried. She opened our bedroom door and called down the hallway. "Joyce, come quick!"

"The baby's trying to come out," I cried. "It's tearing me apart." Wrapping my arms around my stomach, I rolled to a fetal position. "It hurts bad. I must be dying."

"No, you're not." Vesta gripped my hand. "You can't."

Just then Joyce shoved her aside. "Go gather towels. Fill the big stockpot with water and put it on to boil." She stuck her head out the door and bellowed at Dirk, "Call Ina. Montana's in labor."

"It's not time yet. I have three more weeks." I cried.

"Babies can't tell time, you little twit. Don't you know nothing?" Joyce spewed her verbal venom.

"I know there's a place in hell for people like you." I couldn't believe I said that. Vesta sucked in a flabbergasted breath and nearly choked. At that point, I was sure I was dying and had no reason to care what she did to me. I saw Joyce's open palm coming at my face, but I never felt the slap. *Was I already dead?*

Eons later, Ina arrived. She placed a large suitcase on the dresser, opened it, and pulled out things like straps, large pieces of cotton, and strange-looking metal instruments. Hopefully, something in that case of hers would get my baby out of me and stop my pain.

She gave me a shot and instantly the room began to swirl. I hoped I would go to sleep until it was all over, but it wasn't to be. Ina barked orders at Vesta and Joyce and me.

"Take deep breaths, Montana."

She had to be kidding. I couldn't even catch my breath, let alone take deep ones. The pain would stop, and I'd think it was over, only to be hammered again.

"Montana, listen to me," she said. "Count to fifteen. One, two, three . . ." she counted for me. When she got to fifteen, the pain magically started to subside. It quickly started again and this time I counted, too.

Ina spread my legs. "The baby is backward. I'm going to try to turn it." She grunted.

I could tell she was working hard. On our farm, I had helped Joe pull calves from cows during hard births. Ina didn't have to tell me my baby and I were in trouble, and she wasn't able to help us.

"Get an ambulance," she shouted.

Joyce raced from the room only to return moments later with Dirk.

"We can't take her to a hospital," he said. "We don't have the money to pay for it, and that baby has already been promised. Now, you do whatever you need to get it into this world alive and well, and you do it right here in this house."

"Listen, you son of a bitch, if we don't get this child to the hospital right now, she and her baby are going to die. The people who are adopting the baby knew from the beginning something like this could happen. After you call the ambulance, you call Marna and tell her to get Mr. Cullen to meet us at the hospital. Montana will be checked in under his wife's name. Do it now."

Ina's tone of voice left no doubt she was in charge. Dirk hurried away.

I focused on her words that I would be someone's wife. Whose wife? Had my imaginary husband come home from war?

"I'm going to give you some more medicine. It'll make you sleep." Ina pressed her gentle hand against my cheek where Joyce had slapped me and, for a second, Ina glared at Joyce. When she looked back at me, her expression was soft and kind again.

"When you wake up, you'll be in the hospital. This is important, Montana. You have to listen to me. You will tell everyone your name is Grace Cullen. Do you understand? They must believe you are Grace Cullen. Say it for me."

"Grace Cullen," I said.

Ina gave me another shot. My tongue grew thick, and I could taste the bitterness of the drug.

"What's your name?" she asked.

"Grace Cullen. Grace Cullen. Grace Cul . . ."

"Mrs. Cullen." Someone was shaking me and calling me by the wrong name. "Mrs. Cullen, your baby is here. She's hungry. Wake up and meet your daughter."

Slowly my sleepy, fuzzy mind came to life. "My daughter?" I mumbled.

"Yeah, let me help you." The nurse adjusted my bed to a sitting position.

She reached into a plastic bin and handed me a tiny pink bundle. I moved the blanket aside and looked down into the sweetest face I'd ever seen. My heart literally ached from all the love I had for my baby girl. She opened her eyes, and I swear she smiled at me. How could anything so sweet come from that hateful, ugly act with Dirk?

"Hello, Berryanne," I whispered. "I'm your mommy." The words choked me, and tears stung my eyes. Berryanne scrunched her face and began to wail. I looked at the nurse. "What's wrong with her?"

"She's hungry." The woman pulled down one side of my gown. "Here, let me help you." She gently placed the baby's face against my exposed breast. Instinctively, Berryanne latched on and suckled like a piglet on a sow. Although there was some pain involved, it was the greatest sensation I'd ever known.

"You're doing good," the nurse said. "My name is Natalie. Press your call button if you need me."

On her way out the door, she passed Ina.

"Look, Berryanne is eating." I motioned for Ina to come to us. "Isn't it wonderful?"

"You haven't told anyone your real name, have you?" She appeared angry.

I shook my head. "Did I do something wrong?" My heart fell. How could anything that made me feel so needed be wrong?

"No, Montana, you did nothing." Her tone did little to reassure me. "We have to talk. There are things you *must* understand. These are unusual circumstances. You should have had the baby at the Spade's, and she should have been taken immediately to her new parents. But the birth was too difficult. We had to bring you here. You were checked into the hospital under the name of Grace Doris Cullen. For the next two days, you will go by that name. Your husband's name is James. You can't tell anyone who you really are or that when you leave here, your baby will be placed with an adoptive family. Do you understand everything I've said?"

I drew Berryanne closer to me as if to say *she's mine*.

"You've known all along, Mont—Grace, that you couldn't keep the baby. Didn't you?"

My lower lip quivered, but I nodded in agreement.

"None of that has changed. The only difference is you will have to pretend to be Mrs. Cullen until you are discharged from the hospital on the day after tomorrow. Jim Cullen will be by every afternoon so the staff doesn't get suspicious. Do you have any questions?"

I glanced down at Berryanne, who was sleeping, but continuing to eat. "If I'm not here, who will feed her?"

"She'll be given formula from a bottle. Don't worry. She's going to a good family. She'll be well taken care of."

How would I be able to face life without my baby? How would I ever be able to let them take Berryanne from my arms? I couldn't let that happen. She filled a huge hole in my heart. She needed me and more than anything, I needed her.

Phillip Kane had listened with great interest to my story of Berryanne's birth. Thankfully, he hadn't interrupted me because if he had I might not have been able to continue. I had talked so long my throat was dry and raw.

A few minutes after one in the afternoon, Phillip's pager went off. He glanced down at it.

"I'm due in court in an hour. We'll call it quits for today." He stuffed the notepad into his briefcase.

Reaching across the table, he took my hand. "Montana, you

are a phenomenal woman. Any one of the things you've been through would have brought most women to their knees. But you survived, and you're going to survive this, too. Trust me."

"I do trust you to do what's best for me." I squeezed his hand. "I just want you to understand, whatever my punishment is for killing Harland, the burden falls on me for doing it, not on you for not getting me off. I have no reason to want to be free. I have a price to pay and even if that means with my life, I'm ready to face it." I lifted my chin a little higher and looked into Phillip's bewildered stare.

"I'm going to do everything I can to see that doesn't happen, and you promised to help me," he said. He released my hand and held the door open for me. Sorensen led me back to my cell.

When I was alone again, I thought about what Phillip had said about my promise to help him. He wanted to find the magical formula to convince the jury I was a wonderful person, and that it was okay for me to kill a not-so-wonderful person. Phillip had more faith in me than I deserved.

Tomorrow, when I told him the rest of my story, his belief in me would crumble. It would have to after he found out Berryanne was dead, and it was all my fault.

Chapter 4

THE MORNING DIN STARTED SHORTLY AFTER SUNRISE. I'D been awake for hours, tossing and turning, pacing the short space of my confines, or sitting on the edge of the hard, smelly cot listening to someone in a neighboring cell cry from deep inside a broken heart.

I wished I could shed tears. Just cry until my soul was cleansed of the hatred I felt for Harland for killing my dreams. And rid my soul of the loathing I had for myself because I'd waited so long to take my life back from his evil hands.

A female guard opened a cell door a short distance from mine.

"Bircher," she said, "you made bail. Let's go."

I listened to their footsteps disappear down the corridor. Being bailed out wasn't an option for me. I had no family, the deed to my house had only Harland's name on it, and other than the money I'd hidden in a safe-deposit box, I had no cash. The prosecuting attorney had declared me a flight risk. A ridiculous notion, to my way of thinking.

Little did he know I'd made my one and only attempt at

freedom. And I'd succeeded. I had rid myself of the living, breathing monster who'd controlled my every move for the past ten years.

Despite Phillip's insistence that I deserved mercy from the court, I didn't believe it or even want it. *An eye for an eye.* I took Harland's life and I deserved to pay with mine. More than that, I didn't want to spend another minute talking about miserable events in my life. The pain cut deeper each time I even thought about Berryanne. Telling her story could possibly push me into a hole I'd never climb out of.

At breakfast, as I picked through my runny scrambled eggs, I decided to stop the painful recounting of events and demand Phillip enter a plea of guilty on my behalf. With that done, I could leave it all behind me and accept the fate I deserved. No trial. No jury. Never having to speak Berryanne's name aloud again.

Phillip waited for me in the conference room. With papers scattered over the long table, he scribbled ragged notes across a yellow legal pad. He stood and pulled a chair out next to him. I ignored the offered seat and took one across from him.

With my hands folded on the table, I sat ramrod straight and stared at him defiantly. For the first time, I saw beyond the deep brown of his eyes and into the soul of a man with a velvet heart. For this man with a mission, allowing me to enter a guilty plea and close the cell door behind me forever would not be an option. He wanted to save me in a way he couldn't save his mother. How strange that I could root for him to succeed for his mother more than for myself.

Suddenly I realized he was looking at me over his glasses. "Good morning." He smiled widely. "You looked like you were a million miles away."

Uncomfortable at being caught thinking about him, I glanced away. "I was a lot closer than that. I want to plead guilty and get this all over with."

I expected him to look surprised, but he didn't. His steadfast smile melted the stiffness in my shoulders.

"There will be days when you'll feel like that," he said, his voice somewhat reassuring. "I can't say it enough, but you must believe you're doing the right thing. You deserve another chance at life, and that's exactly what we are going to work for. We'll do it together."

I leaned back in my seat and crossed my arms over my chest. I figured that was what he'd say, but my will to fight just wasn't there, especially when nothing could change the inevitable—a life or death sentence. Declare my guilt and get it over. That's all I wanted.

I started to state my case to my honorable counsel, but he stopped me.

"Regardless of how you feel, you deserve to have your story heard and be judged by a jury. You have to give the system a chance to do its job."

I almost laughed out loud. "The system hasn't helped me much so far."

"I know that, but I hope I can change it for other women in your position. My dream is to have a special, safe home in every town, a place where a battered woman can take refuge from her abuser. I believe with all my heart it's a real possibility.

"Hopefully, with hard work and a little luck, you'll be acquitted. Maybe then you can help other battered women, too."

"Luck is something I've never had much of. I don't expect that to change now." I forced a smile. "And I can't even begin to imagine how I could help someone else when I couldn't help myself."

"We'll see," Phillip said with assurance.

I wasn't so sure, but I let his comment pass.

"We were at a very important point in the details of what led up to you kil—" He stopped. "Let's see if we can find a softer way of referring to the incident that landed you where you are today."

"There's no way to soften it. I killed, murdered, snuffed out Harland. He's dead and gone, and, I assume, buried."

Phillip's demeanor changed. "I want you to stop beating yourself up. Harland did enough of that, and there's no reason for you to continue, now that he's out of the picture." Phillip came around the table and sat beside me, taking my hands in his. "Let's get past this part. You are worth saving; I'm going to do everything in my power to do it."

I pulled my hands away and folded them in my lap.

"Right now you are facing one of two possible punishments. What's wrong with laying the extenuating circumstances on the table for a jury to see and then decide your punishment? In the end you could still be facing life in prison or death, but you could also be facing the life you deserve."

He jumped to his feet and moved back to his legal pad. "Finish your story. You were in the hospital under another woman's name and had just given birth to a baby who would be taken away for adoption."

Did I dare believe I deserved another chance at a good life? How could I not when Phillip's conviction filled every word he said? With that in mind, I took the painful journey back to when my precious daughter was born.

Late in the evening, the midwife Ina came into my hospital room. She found me alone and deep in self-pity, uttering useless prayers, and staring out the window at the dark sky.

"Montana?"

I jumped.

She pushed my hair back and handed me a tissue from the bedside table. I must have been a terrible mess with tears and snot streaming down my face. Quickly, I wiped it all away. If only I could so easily wipe away the pain causing the wretched sobs aching at the back of my throat.

Ina held up a black satchel, possibly an old doctor's bag she once used to carry her midwife instruments. "Here are the clothes you and the baby will wear when you leave the hospital in the morning. The nurses will bring the baby to you, and you'll dress her. Once you are released, she'll be given to her new parents, and I'll take you back to the Spade's home."

It took a moment for my sixteen-year-old mind to absorb the actual meaning of Ina's words. My baby was going to be taken from me. Ina had to be crazy if she thought I'd willingly hand my baby over without a fight.

At the mere thought, I shuddered violently. Steeling my heart, I prepared for the fight I sensed lay ahead. Suddenly, panic and despair seized me.

"I don't want to give her away. I want her with me," I screamed at Ina. "You can't have her. And I won't go back to that house again. You know what Dirk did to me. You know he'll do it again. I can't go back to that. Just let me take my baby, and I'll find a place to live on my own."

My body shook so hard my teeth chattered. Ina pulled me against her. "You can't do that. You can't make a living. You have nowhere to live. You're underage. You and your baby will starve to death. Is that what you want?"

I jerked away from Ina. "I wouldn't let that happen. I'll find a way to get by."

"You might be able to eke out an existence for yourself, but while you're doing that, who will watch the baby? And with the miserable amount of money someone your age could make, what kind of life would your daughter have? The people who are waiting to take her in are rich. They'll see she wants for nothing. She'll have the finest of everything, including a college education. Don't you want that for her?"

I slumped as deeply into the pillow as I could. I wanted it to swallow me whole so I didn't have to look at Ina another second. I could tell by her tone and the sad look in her eyes she was speaking the truth. The antiseptic smell of the hospital room and the scent of my own fear gagged me. Tears burned at the back of my eyes. My perfect baby girl could have all the things I'd only dreamed of, and all I had to do was give her away. God help me, I couldn't do it.

"I'll be back in the morning. You know it's for the best. You're no more than a child yourself." Then Ina did something that caught me off guard. She kissed my forehead and whispered, "Berryanne will have a better chance in life because of your selflessness. I'll watch after her for you and make sure she is always loved and cared for.

"And, so you know, Dirk Spade will never touch you or any other girl again. This is my promise to you, my dear, sweet Montana."

Ina pulled away and left quickly, but not before I saw the tears running down her cheeks. I touched my face where hers had been. Her tears dampened my skin. Her sincerity shocked me. She'd actually called my baby by the name I gave her. *Ber-*

ryanne. The sweet sound lingered in my mind long after Ina's tears evaporated from my cheek. I didn't want to disappoint the only adult who'd shown me kindness, but I couldn't let my baby be taken away.

After staring at the green wall for several minutes and counting the time by the loud ticks of the round clock, I conjured up a half-baked idea. As quickly as possible, I dressed in the street clothes Ina had brought for me to wear back to the Spade's house in the morning. Patiently, I sat in the bathroom and waited for the nurse to bring Berryanne to be fed.

"Mrs. Cullen?" The nurse tapped lightly on the bathroom door. "Your baby is here. She's hungry." The doorknob twisted, but I'd locked it in anticipation of that happening.

"I'll be out in a minute," I called. "Just leave the baby in her crib."

"Everything okay?" the woman asked.

"Uh, sure . . . just using the bathroom." I flushed the toilet, washed my hands, and pressed my ear to the door. When I didn't hear anything, I peeked out. The hallway door was closed, and Berryanne lay quietly in the bassinet, waiting for her mama to feed her.

I hoped she would remain quiet for a few more minutes. As quickly as possible, I stuffed diapers and sanitary napkins into the bottom of the satchel. I tugged a thin blanket from my bed and wrapped it around my shoulders.

Berryanne fit nicely on the makeshift mattress inside the old doctor's bag, and I still had room to zip the top enough to hide her away, yet allow air to enter. As if sensing how important it was for her to be quiet, my precious baby didn't make a sound.

I took a quick glance up and down the corridor. A nurse came out of a room two doors from mine and disappeared behind a counter at the nurses' station. I clutched the bag in my arms and hurried to the stairwell marked *Emergency Exit*.

I prayed harder than I ever had in my life. *Please don't let any bells or whistles sound an alarm.* Taking a deep breath, I pushed on the door. It opened with no fanfare. I eased it closed and slowly made my way down the stairs. After descending two flights, I still had three to go.

My shaky legs refused to move on their own, and my knees threatened to buckle with every step. I couldn't let fear or the aftereffects of childbirth paralyze me. I pushed on and on until I reached the first floor.

Through a small window I saw people passing. Even at the late hour, there were too many for me to step into their flow of traffic. I couldn't chance wobbling or even passing out. There was one more flight of stairs leading to a lower level. I had to face those and hope I could find a door to the outside.

I made it down the last steps and then slumped into a corner under the stairs. In the distance I heard machines running, maybe heating units. Yet no heat reached the cold floor where I sat. Chills shuddered through my body. As I took Berryanne from her cocoon, I shook so hard I feared I might drop her.

After I laid her on my lap, I lifted her to my exposed breast, the hospital blanket sheltering us. Fascinated, I watched my baby girl suckle, like a scene I'd witnessed many times back home on the farm, but until that moment, I had no idea what the circle of life was all about. The mama pig, or cow, nurtured her babies until they could survive without her, then they were on their own, growing to adulthood and moving on to have babies of their own.

I wanted to be in that cycle of Berryanne's life, and the only way it could happen was for us to disappear into the night. I had to get moving before someone found us. Quickly, I adjusted my clothes and tried unsuccessfully to burp the baby.

The muffled sound of a door closing somewhere on the basement floor filled me with an urgency to get Berryanne hidden again. After I kissed her cheek and squeezed her gently, I placed her carefully into her hiding place.

"I'll take care of you, sweetheart. I promise," I whispered. On trembling legs, I stood, but had to hold on to the wall until my head quit spinning. When the world stopped shifting around me, I picked up the bag and moved as fast as I could in the opposite direction of the approaching footsteps. The hallway stretched forever in front of me.

Two large doors blocked the end of the corridor. A sign across them announced I'd arrived at the morgue and only authorized personnel could enter. I stopped, wondering what I should do next. I didn't have to look behind me to know someone had turned the corner, and I was now in their sight.

"Hey! What are you doing down here?" a man hollered.

My pounding heart drowned out anything else he might have said. Just before I reached the morgue doors, another hall went to the right. A short distance ahead, I saw a beautiful vision—an exit door. From somewhere deep in my soul, I found the strength to make it there and throw my body against the bar to open the door. An alarm shrilled. I never missed a step. I raced across the street into the parking lot and to an elevator.

The loud alarm and the jostling around inside her cramped bed started Berryanne wailing. I pushed the button several times in rapid succession. The doors slid open. Inside the elevator, I resumed my frantic pushing of the button. Slowly the doors squeaked shut. I selected the sixth and top floor of the garage. While the ancient car moved upward, I freed Berryanne and whispered to her and rocked her until she quieted.

I had stolen my own baby, made a quick, and so far successful escape, but I had absolutely no idea where I would go from there. I hadn't given much thought past making my exit.

The elevator's silver doors parted. A blast of late September air assaulted me and Berryanne. She sucked in a sharp breath. I grasped her against my chest, protecting her from the cold air.

Late at night the parking lot was almost deserted. I crept to the guardrail and slowly looked down to the door across the street where I'd made my way out of the hospital. Surprised, I didn't see any hospital personnel frantically searching the bushes for me and my baby. Relief eased some of the panic gripping my insides. Now, all I had to do was get completely away from the hospital before the nurse discovered Berryanne and I were gone.

I hurried back to the elevator and rode down to the first floor. Once there, I wrapped my tiny girl in the hospital blanket and held her next to me. We left by a back street. Lights from apartments and a few porches made a patchwork of a path through the dark alley.

Near an overflowing dumpster, two cats fought a battle royal, screeching and squalling. As I neared, they sprinted away, almost tripping me. The stench of decaying garbage filled the air. I hugged Berryanne closer so she wouldn't have to smell it. From a second-story open window, a man yelled for someone to shut up, followed by a door slam. Stark fear pounded inside my head, making it hard to think, to make rational decisions.

A little voice told me none of this was rational, but I refused to listen. I walked faster and faster trying to escape anyone who might be after us and to outrun the righteous voices screaming in my brain. My legs shook. Weakness slowed my movement. What if I passed out? What if I fell with the baby? I squeezed her tighter. She whimpered.

I loosened my grip and stopped. Where was I going? I didn't know, but I couldn't go much longer running through the night, in the cold, in my weakened state. What good would I be to Berryanne?

Up ahead on the corner, I saw a business still open, bright with lights. Slowly, trembling, I made my way there. Through the frosted window I saw clothes tumbling in two dryers. Inside the Laundromat, I slumped into a hard wooden chair tucked in a corner. The humid, warm air burned my skin.

A young woman reading a magazine sat a short distance away. She averted her gaze and twisted in her seat, turning her back on me. I'm sure my unkempt hair, baggy dress, and the thermal blanket draped around my shoulders painted a picture of a homeless woman who was subjecting her baby to the dangers of the cold night and the dark streets. That's exactly what I was, except I wasn't a woman, but a child of barely sixteen years, who knew nothing about taking care of herself, let alone a two-day-old baby. My whole body ached with humiliation and shame.

As hard as I fought, I couldn't hold back the tears. Tears for myself and for Berryanne. One lone drop fell from my cheek onto hers, startling her awake. She started crying. I hid my breast under the blanket and pulled her to me so she could eat. That was something I could give my baby. Nourishment and love. I could give Berryanne love.

With that thought, determination straightened my spine and sat me a little taller. I peeked inside her cocoon. My precious baby girl fluttered her eyelids in a wink that gave me the courage to go on. I formulated the next stage of my plan. Somehow I had to get to the barn out back of the Spade's house. There I would be able to get Vesta's help.

As Berryanne quietly ate, the unfriendly woman shoved her clothes into two blue plastic baskets and stacked them together. I played a mind game of connecting the dirty spots on the old, beige floor and pretended not to notice that, until she disappeared through the door, the woman stared at me. I heard her car start and finally disappear. Only then did I take stock of my surroundings.

The large room was filled with rows of dryers, washing machines, folding tables, and vending machines with soap powders, but no other people. Maybe I could stay until daylight came. Then I could walk to the Spade's. How could I do that? I knew the address, but I had no idea where I was or which way to go. Childbirth had stolen my physical strength, and with no food, my weakness would only get worse. Without nourishment, how long would my body produce milk for Berryanne?

Apparently, the overwhelming thoughts and fears numbed my brain. Frozen in the moment, I didn't realize another woman had approached me until she laid her hand on my shoulder. I jumped and clutched Berryanne closer to me.

"Are you okay, missy?" The woman shook me slightly.

"Uh, yes, I'm fine."

"What are you doing out this time of night with such a tiny baby?"

That was only the tip of the iceberg of questions I had no credible answers for. I looked into the woman's soft blue eyes. Kindness stared back at me, and I relaxed a little.

I tucked my left hand under the baby to hide the fact I had no wedding ring. "My husband is on the warpath. I had to get away until he cools down." *God please forgive my lies.*

"Oh, you poor thing. Should I call the police?"

"No," I answered.

"Are you sure?"

"Yes, I'll just go to my friend's house until the morning."

Indecision crossed the woman's face. My heart sank. What should I do next? Only a miracle would get me out of the mess I'd gotten Berryanne and me into.

"Well, honey, it's time for me to close up. I can't leave you in here. Can I drop you somewhere?"

Thank God, she could take me to Vesta's. "You could drop me at my friend's. If I can get to her house, she'll be able to help me."

"Where does she live?"

"1775 Barnes Highway." I held my breath.

"That's really out of my way. It's so late, and I have to get home to my kids. I don't like to leave them alone any longer than I have to. I'm so sorry." She held the door open for me.

I adjusted my clothes and bundled Berryanne. The air blasted icy cold against my warm face. Tears stung my eyes. The Laundromat sat on the corner of the alley I'd walked through and a major street. At midnight, not many cars passed by. With no idea which direction I should go, I started walking along the four-lane highway. Maybe I'd come to something I recognized or to a filling station where I could ask directions to Barnes Highway.

After I'd walked several blocks, I sat in a vacant doorway and changed Berryanne's diaper. "Don't worry, sweetheart, we're going to be just fine. Mommy will take care of you today and forever. I promise." Even as I spoke, I knew it would take a miracle to do it.

I rested only a few minutes and was on my way again. Stepping off the curb, crossing each side street, and hoisting myself, Berryanne, and the satchel back onto the paved sidewalk took every ounce of power within me. I'd only gone a short distance when a car pulled to a stop beside me. I was afraid to look at the driver. Instead I picked up my pace. The car followed.

"Hey, you. Stop," a woman's voice called out.

I glanced at her. It was the lady from the Laundromat.

"Come on, get in. I can't let you and that baby go traipsing off in the night. Besides, at this rate, you'll never get there. Barnes Highway is behind you."

My miracle had arrived.

"My name is Lilly," the woman said.

"Thank you, Lilly."

"What's your name?"

"Montana." Should I have given a fake name? Why? Lilly would drop me off, and I'd never see her again.

"And the baby? What's her name?" Lilly asked.

"Berryanne." My voice cracked with pride.

"That's a very pretty name."

"Thank you." Those were the last words spoken on our twenty-minute ride until the Spade's mailbox came into sight. "Stop at the next driveway, please. That's where my friend lives."

Lilly pulled into the lane leading to the main house. "Just stop here, please." Panic strained my voice.

She stopped. "I don't mind taking you to the front door. Looks like it's quite a hike up there, and in the dark it won't be easy."

I opened the door. "The car lights will wake up the whole house. I'm just going to knock on my friend's window." I got out and then leaned back in. "I can't thank you enough."

Lilly nodded. "Just be safe and take good care of that baby."

As I trekked the incline of the lane, Lilly's headlights brightened my way. Once I'd reached the top and stood at the edge of the Spade's front yard, the lights disappeared. Darkness shrouded us. With weary, uneasy steps, I found my way to the back of the huge house. Even though I wasn't in the bedroom with her, Vesta had my night-light on, making her window easy to find in the dark.

I tapped lightly on the pane and said a silent prayer I wouldn't wake the Spade's. Unfortunately, I hadn't knocked loud enough to even wake Vesta. I tried again. Harder and louder this time. Her eyes opened, and she looked my way. I pressed my nose against the glass so she'd see it was me. Quickly, she scrambled from under the covers and threw open the window.

"What are you doing here?" Vesta visibly shook.

Before I could answer, she pulled back the blanket edge and looked at Berryanne. "Oh my God, Montana. You kidnapped the baby and ran away," she whispered, but her voice vibrated with panic. "You're going to be in so much trouble."

"I don't care. I can't give my baby away. She's part of me. I'm part of her. We belong together." My broken heart weighted my voice. Vesta leaned through the open window and hugged me and Berryanne. We cried together, softly, quietly holding each other as if our lives depended on it. They quite possibly did, because I had no idea what the authorities would do to us if we were caught.

Suddenly, a door closed down the hallway. "Someone's in the bathroom," Vesta whispered. "You go to the barn. I'll bring you some blankets and something to eat."

I shook my head. "What if Dirk finds me?"

"He won't." Vesta shoved me back from the opening. "I'll

be out there as soon as I can get away without anyone hearing me. Go."

She closed the window, and I hurried on to the barn, stumbling once, but righting myself before Berryanne and I went tail over teacup. An animal skittered away, tramping through the crisp fallen leaves and breaking twigs. I stopped short, my heart lodged in my throat. Staring deep into the darkness, I strained to see what lay ahead, but I could see nothing. Not even a hand in front of my face, should Dirk reach out to slap me.

Berryanne began to whimper. I prayed so hard the wind wouldn't carry her cries back to the house that my jaws ached. Finally, I felt the barn rise from the blackness in front of me. I ran my hand over the weathered boards until I touched the hasp. Once inside, I found and lit the lantern Vesta and I used on our secret missions to the barn. Old and abandoned except for unused furniture, it had once made a perfect hideout for me and my friend. Perfect until Dirk made it a dirty place.

Vesta and I didn't venture out there now unless Dirk demanded one of us go for a made-up reason. But we always knew what waited there for us. Ina had promised I never had to worry about that again, but I doubted she could keep him away forever. That was another reason why I had to get completely away from the terrible place and take Berryanne with me. To do that, I would need Vesta's help.

She had to go with me. We both had to escape and make a better life for ourselves. I settled onto the cold, hard ground and changed Berryanne's diaper. I had just nudged my nipple into her tiny mouth when the door swung open. I slumped back into the shadows.

"It's me." Vesta dropped to her knees beside me. She pulled the blanket back and watched wide-eyed as my baby ate at my breast.

"Does that hurt?" Vesta asked.

I shook my head. "No, it makes me feel important to someone for the first time in my life. At first, I didn't know what to do, but she did. She's smart. She knew how to eat, and she didn't cry when I was sneaking her out of the hospital. It was like she knew it was for her own good." I smiled down into her face. "Can you believe it, Vesta? I'm a mother. Berryanne is mine forever."

Vesta grabbed my shoulders firmly. Pain shot through them. I tried to shake free of her hurtful grasp, but she held tight.

"Montana, you know you can't keep that baby. You're probably going to jail for kidnapping. You have to let me tell Joyce so we can get the baby back where she belongs. She's already been adopted out." Vesta shook me. "Now, snap out of it. I'm going to go get Joyce."

I grabbed her arm. "You can't do that. You're my friend. I want you to run away with me. Please. You and Berryanne are all I have in this world. Don't let them take her away from me. Please, I'm begging you."

Chapter 5

VESTA SAGGED BACK ONTO THE COLD, HARD GROUND. THE dim lantern light reflected eerily on the weathered barn walls, but did nothing to hide the misery playing across my dear friend's face. Selfishly, I wanted her to ignore what she felt was right and plunge headfirst into a dark pond, having no idea what lay beneath. I needed her help, but did I have the right to ask such a thing? It wasn't fair of me to ask Vesta to do something that would surely cause her a multitude of problems. I opened my mouth to relieve her of the decision, but she stopped me.

"Okay. I don't think for a minute you can get away with this, but . . . I'll do what I can to help."

My strumming nerves quieted to a low hum. I released a ragged breath and lowered my gaze to Berryanne. She'd finished eating and slept soundly. After I nestled her in a makeshift bed, I looked back at Vesta.

"Thank you for agreeing to help me even though I don't have a clue what to do next."

As if looking inside me, she stared deeply into my eyes. "You're so brave, Montana. I could never have done what you did."

"Brave? I've never been so frightened in my life." Fear still tore at my insides. With each icy stab, my determination doubled. I had to do whatever it took to keep my baby with me. I loved her so much it hurt. I couldn't imagine life without her.

Vesta pulled a fried pork chop and a baked sweet potato from a bag she'd brought from the house. I snatched them like I was starving to death. Even cold they tasted wonderful.

"Slow down," Vesta said. "You'll make yourself sick." She ran her finger along the baby's cheek.

"She's beautiful, isn't she?" I asked.

"Yes, she is. Thank God she looks like you and not that ugly—"

A moan rippled from inside me. Dirk had no place mixed with thoughts of my baby.

Instant remorse darkened Vesta's eyes. "I'm so sorry," she apologized through a constricted throat. "I'll never refer to that son of a bitch and your beautiful daughter in the same breath ever again."

"It's okay. I don't ever think of him with any connection to Berryanne. She's my baby. A true gift from God, and that's all that matters." I spoke from the bottom of my heart. Since the first moment I laid eyes on her, my daughter belonged to no one but me. And I intended to keep it that way.

"Are you going to run away with me?" I cut to the chase. "I have to make plans. Will you be part of them?"

Vesta paused for an immeasurable amount of time. Sadly, I sensed what her answer would be.

"No, Montana, I won't go with you. I have less than two years to be tied up in the foster care system and then I'll be free. I can't take a chance on going to jail for kidnapping." She paused as if she had something important to say. "Please let me get Joyce. If you turn yourself in, your actions will probably be chalked up to fear and desperation."

I shook my head vehemently. "I can't do that. I'm getting out of here with or without your help."

"Please don't be mad. I didn't say I wouldn't help you." Vesta reached into a pocket of her robe and pulled out a wad of money. "Here. Take this." She shoved the bills into my hand.

I stared down at the money. "Where did you get this?"

She twisted her hands in her lap and looked like the weight of the world rested on her shoulders.

"You stole it from Joyce's secret hiding place, didn't you?"

Vesta didn't answer, but I knew I was right. I knew Vesta had jimmied the latch on Joyce's rough-wood keepsake box where she hid money; an old, tarnished wedding band; and a few small items that evidently held some kind of sentiment for Joyce. Of course Vesta and I couldn't ask why Joyce kept a newspaper clipping of a wedding announcement of two people whose names we'd never heard her mention. Or why she kept a lock of dark brown hair fastened to a piece of blue paper with yellowed tape.

"I can't take this." I shoved the money back at Vesta. "Joyce'll know you took it. I'd hate to think what she would do to you."

Vesta pushed my hand away from her. "It's only thirty dollars. She has a lot more than that in there. Unless she counts her money daily, it'll take her a while to miss it."

"But—"

"When and if the time comes, I'll handle the situation with Joyce. You take care of that precious baby and yourself." She rose. "I've got to get back in the house. The sun'll be up soon.

You stay out of sight, and I'll come back tonight."

"Oh, no, I can't stay here. I have to leave before the Spades get up."

"No, you don't. Old Dirk hasn't been out here since Ina threatened him with jail if he bothered any girl in his custody again. Now the only reason he has to come out here is if he intends to do some work, and we both know that ain't going to happen." Vesta snickered. "Oh, and Ina told Joyce that if she stood by with her head up her ass and let Dirk bother any girl again, she'd have her arrested, too."

"Oh my God." I nearly choked on my shock. "What did they say to Ina?"

"Not a thing, but Joyce gasped so hard I thought she was going to suck the paint off the wall."

I laughed for the first time in days. Vesta always made me laugh.

She set a Mason jar close to me. "Drink as much water as you can. You need it so you'll have milk for the baby."

She lifted the old lantern. "This is out of kerosene. It'll go out soon." She handed me a flashlight and rose. "Keep this here. I'll be back as soon as I can after dark tonight. In the meantime you rest so you'll have the strength to leave. Somehow, I'll find a way to get you out of here."

Vesta eased the barn door closed behind her. Even though it made only a slight thump in the silent predawn air, isolation and fear crashed violently through my body and left an ache in my heart and hurting in my lower stomach. While Vesta was with me, I could ignore the burning pain, which intensified with each passing hour. But left alone in the deafening quiet, the intense throbbing took on a life of its own. I wrapped my arms tightly across my stomach and prayed for relief.

I'm not sure if I passed out from the agony or mercifully fallen asleep. But when I awoke I felt better. Streaks of sunlight shone through the cracks in the weather-beaten barn and slashed ribbons of light across Berryanne's sweet face. Her tiny cries reminded me of a weak kitten. I had to feed her before she began to cry loudly, but I also had to use the bathroom.

Quickly, I moved to a corner of the barn, swatting spider webs aside. On unsteady legs, I relieved myself and cleaned up as best I could with only the few supplies I'd brought from the hospital. Several times pain ripped through my belly, and I wondered if it was natural to be in so much discomfort. Or could I have torn my insides out because of the hurried, physical way I had left the hospital?

After changing Berryanne's diaper, I let her eat all she would and then laid her back into her warm and comfy nest. Outside a car door slammed. Through a crack I saw Ina and a man in a business suit walking to the front porch of the old farmhouse. The man wasn't Mr. Cullen, who was to adopt my baby. The guy must be a policeman who'd come to find and arrest me for kidnapping. How could that be? I'd never signed any papers agreeing to give my baby away, so how could I be in trouble for taking what rightfully belonged to me?

That glimmer of hope was short lived. I still had two more years as a ward of the courts. No way I'd be allowed to keep my baby.

Ina and the man went into the house, and I stayed glued to my spot, watching for a sign that someone would be coming in the direction of the barn. When they came back outside, Dirk and Joyce were with them. They stood in a huddle for a few more minutes, and then the stranger and Ina drove away. Dirk piled into his car and sped down the lane, spewing gravel into the air.

For a moment, Joyce shaded her eyes from the bright morning sun and stared at the barn. Even though there was no way she could see me through the tiny slit, a knee-jerk reaction made me jump back. When I dared look again, she was going into the house. I breathed a huge sigh of relief.

As the day dragged on, Berryanne alternated between sleeping and making tiny noises to signal her hunger. Between feedings, I curled into a fetal position and tried to pray away the pain growing in my stomach. I swallowed continuously to keep the queasiness from making me throw up. Chills shook my whole body.

Just before the sun set, I fell asleep and dreamed of my mama cooking dinner in the kitchen while I gathered eggs and fed my goat, Ally, in the barnyard. My heart fluttered with the joy of being in a place I'd loved before the ugliness of life took it all away. Wrapped in the warmth of my mother's love, I floated from the henhouse to the barn, where the air was filled with the sweet scent of fresh hay. I dropped to my knees and buried my face in the straw.

Suddenly, I was shaken awake.

"Wake up, Montana. Please wake up," Vesta called to me, but I didn't want to open my eyes. I didn't want the euphoria of being back on our farm to be snatched away. But it was too late. Instead of the glorious smell of clean hay, I gagged on the odor of the mud-caked straw scattered on the ground inside the Spade's barn. The nausea that had plagued me most of the day tripled its force, and my stomach gave way to dry heaves so powerful I thought I might throw up my guts.

"Montana, you're bleeding." Vesta shined the flashlight over me. "I've got to get help." She handed me the light and then ran from the barn.

I raised enough to see my dress and the blanket under me soaked with blood. Panic crashed down on me. My gaze snapped to Berryanne. She lay sleeping just a few feet from me. She looked so tiny, so fragile, and so pale. My wavy vision distorted her face. I reached for her but never made it. My world went black.

"That's enough for today, Montana." Phillip started gathering his papers from the long table. The big clock on the wall showed 3:15. I'd been pouring my heart out to my attorney for hours in the conference room at the county jail.

As if I'd been shoveling dirt all day, my body ached. My heart pounded painfully inside my chest like a bird wanting to fly away. Years separated me from the saga I'd been telling Phillip, but my mind hurt as if it were just yesterday.

Phillip was right. It was time to stop before my heart exploded with sadness.

Early the next morning, I received word Phillip wouldn't be coming to the jail that day. It was probably just as well because my head throbbed so hard it hurt to open my eyes. Around lunch time, Sorensen, the guard on the day shift, stopped by my cell.

"Jeffers?" Her voice startled me.

I sat up slowly and shaded my eyes from the sunlight blasting through the windows directly across from my cell. "Yes?"

"Somethin' wrong with you?" Sorensen's rough voice

jabbed painfully in my ears.

"Just a headache." One of the worst I'd ever had. "Could I get something for it?"

She walked away and then, in a few minutes, returned with another guard. "Rivers here is going to take you to the infirmary. You're not looking too good."

Rivers' petite frame shrank even more when standing next to Sorensen's six-foot height. Her size left no doubt she could handle any situation hurled her way, but I couldn't picture Rivers taking control of an unruly prisoner. Even I dwarfed her. She escorted me to the in-house clinic.

Being the only patient there at the time, the doctor saw me right away. Rivers waited in a corner of the small examining room.

"How long have you had a headache?" Dr. Michaels asked with the bedside manner of a toad.

"This one started about four this morning." I sat very still and answered as quietly as I could.

"This one? What's that supposed to mean?" Sarcasm dripped from his voice. Perhaps he thought I was there for a fix. Why not? I'm sure he'd seen it many times.

According to the framed document on the wall, he'd been at the county jail for fifteen years. He looked old enough to have retirement nipping at his heels, but I had a feeling he was younger than he appeared.

"I've had migraines for several years." They'd started sometime during the sixth year Harland and I were married. Shortly after he'd bashed my head against our tile bathroom floor. If memory serves me, the cause of my punishment was because there was no toilet paper on the roll. Something that never happened again during our marriage.

"Ever seen a doctor about them?" Dr. Michaels asked.

"Once, but all he did was give me pills that did nothing to relieve the pain."

Somehow Harland had access to a drug he'd inject into me when the headache put me down. I never knew what it was, but I knew it would immobilize me for about twenty-four hours. The aftereffects of the shot were worse than the headache, but the more I complained, the more Harland seemed to enjoy giving them to me. Eventually, I hid the migraines from Harland, but sometimes he knew anyway.

Dr. Michaels shone a light into my eyes, and pain exploded like shards of glass. I cringed. He listened to my heart and looked into my ears. When he gently squeezed my shoulder, I saw the first sign he was capable of compassion. He removed something from a locked metal cabinet. When he turned and I saw he had a vial and syringe, terror flooded through me.

"I don't want a shot." Terror and memories of other shots nearly paralyzed my vocal cords.

"It won't hurt. It'll take the edge off the pain. I'm sure it's all been brought on by tension, and with your situation, that's to be expected."

He filled the syringe and moved closer to me. I slid from the table and out of his reach. "No, I don't want that. Just give me Tylenol, and let me rest for a while."

I'd taken major steps to see that no one ever did anything to me against my will again. That included being shot up with drugs that made me lose control of my thoughts. That had happened for the last time in my life.

I continued to back away. He followed me around the table. From behind, Rivers grabbed my arms. Fear caused me to struggle against her powerful grasp. The more I resisted and begged her to stop, the tighter she held me. She slammed me face first onto the examining table, and in a matter of seconds my hands were secured with handcuffs. Just another reminder of Harland and his abuse.

Unable to move, screams ripped from my throat, and I couldn't stop them. I just didn't want to be hurt anymore. Why couldn't they understand that?

When I felt the stick in my upper arm, I gave up and collapsed against the tearstained paper covering the table. I shook from fear and from the sobs racking my body. The guard and the doctor waited patiently for the drug to work its wonders. Finally, I stopped crying and stood upright.

"Better get her back to her cell while she can still walk. I gave her a pretty hefty dose of Demerol. She'll probably sleep the rest of the afternoon."

Rivers held my arm to steady me all the way back to my cell. Once there, she removed my handcuffs and helped me onto my cot. The drug had kicked in completely. I didn't feel the pain in my head anymore, nor could I feel my legs or my hands.

As I slipped into a dark place, all too familiar to me, all I could think about was how looks could be deceiving. Guard Rivers may have appeared meek and mild, but she had proven she was a force to be reckoned with when she subdued me. I was no match for either her mighty strength or that of the Demerol.

When I was taken to the conference room around ten the next morning, Phillip wasn't there yet. A strange sensation of disappointment filled me. Until that moment, I hadn't realized how much I looked forward to seeing his smile or how much it eased my anxiety. Even though he forced me to speak aloud bits of my life I wanted desperately to forget, somehow he made it all less frightening. He understood my situation in a way no one else ever could. The more I recognized his caring as genuine, the more my trepidation of having my story known gave way to trusting Phillip's promise that it was the right thing to do.

But it was more than how he handled my case. It was also that I'd never met a man like him in all my life. His actions were not totally self-serving. Yes, he wanted to serve justice for his mother, but I believed he also truly cared what happened to me. He understood what I'd been through. His kind words and gentle voice warmed my chilled heart.

Still groggy from the drugs I'd been injected with, I rested my head on my folded arms. The door opened and I snapped to attention, sitting straighter in my seat. Phillip stopped short and mischief danced in his eyes.

"Wow. I didn't expect to see you looking so chipper this morning," he said and laid his briefcase on the table. "You're so bright and smiley."

Smiley? He was right. I was smiling. Instantly, I stopped. "I'm sorry. I guess with what I've done, I really don't have any right to smile."

Phillip sat across from me. "Okay, let's not become a martyr. If anyone has a right to some moments of happiness, however fleeting, I'd say it's you. Besides, it's much nicer looking at your smile than when your face shows your heart has no glimmer of hope for redemption. So, please feel free to smile anytime you like."

Halfheartedly I nodded and smiled weakly.

He grinned. "That's better." He began to pull folders from his briefcase and place them on the table.

"I understand you had an unfortunate incident in the infirmary yesterday. Were you hurt?"

"Just my dignity."

"What about your shoulder?" he asked.

How did he know about my shoulder, where Harland had shoved me into the corner of the dresser moments before I shot him? I hadn't told him about it, and I'd taken care to make sure it was hidden beneath my prison-issued clothing.

"No, it doesn't hurt much anymore, but how did you know about that? I never told you about my shoulder being hurt."

"I saw the pictures."

"What pictures?"

He frowned. "The ones they took of your injuries when you were booked. Don't you remember?"

"I remember that I was naked. Surely you didn't see those." I could feel the heat rising in my cheeks.

"Yes." His gaze stayed centered on the folders.

My mind flashed back to those degrading minutes when I'd been photographed and strip-searched. All I could remember about that time was I thought I should feel embarrassed, but Harland had stolen my ability to do that. Suddenly, my mind tore down that wall. Shame and mortification gushed through me with the force of water through a broken dam.

"Oh my God." I buried my face in my hands. "Will the humiliation ever stop?"

I felt his warm hand settle on my shoulder. His touch brought calm with it.

"You have nothing to be ashamed of. You were hurt by someone bigger than you. But you took your life back, Montana, and you're willing to pay the price for what you did.

"Those pictures will help prove you'd suffered years of abuse

84

by a monster that had enough presence of mind to torture your body in places hidden by clothing. He was an evil being who actually calculated ways of administering pain and suffering." Phillip sat down across from me.

"In a few days we have to go before the judge and make a plea, and I want your head and heart in the same place. You knew the only way you would walk out of the house that night was if Harland was dead. We will make the court understand that, and those new and old bruises and telltale scars visible in those pictures will do it."

Lord, Phillip made it all sound plausible, but still I couldn't let my heart have expectations that would only be taken away. Each thread of hope he gave me was broken by the anguish inside me. I wanted to believe there was a reason to look beyond my present state of being, but harsh realities wouldn't let me do it.

My eyes filled with unwanted tears. To hide them, I buried my face in my trembling hands. Giving in to crying was as embarrassing as the naked pictures the guards had taken of me. I roughly rubbed the heel of my hands against my eyes to shut off the waterworks. Once I was sure I could look at Phillip without falling into a blubbering heap, I moved my hands away and found him waiting patiently for me to regain my composure.

"You are so tolerant of my mood swings." I tried to make light of my meltdown. "I can't even begin to understand why."

Thoughtfulness shown brightly from his brown eyes. "You don't have to understand it. Just believe in yourself."

I shrugged.

Phillip knocked on the door and asked if the guard could get us some coffee. Sorensen returned quickly and set a cup in front of me.

"Thanks," I said and the guard smiled.

"Sure, hon." Sorensen left.

"How's your headache?" Phillip loosened his tie and leaned against the wall.

"It's gone, for now."

"Why didn't you want the medication to get rid of the pain?" He took a sip of coffee.

"It's a long story."

"I'm not going anywhere. Are you?"

"I guess not." His encouragement was reassuring. "I've suffered with severe headaches for the last few years. They started right around the time Harland bashed my head into a tile floor. After days of suffering he finally took me for medical help, but forced me to tell the doctor I'd slipped and hit my head. The doctor gave me some pills and set up a series of tests to find out what was wrong."

Phillip returned to his seat. He laced his fingers behind his head and leaned back until the front legs of the chair were off the floor. "What did he find?"

"I never went for the tests. Harland didn't want to take a chance of anyone finding out what really happened. The headaches continued, and one day he came home with a needle and a bottle of some kind of drug. He injected me with it, and I was knocked out for a whole day. Then for several hours after I woke up, I'd shake and feel like my skin was crawling."

"What was the drug?" Phillips leaned forward, banging his chair to the floor and met my gaze with an angry stare. "What did that bastard give you?"

"I . . . I'm not sure."

Phillip swore loudly and startled me. When I jumped, he reached across the table and took my hands. "I'm sorry. I didn't mean to frighten you." Quickly, he let go and stood, leaving me with a feeling of loss. He rounded the table to look out the window. "So you don't know what he gave you?" His tone had returned to normal.

"I don't have any idea. I just know the aftereffects were worse than the pain. Finally, I learned to live with the headaches, and I hid them as much as possible. I didn't want shots from Harland, and I didn't want any from Dr. Michaels, either, but I had no choice. I guess I'd been so tuned in to the fact Harland was gone, and that I'd never be under his control again, I thought I was free of anyone's control." I sighed. "I had a rude awakening about how wrong I was. I'm in jail. My every move is monitored. I'm at the mercy of almost everyone around me. What I have to realize is that as long as I do what's expected of me, I won't be hurt. With Harland, nothing could have been farther from the truth. No matter what I did, it was *never* the right thing, and the price I paid was always high and painful."

"Well, if we work really hard at it, maybe you won't have to kowtow to anyone ever again. And speaking of that, are you feeling well enough to get back to work? Or, would you like to go back to your cell and rest for the remainder of the day?"

I didn't want to talk about Berryanne anymore. The pain was too great, but I didn't want to go back to my cell and put off having to do the inevitable the next day anyway. Besides, leaving the conference room would also mean leaving Phillip for another day. For some reason I didn't want to explore, I didn't want that, either. "I'm ready," I said.

Phillip returned to his seat. "Okay, you were in the barn bleeding, and Vesta went to get help. Pick it up from there."

"I'm not sure how long I was passed out before Vesta returned. I don't remember much about that time. It was so horrendous I believe I've blocked most of it out."

"What do you remember?"

"I remember coming to in that stinking barn and looking up at Dirk towering over me. For a second, I thought he was there to rape me, but then I saw Joyce and Vesta beside him. I couldn't sit up, but I managed to pull Berryanne into my arms. I was weak, but I held her so tight Dirk couldn't take her.

"About that time Ina arrived. I had no strength left, and she easily lifted my baby away from me. I can still feel the vibration in the back of my throat from my scream. I wanted my baby, but Ina handed Berryanne to Joyce, who quickly left the barn. They didn't care how much I screamed, or how much my arms ached with emptiness, or how much my heart hurt as it crumbled into pieces. No one cared. They just took my precious baby and gave her to total strangers."

"Do you remember going back to the hospital?"

"Yeah, but for some reason, I don't think it was the same hospital. It's like I said, after that, I lost about a year of my memory. I guess I blocked it to keep from losing my mind."

"Your mind seems to be working well now. That's what's important." His voice rang with encouragement.

"If you walked out the door and told anyone else that, I'm sure you would meet with opposition. Everyone thinks I'm a raving lunatic. I killed a man who had pulled me from poverty and gave me the world. He built a children's wing at the hospital and gave to a lot of charities right here in the community. No one ever saw the abuse, so no one will see me as anything other than a crazy woman who killed the town's hero."

"Well . . . we'll let them know what you are really made of and, at the same time, introduce them to the real Harland Jeffers.

"You said you don't remember the time following Berryanne's birth. I spent several hours at the hospital yesterday.

You were right. You weren't taken back to the same hospital. The medical records of Grace Cullen at Hudson General where you gave birth showed you were released by the hospital the morning after you ran away. It showed you were transferred to a clinic in Burton County, and Ina Carver signed you out."

"Ina was the midwife who was to deliver my baby at home," I explained.

"Yeah." Phillip nodded. "I figure she went back to the hospital and took care of the paperwork so no one would ask questions. I'm not sure how she kept it from being a police matter when you disappeared along with the baby into the dead of night, but somehow she did it."

I didn't try to hide my confusion. "I don't understand how all the events during that time now seem so diabolical. Why so much secrecy, and why did I have to lie about who I was?"

"I don't have an answer to that, yet." Phillip pulled more papers from his briefcase. "I didn't have any trouble getting the medical records at Hudson, but the clinic in Burton closed several years ago, and all their records are in a data storage bank. It'll take a few days for me to get the documentation from the court so I can get a copy of the medical records." Phillip gathered his things.

"Are we through already?" I hated the desperation that had seeped into my voice.

He looked at me long and hard. "I wish I could get bail set for you, but the district attorney is adamant you are a flight risk, and the judge agrees. I'm working on a speedy trial, but I have to have your defense solidified before then."

"I understand. I've said it before; I did the crime, and I expect to pay for it, but once in a while a little wistful thinking sneaks in."

He patted my shoulder. "There's nothing wrong with that. And I'm sure it's lonely when you return to your cell."

I tried to smile, but I was sure I missed the mark of looking cheerful. "I've lived with loneliness for many years. My family is gone, and Harland made sure I had no friends. At least in my cell, I can hear inmates' and guards' voices, know others are close by, and not have to fear being slapped because of a wrong move. It's a solitude I can live with."

Phillip checked his watch. "I have to leave for today. I'm temporarily moving my office here to Pinehurst so I don't have that hour drive to and from Camden every day. I'm taking the weekend to get set up, and I need to meet with the partners of my firm. They've agreed to take care of some of my tax cases so I can concentrate on your trial. I'll be back first thing Monday morning. We'll be in court around 10:00 a.m. to enter a not guilty plea."

"I'm having a hard time understanding how I can deliberately shoot Harland, yet you want me to plead not guilty. I *am* guilty, and I feel like a liar saying anything different."

"Harland was a lawyer. I know you understand some of the workings of the legal system."

"Oh, I do understand. I just don't want to get my hopes up."

"Why not? What purpose would it serve to keep your hopes down? You have to believe you deserve a better life than what you've left behind. I barely know you, but I'm convinced you're worth the effort."

His words built a fire beneath my self-confidence and melted a large portion of my heart.

Chapter 6

I SPENT THE WHOLE WEEKEND THINKING ABOUT PHILLIP DE-
claring I was worth the effort to work for a better life. Even
though I knew deep in my soul I had a price to pay, every once
in a while he forced me to see a spark of hope. Granted, it was
fleeting. But each time I let Phillip's optimism penetrate the
steel wall I'd built around my heart, a little of the facade crumbled. Then reality flooded back. It would take all my energy to
put the barricade back up.

I spent the two days since I'd last seen Phillip compartmen-
talizing each thought and each emotion battling inside me. I
had to pay a debt to society. Yet my attorney thought my actions were justified. He was convinced all he had to do was
stand before twelve jurors and lay out my pathetic life in such a
way they'd feel sorry for me and basically give me their stamp of
approval for killing Harland. All I had to do for Phillip to per-
form that magic trick was tell him, and at the same time relive,
the events that had scarred my soul.

The heavy thoughts burned deeply into the pit of my stomach, and just when I thought I would vomit, I'd hear Phillip's voice in my head assuring me a positive outcome was truly possible.

By lights out on Sunday evening, I was exhausted. I figured I'd fall asleep quickly, but that wasn't the case. In the quiet of my cell, my thoughts ricocheted loudly through my brain. If a total stranger like Phillip had so much faith in me, the least I could do was give him something to work with. So I lay on my cot and tried my best to remember the year I'd lost following my baby being taken away, but it didn't come easily. Was it because I couldn't or because I didn't want to remember? I pushed myself to find the answer.

For the first few months, I'm sure I walked through each day doing exactly what was expected of me, because I don't remember being punished. I'm sure I executed my chores as I knew I should. Evidently, I ate enough to stay alive, but short-lived visions of a frail, painfully thin young girl, who had matured way before her time, haunted my dreams. Dark circles around her eyes, sunken cheeks, and lifeless eyes stared back at me from a veined bathroom mirror.

Through the years, I always knew that empty shell of a woman had to be me, but I never allowed myself to think about it. I didn't want to remember those days when anguish tortured my heart. Or the nights when Vesta had to hold me in her arms and soothe my mind with a lullaby before I could fall asleep, only to have the nightmares of that pathetic young girl searching everywhere for something she'd lost, but never quite sure what.

But in the darkness of my stark, desolate jail cell, I had to meet it all head-on. I had closed out a full year of my life. Was it because of losing Berryanne, or was it a respite to prepare me for the horrendous happenings awaiting me? Or was it merely a way to survive?

What were my first recollections following that time? It had to be the day Vesta left the Spade's for good.

"It's only one more year, Montana," Vesta told me. "I'll have all this being-on-our-own stuff figured out by the time you get cut loose from foster care. You'll come to stay with me."

That relieved some of my dread of being left behind and even gave me something to look forward to for a few moments, and then real fear kicked in. "You'll forget all about me. You'll probably be married by then." Panic crawled through me, and I shook violently.

She gripped my shoulders firmly and from arms' length, stared into my eyes. "No, I won't. I'll come and visit you every chance I get until you're eighteen and allowed to leave this hellhole.

"We may not be bound by blood, but in my heart, you are my sister. Nothing can change that. You'll never be far from my thoughts." God bless Vesta for knowing what I needed to hear.

I breathed in comfort from Vesta's declaration. A cry of relief crossed my lips. "You're right, we are sisters. I'll carry you here," I placed my hand over my heart, "until we can be together again."

As Vesta was driven away by the social worker, she continued to wave until she was out of sight. I wanted to run after them and make them take me, too. Even though my brain wobbled on the precarious edge of insanity, I clung to my last shred of control to face the next twelve months. At the time, I didn't believe I could ever feel so lonely. Little did I know, it was only a hint of what lay ahead.

In the end, the one thing Vesta's leaving did for me was give me something to look forward to. When I turned eighteen, I'd leave the less than welcoming arms of the Spade's and head right to wherever Vesta had landed. Anticipation would out-weigh the loneliness. It had to, or I would die.

Monday morning I awoke filled with eagerness and fear for my court appointment. Until I entered my plea, no date would be set for the trial. Not that I'd originally expected a trial. I thought I'd say I was guilty, which was pretty obvious to everyone who'd heard my confession and witnessed my hatred toward my dead husband's body. After that, I would immediately start serving my sentence in prison either as a lifer or a woman on death row. That seemed so much easier than even thinking about convincing anyone I was a victim of abuse and should be set free.

But life in the form of Phillip Kane had intervened and partially convinced me to say I wasn't guilty because I'd killed Harland in self-defense. I truly believed that eventually it would have come down to Harland or me, but I always assumed it would be me.

Then I had found Berryanne's adoption papers hidden in his private drawer and quickly realized how much of a lie my life had been. For the first time, I hated Harland more for the emotional abuse than for the physical. His death did not change it.

Even though I feared for my life on a daily basis, it took a while before I grew to hate Harland, mainly because I had stupidly bought into the things he touted as reasons why I should be grateful to him, like food, clothing, and a roof over my head. I *was* grateful for those things and I tried to show him. But when it came to manipulating my mind and soul where my baby was concerned, hatred outweighed the fear of dying. Suddenly, my brain, raging with survival instinct, told my body what to do and the matter was taken out of my hands.

In a split second, I made the decision. Moments later Harland lay dead and, God help me, I couldn't feel remorse for taking his life. How could all that culminate in a not guilty plea? The knots in my stomach told me it couldn't, and I'd be foolish to believe otherwise.

Entering the courtroom, I was met by Phillip's reassuring smile. A small amount of the doubt plaguing my thoughts melted away, and I allowed him to do what he thought was right.

The room was filled with people chattering and pointing at me. In the middle of the crowded benches sat Vesta. She waved. Her mouth was tight and grim. I started to wave back, but was quickly reminded my hands were shackled at my waist.

"I'm okay," I mouthed, hoping to relieve some of her despair, but her face plainly showed her feeling of helplessness.

At the front of the room, court officers scrambled to make ready for the Honorable Davidson Kent to enter. Chairs scraped, papers rustled, and whispers buzzed from every corner. The high luster of the wooden judge's bench and railings glistened under the milk-glass chandeliers. A blend of linseed oil, beeswax, and turpentine had been used to shine the wood. I knew that because I used to help my mother make that same mixture to polish our furniture. The subtle, clean smell comforted me and made me feel my mother was nearby.

Phillip shuffled through pages of documents. For the first time, I didn't voice my uncertainties about pleading self-defense. Instead, I took a wait-and-see attitude. It came easier than I thought. But then again, wasn't it what I'd done every day for the past ten years? I waited to see if I would live another day. I'd escaped death by Harland's hands, but from the grave, he still controlled my fate.

The judge's chamber door opened and the room quieted. Judge Kent took his seat behind the bench. His gaze scanned the immediate area and came to rest on me. I swallowed hard, but maintained eye contact with him. Although his poker face remained hard and unreadable, his soft brown eyes eased some of the anxiety and fear constricting the muscles in my throat.

After a short discussion with the bailiff, Judge Kent banged the gavel and looked at Phillip.

The court clerk read the charges. "Case number 763 on the docket. The State of North Carolina verses Montana Jeffers. The charge is murder."

He handed the case file to the judge, who studied it for a moment before looking at me.

"How does the defendant plead?"

Phillip took my arm and helped me to my feet.

"Not guilty, Your Honor." I'd said those words, but I never felt them pass my throat. They did, however, cause bitterness in my mouth. I'd lied in a court of law, and I was supposed to believe it was the right thing to do.

Just as I turned to beg Phillip to take back my plea, he squeezed my arm in a reassuring way and spoke to the judge.

"I request bail be set and Montana Jeffers be released on her own recognizance."

The prosecuting attorney sprang to his feet started to speak, but Phillip cut him off.

"Your Honor, Mrs. Jeffers is not a threat to society. She has friends she can stay with."

"Not a threat to society?" District Attorney Donovan's voice vibrated with anger. "I think anyone who murders her husband in cold blood is truly a threat to society. Your Honor, I object to bail being set. Mrs. Jeffers has no job, no home, and should definitely be considered a flight risk. I ask for remand."

Instantly the Judge agreed. "So ordered. Court is adjourned."

The gavel banged. I nearly jumped out of my skin.

That quickly the proceedings were over, and I was sent back into the care of Guard Sorensen. She marched me to the conference room and removed my handcuffs. Phillip awaited me.

"Come on in, Montana." He pulled out the chair next to him.

"What happens now?" I accepted the seat.

"I'll be advised when the trial date is set. In the meantime, you and I will continue to prepare your defense."

"Will it be added to the docket for next week? I'd like to get this over with as soon as possible."

He shook his head. "The old saying that the wheels of justice move slowly is very true."

My features must have wilted with disappointment. Phillip quickly added, "I'll do everything I can to speed it along."

"I hope so. I want the trial behind me as soon as possible." I didn't want to postpone the inevitable.

Phillip's bright eyes darkened. "I want it behind you, too, so you can begin living the life you deserve." He smiled. "Let's get to work on that."

My heart took an extra beat, and there it was again. That flicker of hope I'd fought so hard to keep at bay. I offered a weak smile and plunged headfirst into the task at hand—getting rid of the dark skeletons in my closet—one bone at a time.

"I've already told you I don't remember much about the year following the loss of my baby. It wasn't until after Vesta was turned out into the world and I was left behind at the Spade's, that I have any recollection."

"Did Dirk pose a threat to you during that time?" Phillip asked.

I didn't have to think long. "No, he didn't cause me any more grief. As a matter of fact, he totally ignored me, which was just fine. It was a lonely time because I had no one to talk to. Also, I wasn't permitted to go back to school after I'd dropped out to have my baby. So, except for Vesta when she came to visit, Joyce was the only person I talked to and that was only when necessary." Vesta's visits were the only bright spots during that time.

"How often did you see Vesta?"

"At the most, once a month. She worked all day and went to beauty school in the evening. She had little free time." A smile pulled at the corners of my mouth. "I'd be so starved for someone to talk to, I'd barely let her get a word in."

Phillip chuckled. "I can only imagine."

With the way his coffee-colored eyes danced when he smiled, I wondered how bright they would be if he broke into full-fledged laughter. I looked forward to seeing that sometime.

"How long before you went to live with Vesta?"

"It was a whole year." It felt like a lifetime.

"So Dirk left you alone. Was there anything remarkable about that period of your life? Lessons learned?"

"I never thought of it as a lesson learned, but there was a strange occurrence that gave me a new perspective on Joyce Spade." I chewed on my bottom lip. Phillip gestured for me to continue. It had been years since I'd allowed myself to think about anything connected with the Spade's. Strange, but now that I was giving myself permission for memories to work their way back in, I remembered several things that revealed Joyce was also a victim of Dirk's abuse.

I relayed those moments to Phillip. On the occasions when Vesta and I had been alone in the house while the Spades ran errands, we would jimmy the lock on the box that held Joyce's secrets. We'd guess what all the bits of memorabilia meant to Joyce. We also relocked it and replaced it in its hiding place and no one was ever the wiser. We never stole anything. We just enjoyed the adrenaline rush of getting away with something.

After Vesta left, I didn't have the desire, or the nerve for that matter, to delve into Joyce's privacy. A few months before my time was up, I went to the kitchen and found her sitting with her back to me. Although I couldn't see her face, her body movements made it obvious she was crying.

I moved closer to her. "Joyce?"

She jumped. After she shoved the items back inside the box, she slammed the lid and dried her tears on a kitchen towel. In her haste to close the box, a paper slid from the table and floated to the floor. I bent to pick it up.

"What's going on here?" Dirk's voice boomed from the doorway.

Joyce and I both bolted upright. We turned to face him. Stepping closer to her, I hoped our bodies hid the box behind us. Her body trembled and her skirt danced against my leg. Even I wasn't that afraid.

"Well? What's that behind you?" he demanded.

We hadn't succeeded in keeping it hidden. Joyce emitted an anguished moan, reminding me of a petrified kitten. Her body shook even harder. I knew the same fear all too well, and the depth of hers chilled me. Suddenly, sorrow for the pitiful, terrified woman shoved me into action. I snatched the box from the table and hugged it to my chest.

"This is mine," I shouted at Joyce and then turned to Dirk. "She had no right going through my stuff." I stormed to my room and slammed the door behind me. Once there I hurriedly stuffed the lone piece of paper I'd retrieved from the floor inside the box and clicked the lock shut. As a chill shivered through me, I realized what a chance I'd taken. Surely Dirk would use his strap on me. I wrapped my arms across my chest trying to ward off the coldness surrounding me and waited for the wrath of Dirk to rain down.

I plainly heard him shouting at Joyce. "Are you going to let her talk to you that way? She needs a strap to her ass to teach her respect."

After a short hesitation, Joyce said something, but I couldn't understand her. Evidently, she played down my verbal attack, because Dirk snapped back, "You're stupid to let her get away with that. Take this in there and show her whose house this is."

There was another lull in the exchange.

"Now," Dirk bellowed.

Involuntarily, I jumped several inches off the mattress. The sound of my rapidly beating heart pounded in my ears.

A few seconds later, my door opened and a sad-eyed Joyce stepped into the room and closed the door behind her. She held Dirk's wide, thick belt in her shaking hands. Short of telling Dirk the box belonged to Joyce, I could see no way out of being punished. I braced myself for what was to come.

She pointed to the edge of the bed and I knew I was expected to lean over it. As I moved into the position, she took a blouse from the back of a chair and hung the garment over the door handle preventing any peeking through the keyhole.

I heard Dirk grunt from the opposite side of the door, confirming what Joyce and I suspected. She moved next to the bed and swung the belt, striking it loudly against the mattress, completely missing me. Twice more she struck and each time I released a soft grunt, not to add sound effects to her charade, but because of the anticipation of pain and surprise at not receiving it. Quickly, and without a word, she left the room.

A lump grew in my throat. Joyce took a big risk not following through with the punishment Dirk had demanded she give me. Gratitude for what she'd done melted the knot in my throat and spread warm appreciation through my stomach. I was happy to know there was a heart inside the cold woman.

Shortly, the back door slammed. With my heart pounding loudly, I peeked out my bedroom window and saw Dirk tramping across the yard in the direction of the henhouse. Each heavy step showed the depth of his anger. When he reached the coop, he grabbed a bucket of feed and spread handfuls on the ground.

I picked up Joyce's box and hurried to the kitchen. I found her huddled against a wall, trembling and with tears streaming down her face. When she saw me, I held out the box. She straightened and took it from me.

"Thank you," Joyce said.

"Thank you," I told her. We never discussed the matter again, but from that moment things were different between us. We weren't friends, but at least she never again displayed her obvious hatred for me. That made things a little easier and, for that I was grateful.

I didn't fear Dirk anymore, and Joyce and I had formed a truce of sorts. Vesta came to visit at least once a month, and she always brought news of the life I'd be living when I left the Spades. All that made my last year in foster care at least bearable. It even helped the time pass more quickly.

The week before I would be sent out into the world, Joyce went to town for groceries and her usual weekly errands. When she returned, I immediately put the groceries away, and she disappeared to the back of the house. By the time she appeared again, potatoes were peeled and already boiling and pork chops sizzled in hot oil.

"I'll take over from here. You need to clean out your drawers and closet and start packing. You'll be leaving on Wednesday morning," she told me.

I probably just wanted to believe someone would miss me, but I thought I heard regret in her voice. I waited to see if she had more to say, but she didn't, and I didn't have anything to say, either. I suppose I should have said I was grateful for being able to stay in their home, but for the life of me, the words wouldn't come. Too many unhappy and life-changing things had happened during my stay. And some times it was better to say nothing at all.

In my room, I found an old suitcase. Inside it were two new dresses, two pair of slacks and two tops, three brassieres, and three pair of underwear. My first thought was that foster care had given me the things, but then I remembered just the year before Vesta had not received anything new. She left with only the things she had collected over the past few years.

There was only one other explanation. I stared at the clothes, speechless, yet touched by Joyce's offering. I couldn't be sure if she had made the move because she liked me, because she felt sorry for me, or if she felt she owed me something for saving her from Dirk when he caught us with her keepsake box.

Whatever her reasoning, I knew it would never be spoken of, nor would Dirk ever know Joyce had done something nice for me. I wouldn't do anything to give her away.

Arrangements had been made for Vesta to come and collect me and my belongings. I thought it best to wear something old in case Dirk was observant enough to notice. I needn't have worried. He had left early that morning and hadn't returned.

For about an hour, I'd waited on the front porch. Joyce was inside. An older model black Chevrolet topped the hill at the end of the lane that led to the Spade's house. Vesta sat behind the steering wheel. She smiled from ear to ear and so did I. Ignoring the steps, I jumped from the porch and ran to the driver's side.

"Where did you get this?" I squealed and bounced up and down like a kangaroo.

Vesta climbed out and hugged me like it had been years since we last saw each other. "My boss loaned me the money to get it. Ain't she beautiful?" She ran her hand over the fender. "And she runs great."

"She's more than beautiful. I can't wait to see how she rides and how you drive. Will you teach me?" I was so lost in my own little world, basking in the joy that I was making a move to a new home and a new beginning I hadn't even noticed Joyce had come out of the house.

She handed me my suitcase. What should I say to her? I searched my mind and my heart, but nothing came. I took the suitcase and while Vesta unlocked the trunk, I looked at Joyce. Like always, her eyes were cold and empty. When I first arrived, I mistook the look as hatred and possibly evil. During the nearly three years I'd lived with her, I came to realize her lackluster gaze was nothing more than a facade to hide the unhappiness and disappointment with her own life.

Living in a loveless marriage had killed Joyce's soul. It was in my power to never have to live like that. At that very moment, I made a pledge to myself to see I never did.

Joyce broke my reverie. "Have a good life, Montana." I thought for a moment she was going to break into tears or maybe even hug me. But then she turned and slowly made her way up the steps and onto the porch.

"Thank you for giving me a place to live, Joyce," I called to her as the screen door slammed behind her. I'm not sure she even heard me.

Vesta took my bag. My chariot awaited. I hurried around the car and got in. Vesta backed into the lane and then ground the gears trying to shift. "This takes some getting used to." She laughed.

I was so thrilled to be leaving with her, I'd have pushed the car to the highway. By the time we got to the bottom of the hill and pulled onto the main road, Vesta had the gears synchronized and engine humming. We buzzed along. Trees and road signs blinked in and out of my sight. I was drinking it all in. Each mile took me farther from the Spade's and closer to my new home. Excitement left me giddy.

Suddenly, I saw a car partially hidden by a group of pine trees. A man sat on the hood watching the passing cars. We sped by him so fast that at first I thought I imagined him, but once my heart quieted I knew it was real.

"That was Dirk parked back there," I said.

"Yeah, I saw him." Vesta straightened her rearview mirror. "He's pulling onto the highway."

Panic knotted my insides. "You mean he's following us? I don't want him to know where we live."

Vesta squeezed my hand. "Calm down. He's going the other way. I'm sure he just didn't want to go home until he was sure he was really shed of us." She burst out laughing.

I needed an extra moment to get past the scare I'd had, but soon Vesta's infectious giggling helped my heart slow its pounding and urged me to find a glint of humor in her kidding. I joined her with deep, throaty laughter, but we both knew it was forced. I was terrified of what I'd left behind and even more of what lay ahead.

Only one thing eased my trepidation—being on my own, I could look for Berryanne.

"Welcome to your new home." Vesta entered our garage apartment and made a grand gesture for me to follow.

One step into the room and I could take in every inch of living space with a single sweeping glance. The living room was L-shaped with a dining area at one end that extended into a small kitchen. Straight across from the entrance was a door to the bedroom with twin beds and the bathroom.

I walked through the apartment, taking in everything Vesta had done to make the tiny place a home. The tattered sofa was partially covered with a worn quilt, and gold brocade curtains hung over two windows. The sun had faded the color and age had frayed the hems.

A tie-dyed scarf covered a lampshade next to an overstuffed chair also battered with age. I ran my hand over the mismatched chairs surrounding a dining table topped with an embroidered cloth and a Mason jar filled with wildflowers. Suddenly, my legs folded beneath me, and I sank to the floor. Burying my face in my hands, I sobbed uncontrollably.

"My God, Montana, what's wrong?" Vesta stooped beside me and rubbed my back like a mother consoling her child. The sharp stab of missing my own mother, the anticipation of what lay ahead, and the uncertainty of whether I'd survive the big world on my own, tumbled inside me like clothes in a dryer. I cried harder.

"Are you sick?" She pulled my hands away from my face and forced me to look at her.

Sick? As if I'd been slapped, I stopped crying. "Oh, Vesta, my dear friend, I'm way too happy to be sick. This is the most beautiful place I've ever seen." I used my shirttail to dry away the waterworks drowning my face. "I'm so proud of how well you've survived on your own. And so thankful you've cared enough to take me in. I don't know what I would have done without you."

"I guess you aren't going to be happy until you have me bawling, too." She rose and pulled me to my feet. "Let's get you settled in and then we'll go over to the café so you can meet with Shirley and Cal. They're anxious to get you on the schedule. Shirley's having surgery next week, and she hopes to have you going strong by then."

My head spun. So many things going on at one time. I'd barely had time to enjoy the excitement of being in my new home, and now I'd be facing the working world. "What if I can't do the job?"

Vesta laughed. "Sometimes you are so funny. If I can be a waitress, so can you." She turned me toward the bathroom and shoved me. "Go wash up and put a cold rag on your face for a few minutes. Your crying eyes make you look like a howler monkey."

A giggle trickled past my lips. I wished I had her confidence, but right then the most I could hope for was to not dissolve into tears while talking to the owners of the café where I hoped to work. Right then, even though self-assurance may have been elusive, joy and satisfaction filled my heart. The heavy sadness of the past few years disappeared. And, except for the dark shadow across my heart left by Berryanne, I was truly happy.

I'd worried needlessly about whether I'd be able to do a good job as a waitress. Shirley and Cal declared me a natural. Between my brother and the Spade's, I'd been waiting on people for years. The biggest difference between them and the patrons of Shirley's Home Cooking Café was the patrons appreciated what I did; they smiled, and they tipped me. I loved the work and the new friends, but most of all I appreciated every breath of freedom. I didn't intend to waste a moment of it.

Vesta and I worked the breakfast and lunch crowd at the café. We were there at five to set up and could depend on a line of hungry men waiting for us to unlock the door promptly at six. Several were construction workers in town for as long as it took to replace the Branson Bridge crossing the Conway River, but according to Dan White, the head man, the project wouldn't be finished for another eighteen months. Until then, I was happy they were a hungry bunch. Shirley assured me that when they were gone, another group would be there to replace them.

The one morning crowd we could always depend on was a group of retired men who called themselves the *Over What Hill? Gang.* They had their own coffee cups, which hung on a rack Cal had put on the wall for their use. The men were like a scale that tipped one way one day and the other the next, depending on what the headlines said that morning. They were either laughing at everything or arguing over nothing.

Either way, I found them refreshing in my way-too-serious life.

"That's my goal," I said to Vesta as we stood behind the counter waiting for Cal to send out the next order.

"What goal would that be?" She slathered butter on a short stack.

"I want to grow old like those guys over there and never be afraid to say what's on my mind." I never wanted to bow down or fear anyone again.

"You don't have to be old to do that. Do it now. You might find it exhilarating." Arms laden with platters of breakfast food, Vesta moved past me.

I watched her set each order in front of the right person. No mix-ups. No confusion. She knew her stuff and was really good at it. She knew exactly which one needed more coffee, more hot tea, or more milk. I copied her style as closely as I could, but no one waitressed like Vesta.

"You know what, my beautiful Vesta?" Round-faced Mike Lamb flashed his yellowed teeth at her. I delivered my order to the men at booth six, but I listened to what was transpiring at the retirees' table.

"If I were forty years younger," Mike continued, "I'd be chasing you around this place and, boy, when I caught you, we'd be in for a good old time." His announcement started an uproar with the others.

"Don't worry about him, sweetness." George Baumgartner elbowed Mike. "If he caught you, he wouldn't know what to do without the rest of us there giving him step-by-step instructions."

A good-looking man, much closer to my age, listened to the carryings-on at the next table and looked at me over the top of his coffee mug. His green eyes sparkled with laughter. When he set the cup down, his mouth sported a beautiful smile.

"I've been listening to those ol' farts. They live in the world they left behind a long time ago," Mr. Sparkling Green Eyes said. "None of them would know what to do with a pretty young thing like her." He nodded in Vesta's direction. "Or you, either."

Heat rose to my cheeks, and I was sure neon colors flashed across the rest of my face. Shyly, I hurried back to the counter and pretended to be very busy. When I dared glance in the direction of the good-looking man, he winked, and I knocked a cup of hot coffee onto the floor.

"Smooth, Montana, smooth." Vesta knelt beside me and sopped up the liquid while I dropped the chunks of the ceramic mug into the trash pail. "He can't bite you from over there." She peeked over the counter. "Although, if I were you, I'd go over there and bite him."

"Shhh, Vesta. He'll hear you." I rose and found him standing at the end of the counter with cash in his hand. *Please let the ground open and swallow me whole.*

"You didn't leave my ticket, but I think this'll cover it." He handed me the money, and I took it without ever making eye contact.

He lifted my chin and forced me to look at him. "See ya around . . ." He glanced at my name tag. ". . . Montana." There was a hint of laughter in his voice, not mocking, but very seductive. My body tingled in response.

All I could manage was a nod, but as soon as the bell signaled the closing of the door, Vesta and I giggled like schoolgirls. "Montana's got a boyfriend," she teased.

"No, I don't. He probably thinks I'm the silliest girl he's ever seen." I rang up his charges at the register, made the change, and counted the substantial tip he had left. Slipping it into my apron pocket, I fingered it like a good-luck charm and felt giddy with excitement.

I didn't even know the man's name, but my body buzzed with expectation. I wanted to get to know him better and possibly prove that a man and woman could have a gentle relationship as opposed to demeaning and painful rutting.

Suddenly, the excitement died and was replaced with disgust. Disgust for anything connected to intimacy between a man and a woman. What had I been thinking? I wanted no part of what Vesta deemed the greatest feeling in the world. For me, sex meant nothing but pain and heartache. I'd had all of that I ever wanted.

I pulled a folded bill out of my pocket and twirled it in my fingers. Moments before I had allowed my judgment to be clouded by a man with alluring features. Now I was back on track. The only good thing I had reaped from a relationship with a man was my precious baby girl and even that had left deep scars in my heart. I had no intention of ever facing that type of sadness again. And that included Mr. Green Eyes and his dazzling smile.

Chapter 7

DURING THE YEAR I'D BEEN ON MY OWN, I SPENT MOST NIGHTS cleaning the garage apartment Vesta and I shared and watching one of three channels on a small black-and-white television. Four nights a week, Vesta attended the local beauty school.

With only a few weeks left until she graduated, I found myself dreading her career change from waitress to beautician. I liked working with her at the café, and I knew her leaving would make me sad. I'd become very good at my job and no longer depended on Vesta for guidance, but I would miss her good-humored banter with the customers, our private jokes—usually at the expense of those same customers—but most of all, I'd miss having her there.

While watching an episode of *Peyton Place*, melancholy thoughts of my own family, all dead or snatched from my arms, forced tears from my eyes. Deep in a crying jag, I didn't hear Vesta enter the front door.

"Montana?" she whispered.

I jumped like I'd been shot. "Vesta. You scared me." I

desperately tried to wipe away my tears, but couldn't. The tears just kept coming.

Vesta took a seat and put her arms around me. That was the first time since I'd arrived she'd had to console me. She rocked me, and I emptied my heartache on her shoulder. Only after I'd cried it all out did she say anything.

"Do you want to talk about it?" she asked as she dug a tissue from her handbag.

Did I? What did I have to talk about? Vesta knew all about my life. She'd done all she could to put me on track, to make it better. And how did I repay her?

"I'm sorry, Vesta." I wiped my face and blew my nose. "You've done so much for me, and here I am swimming around in a big ol' pool of self-pity."

"I think we're all allowed to do that at some point in time. What's going on right now in your mind or heart that's brought on the waterworks?"

"Just feeling sorry for myself, I guess." I crossed my arms. "Sometimes I can still feel Berryanne against my chest, and I don't think I can go on another day."

"Then go find her and bring her home." My friend made it sound so simple, but that could never happen.

Every word Ina had said the day she took Berryane from me was true. I barely made enough money to feed myself. How could I work and take care of a baby, too? What did I have to offer her? Nothing.

"She deserves the best out of life. I could never give her any-thing. I'm not very smart. I never even finished high school." I stood to put distance between my friend and me. Her mother-ing made it too easy for me to give way to more crying. "It's for the best." I swiped away a stray tear. "I have to remember that, since I can't change any of it."

Again, Vesta dug in her handbag. "First of all, you may not have a diploma, but you are not a dummy. You can go back to school."

She handed me a brochure.

"What's this?" I asked.

"It's an application for adult night classes where I go. They're starting a class to prepare you to take the GED test and then get your diploma."

I glanced through the information. It sounded fairly simple, and I definitely had the time.

"Well, what do you think?" Vesta asked.

"Getting my diploma would be wonderful." Was it really possible?

"It may be a step toward getting your baby back, too. Think about it." She squeezed my hand encouragingly and then disappeared into the bedroom.

I stared at the paper. With tightness banding my heart, I wrapped my arms across my chest. Was there a chance I might hold Berryanne again? A burning sensation loosened the imaginary hold I had on my baby. I shook my head. No, that could never happen. She was better off where she was and a high school diploma wouldn't change it. Taking the GED test would be for me and me alone.

Two weeks later, I started classes. Two hours a night, Tuesday and Thursday evenings. It was a six-week review of things I was expected to know for the final test. Much to my surprise, I zipped right through all of it. Some of it I remembered from school, but what I hadn't learned before, I picked up easily.

A small patch of confidence began to grow inside me. I liked the way it felt. I hoped, as time went by, I could cultivate it and benefit from its development.

During the next few weeks, I easily floated through my workday at the café, feeling a little cocky about my effort to get my diploma. By the time Vesta had worked her two-week notice and put in her first few days as a certified hairdresser, I had taken her place with the *What Hill?* group of retired gentlemen. Getting the orders right before I carried them to the tables proved to be easier than deflecting the men's wandering hands.

"That's my butt, Mr. Lauder." I tried to be as cordial as possible. I didn't want to be touched, but I didn't want to lose my tips, either. "No one touches it without my permission."

"May I have permission to touch it?" Mr. Lauder had the nerve to ask. Of course, this brought uproarious laughter from the other old coots, and heat as hot as Cal's griddle rose to my face.

"Good one, Mr. Lauder, but the answer is *no*." I glanced around the table at the other old men who found humor in watching grass grow. "That goes for the rest of you, too, understand?"

They all nodded. I believe I heard their arthritic necks creaking.

"Good. Now that we understand each other, who wants more coffee?" I scurried back to the pass-through window separating Cal from the rest of the room. His grin shone brightly. When I gave him a glare, he returned to his work at hand, but I plainly heard his snicker.

Cal had hired a waitress to take Vesta's place. Maria was in her late thirties, married with two children. Her husband was part of the construction crew building the new bridge. She'd been a waitress since high school and knew her way around a dining room.

Behind the counter, I swept crumbs and bits of food into a pile. Maria stood next to me. "That man over there wants you to wait on him," she whispered.

I turned, expecting to see her pointing at one of the old men, but instead I saw the man with the beautiful green eyes and delicious-looking smile staring at me. My heart dropped, skipped a beat, and may have even flipped. I'm not sure what all it did, but I know it felt good.

I strolled over to his table. "What would you like?"

He looked at the menu. "Cal's big breakfast, eggs over medium, bacon, crisp, and," he looked up and smiled, "a date with you."

I stopped mid-pencil stroke and stared at him. My mouth was probably hanging open. "I beg your pardon."

"Date. You know, I pick you up. We go out to a movie or for a burger and fries. Ever heard of one?"

Oh, I had heard of one. I'd just never been on one. Being asked on my first date set me back a little.

"Sure, but I don't think I'll be free that day."

"What day? I didn't say when." He pinched his lips together to stifle a smile.

I continued to write his order using abbreviations, but being a little bum-fuzzled by his question, heaven only knew if he'd get what he ordered or something weird from my short-order chicken scratching.

"Okay, when?"

"How about Friday night?"

"I'm busy Friday night."

"Do you have a good reason for not wanting to go out with me?" This time he didn't have to struggle not to smile.

"I don't know you, for starters. I work here all day and go to school two nights a week. The other nights I spend studying, and then on Friday night I have to wash my hair. Good enough reasons?" As my fist went to my hip, I stared him down.

"Very good reasons. Give me your address, and I'll be at your house at seven thirty Friday to wash your hair for you."

Now I had to struggle to keep from laughing. Okay, so he was charming in a comical sort of way, and then there was the extra added attraction of his bright eyes and captivating smile. "How about you take me out for a bite to eat and have me home early enough for me to wash my hair?" Good heavens, what was I doing? I didn't know anything about dating. I'd be like a fish abandoned by an outgoing tide. Floundering around on the sand. Totally out of my comfort zone.

"Sure you don't want me to wash your hair for you?" He wiggled his fingers up my forearm. "They don't call me Happy Hands for nothing."

Instinctively, I stepped out of his reach. "I'm sure, but keep your Happy Hands to yourself." Making my way around the tables back to the window to place his order, an uneasy thought shivered its way through me. I didn't even know his name. I certainly couldn't call him Happy Hands or Mr. Green Eyes. Would he expect me to be an experienced woman with no morals?

In my own thoughts, I was still a girl who had been forced into adulthood by a string of appalling and frightening events. Although I was no longer a virgin, and I'd brought a child into the world, my innocence in matters of relationships between men and women could send Happy Hands running for his life.

What were we talking about, really? He asked to take me out. Yet I assumed it would entail climbing into bed with him. That didn't have to be his intention. Did it? I placed his order, made a pot of coffee, and turned to another table to take an order. Mr. Green Eyes was staring at me with a smile as wide as a quarter moon.

I averted my gaze long enough to make a round of refills, but then I had to go back to his table to deliver his order and give him more coffee.

"My name is Eddie Shannon, and I promise not to take advantage of you on our first date. Will that erase the deer-in-the-headlights look you've had since you agreed to go out with me?"

It was as if Eddie had read my mind. I started to defend myself, but why? He'd hit the nail on the head. Insightfulness was a trait Vesta swore no man possessed. Maybe Eddie proved her wrong.

"Thanks, it did ease my mind. Will you be in tomorrow?"

"No, I'm working on the other side of the bridge tomorrow and Friday. I need to know where you live." He glanced at my name badge. "Montana. Are you from Montana?"

I shook my head. "No, it's a place my mama always wanted to go, but she never made it." A lump rose in my throat. I swallowed it away.

I scribbled my address on a napkin and handed it to him. "It's the garage apartment behind a pale blue, two-story house at the corner of McCarthy and Nelson. I'll be ready at seven thirty." I left his bill on the table and went to retrieve my next order. I kept my back to Eddie as much as possible. When I dared look in the direction of his table, he was gone and had left me with an odd sense of disappointment.

When Vesta came in from work, I was bouncing around like a schoolgirl. I told her about my exchange with Eddie that morning.

"You have a date with Mr. Green Eyes? How exciting. I remember how interested he was in you and how fluttery you got being around him. Has he been back a lot since I quit working there?"

"No, today was the first time."

"Is he working on the bridge?"

"Not sure. He said he wouldn't be in again this week because he has to work on the other side of the bridge, but he didn't say he was actually working on the bridge."

"What's his name?" Vesta brushed the tease from her shag.

"Eddie Shannon."

"Hm, sounds like a singer we'd see on *American Bandstand*." Vesta used her hairbrush as a microphone. "And here he is with his latest hit, Eddieeee Shannonnn." She made a grand gesture.

"Knock it off. You're making me even more nervous than I already am."

"Where's he taking you?" She went back to taking care of her hair.

"He didn't say exactly; just that we'd go out for a bite to eat. At some point he did mention a burger and fries. What should I wear?"

"Clothes. At least at the start of the date." Pure orneriness filled Vesta's laughter, but her remark added to my apprehension. I didn't want to be in a position to worry about keeping my clothes on.

"There'll be none of that. Eddie assured me he wouldn't get fresh on the first date."

"You asked him that?" Her eyes were as big as moon pies.

"No, I think he saw the fear on my face and wanted me to

relax."

"Oh, Lordy, you're a pip, Montana. That's one of the greatest lines I've ever heard. Men will tell you anything to get a chance to get into your pants. I guess the reason they don't ever say anything like that to me is they're usually trying to keep me out of their pants."

I gave her a playful shove. "You're awful, Vesta, and I'm not listening to you anymore." I put my fingers in my ears and hummed my way to the bathroom.

Friday night, Vesta had laid some clothes on the bed. "Here, try these on." She handed me a light blue, A-line skirt and a white gypsy blouse. Anticipation shoved me into action. I shimmied out of my clothes and into Vesta's. They fit perfectly.

"You look great, kiddo." Vesta walked around me. She motioned to my bed. "Sit and let me fix your hair." She twisted and pulled every strand of my dark hair into a ponytail and then formed individual curls from my crown trailing down the back of my head. "Your hair is so shiny. It's dark but has a hint of chestnut ribboned through it. I've always loved the way the sun bounces off it."

She dug around in her makeup bag and painted my face with foundation, powder blue eye shadow, and pale pink lipstick.

"Take a look." She stepped aside so I could see in the bureau mirror. I rose on tiptoes to try to see the whole effect. Climbing onto my bed, I could finally get a complete look at the new me. I looked grown-up. Maybe even pretty.

"Whatcha think?" Vesta fussed with my skirt hem, pulling it even all the way around.

"Who's that looking back at me?" I jested.

"That is the woman who is going to go on her first date, and the woman who is going to start Eddie Shannon's heart to pumping."

"Do you really think I'm capable of doing that?"

"Of course you are. Look at yourself. The skin on your face is as smooth as a baby's hinny butt."

I rubbed my hand over my cheek. "Is that a good thing?"

"Yes, my dear it is. Look how the slight hint of olive complexion brings out the rich warmth of those big brown eyes."

Vesta ran her fingers over my collarbone. "You have the right amount of flesh peeking from your blouse. I'd kill to have your beautiful skin. And while I'm killing you off for body parts, your tiny waist would look good on me, too." Vesta laughed.

I couldn't really see all my attributes. I'd have to trust my friend on those things. Right then I had to deal with the butterflies fluttering through my stomach. I closed my eyes and took deep calming breaths. If I hyperventilated just thinking about going out with Eddie, how would I be able to spend a whole evening with him?

"Wow. You look great." Eddie opened the passenger door of his white and silver Chevy.

I thanked him, climbed in, and made sure Vesta's skirt didn't get caught in the door. Soon we were backing out of the driveway with her waving good-bye from the landing outside our apartment. She'd fixed my hair, done my makeup, and proudly sent me off on my first date ever. A fact she and I didn't mention to Eddie. He didn't need to know that, and I certainly didn't want to admit it.

"Where are we going?" I asked.

"I thought we'd go to Howey's in Jefferson, if that's okay."

He made a sharp right turn, and I had to grab the door handle to keep from falling in his direction.

"Sure, I've never been there."

He glanced my way and smiled. "I have a feeling there are a lot of places you haven't been. Am I right?"

Heat rose to my face. "Yes, you're right. I'm fresh off the mountain and fairly new here in town." I didn't want to talk about myself. Too many "poor Montana" moments. I'd rather Eddie tell me what made a devilishly handsome fellow like him tick.

"What about you?" I asked. "Where are you from?"

"Out west. My mom and baby sister still live there."

"What about your father?" I asked and instantly regretted it. Eddie's jaw line tightened, and he gripped the steering wheel hard enough to turn his knuckles white.

"I'm sorry. That's none of my business."

"I don't mind. I just haven't thought about him for a long while. He left when I was thirteen and never came back."

"That must have been hard on your mom."

"She never quite got over it. She slipped into a depression. Over the years it's wreaked havoc with her health. The last twelve months have been the worst. My sister graduated from high school last spring and now she takes care of Mom."

"Does your sister have a job as well as watching your mom?" Again, not my business, but I was interested in everything that touched Eddie's life.

"I keep just enough of my paycheck to pay for my room and to eat on. I send the rest home to Mom and Betsy."

Instant guilt pressed into my heart. "Oh, my. You shouldn't be taking me out to eat. You need all your money."

"A man's gotta have some entertainment. I kept a little extra so I could have the honor of eating dinner with the prettiest girl in town." He emphasized his declaration with a huge smile.

Intense pleasure warmed its way through me. He thought I was pretty. Hearing it for the first time, I was sure I'd cherish it forever. "Thank you," I said. "No one has ever said that to me before."

"Were all the men blind on that mountain you came from?"

I giggled, but didn't answer. Eddie had parked and made his way around the car. I fiddled with my purse to give him time to open the door for me.

Howey's turned out to be a pizza parlor and bar. We sat across from each other in a booth near the back of the restaurant. After we had ordered a medium pepperoni pizza and a pitcher of soda, I couldn't think of anything to say. I picked my nails, tapped my fingers, and had just started to shred the corner of my napkin when Eddie reached out and took my hands.

"You're really nervous, aren't you?" He whispered so the people at the next table didn't hear him.

I appreciated his thoughtfulness. "Just a little."

"A first date is always awkward."

Was it that obvious? "How did you know? Do I have it stamped on my forehead?"

Evidently it took a few seconds for it to dawn on Eddie what I was saying, but when it did, his expression went from confused to amused in thirty seconds.

A few moments after that, I realized he meant *any* first date. Before I could pray for a hole to open and suck me under the table, Eddie left his side of the booth and slid in close to me.

"Are you telling me this is your very first date?" He whispered near my ear, sending a tremor of delight through me.

"I'm afraid so."

"How old are you?" Eddie asked.

"Almost twenty."

He sighed and leaned back. "You know, I think it's kinda sweet. I guess you were saving yourself for me." His low, gentle whisper and courteous smile calmed my racing heart to somewhere near a normal beat.

Without overanalyzing, I knew he was trying to make light of the situation, trying to help me relax. At least that's what my jittery insides told me.

I looked into his eyes and wondered if the kindness I saw there was real or only a figment of my imagination. Did I want to believe a man could possess the ability to care for me or, at the very least, not look at me with loathing?

The waitress delivered our pizza. Eddie switched back to the other side of the table and, using a spatula, lifted a piece of the pie onto my plate. The warmth of his smile carried through his voice. "We'll take it easy. I wouldn't want to scare you off. You let me know when you feel comfortable with me."

I wanted to shout that I'd never felt more comfortable with any other man in my entire life. Nor had I ever wanted to be as close as we'd been before he moved back to his side of the table. And never had I ever wanted to taste lips like the ones framing his amazing mouth.

After we ate, we cruised the main thoroughfare. The McCoys sang "Hang on Sloopy" on the radio and warm air whipped my hair around my face.

"Move over here and the wind won't muss your beautiful curls." Eddie took my hand and persuaded me to slide next to him. Truth be told, it didn't take too much to get me to move over. I'd been racking my brain for a way to do it anyway.

With me beside him, Eddie put his arm around the back of the seat and within seconds his hand rested on my shoulder. A feeling of wanting more pulled me like a magnet against him, and I settled comfortably in the warm circle of his arm.

We made a few more turns up and down the avenue, and then Eddie stopped at the park along the bank of the Conway River. There were benches next to a walkway where people sat during the day to eat lunch, read, or just escape their lives for a little while. In the daylight, the river glowed with sunlight, and geese played along the shoreline. But in the dark, it was hard to see. Luckily, the full moon gave some light. Eddie held my hand tightly and led the way to a nearby bench.

Frogs and crickets sang their night chorus. Jasmine lingered sweetly in the air, rounding out the perfect evening.

For at least an hour, we sat side by side, our fingers intertwined, my pulse alternating between a slow pace when Eddie looked out over the river and racing when he looked my way and his soft breath grazed my cheek.

If I had to repeat what we talked about during the hour we sat on the hard seat in the damp night air, I would be hard-pressed to do it. But if I had to tell you the moment I fell in love with Eddie Shannon, it wouldn't be when he lifted my face to him and his mouth claimed mine, slowly and thoughtfully. Or, when his tongue explored the crevices of my mouth and a thousand shards of desire exploded through my body. It would be when he broke our connection, allowing the cool air to pass over my swollen lips; and with the moonbeams dancing in his eyes, I saw heart-stopping tenderness. As my heart turned over in response, I knew, from that day forward, Eddie Shannon would be my one true love.

Two weeks after my wonderful date with Eddie, I sat on the outside stairs leading to my apartment. A faint breeze caressed my warm skin, and I enjoyed being off my feet and not having to think about refilling coffee cups or dodging advances by one of the *What Hill?* gang. Vesta had just left on a date with her steady boyfriend, Mitch, and I was feeling lost and alone.

I hadn't heard a word from Eddie since our first date. We said our good-byes on the very steps where I sat, and he drove off into the night. For the first week, I'd managed to make excuses, like he worked late, and since I didn't have a home phone, he had no way to call. When my ability to invent reasons why Eddie had stolen my heart and then disappeared had faded, I faced reality—the kisses we shared meant more to me than they did him. My naiveté translated to inexperience, and that wasn't what he was looking for.

He'd said I was pretty. When he had pulled me close to him and kissed me, I'd felt his heart pound against my chest. Yet, none of that had affected him the way it had me. Evidently, being more experienced gave you the ability to say and do things that could be interpreted as deep passion with someone like me, when in reality I'd been erased from his memory by the time he'd backed out of the driveway.

In the future, I'd remember I'd allowed my emotions to run wild and been hurt in the process. Thank goodness I'd learned my lesson quickly. Where men were concerned, I lacked the judgment to interpret their intentions. I would not put myself in that position again.

Silently, I repeated my affirmation several times and then once aloud to the rising wind. "You're the only one who can take care of your heart. Guard it, protect it, and never give it away completely."

"Hi, Montana." Eddie Shannon materialized from the dusky haze that had closed in around me. "Was that little speech for me?"

I focused on his face, looking for a sign of why he was there or, better yet, what had taken him so long. "No, it was for me." I remained seated, fearful that if I tried to stand, my shaking legs would betray me.

"I'm sorry I haven't been back. It wasn't because I didn't want to, but my boss sent me to Webster to work on another job. I just got back to town about an hour ago." He held out his hand, and I couldn't take it fast enough.

Pulling me into his arms, he kissed away my disappointment and filled me with a welcome wave of excitement and renewed my faith in my judgment. Although he hadn't said it yet, Eddie Shannon loved me. I felt it to the tips of my toes.

Eddie and I hung out at my apartment that night, and we went on a picnic on Saturday and to a movie in the evening. Our two days together intensified my attraction to Eddie. I had the whole head-spinning, breath-catching, heart-fluttering thing going on. Nothing could or ever would feel as good as being locked in his arms.

He wanted so much more, and so did I, but fear and vivid memories of horrific encounters with Joe and Dirk pounded through my mind and tamped down the desire strumming through my body. I reminded myself over and over again Joe and Dirk were no more than animals, and Eddie Shannon possessed kindness and gentleness.

I couldn't bring myself to explain to Eddie my body's reaction to any intimate touch. Defending myself or my actions never became an issue. Eddie sensed my uneasiness with intimacy.

"Montana, I would never force you to do anything you didn't want. That is a promise I can and do make to you. That doesn't mean I won't go out of my mind from wanting you, and make a move you don't want. But at the first sign of resistance, I'll back off. Understand?"

"I'm sorry I'm not more—" I started to say "worldlier," but his kiss stifled my apology. His gentleness confirmed his vow to be sincere. For the rest of our time together, Eddie lavished me with attention and never caused me to feel uncomfortable with our degree of intimacy.

When he left, he promised to call me at the café sometime during the week to make plans for next weekend, but it didn't happen.

After not hearing a word from Eddie for the next two weeks, I slid into a painfully reclusive cocoon. I did my job at the café. I waded through homework assignments, classes on Tuesday and Thursday. But the spark Eddie brought into my life was fading fast, and there didn't appear to be anything I could do about it.

I couldn't call his boss and ask about Eddie. What if he decided my virtue was more than he wanted to deal with? How embarrassing would that be? No, I needed to face the fact I'd put more stock in our one-sided relationship than he had. It meant more to me, and I had to move on without Eddie.

Even if he reappeared, I couldn't allow him back into my life, because his leaving left scars as painful as others I'd received. So, again, I repeated my affirmation to steer clear of Eddie Shannon, should he ever show up.

Evidently, making rock hard decisions and sticking with them was not my forte. Within three weeks of my vow to steer clear of Mr. Green Eyes, I found myself huddled in the backseat of Eddie Shannon's '57 white and silver Chevy. Our clothes and body parts jumbled into one mass.

Hopefully, the steamed windows would keep anyone else at the Fun-Land Drive-In from seeing us, but for some strange and unknown reason, I chose not to worry about it. My fear lay deeply rooted in my stomach, causing me to sweat and feel light-headed. My body and mind couldn't agree on what should be happening. I ached to have Eddie's hands all over me. I wanted to kiss his beautifully suntanned body, but when it came down to having sex with him, I had trouble separating him from the only other men I'd known in that way. Yet something deep inside me told me Eddie wasn't like the others. I relaxed and gave into the wonderful sensations his touch sent through my entire body.

Once my blouse and brassiere hit the floorboard, Eddie lowered his bare chest against me. I swear our hearts beat as one. His mouth covered mine. His deep exploring kiss intensified the electricity vibrating through my entire body. I returned his passion with an eagerness I'd never known possible. I tasted the sweetness of his moist lips as if it were nectar from the gods.

My response accelerated Eddie's enthusiasm and his movements. Hurriedly, he removed his jeans and almost violently pulled mine down. Through ragged breaths, I mumbled *no,* and he obediently pulled away, allowing cool air to chill my bare skin, but I couldn't stand not having him next to me. I pulled him back down and held on as if my life depended on it. And in a way it did, because in my cracked mind, if I couldn't give my-self to Eddie Shannon, the greatest man on the face of the earth, I would never be able to have a relationship with any man.

Chapter 8

ONCE WE WERE IN THE HEAT OF THE MOMENT, I DIDN'T WANT to stop, but Eddie broke away from my arms. He leaned into the front seat and opened the glove compartment. I tried to pull him back.

"Give me a second," he said, as breathless as I felt. He shuffled around for what seemed an eternity, and then lowered himself back on top of me. Right there, in the backseat of his Chevy, Eddie and I made love.

I didn't dare allow thoughts of my other sexual experiences to seep into my brain. They were so different from what I'd just experienced. Eddie's unselfish consideration of me and my needs and his tender touch painted a whole new picture of what love and making love was all about.

It wasn't until we were dressed and he'd gone to the concession stand to get us popcorn and sodas that the real impact of what we'd done hit me. What if I got pregnant again? What if he didn't love me enough to marry me? What if another baby was taken away from me?

I pressed my hands to my stomach and prayed with every fiber of hope I could muster. *Please, God, don't let me be pregnant. I can't go through that again.*

A maelstrom whirled in my stomach, and I thought I might be sick. What had I done? This time I wasn't forced to have sex, but had craved it, had lusted for Eddie, and in the end gave in to the one thing that could possibly bring another round of the most unbearable misery.

By the time Eddie returned to the car, I had worked myself into a frenzy. My breath caught in my throat, and panic rioted inside me.

The overhead light came on, and Eddie only needed a quick glance at my face to realize something was terribly wrong. He set the popcorn and soda on the front seat and climbed into the back with me.

"Are you okay?" He put his arm around me.

"No, I'm scared." My voice quaked.

"Of what? Did something happen while I was gone?"

I didn't know what to say. I couldn't tell him I'd been stupid to do what we just did. I wanted it as much as he did. At one point, I'd even begged him to make love to me. Now, during a quick trip to the concession stand, I'd become distraught and sorry it happened. No, I couldn't say that.

"What is it, Montana? You were so happy when I left to go get something to eat." His gentle voice blanketed me and encouraged me to tell him everything, but I couldn't tell him all of it. I couldn't tell him about Dirk and Berryanne. So, instead I chose to tell him only the part that pertained to him.

"After you left, I got to wondering what would happen if I got pregnant. Then I felt stupid to have gotten so carried away and for not using my head. What *would* happen if I got pregnant?" Imagining what his answer would be, sheer fear swept through me.

"You amaze me," Eddie said with a tremor in his voice. With only the light of the huge picture screen to see by, I looked into his eyes and drank in the reassurance I saw there.

"I would never take the chance of getting you pregnant." He pulled me close to him and whispered against my hair, "I used a rubber. That's what I got out of the glove compartment."

I shivered despite the warmth inside the car. Why hadn't I thought of that? Joe and Dirk had always been so driven by their own needs, they never thought of using protection. But Eddie had. He had because he was a different kind of person who cared enough about me to do right.

"I'm glad one of us thought of that," I said, hoping I sounded like I knew what I was talking about. Other than what Vesta had told me, I knew so little about things of that nature. I vividly remember lying in bed one night when we were still at the Spade's and Vesta telling me about rubbers. It all sounded so silly, I thought she made it up. Guess I needed to pay more attention when she talked. At the thought, I giggled.

"Are you laughing?" Eddie pulled back to look at me.

"Yes, I am." I pecked him on the cheek. "I'm just very happy. Where's the popcorn?"

Remembering the feel of Eddie's arms sustained me for the first week after our night at the movies. By the second week and still no word from him, the memory began to fade. I reminded myself that the other times he'd been absent he had returned after two weeks. His boss had probably sent him to another town, like the other times. Even on Friday of the third week, I still danced around the chance that Eddie Shannon might not be coming back. I stayed busy studying for my GED exam, which I would be taking the following morning.

After I'd finished the test, I went by the café even though I had the day off. I told myself I wanted to make sure Maria and Cal weren't swamped without me there, but if I wanted to be truthful with myself, it was to see if Eddie had left a message.

Cal saw me enter and he nodded. "Just can't stay away from us, can you?" he called over the clamor of dishes and loud voices.

"How'd you do on the test?" Maria asked.

"They'll mail me the results sometime next week. I think I did pretty good, though."

Cal handed me a business card. "A man dressed in a fancy suit left this for you. Said it was important you call him when you can."

"Casper Lockwood. Commercial Insurance Specialist," I read. "Did he say what it's about?"

"No, just that he wanted to talk to you." Cal set a plate in the window. "Order up, Maria."

I went into Cal's office and called Mr. Lockwood. "Hi, this is Montana Parsons at the café. My boss said you wanted me to call you. Is something wrong?"

"Oh, no. I didn't mean to alarm you. I need a secretary, and you were recommended to me."

"Me?" Surely there'd been a mistake. I'd never worked in an office and didn't know the first thing about being a secretary. Who recommended me?

"You are the Montana who took classes at the high school recently, right?" Through the phone, I heard a lighter click and cigarette deep inhalation.

"Well, yes, but it was just so I could get my GED."

"Yeah, I know. Sometimes the school recommends students for jobs. I asked for someone who could answer phones, has a pretty good grasp of math, personable, not lazy, and capable of learning as they go. The assistant principal in charge of the adult classes said you would more than fit the bill. Are you interested?"

"I don't know. This is kind of sudden. Cal has been really good to me." I glanced into the next room where he was flipping burgers and grilling cheese sandwiches. "I'd hate to leave him."

"I have a good idea what you are making there and, if you turn out to be good at the job, I'm prepared to double what you're making now. Plus, I can offer benefits like good health insurance. Do you have that there?" Mr. Lockwood certainly made his offer very interesting.

"Are you still there, Miss Parsons?"

"Yes, I need to think about it. When would you need to know?" Was I giving this proposition credence? How could I? I owed so much to Cal.

"I'll be here in my office until four. I need to know before I leave today. I need someone Monday morning. I hope you'll make the right decision."

Mr. Lockwood's offer left me reeling. It wasn't every day a woman my age with no experience had a job like that dropped in her lap. I could learn as I went along and make twice the money I was making standing on my feet for nine or ten hours a day. But I didn't want to leave Cal in a bind.

I looked up and found him standing in the doorway. "You can't afford to turn this down, Montana." He folded his arms and leaned against the doorjamb.

"You know what he wanted?" That puzzled me.

"He asked about you. If you were dependable, if you were good with money, and how much you made. That kind of gave me a hint."

"And you told him how much I made."

"Of course. Since I'd figured out he was trying to steal you away, I added a little more to it and way overestimated your tips. If I was going to lose you, I wanted to be sure you were well compensated." He laughed his usual full, deep laugh.

"Well, he doubled what you told him, but you've been so good to me. You gave me a job when I didn't know anything. I can't leave you."

"Sure you can. You're fired." Cal pointed at the phone. "Call him back and tell him you'll take the job, and then get out of here. I have work to do."

"What if I can't do the job he wants me to do?" I asked Cal.

"I have no doubt you can do the job, but if you can't or just don't like it, you come on back here." He glanced around the door into the kitchen. "Ah, burgers are burning." He hurried away.

I called Mr. Lockwood back and told him I'd be able to start on Monday morning. He gave me the address, and then added, "Be here at eight."

I walked home from the café with a whirlwind of confusion swirling around me. I was fairly sure I'd passed my GED test. I'd been offered and accepted a job that had come out of the clear blue sky and at more than twice the salary I'd been making at Cal's. Because he cared about the waitresses who worked for him and wanted what was best for them, Cal had insisted I take the job.

It was all wonderful and exciting, yet I missed Eddie, and I was consumed with the painful thought I might never see him again.

Vesta was thrilled for me and the upward swing my life had suddenly taken. On the following Friday evening, when I arrived home at the end of my first full week at Lockwood Insurance Agency, she and Mitch had dinner and a cake waiting for me. Their celebration was meant to bring me happiness, but I wished Eddie had been there if for no other reason than to tell me why he'd allowed me to fall in love with him and then left me.

During dinner, Vesta kept looking at her watch and giggling for no apparent reason.

"Is there something going on I should know about?" I asked her. When Vesta acted that way, it could be anything.

"Actually, there are a couple of things." She glanced at Mitch and giggled again.

"Mitch and I are going to get married."

I nearly choked on my roast beef. "You are?" I jumped up and rounded the table to give both of them a hug. "When did you decide this?" I returned to my seat.

Again, Vesta giggled and this time Mitch laughed along with her. "Today," Vesta said, "when the doctor announced that the rabbit died." They leaned over and kissed.

"You're going to have a baby?" That deserved another hug. "This is so exciting. When?"

"In about seven months. Can you believe it, Montana? I'm going to be a mother."

I squeezed her hand. "You'll be a good one, Vesta. Look at how you've taken care of me. Guiding me every step of the way into the real world. I'll never forget everything you've done for me."

"I'm getting married and having a baby. I'm not dropping off the face of the earth. Remember, we will always be sisters in our hearts. No matter what happens." She nodded at my plate. "Eat your broccoli."

The three of us broke into laughter, which was quickly interrupted by a car door slamming in the driveway below. Vesta looked at me.

"Get the door, will ya? I'm sure it's for you."

No one had knocked yet. I assumed she was kidding around, but I soon found out she was right. As the knock sounded, I opened the door. Eddie Shannon stood on the other side. Lost in indecision about what I should do or say, I just stared at him.

"Hi, Montana." His arm snaked out and pulled me to him. I didn't put my arms around him, nor did I kiss him back when his mouth touched mine.

He released me and took a step back. "Aren't you glad to see me?"

"Should I be, Eddie? You come along, fill me full of expectations, and then disappear for weeks at a time and never once let me hear from you. I don't want to have a relationship like that. It's too unstable for me." I started to close the door, but he stopped me.

"I understand. Just give me a few minutes to explain."

At that moment, Vesta came up behind me. "Are you going to ask him in, Montana? He was here earlier, and I invited him to come by for cake."

I stepped aside to let him in. He glanced at Vesta. "Montana and I need to talk first. We'll be right in." He took my hand and pulled me onto the landing with him. We went down a few steps and sat down.

"What's your excuse for not letting me hear from you this time, Eddie?" I asked.

"My mom took a turn for the worse. I took two weeks off work to go home and help my sister. Mom had to have surgery on her heart. It was touch and go for a while. Today was my first day back at work. I went by the café, and when you weren't there, I came by here. Vesta told me you got a new job. That's terrific."

I felt crummy for doubting him. "I'm sorry about your mother. I just wish you would have let me know."

"Things were too hectic and uncertain. Mom and Betsy don't have a telephone. I have to call my uncle every few days to make sure they're okay. I'm sorry, Montana. I knew you'd be upset, especially after what happened our last night together. I've thought of you every day and wanted so much to be with you. And I would have been, but I had to wait until Mom was home from the hospital and stable enough for me to leave her." He rubbed his brow.

"She has to have more surgery," he said with sadness in his voice. "I hated to leave my sister with so much responsibility, but I had to come back to work. I'm not sure how I'm ever going to pay Mom's doctor and hospital bills."

Way in the back of my throat, the major lump of misgivings about Eddie dissolved. What was done was done, but I didn't want to go through the period of not knowing ever again.

"I understand, but I'm not sure my heart can take another time like that. I answer the phones at my new job. You've got to promise me you'll call me there once in a while."

"I will, but you have to trust that I'll be here every weekend I can. And if I don't show up, I'll damn sure have a good reason for not being here. During the next few weeks I'm going to be working overtime. We're behind on the contract to complete the bridge. The company owner is putting a lot of pressure on my boss. He asked for volunteers to work double shifts, and I'll be doing that because I need the money for the surgery Mom has to have."

Of course I forgave Eddie for being gone so long and not calling. Why wouldn't I? I loved him and wanted to be with him even if I couldn't be certain when that was.

Vesta, Mitch, Eddie, and I spent the rest of the evening together. We ate cake and danced to scratchy LPs on the record player. And for a short period in time, I was happier than I'd ever been.

The next day, Eddie came by, and he and I decided to walk to the café to have lunch. We strolled hand in hand along the boulevard with the sun shining high in the sky. The bright light danced on wildflowers in a deserted lot between two run-down cookie-cutter houses. On the porch of one of the two-story dwellings, a middle-aged man sat on a dilapidated couch, a dog sleeping at his feet.

As we approached, the dog jumped up and bared his teeth. Instinctively, Eddie stepped in front and put his hand out to protect me. The man kicked the dog sharply in the gut. As the animal tumbled down the stairs, Eddie swore under his breath.

The poor animal made his way back up the steps to the porch. The man kicked him again. This time Eddie couldn't hold back.

"You son of a bitch," he shouted at the man. "What the hell is wrong with you?"

"Mind your own business." The man spat his words at Eddie. "That's my dog and I'll kick its ass if I want to and no piss ant like you is going to stop me."

When Eddie stepped forward, fear caused me to grab his arm. "Don't. He's not worth the powder it would take to blow him off the face of the earth. Let it go."

Eddie was visibly shaken, but stopped in his tracks. "I'll give you five dollars for that dog." He pulled his wallet from his back pocket.

"Make it ten, and you got a deal." The man grinned, exposing missing front teeth.

"Here, seven is all I have." Eddie thrust the money at him.

The man took it, and Eddie slowly presented the back of his hand for the dog to smell.

"Here you go, boy." The dog accepted the peace offering and swiped his tongue over Eddie's hand. He scratched the pooch behind his ear, and they were instant friends. "Come on, fellow," he called, and the dog walked with us down the street.

When we were out of earshot of the horrible man, I held on to Eddie's arm. "That was a very noble thing you did back there. I'm so proud of you."

He planted a quick kiss on my forehead. "I hope you're proud enough to skip lunch. I had to send extra home this week to Mom and Betsy, and I just gave that creep back there the money I'd set aside to buy our lunch."

Eddie possessed a kindness I'd not experienced before.

"Lunch is on me today. Yesterday, I got the biggest paycheck I've ever received. And I'd be honored to buy you lunch, Mr. Shannon. We'll even save some scraps for this precious beast you just saved. What are you going to call him?"

"Finding a name for him is the least of my worries. I'm not allowed to have a dog in the motel where I stay, and I never know if I'll be coming back to the same motel or be sent to another job site. Sometimes my gallant efforts are misguided."

As if he understood exactly what Eddie and I were talking about and what was at risk for him, the dog came around Eddie to me and looked up with sad eyes. I gave him a gratuitous scratch under his chin and tried to shoo him away. He would not budge. Instead, he whined pitifully. I crumbled under the pressure. "He can stay with me until you find another sucker to take him. Okay?"

The dog wagged his tail, and I scratched his belly. Eddie started to whine like the dog. "I need my belly scratched, too."

"Let's eat first and then we'll talk about that."

The dog waited obediently on the sidewalk while Eddie and I ate lunch. Over our burgers and fries, we decided to call him Scratch, and Eddie decided to try to find someone else to take care of him.

Eddie made it a point to call me at least once a week at my job. The calls were short, but enough to assure me I was in his thoughts as much as he was in mine. I didn't get to see him every weekend for a range of reasons, such as he had to go to a different town to work, he had to work double shifts, or he had to go home to help his sister and mother. But at least with the phone calls, I knew whether or not to expect him.

Within three weeks of Vesta and Mitch's announcement, they were married by my boss, Casper Lockwood, who was a notary. Mitch's brother and I served as witnesses. The bride and groom moved into a small two-bedroom house on Crow Street. Vesta tried to convince me to move in with them, but I was making enough money to pay my own way and the newlyweds needed to be alone. So, I kept the place I'd called home since my release from foster care.

Vesta took the few pieces of furniture she had bought to fill the partially furnished apartment, like her twin bed, her television, and record player. I invested in a full-sized bed for my bedroom and moved my twin bed to the storage area in the garage below.

I had my own place, a high school diploma, a good job, and a wonderful boyfriend. I, Montana Inez Parsons, was on top of the world. And for the next three months things continued to go very well.

I liked to arrive at my office at least a half hour before Mr. Lockwood. I'd make coffee, empty trash cans, and water flowers. When my boss arrived at eight o'clock, he always bombarded me with a list of appointments to set up, files to pull, and copies to make. I liked to be ready for whatever tasks he had in store for me.

My three-month anniversary at my new job was also the end of my ninety-day probation period, and if Mr. Lockwood liked the job I'd been doing, I would get a raise.

When he arrived, prompt as usual, he barked about ten orders in the span of three minutes. He appeared a little more harried than usual. And a lot more jumpy. Before I could ask if something was wrong, he enlightened me.

"Harland Jeffers called me at home last night and said he'd be here this morning to file a death claim for his mother. While he's here, he wants to do his quarterly inspection of his portfolio. He wants to rearrange some of the beneficiaries on his policies." Mr. Lockwood ran a finger over the edge of my desk and inspected it for dust. Since I made it a point to keep the reception area clean, he found none.

I'd seen Mr. Jeffers's name in correspondence and on several files in Mr. Lockwood's office. His name meant nothing to me, but it certainly made my boss jump to attention. I pulled all the files I could find, which were numerous, and deposited them on a table in the conference room. I filled a carafe and gathered the necessary things for Mr. Lockwood and his client to have hot coffee. After making sure there were notepads, pencils, and pens on the table, I felt everything was in order.

At my desk, I made a special effort to be busy, and waited for the arrival of the one person who appeared to strike fear in Mr. Lockwood's heart.

I didn't have to wait long. When the door opened, I donned my friendliest smile and greeted a younger and much better-looking man than I'd expected.

"Good morning. May I help you?" I asked in the most pleasant voice I possessed.

He smiled, exposing straight white teeth, a striking contrast to his olive skin. He wore his thick, tawny hair shorter than most men his age, and as he strode my way, his broad shoulders and confident step commanded my attention. And believe me, he got it.

"I'm Harland Jeffers. I'm here to see Casper."

I extended my hand. He took it and held it a beat beyond a normal handshake, unnerving me slightly.

"It's nice to meet you, Montana."

I pulled my hand free. My name tripped melodiously from his tongue, but how had he known it? I hadn't told him.

"How—?" was all I managed to stammer.

He pointed at my nameplate on the front of my desk. Feeling foolish, I sensed the heat rise in my cheeks. Seeing amusement in his eyes, I had to laugh.

"Is Casper treating you well?" he asked.

Before I could answer, Mr. Lockwood entered the room. "She's doing an exemplary job. As a matter of fact, she's due for a raise today."

"Well, good for you," Mr. Jeffers said. "You let me know if he gets out of line." He winked at me.

Mr. Lockwood's face turned purple, and I was embarrassed for him. He'd never given the slightest hint he might get out of line. I thought I should defend him, but chose to let it drop and not emphasize the uneasy situation.

The two men spent a good two hours in the conference room. I was called in only once to witness Mr. Jeffers's signature on several policy changes. I then returned to my desk and was hard at work when they finally materialized from behind the door. Mr. Lockwood's arms were laden with the stack of folders I'd pulled earlier. He plopped them down on my desk.

"Try to get these changes written up and sent to the home office in today's mail," he instructed.

"Yes, sir. They'll be done today," I assured him.

"Will they be done in time for you to go to dinner with me, Montana?" Mr. Jeffers asked.

Although flattered, I didn't feel it would be appropriate for me to go on a date, mainly because Eddie and I had an understanding. I wouldn't do anything to jeopardize our relationship.

"I'm sorry, Mr. Jeffers, but I have a steady boyfriend." I smiled widely. "But thank you, anyway."

Stern disappointment flashed across his face, but only for a fleeting moment. Quickly, his kind expression returned along with his wide smile.

"Well, if you ever send him down the road, let me know." He turned to my boss. "You say I can look for a check from my mother's policy within the next three weeks?"

"Yes. Montana will send the request right away. It shouldn't be longer than that."

"You'll take care of it for me, won't you, sweetheart?" His right brow rose slightly.

"Of course, Mr. Jeffers."

"Call me Harland." He winked and then, with fluid steps, left the building. The room felt as if he'd taken all the oxygen with him.

Back then, the dizzy feeling he left me with confused me. In retrospect, I should have known in that moment my life had changed.

Chapter 9

INSIDE THE JAIL CONFERENCE ROOM, PHILLIP KANE HAD LIStened to me ramble for hours with no interjections or questions. The whole time, my heart had ridden an emotional roller coaster. By the end of the day, my body ached as if it had suffered one of Harland's beatings. I rubbed a kink in my neck and paced the room to relieve some of the stiffness locking the joints of my exhausted body.

"You knew from the first time you met Harland Jeffers he was going to cause you problems?" Phillip asked. He, too, stood and stretched.

"At that time, I never thought of it as trouble. It was just a niggling sense of drastic change. Things were going so well for me at the time; I never associated the feeling with something frightening." I forced a smile and Philip returned it, removing some of the dark funk I was in.

Suddenly, I was shaken by the fact that I put so much stock in a man's smile. It was the first thing I noticed in the opposite sex. For some outlandish reason, I associated a smile with a happy and trustworthy heart. After Harland, I couldn't believe I was so trusting of another smile, but a quick glance at Phillip's and I saw things in it I had never seen in Harland's—sincerity, compassion, understanding, and real concern for me.

"I know you're tired, but I'd like to ask a few follow-up questions and then we'll call it a day." Phillip moved back to his seat and pulled his legal pad to him. "What happened to Eddie?"

Even after all those years, I couldn't think about that time without a stab of pain in my heart. "I loved Eddie, and I still mourn the loss of his love." I sat on the edge of the long table, my back to Phillip.

"Eddie died?" he asked.

I turned around, cocking my leg on the table. "I probably could have handled his death better than his betrayal." I swallowed a knot of sadness. "A few days after I met Harland, Eddie phoned to say he'd be at my house Friday night at seven, and he had a surprise for me."

"What was it?" Phillip asked.

"He gave me a small, velvet jewelry box, and inside was an engagement ring. It was beautiful. The whole weekend was magical."

"So what happened?" Phillip folded his arms across his chest. His gaze never left mine.

"I made the crucial mistake of telling Eddie about being raped by Joe and Dirk and, of course, about my pregnancy and having to give my daughter away." I slid off the table and went to look out the window. I didn't want Phillip to see the pain I was sure darkened my face.

"I felt Eddie needed to know everything. He held me, and we cried together. I truly thought he understood and accepted my past. Before he left that Sunday evening, we made plans for him to pick me up the following Friday. His home was two hundred miles away, and he was going to take me to meet his mother and sister."

"Did you get to meet them?"

I nibbled at my bottom lip and slowly shook my head. "No, not only didn't I get to meet them, I never saw Eddie again."

Phillip's eyes darkened and anger flashed across his face. "You mean to tell me Eddie Shannon gave you an engagement ring, asked you to marry him, planned for you to meet his family, and then rode off, never to be heard from again?"

"That pretty much sums it up." Way too simple an explanation for the humiliation and hurt I felt when I realized my life had so repulsed Eddie he'd run away forever.

Phillip's demeanor changed. "Did you try to find him? Maybe he was killed in a car or construction accident."

"Yes, I tried." Even after ten years, the truth left a bitter taste in my mouth. "For the first couple of weeks, I made the usual excuses. He'd been sent out of town, worked double shifts, or his mother had taken ill. After six weeks I figured only death would keep him away, so I called information and got the number for his Uncle Pi, who lived next door to Eddie's mother."

"Could he shed any light on the matter?"

"I asked if Eddie happened to be at his mother's house. Uncle Pi said his nephew was working and wouldn't be in until after six o'clock, but that Eddie's wife was home and did I want to talk to her." Just thinking about it still made me sad. I sat down.

"What?" Anger filled Phillip's voice. "That son of a bitch was married and stringing you along? Even gave you a ring? I suppose he bought it at the dime store."

That was the ironic part of the whole thing. "The ring had belonged to his grandmother, and I thought he might come

149

back after it. I wouldn't have felt right selling it. Besides, it was a link to a happy time of my life, however short lived. A few weeks before Harland . . . died, I discovered why I'd kept it all those years and had never let him see it. I sold it to a jeweler for fifteen hundred dollars and put the money with my stash to make my great escape.

"At the time, I felt Eddie was my guardian angel and had lent a helping hand for me to get away from Harland. Of course, we all know I screwed up my one chance at freedom. Royally."

"Had he, in fact, been married the whole time?" Phillip asked.

I stood and deliberately stared at my hands. "I don't know. When his uncle asked if I wanted to talk to his wife, my brain and mouth refused to work together. I just hung up."

"Damn him to hell." Phillip pounded his fist on the long conference table. Instant fear tore at my insides. I recoiled against the nearest wall.

Before I could form a reasonable thought, Phillip was at my side. I'd been on the receiving end of a bad temper too many times, and I knew exactly where it could lead. Had I misjudged yet another man?

He reached out to touch me. I drew back.

"I didn't mean to frighten you, Montana. I swear I don't usually react like that, but I was just so angry over the way that bastard treated you."

I studied the set of his jawline and looked into his eyes. Deep in his velvet gaze, I saw true regret. Although my instincts about men had proven to be wrong in the past, this time I had it right. Phillip Kane wasn't a threat to me. In many ways, he was my redeemer.

I threw myself into his arms and clung to him with all my might. He buried his lips in my hair and whispered in my ear,

"You don't deserve any of this." He kissed my ear and, until I quit shaking, Phillip held me.

In my jail cell that night, I was exhausted. My heart hurt from digging up memories I'd buried long ago. All I wanted to do was go to sleep, but after an hour of tossing and turning, I realized it wasn't going to happen. I sat on the edge of my cot and flipped on my reading light.

Before he'd left that afternoon, Phillip gave me a spiral notebook and pen. He had to go to his main office for a couple of days. Until I saw him again, he wanted me to try to recall, step by step, how I'd come to marry Harland and how and when the abuse started.

"Try to remember certain incidents that show the level of abuse," Phillip had said.

It wouldn't be hard. From my ten-year marriage, those were the things I remembered most.

I pulled the notebook and pen from under the mattress. While sitting on the bed, I could comfortably write on the fold-down tabletop attached to the wall. I thought hard about what I wanted to say, where I wanted to start, and what good rehashing all of it would do.

I clicked the pen in and out. Out and in. Paced the tiny cell. Sat back down and numbered the top of the page. #1. Yet words were as elusive as sleep.

Everything that came to mind about Harland and our relationship translated to one thing—Eddie had broken my heart and, in the beginning, Harland made it all better. That was the first sentence I wrote, and from there I couldn't stop.

Harland had dropped by my office twice during the six weeks before I found out what happened to Eddie. The day I called his uncle, Harland showed up for the third time. It was the charm.

For our first date, he took me to a fancy restaurant and spent more money for that one meal than I made in three days working for Mr. Lockwood. Harland was smart and had a great sense of humor. He lightened my heart and made me smile. The difference between the world I'd come from and the one Harland presented gave me hope that evil didn't necessarily lurk around every corner.

One bright sunny day, my boss handed me a folder to file. "I understand you're dating Harland Jeffers," he said nonchalantly.

"I've gone out with him a few times." He looked unusually stern. "Is there a problem?"

"Not yet. I hope there won't be one." His tone bordered on reprimand. It startled me.

"I don't understand." That was putting it mildly.

"Harland has his finger in a lot of pies in this town. He sits on several boards as a legal advisor for the Police Benevolent League, the library, and he's a past president of the Chamber of Commerce. He owns a fortune in rental property, and now that his mother is dead, he's picked up where she left off with several charities and building the new children's wing at the hospital."

Was Mr. Lockwood trying to sell me on Harland or trying to scare me away?

"That's quite an impressive lineup. I know he's a partner at the Jeffers and Knightly law firm, but we've never discussed his job beyond that. Are you trying to make a point?"

"My agency holds the policies for every cent of insurance

Harland has. It would be devastating should he become unhappy with anything connected to my business." His tone seemed to hold a warning.

Mr. Lockwood's obvious stress level bordered on panic, and although Harland had taken my mind off Eddie, I could easily stop seeing him if it meant so much to my boss. "I've had a couple of enjoyable dates with Harland, but I'm not looking for a permanent situation, and I'm sure he isn't, either. If it would make things easier for you, I'll stop seeing him," I volunteered.

"No." His sharp response came so quickly I jumped. "You *can't* stop seeing him. We talked this morning, and he's quite taken with you. It would be best if nothing happened to change that."

I didn't like the implication in my boss's statement. "Does my job depend on my dating Harland Jeffers?"

"Both our jobs depend on it." Mr. Lockwood disappeared into his office and closed the door behind him.

"What the hell was that all about?" I asked the troll with purple hair stuck on the end of a pencil in the holder on my desk. I rubbed the pencil between my hands and watched his hair form a point, then shook my head to clear the bad vibes from the conversation I'd just had with my boss. I didn't understand, but it gave me an instant headache.

Later that afternoon, shortly before closing time, Harland called.

"Hi, sweet thing, there's a new movie at the Monitor. I'll pick you up around seven," he told me.

I'm not sure if it was the fact he didn't *ask* me to go out or if the remnants of my conversation with Mr. Lockwood left me a little punch-drunk. Whatever the reason, I didn't want to go out at all that night.

"Sorry, Harland. I've had a pretty rough day. I think I'll

stay in tonight. Maybe next time. I've gotta run." I hung up the phone.

Half an hour later I locked the door on my way out of the office. Mr. Lockwood had left ahead of me. The sky spit a light mist, but moving dark clouds threatened more. I opened my umbrella and hurried along the sidewalk as fast as I could. I had a half mile to walk to my apartment. Not so far on a bright, sunny day, but forever with lightning flashing across the murky sky.

I'd only gone two blocks when a car pulled alongside me and stopped. Harland leaned across the passenger seat and shoved the door open. "Get in before you get soaked," he called.

I didn't want to get in, but I didn't want to get wet, either. I got in and pulled the door closed.

"Thanks," I said. "I really think I could have made it home before the hard rain came."

"I'm sure you could have, but since I'm going your way, this works out better." Harland drove down the driveway past my landlord's house and pulled his Lincoln to a stop at the bottom of the steps. "How about you run upstairs and freshen up and then hurry back and we'll go get a bite to eat."

"I'm tired. I just want to relax, watch some television, and go to bed early. I appreciate the offer." I started to get out.

Harland grasped my arm. "I knew I made a mistake giving you that television. I'm not taking no for an answer. Now hurry up before that bad old thunderhead breaks and you get your beautiful hair all wet."

Vesta had taken the television with her and Harland gave me an old one of his, but that shouldn't mean he owned me.

When I started to present my final argument, he placed his finger to my lips. "Please."

Harland had been very close to his mother, and she'd died

only a few months before. I was sure he was lonely, and loneliness was no fun. Besides, I had to eat anyway. So I caved. "Okay. I'll be back in a few minutes."

Scratch, the dog Eddie had put into my custody, waited impatiently inside my apartment. As soon as I opened the door, the dog zoomed past me and down the stairs. By the time I'd gone to the bathroom, washed up, run a brush through my hair, and painted my lips with shimmering pink lipstick, Scratch was clawing at the door to get back in.

"Perfect timing, little fellow." I took a second to ruffle his curly hair. "I'll be back soon. You keep an eye on everything around here." Since it would be dark when I returned, I left a table lamp on for Scratch. And for me.

I was tired, but more than that I didn't like the feeling of not being able to make my own decision. So as soon as Harland and I finished eating, I insisted he take me home. He wanted to walk me to my door, but the rain was pouring down and lightning was veining the sky.

"No, there's no need for you to get wet, too. Thanks for dinner."

Harland leaned close and pressed his strong, hard lips against mine. I kissed him back, but when he drew me to him, I pulled away so quickly I knocked my purse into the floorboard.

"Things are going too fast, Harland. I'm not interested in anything heavy."

He reached into the floorboard and gathered the spilled contents of my purse. "I can understand that. You appear to have some growing up to do. Why don't you give me a call when you're ready for a mature relationship?" He leaned over me and opened my door. "Good-bye."

Dumbfounded, I got out of the car and didn't wait to open

an umbrella. I took the steps two at a time and got into the apartment as quickly as possible. Once inside, I shivered from the rain and the unsettling feeling washing coldly through my body. By taking a stand, I'd offended Harland. I hadn't meant to do that, especially since my boss had emphasized keeping Harland happy. I was sorry, but really couldn't do anything about it. Harland had made the decision.

After I'd changed out of my clothes and put on blue baby doll pajamas, I wrapped my chilled body in my warm chenille robe. Suddenly Scratch ran to the door and emitted a low growl. The wooden floor beneath my feet vibrated letting me know someone was climbing the outside stairs leading to my apartment.

I stared at the thin lace curtain covering the window in the top half of the door. Whoever was out there could plainly see into the room where I stood. I waited for a knock. None came. Lightning flashed, illuminating a silhouette of a man on the landing.

Icy fear burned in the pit of my stomach. I had no phone to call for help. My only neighbor was my landlord, and he was so deaf he'd never hear my cries for help. I had to know who was out there. I edged my way quietly to the door, flipped on the porch light, and pulled back the curtain.

Harland squinted in the blast of bright light. He held up my wallet.

"You lost this when your pocketbook fell," he called through the closed door.

A huge sigh of relief escaped my lips. I clutched the neck of my robe and then opened the door enough to retrieve my wallet. "Thank you," I said. "And thank you for dinner. I really enjoyed the time we spent at the restaurant."

He smiled faintly. "Me, too. Listen, I'm sorry for the way I acted in the car. I was a real jerk. I guess I'm just disappointed that I'm a little more certain of where I'd like to see our relationship go than you are. I promise I'll back off and let you set the pace. Okay?"

Immeasurable relief flowed through me. I'd been handed the right to make decisions about things that affected my life. To call the shots about what I did and did not want. It was an exhilarating feeling, and I liked it. Besides, I really liked spending time with Harland, and I'd hate it if we stopped seeing each other.

For the next few weeks, I didn't have to exercise my right to say no. Every date Harland invited me on offered a new and exciting experience, and I was glad to go. When he dropped me off, he never tried to come inside my apartment, and I never invited him. After I'd verbalized my sincere thanks for whatever the occasion, he would place a chaste kiss on my lips and leave.

It was a comfortable arrangement, and I was having the time of my life.

Harland called my office during the middle of the week. "I've been asked to speak at a Kiwanis gala on Saturday. It would be really nice if I had a beautiful lady on my arm."

I waited a moment to see if he was going to ask if I'd like to go, but he didn't, and I'd pretty much accepted that wasn't part of his chemistry. He probably didn't even realize it might be looked upon as rude. I gave him the benefit of the doubt.

"I don't have a lot of dressy clothes. I'll have to see what I can come up with."

Harland didn't give me the chance to decide what to wear. "A dark cocktail dress will be fine. Preferably black. Not too short. Just a little above your knees. And try a darker shade of lipstick. I'm not real crazy about the pink you've been wearing."

"Well . . ."

"Well, what?"

"You never said what color my underwear should be." I giggled, but silence was all I heard on the other end of the line. "Harland? It was a joke. You know, ha ha ha."

"Of course that's how I took it, but you have to understand my mother and I have maintained a certain public personae. If you are with me, it's important you present the same image. I was simply trying to keep you from being embarrassed later."

At first his thoughtfulness for my comfort warmed me, but his next words left me cold and bewildered.

"I'm sure you understand, and we won't have this conversation again. I'll pick you up at seven fifteen Saturday evening."

"Okay," was all I could manage with disbelief lodged in my throat. I hung up the phone and continued to stare. I liked Harland and enjoyed being with him, but once in a while, his arrogance raised its ugly head. By all accounts, he was a very good lawyer and undoubtedly needed to have a sharp tongue to badger witnesses to say what he wanted. But he didn't need to use those tactics on me.

Now what do I do? Go anyway, or call him and tell him no?

The phone rang. I snatched it from its cradle before the first ring ended.

"Lockwood Insurance Agency," I answered with a sharp-edged tone.

"Montana?" It was Vesta. "Are you all right?"

"I guess. I'm just feeling a little jumpy about Harland and me. It's no big deal." As time went by, it was becoming *some* kind of a deal, but I wasn't sure what. Regardless, I had to evaluate what Harland stood for and if he fit in my plans for the future. My feelings for him were growing stronger every day, but I wasn't sure we were compatible.

"According to you, he's Mr. Wonderful. Has he fallen off his pedestal?" Vesta laughed quietly.

She always looked at things logically. Maybe I needed to lay my uneasiness on the table for Vesta to give me her two cents' worth. I looked around to make sure Mr. Lockwood hadn't walked up behind me.

"The bottom line is Harland acts like I'm his possession. When I tell him I don't want to do something, he won't take no for an answer."

"You mean he's forced you to have sex?"

"No, nothing like that. He tried to hug me once. I told him he was rushing me. He said he'd wait until I was ready."

"So, what did he do wrong?" Vesta seemed irritated.

"He doesn't ask me to go out. He just calls and says he'll pick me up at a certain time on a certain day and expects me to be ready."

"You mean you don't want to go out with him?"

"I want to go out with him, but I'd like to be asked."

"Do you like the places he takes you?"

"Yes, we've been to a political picnic, a movie, a dinner theater in Webster, and a cocktail party at the mayor's house. He just called and told me I was going to a Kiwanis dinner on Saturday night. He also told me in detail what to wear. He said he has an image he and his mother have built and need to maintain. Since I'll be with him, I'd be expected to reflect the same image."

"What he told you to wear . . . was it really sexy or, even better, sleazy?"

"No, nothing like that. It was very conservative, actually. Basic black cocktail dress, right at my knee, and a different shade of lipstick."

"Let me see if I have this right. You've said this man is very good-looking; he's a rich lawyer. He takes you to fun and interesting places. You've been seeing him for a while and he has respected your wishes, leaving your virtue intact. And because he suggests what you should wear to a place you've never been before, you want to send him down the road. Do I have all that right?"

"It's not that—" Another line lit up. "Hang on." I put Vesta on hold and answered the other line. I buzzed the call through to Mr. Lockwood's office, and waited for him to pick up. My brief break from Vesta's analysis of my situation had apparently cleared my thinking. She was right. I flipped back to her.

"I'm back. I understand what you're saying, but I've been wondering if I could live with someone like that. You know, a person who has to be in charge of everything."

"It's called being a man, Montana." She did sarcasm so well.

"Oh, Vesta, just because you've been married almost a year doesn't mean you know all about men. Mitch would never tell you what to wear or tell you to do something without asking you first. He seems to be perfect."

"Let me tell you about my man. He's poor, he leaves the cap off the toothpaste, and he farts at the table. Wanna trade?"

I broke up laughing and placed my hand over my mouth so Mr. Lockwood wouldn't hear me. "You're crazy, Vesta. That's why I love you. I have to get back to work."

"Wait. Do you have something to wear Saturday night?" she asked.

"Just the same dress I wore to the mayor's house. You know

the blue polka-dotted one I bought in the bargain basement at Turner's."

"Will you be home tonight?"

"Yes, unless Harland comes by and takes me somewhere." I chuckled.

"I have a dress I think will be perfect for Saturday night. Mitch is working late. I'll swing by the Biff-Burger Drive-In and pick us up something to eat. We haven't had dinner together in a long time."

"That really sounds good. I've missed you."

When Vesta showed up at my home that night, we ate while the food was still hot. As I took my last bite, I accidentally dribbled a blob of thin barbeque sauce onto my white cotton blouse. Quickly, I used a damp towel and rubbed at the spot. It did nothing but smear the red sauce into a bigger smudge.

From the driveway below, a car door slammed. Vesta looked out the window and the floor began to vibrate.

"Who is it?" I asked, still wiping at the stain on my shirt.

"From all your descriptions, I'd say it's Harland Jeffers."

My heart dropped to my stomach. I had on cutoff jeans, a white blouse with barbeque sauce all over it, and I was as barefooted as a yard dog.

I waved my hands up and down in front of me. "Wonder how this outfit will fit into his public image?" I asked Vesta.

She hurried around the end of the couch to stand next to me in the middle of the living room floor. "You're not in public. You're in your own home. Not his business."

As Harland took the last step onto the small porch outside

my open door, he stared through the screen at Vesta and me standing like soldiers side by side at full attention. Embarrassed, I started to laugh. Vesta pushed by me and shoved the screen door open.

"Come on in." She grabbed Harland's arm and pulled him over the threshold. "You must be Harland." She held out her hand, and he took it. "I'm Montana's friend Vesta."

He gave me a scowling, sideways glance, then looked back at her. "It's a pleasure to meet you. Did I interrupt something?" Quickly his gaze scanned my barbeque stain and then locked with mine. Finally, he smiled.

"No, you didn't interrupt anything. Vesta brought us dinner, and we've just been catching up on old times. Please come in. Have a seat."

"No, I can't stay. I'm having a telephone put in for you tomorrow, and I need a key to let the phone company in to install it." The confident set of his shoulders told me there wouldn't be a discussion, but by the way my spine automatically stiffened it made me think there should be.

"If I could afford a telephone, I'd already have one, Harland." Steel edged my tone.

Color drained from his face. At first I thought he was going to verbally lash out at me, but then I realized I'd embarrassed him in front of Vesta. He recovered quickly.

"I'm sorry. Let me start over." Laughter filled his voice. "I'd like to be able to call you and talk to you without being interrupted by customers or other ringing lines. The best solution I could come up with was to have a phone installed here for you. I intended for it to be a present from me to you. The monthly bill will come to my office."

"I can't let you do that," I argued.

"Well, I think it's a wonderful gesture." Vesta gripped my forearm and squeezed. "I'd like to be able to talk to you, too, without being put on hold a few dozen times."

I glared at her. She released me and busied herself clearing hamburger wrappers from the table.

I took Harland's arm and led him outside. "I don't know if that's a good idea. It makes more of a statement about us as a couple than I think it should."

"That's my point. I know all I need to know about you, but I want you to get to know me better. I don't see that happening with us only seeing each other once a week. Or with me calling you at your job and having to hurry and spit out what I want to say before you have to answer another line or hang up to help a customer. Is that too much to ask?" His hard expression relaxed into a smile.

That explained why he always told me what he wanted instead of asking. He didn't feel he had time for it. So he'd lay out the plan and eliminate the small talk. I certainly felt better about the situation. Also, I did miss being able to talk with Vesta as long as I wanted to. She had the same complaint as Harland.

"Okay, you can have it put in. It may take me a couple of months, but I'll figure out a way to pay the bill."

He started to object, but I didn't let him.

"That's the only way I'll agree to it."

He nodded and held out his hand. "How about that key? Do you have an extra one I could use tomorrow?"

"I still have the one I had when I lived here," Vesta called from inside the house.

As warm blood made its way to my cheeks, I rolled my eyes at Harland. "She may be nosy," I snickered, "but she's my best friend."

He smiled and my body warmed. Vesta appeared at the door and handed him the key. He took it, placed a quick kiss on my cheek, and descended the stairs. I shoved Vesta back inside.

"What do you think?" I couldn't wait to hear what my wise, all-knowing friend had to say.

"You want to know if I think he's a keeper? Let's put it this way; if you don't grab up that cute, rich, caring man who appears to think the sun rises and sets on you, then you should be locked up."

Sitting in my jail cell, I stared at the notebook I'd been writing in for several hours. The words blurred, except for Vesta's declaration that if I didn't continue my relationship with Harland, I should be locked up. Neither I nor my dear friend could have ever dreamed that *getting* mixed up with him would have the same result.

$\mathcal{C}$hapter 10

THE NEXT MORNING, I RETURNED TO WRITING EVERYTHING I could about my walk to the dark side of Harland Jeffers. As I thought about the first stages of our association, I was shocked and embarrassed that I hadn't seen the signs. They were there as plain as the bruises and broken bones I would receive later. Yet I never saw his constant demand for my perfection as anything more than my lack of knowing about proper etiquette or how to make a man happy. I was the one who was broken. I was the one who needed fixing.

The evening of the Kiwanis function, Vesta helped me slip her black cocktail dress over perfectly curled hair and down over my squeaky clean body. As she zipped me up, I placed my hands on my narrow waist and rose on tiptoes to look into the mirror. My hem was exactly where Harland had said it should be. I licked my red lips and hoped the new color would please him. Vesta gave me one last squirt of powerful, magnolia-scented cologne.

"Here." She placed a gold chain with a small angel pendant

around my neck. "That should do it." She spun me around. "You look like a million bucks waiting to be spent."

Excitement buzzed through every fiber of my body. I stared at the unfamiliar woman looking back at me from the dresser mirror. "You made me look so pretty," I said.

"I had nothing to do with it, you moron. You were born like that." Vesta pulled her keys from her purse and headed for the door. "I want you to call me as soon as you get in tonight." She pointed to the newly installed, black telephone sitting on an end table. "No matter what time. Promise?"

"Yes, if you're sure Mitch won't get mad at me."

"He'll probably be waiting with me to hear the details, too." Vesta giggled as she made her way down the stairs.

I paced from the window overlooking the driveway below to the bedroom for another look into the mirror. I couldn't believe it. I felt like a queen.

Surely Harland would be pleased. I'd tried to dress as he'd asked. He hadn't mentioned what kind of neckline he liked, but Vesta assured me any man worth having would be delighted for his woman to have just the right amount of cleavage peeking from a V-neckline. The pendant rested between the swell of my breasts. My guardian angel. I wasn't sure why I thought I needed a guardian, but I was glad she was there.

Harland arrived on time. When he first came into the apartment, he looked me up and down. A few seconds later, he stepped close enough to kiss my cheek.

"You look nice. Are you ready to go?"

I'm not sure what I expected from Harland, but *nice* wasn't it. His lukewarm reaction to my hours of meticulously dressing especially for him dissolved my feeling of enchantment. I picked up the black, beaded clutch Vesta had insisted was the perfect accessory for my new, sophisticated look. As I followed Harland to the car, I rubbed my guardian angel between my fingers and prayed the evening wouldn't be a complete disaster.

"You look very handsome," I said. Of course, he always did, no matter where we were going. He didn't acknowledge my compliment, simply stared at the road ahead. I had the feeling I should sit quietly and speak only when spoken to. However, I shoved past that just to show Mr. Harland Jeffers I didn't have to bow down to his rude mood swings.

"If you're pouting about something and you expect me to figure it out, you'll have a long wait ahead of you. I haven't a clue what's put that sour look on your face."

His gaze snapped in my direction. His glare locked on my face, chilling me to the bone. I shivered. Harland pulled into the driveway of a sprawling, ranch-style home with a lush, green, perfectly manicured yard. The drive circled in front of the house, which was hidden by a brick wall with a wrought-iron entrance gate, but we drove to the right side of the house where one of three garage doors was already rolling open. We pulled inside.

Harland spoke his first words since he'd picked me up. "I'll be right back." He disappeared into the house.

A second beige Lincoln occupied the last stall of the garage. The middle bay was empty. On the wall facing the street, white curtains adorned the windows. Floor-to-ceiling cabinets lined another wall. Everything neat and orderly. Evidently, Harland's picture of perfection extended to his home, too.

As Harland climbed back into the car he tossed a mint green shawl into my lap. "Here. Put this on. Cover yourself up." He backed out of the garage, and soon we sped along maple-lined streets. Speechless, I stared at the wrap and then looked down at the front of my dress. I would admit I exposed more flesh than usual, but I didn't see it as indecent.

"If you didn't like the way I was dressed, why didn't you say so? I would have changed before we left my place." I hoped the shaking in my voice came across as anger more than apprehension about the situation.

"If I'd wanted you to change, I would have said so. I decided one of Mother's shawls would remedy the situation without an ugly exchange of words." He glanced my way. "I did make the right decision, didn't I?"

"Sure," I mumbled, uncertain what my argument should be. After all, he had wanted to make sure I presented a sophisticated image, not that of a call girl. He tried to tell me this without an argument. So I guess he had made the right choice.

I lightly stroked the green silk shawl decorated with gold beads and white sequins. It was a perfect addition to my outfit. I slipped it around my shoulders and hugged it across my breast. Harland cared about how I looked to other people. He had a good eye for style. Yes, he made decisions for me, but I was beginning to believe he did it because he cared for me. And wasn't I becoming a better, more cultured person as a result?

"This is beautiful, Harland. I guess I've got a lot to learn about what's proper and what isn't." I smiled at him.

He ran his finger along my jaw. "I'll teach you everything you need to know."

Just then he wheeled into the parking lot of the Hyatt Regency. Inside, I was introduced to the president of the Kiwanis Club and his wife, and was escorted to a table near the lectern. The whole time I kept the shawl wrapped tightly to prevent anyone from seeing what I hid beneath it.

Harland shook hands and chatted with several bystanders

before taking a seat next to me. "Smile," he whispered in my ear. "You never know when someone will take your picture."

I did as instructed and kept it in place for the rest of the evening.

Several months passed, and each time I became uncomfortable with something Harland said or did, I'd pacify my apprehension with the mantra I'd adopted. *He doesn't mean anything by it. That's just the way he is.* And the fact that no one else ever heard his sharp criticisms only added to my self-consciousness. Eventually, I came to believe it was me, not him, who had a problem.

As I left work one afternoon, Harland waited in the parking lot with a brand-new white Skylark. He jiggled the keys in front of me.

"It's for you, sweetheart." He handed them to me. "No more walking to and from work."

I'm sure my eyes were as big as moon pies. Whether I should accept the car or not wasn't even something I had to think about. I'd already learned that if Harland gave me something, I had no choice but to take it. I really wanted my own car. He had bought me one. End of discussion.

"Oh, Harland, it's perfect." I threw myself into his arms, and he swung me around like a father would an excited child. "You shouldn't have," I said, but his crestfallen look made me add, "but I'm glad you did. May I drive it now?"

"Of course. It's all yours." Harland opened the door, and I climbed behind the wheel. Vesta had taught me to drive her car, but I'd need a little practice before I'd feel confident enough to hit the road alone.

Harland got in next to me and opened the glove compartment. He pulled out a small black box, and when he opened it, I gasped. "My God, Harland, that's the biggest diamond I've ever seen." The sun glistened through the beautiful gem while my heart danced to the rhythm of each sparkle.

Harland removed the ring from the box and reached for my hand. "Will you marry me, Montana?"

He was good-looking, held in high esteem by the entire town, and was rich and not afraid to spend his money on me. But were those reasons enough to accept a marriage proposal? In my heart, I didn't feel it was right.

When he gave me presents, I accepted, but when he asked me to make a commitment to him for life, I couldn't do it. What kind of woman did that make me? I wasn't sure, but I didn't want to try to figure it out.

"Harland, I can't marry you. I love being with you and doing the things I'd never have a chance to do if not for you, but marriage? It is way too soon for me to even consider it."

Disappointment played plainly across his face.

"I know you don't love me, Montana, but I love you and have since the moment I first laid eyes on you. I've been very patient waiting to win you over. I've tried with all my might to make you happy. I've not tried to force you to have sex with me, but I don't want that kind of relationship any longer. I want you to be my wife. I want you in my bed. I don't give a damn if you love me. That doesn't have to be part of the deal."

Harland and I had barely kissed, yet the words *love, sex, bed, wife* tumbled out of control through my mind and then landed in a heap somewhere inside my brain.

"I didn't say I didn't love you." My voice sounded almost eager.

"Then you do love me?" His question sounded more like a plea.

I didn't want to hurt him, but I couldn't blatantly declare my love for him when I wasn't sure how I really felt.

"I care for you. I'd even go so far as to say I'd like to see our relationship move to a higher level. But declaring love and getting married? I can't do that right now. Don't you understand?" My gaze searched his stone-cold face. I couldn't read his thoughts, and I really wasn't sure I wanted to. We continued to sit motionless, staring at each other. To ease the tension, I leaned back against the headrest and closed my eyes.

"I'm sorry, Harland. I guess this changes everything."

"I guess it does." His voice was cold and exact.

I looked at him, and found he was busy putting the ring back in its box. He slammed it into the glove compartment. From the beginning, Harland's attitude had been his way or not at all. An ache lay heavy in my chest. Since I hadn't said yes to his proposal, I was pretty sure our connection had just been severed.

He got out of the car and came around to open my door. "Scoot over," he said, his voice dry and emotionless. "I'll take you home."

Once we'd changed seats, he started the car and sped out of the parking lot with tires squealing and gravel spewing. I gripped the armrest and closed my eyes, but then relaxed and stared straight ahead. I refused to show any fear, because no matter how bad Harland's temper tantrum got, I wouldn't marry him without loving him completely.

Without a word, Harland dropped me in front of my landlord's house and sped away. I watched him until he'd disappeared. Disappointment filled my heart. I was sure I'd never see Harland again.

The next day I received a large bouquet of white roses. I knew instantly who had sent them. The card read: *Someday you'll be able to shout your love for me from the highest mountain. Until then, I'll be happy just being part of your life. The keys are under the floor mat. I'll pick you up at seven on Friday night. And just so you know, you don't have to wait for my love. You already have it. I love you, Harland.*

I went to the door and looked out into the parking lot. There sat the Skylark. My present from Harland. All along, he'd given me things to make my life better, more enjoyable, like a telephone, a record player, a television, and now a car. Maybe I wasn't madly in love with him, but there was definitely warmness around my heart that grew stronger with each passing day. Was I crazy to keep waiting for that happily-ever-after kind of love in books?

The next few weeks with Harland were magical. I had a good job, my own apartment, and Harland loved me. He made it easy for me to forget the sadness Eddie's disappearance from my life had generated. And, more importantly, Harland made it easy for me to return his love.

Although we only saw each other on weekends, Harland and I talked every night on the phone. It had been installed for several months, but he had yet to let me pay the bill.

Our nightly conversations were lengthy. We never lacked for things to talk about. Mostly we discussed how we had spent our days and what we wanted from the future. On rare occasions, we'd broach the subject of his mother. He never came right out and said he loved her, but it was evident by what he did say that she had been a remarkable woman, and he held her in the highest regard.

"My dad died when I was twelve," Harland told me. "He made the usual soap opera deathbed demand for me to be the man of the house and to take care of my mother." Even through the phone I could hear bitterness in his voice.

"As a child, I'm sure that must have been hard on you."

"Other than material things, the bastard had never taken care of my mother unless it was to give her the back of his hand. Yet he thought he'd pass that task on to his son." His voice seemed to seethe.

"I'm sorry, sweetheart," I whispered.

"Don't be. My mother more than made up for my father's shortcomings." After a short pause, Harland said, "I thought maybe you could come to my house Friday night for dinner." He'd changed the subject to something I found very intriguing.

"Dinner at your house? Do you mean to say I get to enter the inner sanctum of Harland Jeffers's home?" I teased.

"You know what they say—be careful what you wish for." His chuckle wrapped me in pure joy.

Friday night, I drove to Harland's house on Serenity Drive for my first peek into his home. I'd only been there the night he gave me his mother's shawl to wear to the Kiwanis dinner and I'd waited in the car inside the garage.

This time I followed the paved driveway, which curved outside a brick wall with a black entrance gate. After pressing a lighted button next to the gate and while I waited for Harland, I admired the beautiful rosebushes laid out in a formal garden between the wall and the front porch. He'd talked often of his roses and his love for gardening. It plainly showed in the colorful petals of every flower. Harland nurtured things and helped them grow. I was an example of that.

The unstable and mostly sad life I'd always known took a backseat to the happiness I'd found with Harland. I never wanted what I was feeling at that moment to go away.

Suddenly, I realized he was standing at the front door watching me.

"Hi, I was just looking at your beautiful roses."

The gate clicked loudly and when I pushed on it, it opened into the courtyard. Harland closed the space between us with quick, fluid strides, wrapped his arm around my waist, and led me up the path.

"I'm glad you like them. I spend at least a few minutes every evening doing something out here or in the backyard, but I enjoy it."

We entered the house through double doors into a beautiful foyer; a connecting hallway led to other rooms. Some had arched doorways and some had closed doors. At the end of the hallway were sliding glass doors that led to a patio and pool area. From what I could see, it was magnificent and inviting.

Daunted by the bric-a-brac displayed on a library table along one wall, I concentrated on my movements. I certainly didn't want to accidentally knock anything onto the highly polished marble floors.

"Harland, this is all so beautiful." I'm not sure why I felt the need to speak in hushed tones. Maybe because I'd never been in such a grand home, and I thought whispering would give it the reverence it deserved.

"Glad you like it. Let me show you around." Proudly, Harland started his tour right in the entrance. "My dad built this house in the early forties. He always called it a shotgun house because you can come in the front door, walk down the hallway, and go out a back door to the pool without ever going through any other room. If the doors were opened, you could shoot a shotgun through the house and never hit anything." He pretended to do just that.

"The old house I grew up in on our farm was a shotgun house, but believe me it wasn't as elegant as this. Your mother had exquisite taste. Was she a interior decorator?"

"No," Harland said. "She just had an innate sense of beauty and design."

I studied the huge glass case along one side of the hallway filled with knickknacks. "Did you collect all these ceramic birds?" They were beautiful, and at first glance, it was hard to even guess how many there were.

"They belonged to my mother, and they're porcelain." He corrected me with a slightly irritated edge to his voice.

"Sorry," I said. I'd have to be careful lest my ignorance of uppity stuff showed. I nearly giggled out loud, but I'd learned early in our relationship that if Harland spoke in that somber tone, it was better not to try to make light of the situation. "I don't believe I've ever seen anything like them. They're beautiful."

He didn't reply, but stepped around me and swung open white, double doors into an elegant parlor. It could have been featured in one of those *Good Housekeeping* magazines Mama used to pick up occasionally. Everything was neat and shiny, and I couldn't visualize anyone slumping on the gold brocade sofa and propping their feet on the coffee table to watch television.

Evidently, that would never happen because a quick scan of the room told me there was no television.

"Very impressive," I said.

Harland showed me the formal dining room, which was just as eye-catching as the parlor. Two places had been set at the table complete with flowers and candles ready to be lit.

You could enter the kitchen from the dining room or from the hallway near the glass doors leading to the pool. The kitchen was modern and equipped with what appeared to be shiny new appliances.

"My mother had redone the kitchen shortly before she passed away," Harland said. I could see something was baking in the eye-level, built-in oven and the smell was wonderful.

"Did you cook dinner?"

Harland shook his head. "No, Clara cooked something for us." He looked at the timer above the oven. "It should be ready in about ten more minutes. Would you like some wine?"

I still had about four months before I'd be twenty-one, but I didn't think one glass would hurt me. "I'd love some."

While he opened the bottle, I strolled to the sliding doors that led to the pool. He joined me. I took a big gulp of the red wine and emitted a little cough.

"You sip wine. Slowly. Deliberately. Let it linger on your tongue. Let your taste buds come alive with the flavor." Harland took a small drink and appeared to swish it around in his mouth like it was mouthwash. Finally, he swallowed and motioned for me to do the same thing.

I sipped, swished, swallowed, and coughed again. Harland took my glass, still half-full of wine, and carried it back into the kitchen. He dumped the liquid into the sink, washed out the glass, dried it, and put it back into the cabinet.

"It's an acquired taste. We'll try it again some time." Harland took my hand and led me down the hallway. "Come on. Let me show you the guest room."

My mind was still on the wine. I thought it was rude of him to take it away like that and maybe I should tell him so. I also should tell him I didn't foresee me liking it any better at a later date and that I'd rather drink Concord grape juice. I should have . . . but I didn't. Instead, I shoved it out of my mind and followed him with great expectation.

I wasn't disappointed. The guest room was right out of a fairy tale, fit for a queen.

"This was my mother's room, and now I call it the guest room. Of course, no one has slept in it since my mother died, but it's there should company arrive. What do you think?"

"I think the whole place is wonderful. I can't imagine—"

The kitchen timer sounded.

"Dinner's done. Let's go eat," Harland said.

I took one more glance at the white and pale blue furnishings before he pulled me out of the room and escorted me to the dining table.

He pulled out my chair. "Your seat, madame."

I placed my hand over my mouth to stifle a giggle. He removed it.

"Go ahead and laugh. That's something that's been missing in this house for a long time." He planted a kiss on my forehead. "I'll be right back with dinner." A few minutes later, he set a plate in front of me, a very appetizing presentation of baked chicken, rice, and asparagus.

I'd never eaten asparagus before, but I would try it and hope with all my heart it tasted better than the wine.

"You say Clara fixed this for us?" I tasted the vegetable, which was pretty good.

"Yes. She's a good cook, don't you think?"

"I do. I know you told me she had worked for your mother for many years cleaning house and doing the laundry, but you never mentioned that she cooked, too."

"She did everything for Mother. She was more of an assistant than a housekeeper."

"I know your mother was in some type of business, but you never said what she did."

Harland paused for a moment. "I guess you could say Mother was a professional board sitter."

"You mean like a carpenter?" I was kidding, of course, but where his mother was concerned, Harland appeared to have no sense of humor. "That was a joke, Harland."

His puzzled expression gave way to a smile. "Oh, what I meant is she was on boards for several charitable organizations, not only for the city, but throughout the state. Dad left her, or I should say us, a lot of money he'd made in overseas stocks. So Mother put it to good use in helping benefit others, especially where needy children were concerned. You know, like donating the money to build the new children's wing at the county hospital. She was generous like that." A smile pulled at the corners of his mouth. His thoughts appeared to be a million miles away.

When we finished eating, we carried our plates to the kitchen. I offered to wash the dishes, but Harland said no. He fixed me a glass of soda and poured himself another glass of wine. His third, but who was counting. We took our drinks out onto the patio and relaxed on a double lounge chair next to the lighted pool where the clear, blue water rippled in the evening breeze.

The brick wall that enclosed the front of the house totally surrounded the beautiful backyard beyond the pool. Along the back, through another iron gate was a path that led to a wooded area of stately oaks. The roof of a building rose above the wall.

"Is that building on your property?" I asked.

"Yes. I have five acres here. The line goes all the way through that stand of trees down to Six-Mile Creek that runs . . . well, for six miles. The building just outside the gate is my workshop. I keep my lawn and gardening equipment, woodworking tools, and workout equipment back there. It's a nice walk down to the water. We'll do that sometime when you're here in the daytime. There's also a new housing development right at the back of the property." Harland emptied the last drop of wine in his glass and stared intently at the path through the woods.

"I'd like that," I said, but wasn't sure I wanted to. In the dusky shadows, it looked a little eerie to me.

When the sun had completely disappeared, the night sky twinkled with bright stars. Harland and I held hands and talked about everything and nothing. Eventually, as quiet closed around us, I rested my head on his shoulder and wondered if there was any better place on earth than at Harland's side.

More than anything, I wanted to let him know exactly how I felt. He'd been telling me his feelings for weeks. Suddenly, I wasn't afraid to let him know mine.

I shifted slightly to look into his eyes, and I was lost. For the first time since I'd met Harland, I initiated a kiss. When our lips touched, I looped my arms around his neck and pulled him so close I could feel his heart pounding against my chest. Brought on by the knowledge I caused the rapid cadence, my confidence spiraled upward.

I dared to push further and trailed kisses along his neck. Vibrations of a soft moan came from Harland's throat. I held the means to make this powerful man wither under my touch. Egged on by the knowledge, desire flared through my body.

After unbuttoning his shirt, I slipped my hands inside and ran them over his muscular chest. His skin's heat escalated beneath my touch.

"Should we go inside? You do have neighbors." I stared into the darkness over the brick wall surrounding the backyard. A stately home stood close to Harland's property line. Only the second story could be seen above the brick wall.

"That's the Simpsons'. They're out of town, and I don't believe they'd be watching us even if they were home." His lips trembled as if he was fighting a smile.

Slowly he slipped my blouse over my head and paused. I looked into his eyes and saw raw desire mixed with uncertainty. He feared I would pull away as I'd done before. But it wasn't going to happen. I wanted him as much as I knew he wanted me.

I reached behind me and unfastened my brassiere and then tossed it aside. He needed no more invitation. Gently he kneaded my breasts. In case my response to his touch on my flesh and my quivering body left any doubt, I whispered, "Please . . . I want to be yours completely."

"Oh, Montana." My whispered name was almost lost as Harland reclaimed my lips and, at the same time, urged me down onto the chaise lounge. He continued to kiss me with a hunger I understood. I matched his level of desire and brazenly upped the stakes a notch. By the time he'd shoved my skirt to my waist and taken my panties from my hips, I had freed the most intimate part of him from his slacks.

Opening to him, I guided him into me and kneaded handfuls of bare flesh, pulling him to me with all my might. We fit together, combining our bodies until we were one. As our bodies rocked in perfect harmony, my hand ran the length of his back. My fingers ran over a ridge of flesh. A scar of some sort. There wasn't time to wonder how it had gotten there. The thought was quickly replaced by the flow of passion flooding through me.

Although there wasn't the ultimate sensation I'd experienced each time Eddie and I had made love, Harland's shuddering release brought me complete satisfaction. And, as he called my name, I felt his undying love vibrate through my heart and peace settled inside me.

And it all became clear. When Eddie left, he had taken a large chunk of my heart. I never thought I'd ever be able to love another man. Harland proved to me I was still capable of love, and I knew that, no matter how long I looked, no one would ever love me as much as Harland.

With deepest sincerity, I whispered, "I love you, Harland."

Chapter 11

AFTER WE'D MADE LOVE, HARLAND AND I WENT SKINNY-DIP-ping. We played like children. When he swam away from me, the cool water caused chill bumps to cover my flesh, but when he took me in his arms, my body warmed again. He lifted me, and I wrapped my legs around him. While our bodies swayed with the ripple of the water, we kissed and the fire burning in my heart flamed even higher.

Our lips parted, and I whispered again, "I love you, Harland."

"I love you, too," he said and pulled my naked body against him. His muscular arms held me so tightly I could barely breathe.

"You're very strong. Where did you get all those muscles?" I asked as I ran my hand over his shoulder and down his back.

"I lift weights in my workshop. Plus, yard work helps keep me in shape." He flexed.

I squeezed his arm. "I'll bet you got them from pitching prosecuting attorneys out of windows." I splashed water in his face and tried to make a quick getaway.

With little effort, he caught me, raised me over his head, and pitched me back into the water. My painstakingly teased hairdo was ruined. I'm sure I looked like a drowned squirrel. We were both laughing so hard I had trouble catching my breath. It was a good thing his neighbors were gone. I don't think they would appreciate the two of us loudly romping bare-assed naked at three in the morning. We could have turned out the pool light, but I liked watching Harland glide through the clear water.

I pushed my wet, sticky hair out of my eyes. He surfaced and splashed me again, and turned to swim away. It was then I saw the scar I'd felt while we were making love.

"Harland?" I called to him.

He swished back through the water to the shallow end of the pool where I was standing.

"Something wrong?" he asked.

"How did you get that scar on your back?" I had him turn around so I could get a better look. The puckered section of skin was at least six inches long. Marks left by what must have been large stitches dotted each side of the scar. I touched it lightly.

"It's nothing." He spun to face me, causing a mini-whirlpool to swirl around us. "Let's go in. It's really late." He walked up the pool steps and grabbed a couple of large towels out of a cabinet on the patio.

After he'd wrapped one around his waist, he waited for me to climb out of the water and draped a towel around my shoulders. Once inside, I dressed in the crumpled clothes I'd worn earlier and joined Harland in the kitchen. He'd slipped into a robe.

"Are you sure you won't spend the night here? I'll fix you breakfast in bed." He leaned into me until our foreheads touched.

"I have to go. I've stayed too long as it is. I'm sure Scratch is standing at the door with his legs crossed. Poor baby always goes out before bedtime, and it's way past that time."

I slipped my shoes on, put my arms around Harland, and kissed him. My fingers touched the raised scar on his back. I looked at him. "Are you going to tell me what happened here?"

He stared at me for a short time, and I felt he was going to tell me it wasn't my business, but instead he took a seat at the bar that divided the kitchen from the breakfast nook.

"My father put that there." Harland's voice shook and his shoulders slumped. I easily understood how hard it was for him to speak of whatever horrific event had created the scar.

"How did it happen?"

After a short delay, Harland sat up straight and spoke in a tone he probably used when presenting facts to a courtroom.

"That workshop out back used to be my father's. As a matter of fact, his tools are still there, almost where he left them. I wasn't allowed in his building, but one night I thought he was still at the office. I decided to sneak out there to see what the big deal was that kept my father out there for hours."

Harland paced a few steps. I slid into the off-white upholstered booth around the breakfast table.

"That sounds like a typical child," I tried to reassure him. "What did you find?"

"I found dear old Dad screwing Mrs. Simpson. He and the woman who stills lives next door were going at it hot and heavy right there on his workbench."

Harland certainly had my attention. "You poor thing, I take it they saw you."

"Not at first. I think I was in shock. My feet wouldn't move, so I stood there dumbfounded, having no idea what to do." He took a deep breath and exhaled loudly. "Some of the details of that night aren't very clear. I'm not sure if one of them heard me or saw me, but they realized I was there. Mrs. Simpson yelped and slithered from the table like the reptile she is and started trying to get her clothes in the right places." He paused and chuckled, but the sound held no humor.

"It would have been funny, if I hadn't been so afraid of my father's wrath."

"How old were you?"

"I don't remember," he said.

He had already told me he was twelve when his father died. So he had to be younger than that. Many children accidentally saw their parents in the act of having sex, granted, but not necessarily with a neighbor.

"What did that have to do with the scar on your back?"

"I'm not sure you really want to know."

"Yes, I do. Anything that affects you as strongly as this apparently has, I want to know about."

I scooted farther into the booth. Harland took a seat beside me. With his hands folded on the table, he squeezed them together until his knuckles turned white.

"On one side of the workbench my dad had a power saw. The blade stuck up through the table. He used it to plane and miter boards for projects he was always working on, like the curio Mom's birds are in. He was very talented." Harland grew quiet.

"And?" I urged.

"When Mrs. Simpson ran past me, I decided I should get out of there, too, but my dad grabbed me and threw me onto the table. I landed with such force that the saw blade ripped my back open."

Even though I was sitting down, my knees turned to jelly.

"Oh my God, Harland." My heart cried out for the little boy.

"He dragged me off the saw and onto the floor. It wasn't until I hit the ground and rolled to my stomach that I saw the trail of blood I'd left. I must have been screaming, because my mother heard me and came running to see what was wrong.

"She took her robe off to apply pressure to the wound. By the time the blood stopped, the robe was soaked and dripping." He stared at his hands and appeared to be lost in another time.

"I'm so sorry that happened to you." My hands were shaking so hard I had to clench them together to still them. "What did the doctor say?"

Harland's gaze never strayed from his hands, but he seemed to rouse from his thoughts to answer me. "I didn't go to a doctor."

"What? There are stitch marks around the scar." I couldn't imagine what would have kept his parents from taking him to a doctor.

"My dad made my mother sew it closed. He didn't want anyone to know how stupid I'd been playing on a table with something as dangerous as a saw."

"But that wasn't what happened."

"I know, but that was the way my father explained away the bad things he did. He'd lie about them, and expect you to lie about them, too. He was a horrible bastard." Harland shook as if physically detaching himself from his memories. "I don't want to talk about him anymore."

Although I wanted to know everything about Harland, good or bad, I sensed it was time to drop the subject.

"Okay, but I want you to know, I understand what it's like to be betrayed by a family member whom you love and who should love you."

For a few minutes, we sat in silence with only the ticking of the clock on the wall breaking the stillness in the kitchen. Finally, I moved closer to him and he put his arm around me.

"I really have to go," I said.

He kissed the top of my head. "I know. I guess we both need to get some rest. You're sure you'll be okay to drive home this late?"

"I'm wide awake." With the events of the evening, I'd be lucky if I got any sleep even after I got home. Our lovemaking had brought me fulfillment and joy. That alone had my world spinning crazily, but when I thought of the torture Harland suffered at the hands of his own father, my mind wouldn't let go of the image.

Alone inside my car, I let the tears fall for the little boy who had endured all that abuse from his father, but maybe some of the tears were for the girl who had suffered even more from her own brother.

For the next few Friday nights, I went to Harland's for dinner. Afterward, we made love and talked until well after midnight. I never stayed all night because I had to get home to Scratch. Sometimes on Saturday evening, we'd go to a movie and then back to my apartment.

For some reason, Scratch didn't like Harland. He would no sooner walk through the door than the dog retreated to a corner and never take took his eyes off Harland. Normally, I'd end up putting the dog outside during Harland's visit.

One Saturday night, I fixed dinner for Harland. The whole time we were eating, Scratch lay by the door emitting low, but noticeable growls.

"Where'd you get that mutt?" Harland asked. He cut a piece of roast beef, stabbed it with his fork, and shoveled it into his mouth without ever taking his eyes off the dog.

"Eddie rescued him from a man who mistreated him. Scratch is very protective. I don't think he'd ever let anyone hurt me, would you, boy?" I took a bit of beef from my plate and held it close to the floor. He came to me and gently removed the meat from my fingers. "Good boy." I scratched his ear.

"Don't feed that dog from the table." Harland's sharp tone startled me.

Before I could respond, Scratch took an aggressive stance, hackles raised and teeth bared at Harland. I grabbed the dog's collar and strained to hold him back. Harland jumped to his feet. He knocked the chair over backward onto the floor with a loud thud. It only made Scratch more determined to get at Harland.

With the dog snarling and fighting me every inch of the way, I managed to drag him to the door. Once I got him on the porch and out of Harland's sight, Scratch's vicious growls changed to soft whines.

"It's okay, buddy." I petted his head while I moved his dog tag back in place. I'd bought it on a whim shortly after I'd taken in the dog. The man who ran the filling station near my home made keys and engraved dog tags. So I had one made with Scratch's name on it and then attached it to a brand-new collar. I straightened it so his tag once again hung under his neck.

"You're a good boy," I said. Since he'd calmed back to his usual friendly self, I turned him loose to run in the yard and went back inside to Harland. He had righted the chair and was in the process of finishing his meal. I washed my hands and returned to my place at the table.

"You didn't have to be so rude. Just say you'd rather I didn't feed him from the table. That would have taken care of it and not have upset the dog."

From across the table, Harland pointed his knife at me. His icy glare sent shivers down my spine. "Don't you ever talk to me that way," he said.

I was so taken aback it took a moment for me to gather my wits to respond to him.

"I see nothing wrong with me pointing out that sometimes you can be rude." I, too, had a sharp-edged tongue when the situation called for it. "You have no right telling me what I will or will not do inside my own home."

Harland gripped the edge of the table, and for a short moment I thought he was going to tip it over. He didn't, but I had the strong, terrible feeling he could have and would have. I stood ready to catch whatever I could of my cheap dishware.

Harland didn't upset the table. Instead, he stormed to his car and spun his wheels on the small amount of grass I had for a yard. Like a child who stomps his way to his bedroom when he's done something wrong, Harland left with a lot of commotion. At one time, I would have thought it was the last I'd see of him, but past experiences told me it wasn't.

By the time Monday morning rolled around, I'd begun to think that maybe I wouldn't be hearing from Harland again. He hadn't called on Saturday night or all day Sunday, either, as I'd expected he would.

As I did every morning when I got up, I let Scratch out to do his thing while I dressed for work. When I was ready to leave, I expected to find the dog on the porch waiting to be let back in.

He wasn't, so I whistled and called his name several times. In the end, I decided he'd found himself a girlfriend, and he'd be home when I got in from work like he had a couple of times before.

Scratch didn't come home that day, and I hadn't heard a word from Harland. By Tuesday evening when Scratch still wasn't there, I began to worry something had happened to him. I drove through the surrounding neighborhoods calling his name out the window. I walked up and down the streets right by my house, and still I couldn't find Scratch.

And nothing from Harland, either. Uncertainty about whether I'd ever see either one of them again suddenly became a possibility. Loneliness stabbed my heart, and I had to guard my inner feelings from the pain. I'd been alone before and I could be alone again. By the time I got back to the drive leading to my apartment, I'd lost the battle to restrain my tears. They freely ran down my face, and with the way my heart was hurting, I wasn't sure I'd ever stop crying again.

Back at my apartment, I found Harland sitting on my doorstep.

"Hi," he said and then appeared to be waiting to see if I was glad to see him. I desperately tried to keep my sobs inside me where they belonged, but I couldn't. I ran into Harland's open arms and wept aloud.

"I'm sorry," Harland whispered in my ear. "I know I should have called and apologized for the way I left the other night, but early yesterday I had to make an unexpected trip to Raleigh and I just got back an hour ago."

He continued to apologize profusely, and it took me a while to realize he thought that was why I was crying.

"He's gone," was all I could manage to say.

Harland pulled back to look at me. "Who's gone?"

"Scratch."

"The dog? You're crying like this because of a dog?" He was annoyed, but I didn't care. Scratch was the one thing I could always count on. No matter how long I was gone, when I got home he was glad to see me. He never shouted, or criticized, or stormed out leaving me to wonder what I'd done to cause his unhappiness.

"Yes, the dog." I started climbing the stairs, and Harland came behind me. "He's been gone since yesterday morning, and I'm afraid something has happened to him." I stomped my way to the top of the stairs, all the while wiping tears away and struggling to make them stop.

In the living room, Harland turned me to face him. "Can I help you look for the mutt?"

I glared at him.

"Okay, I'm sorry. Let me put that another way—can I help you look for the darling doggie?"

I put away the imaginary daggers I'd been throwing at him with my stare. I might have even smiled at him. He did have a way of making me laugh.

"I don't know where else to look. I've ridden for miles calling his name, and I've walked for the last hour right here in the neighborhood, but I can't find him."

Harland checked his watch and then took a small address book from his pocket and opened it.

"I know the man who runs the dog pound. I'll give him a call." Sitting on the couch next to the phone, Harland dialed a number. He motioned for me to sit next to him.

"George? This is Harland Jeffers. My friend has misplaced her dog, and I was wondering if there's any chance it might have been brought to you today." He paused and listened for a moment.

"What does he look like? He's a mixed breed, but I'd say he has some yellow lab in him. He would have been picked up in the area of McCarthy and Nelson."

Harland covered the receiver and asked me, "Does he have any identifying marks?"

I pictured him vividly in my mind. He was the same color all over his body. "Oh, I know," I said. "He has a leather collar with an engraved name tag that says 'Scratch' on it."

Harland relayed the message and there was a brief pause.

"Okay, I'll tell her. I just thought it was worth a shot. Bye." He hung up the phone and shook his head. "No luck there. He'll keep an eye out over the next few days to see if the dog shows up."

Relief flooded through me. "Thank you and by the way, I missed you, too."

"Look, I came by to apologize for the other night and to tell you I'd been out of town for two days. I am sorry for the way I acted. I love you."

"I love you, Harland, but why did you storm off like that?"

"I have a short fuse. I've always had this fight-or-flight attitude. I inherited it from my father. It works well in a courtroom because I can't flee so every part of my thoughts goes into fighting for the case I'm handling. But with you, I don't want to argue a point with you, so I simply leave. Later I always see I may have overreacted. I hope you'll forgive me."

I threw my arms around him.

"I may not agree with your leaving in the middle of an argument, but I forgive you for it."

Harland pulled the diamond engagement ring from his pocket. "Don't you think it's about time you accepted this? We love each other, we're good in bed, and I don't want to have to keep getting up and leaving in the middle of the night or watching you go off into the darkness."

The diamond was even more beautiful than I remembered. Harland and I were truly in love, and getting engaged was the next logical step. However, I just wasn't ready to get married. I loved having my own home, one I paid for with a job I was good at.

"Harland, I'd love to wear your ring and to be your fiancé, but I don't want to get married tomorrow. I want a little more time to be on my own. It's the one thing I've worked for, and it means a lot to me."

His expression never changed. "Well, I can understand that. How about you say you'll marry me, you take the ring, and then we'll decide on a reasonable engagement period? Would that work for you?"

"Yes, it would." Butterflies danced in my stomach. So that was what happiness felt like. I wanted it to last forever. Harland slipped the ring on my shaking finger. I held my hand out and admired the sparkle of my engagement ring. "It's beautiful. I love it and you, Harland."

I expected him to kiss me in that slow, enchanting way of his. I was disappointed.

"Okay." A smile tipped the corners of his mouth. "What do you consider a reasonable engagement period?"

"I'm not sure. I haven't had time to think about it." I had things to do before I married Harland. The biggest and most important was to find the intestinal fortitude to tell him about Berryanne.

"Let's talk it out. You'll need time to make wedding plans, go shopping, and maybe fix up the bedroom at my house. I guess I should say at *our* house. You'll need to give the landlord notice that you'll be leaving. Pack. And, of course, you'll want to give Mr. Lockwood a decent amount of time to find your replacement."

"Wait. Back up. I don't intend to quit my job. There's no reason for me to do that. What would I do all day? No, that's not part of the deal."

"Of course you'll quit working. You'll have all the money you want. None of the wives of my associates work outside the home. I'd look foolish if my wife was the only one. No, that is out of the question." He paused.

"Look, think about it. I'm going to need your help when it comes to entertaining clients and attending charity functions. You'll see. You'll be too busy to go to work every day. Besides, Clara is getting up there in years. She could use some help now and then. Taking care of the house should keep you busy. And kids. I hope we have kids someday. Surely you'll want to be home with them."

"Well, of course, but that's way in the future, Harland. You're talking like you think I should quit right now."

"All I ask is that you think about it. Will you?"

At the moment, I was thinking hard about it, and he wouldn't like what I was thinking.

"I'll think about it, but not until it gets closer to our actual wedding date."

"And when will that be?" Harland asked.

I felt crowded. I wouldn't be forced to rush to make such an important decision. "I'll let you know when I figure it out."

Two weeks later, on a Friday, I was looking forward to seeing Harland. I'd spent time every day looking for Scratch, but I could feel in every fiber of my body that he wasn't ever coming back. As the day came to an end, and it was time for Mr. Lockwood to give me my paycheck, he called me into his office.

He motioned to a chair. "Have a seat, Montana. I need to talk to you."

His somber tone told me something wasn't right. "Is something wrong?" I asked.

"I'm afraid so. I'm going to have to let you go."

Thinking he must be joking, I laughed, but his pitying gaze told me this was not a kidding matter. He was firing me. The job I'd been so proud of. The one that had allowed me to live on my own. My throat constricted against the sob.

"Why? Not too long ago you gave me a raise. You told me last week I was doing a good job, and if I remember right, you even said you didn't know how you had gotten along without me. What has changed in such a short time?"

"I don't feel I need to explain it to you. I have to restructure my business and cut back where possible. My wife will be working in your place starting on Monday. Your services are no longer needed; however, I'm giving you two-week severance to tide you over until you can find something else." He rose and extended his hand. I just stared at it, unable to move.

Finally, I took the handshake and my check. On the way out I gathered my few belongings, including my troll-topped pencil. I made my way out into the bright sunlight, barely able to see through the tears flooding my eyes. I cried all the way home, but when I climbed the stairs to my apartment and found the door standing open, I sobered and dried away the tears.

"Hello?" I stuck my head inside the door. I didn't hear

any movement, so I made my way into the living room. My heart pounded so loudly I wouldn't have heard anyone had they been there.

Inventory of my meager possessions took only a few minutes. The contents from my lingerie drawer were strewn over the bed. Since I didn't have an overabundance of underwear, it didn't take long to know a couple of pairs of panties were missing. Everything in the bathroom was as it should be.

The pages of my *Modern Romance* magazine were shredded and spread over the coffee table like celebratory confetti. And my television, a generous gift from Harland, was missing. The rabbit ears wrapped with strips of aluminum foil lay on the floor. A screw had been ripped away from the television and was still attached to the discarded antenna wire. At least I could feel some satisfaction that the jerk who had stolen the TV set wouldn't get any reception without the antenna.

Rage set my nerves on fire. I turned quickly and bashed my shin into the corner of the coffee table.

I grabbed my leg and sank to the floor. "Damn," I cried. As I rocked back and forth, my anger fizzled. Someone had invaded my home and took things that belonged to me. They had been breathing the same air I now sucked in to keep from crying. My television was one thing, but my panties were personal. That could only mean the thief was depraved. An eerie feeling crept through my body. What if he was still around? Maybe he was hiding under the bed or in my closet.

I scrambled to my feet, grabbed the telephone from the end table, and stretched the cord until it reached the landing outside the door. I dialed zero and waited for the operator to answer. When she did, I asked for the police department. My next call was to Harland, who arrived shortly after the police.

After they had covered doorjambs and tables and my dresser with black fingerprint dust, one of the officers handed me a card with my case number on it.

"If we find anything, we'll be in touch," he said. "By the way, it looks like they used a crowbar and destroyed the lock on the door. That'll have to be replaced. If you find anything else missing, my number is on my card."

He left, followed closely by the evidence technician, who carried his equipment in a tackle box. Evidently he didn't have any cleaning stuff in there because he left a sticky, smeared, black substance for me to clean up.

"Do you believe this mess?" I halfheartedly made a sweeping hand motion. "It's the perfect ending to my day." I slumped onto the couch. "Mr. Lockwood fired me and then I came home to this."

Harland sat beside me and pulled me into his arms. "It's all right, sweetheart. I'm here. I'll take care of you."

I wilted against him to absorb warmth from his firm, muscular body. I wanted to stay there and let Harland keep the big, bad wolf away from my door, especially since now it wouldn't shut or lock.

"What am I going to do, Harland? I'm afraid to stay here. What if they come back? I can't even move to another place because, as of five o'clock today, I no longer have a job." I didn't want to be reduced to a weak, sniveling woman, but the panic ringing an alarm inside my brain wouldn't let me think straight. The clamoring dug deep into my self-assurance and shattered it. I wanted to be protected, and common sense told me Harland could do that.

Somewhere a short distance from my jail cell, a scuffle broke out, yanking me sharply from my writing. I'd learned by watching that if it wasn't your business, it wasn't your business. So I stayed as far away from the cell door as I could and hoped to stay out of the way of flying objects, or worse, gunfire.

Shortly, the eruption simmered to a verbal exchange of vulgarity I'd only heard when Harland was in one of his rages. Two guards dragged a new inmate past my door and out of sight. Their voices faded, and I was free to go back to recording the experiences that had brought me to my present home, but I was too tired or possibly too afraid to delve into the nightmares that night. I decided to go to bed and pray sleep would come.

Luckily, I slept soundly that night. It was as if my body knew that when day broke, I'd have to write about the most difficult part of life with Harland. The part where he transformed from a stable, caring man to the devil incarnate.

Yes, I needed all the rest I could get to be able to dig horrendous memories from what I'd subconsciously thought of as a safety vault. Replaying through my mind the first few years of my marriage to Harland and then actually transcribing them with ink onto lines of notebook paper would surely leave my heart raw and aching.

So many unspeakable events had plagued our wedded bliss. As each escalated into something worse than the last, I found ways to bury them in a hidden place inside me. Unfortunately, along with each memory, I also buried a bit of my soul until it was all gone, reducing me to nothing but a shell of a woman.

When the sun rose the next morning, I didn't want to delay the inevitable, so I got right to the task at hand—writing more of my memoirs for Phillip.

As I'd feared, the process proved painful. Not from remembering the physical anguish, but because as I pulled each tidbit from its safety vault, I asked myself how I could have been so weak and stupid.

Chapter 12

THE SAFE HAVEN OF MY APARTMENT HAD BEEN DESTROYED. Someone had broken in and stolen some of my personal belongings, but more importantly they'd taken away the protective cocoon I'd been wrapped in, throwing me into the pit of hell.

Of course, at the time, it didn't appear that way. It would be almost three months before I came to the full realization that even with no lock on the door, I would have been safer in that apartment than in the torture chamber Harland called home.

I moved in with Harland that night, and he immediately insisted we go ahead and make our wedding plans. His argument against waiting was that we were "living in sin" in his highly respected and dead mother's house. We loved each other and had planned to eventually marry anyway, so why not just do it?

I probably could have stayed with Vesta, but she had her family and her hair salon to take care of. Her house was small. She didn't need me horning in on her little nest.

I didn't have a reason to say no, but I feared Harland might once I told him about giving my illegitimate child away. Surely that would put a tarnish mark on the public image he and his mother thought of so highly.

Before I would allow him to set a date, I had to tell him about Berryanne.

"I need to talk to you." I sat across from him at a table on the patio.

"This sounds serious." He reached out and took my hands. "What's wrong?"

I hesitated for a moment, gathered my strength, then plunged in before I lost my nerve. "Two years before I was released from the foster home, I had a baby. She was put up for adoption." I'd tried many times to imagine what Harland would say when I told him, but nothing prepared me for his response.

"I know that." Gently he kneaded my hands. "I've known for a long time."

I was speechless. Harland knew my darkest secret and wanted to marry me anyway. He didn't show disgust in his deep gaze, and he hadn't run away like Eddie had.

"How did you know?" My voice cracked.

"Honey, I couldn't marry you and not check out your past. I'm a lawyer. Every day I see men and women who pretend to be someone they aren't just to scam someone else out of money. I'm sorry, but that's the world we live in. Although I was pretty sure you weren't one of those people, I had to make sure. Forgive me?" He feared my disapproval as much as I feared his. I jumped at the chance to reassure him he was right in what he'd done. There was nothing to forgive.

With that major block out of our way, I happily agreed to be married in six weeks. I anticipated spending hours, days, and weeks on the plans for the extravagant wedding Harland insisted on.

"We are both going to have only one wedding. If my mother were still alive, it would be the biggest affair this town has ever seen. As a matter of fact, not long before her death, she went on a campaign to marry me off. She even set up a notebook with ideas for a wedding and the reception." His voice trailed to a whisper. "I think she sensed she wasn't going to be around much longer and wanted to be sure I had someone in my life."

Every word he spoke showed the deep admiration he had for his mother. I wished I could have met the woman who helped make Harland the man he was.

"Did she have someone picked out for you?" I chuckled.

"Yes, Patricia Simpson from next door."

That took me by surprise. I wasn't sure how I felt about my competition living right next door.

"Why didn't you marry her?"

"I was waiting for you." Harland's sincere smile warmed me. "You and I together are going to come as close as we can to having the wedding my mother would have wanted." Harland was more excited than I'd ever seen him.

The time I'd expected to spend on the wedding preparations was cut to almost nothing. Harland took care of everything. All I really needed to do was pick out a dress for me and for my maid of honor, Vesta. Once that was done, I took over re-decorating the only room in the house that needed a woman's touch—Harland's old bedroom, which was now ours.

The room hadn't been painted since he was a boy. Although all the other rooms in the house were done to elegant perfection, his bedroom could have been in a run-down shack at the other end of town. Evidently he'd been a rowdy boy. There were several holes in the walls and the decorative knobs on the head and footboards of the bed were scratched and worn from something being tied to them.

Harland gave me the green light to redo it any way I wanted with only one exception. He wanted to pick out the bed, which he did. I designed the rest of the room around it. By the time our wedding day arrived, the workmen had replaced the damaged Sheetrock, wallpapered, and installed wall-to-wall carpeting.

It wasn't until the furniture was delivered, and I saw the bed in its place, that it dawned on me this one was a king-sized version of the bed Harland had before. The rich, dark wood of the head and foot boards blended nicely with the homey atmosphere of the rest of the room. With our marriage bed in place, the room was complete.

I doubted Cinderella's wedding was as grand as the one Harland, with the help of his dead mother's notes, had prepared for us. I wouldn't have had a clue how to put together something like that, so I was happy he was handling everything. Over five hundred people attended the gala. All of them were friends and associates of Harland's except for Vesta, Mitch, and their baby. They were the only friends and family I had.

Harland had already informed me our honeymoon would have to be put on the back burner, because an upcoming trial made it mandatory he fly to Philadelphia for depositions late Sunday evening. We had Saturday night and part of the day Sunday to enjoy each other's company as man and wife.

Harland never called home while he was in Philadelphia. I didn't even know when to expect him. Late Wednesday afternoon, Mr. Mano, who had worked for the Jefferses for several years, came to clean the pool. When he rang the bell at the gate, I buzzed him in. We waved to each other. He went around the house to do his job. I went to take a shower and dress in something nice in case Harland should return from his trip that evening.

When I stepped from the shower, I sensed there was something amiss, and before I left the bathroom I wrapped a plush lavender towel around my body. In the bedroom, Harland stood with his back to me, suitcase open on the bed.

"Harland," I squealed. I was so happy to see him. When he turned around, I raced to him and threw my arms around his neck. "I'm so glad you're home. Why didn't you let me know when you were coming?"

"Why, so you could make sure your lover was gone?"

A warning bell jangled in my head. Something was terribly wrong.

"What are you talking about?" Stunned, I waited for him to answer.

"Jacque Mano is right outside the back door, and here you are running around with no clothes on."

"I just took a shower. I haven't even spoken to Mr. Mano. I let him in just like I've seen you do. That was the only time I even laid eyes on him today. Why are you acting like this?"

Harland turned to get something from his suitcase. In one swift motion, he spun, grabbed the back of my hair, and stuck a gun to my throat. I struggled to get free. He snapped my head back.

I tried to scream, but he pressed the gun harder against my windpipe. I couldn't force any sound out. Suddenly, the shock of the moment crumbled away, exposing the truth. Harland was going to kill me. My knees trembled. He released me, and I fell to the floor.

Curling into a ball, I protected my head with my arms and prayed God would let me live at least long enough to see my baby one more time. I'm not sure how long I lay there before I realized Harland was no longer towering over me. I dared to steal a look between my fingers. He was gone.

Weak from fear, I somehow managed to get up. After I'd dressed, I sat on the bed and stared at the small roses trailing a vine from the ceiling to the floor on the wallpaper of our bedroom. I concentrated on one flower. The blue one, on the fourth vine from the corner, the third flower down from the ceiling.

I saw it clearly at first—the blue rose, three down, four across—then it blurred in a mist of tears. When darkness closed around me, I hurried to the bathroom and turned on the night-light. I'd slept with one every night since my first repulsive encounter with my brother. If broad daylight held so many evil people, what kind of wickedness lurked in the dark? I didn't want to know. So the light burned every night.

When I came out of the bathroom, Harland had finished unpacking. He placed the pistol inside a dresser drawer, one designed to hold jewelry or other valuables. After locking it, he stuck the key into his pocket.

I moved slowly, cautiously, not knowing what my next move should be. The only thing I knew for sure was I'd never been so afraid in my entire life. The fear wreaking havoc in my brain shielded my heart, momentarily keeping the devastation at bay.

He put his arms around me and placed a gentle kiss on my cheek. "I'm sorry if I overreacted. I just love you so much, I don't want there to ever be a chance you'll leave me for someone else." He stepped around me and went into the bathroom. "It took me a minute to realize that Mr. Mano is too old for you." He spoke loudly above the running water.

I stared blankly at the bathroom door, stunned by this change in him.

"I'm hungry," Harland said. "Let's go out to eat. Where

do you want to go?"

Heartache and confusion ran the gamut. Did Harland truly believe he could wash away what had taken place as easily as he washed his hands?

When he came out of the bathroom, I stood ready for a confrontation.

"What is going on with you? Don't you realize you hurt me, not to mention scared me to death? Now you want to give me a kiss and take me to dinner? What is wrong with you?"

Casually, my husband of four days walked up to me, grabbed my hair, and pulled my head back so I was looking up into his face. Pain radiated through my already throbbing head.

"Don't you ever talk to me like that again, or I'll show you exactly what is wrong with me. If you do things that make me look bad, like strolling through the house naked with the pool man right outside, you have to expect to be punished." He lowered his mouth to mine and kissed me hard. I tried to pull away, but he forced me to keep my lips on his.

He released me, then turned and walked away. "I'll be in the car."

Terrified, I went into the bathroom, splashed water on my face, and brushed my hair. Harland and I went to a nearby restaurant. He talked about his trip to Philadelphia, which he'd taken instead of going on a honeymoon, as if we were like all the other couples in the room. I knew we weren't. I tried to listen to what he was saying, but my mind kept going back to the life-threatening incident inside our bedroom, in our home on Serenity Drive.

That was almost a joke. Our house was anything but serene.

Suddenly, I realized Harland was staring at me, possibly expecting me to remark about something he'd just said.

Terrified of setting him off again, I said, "I'm sorry. I guess my mind was somewhere else."

"I said, smile, Montana, you never know when someone will take your picture."

To avoid Harland possibly making a scene, I did as I was told. But I certainly didn't feel like smiling, or eating, or anything else at that moment. I was lost in a world of indecision, fear, and a broken heart.

I didn't get to leave Harland that night. He watched me constantly, staying by my side every moment. Finally, I accepted I was a prisoner and went to bed, but I couldn't sleep. My heart and mind fought a bitter battle. Why had I put such expectation in having a perfect life with Harland when, given my history, it was never going to be smooth sailing?

By the time daylight returned, so did the old Harland. He was loving, caring, and attentive. There was not one dark shadow hovering in his bright blue eyes. Eventually my defenses dropped. I was even able to forgive him, because he loved me so much he went crazy for a few minutes when he thought he might lose me.

All I had to do was show him every day how much I loved him. Since I did with all my heart, it should be an easy task.

One night somewhere near the fifth month of our marriage, we were lying in bed together. The night-light cast shadows across Harland's face, but I could tell by his uneven breathing he wasn't asleep yet.

"I love you," I whispered and moved closer to him.

He cradled me in his arm and lightly kissed my forehead.

"I was just wondering; shouldn't you be pregnant by now?"

His question caught me off guard. "I don't know. I guess it will happen when it happens."

"It just looks like after five months of marriage plus the two months we were having sex before that . . . well, I think you should already be pregnant."

Someday I wanted another baby, but I'd been extremely busy adjusting to being a wife. And if I was being completely honest, maybe my thoughts were selfish. After all, I already was a mother, and that baby stayed on my mind constantly. Eventually, I wanted Harland's baby, but if it didn't happen for a while, I was okay with that, too.

"I think we need to spend time as a couple before we become a threesome. A baby will come in due time, but in the meantime we have each other."

Harland rolled away from me. Startled by his abruptness, I lay perfectly still until I was sure he was asleep. Guilt kept me from sleeping. Was I wrong to not want a baby right then? What was the real reason I wasn't pregnant? I'd had no problem getting that way with Dirk. Had Berryanne's difficult birth been too much for my body? Was she the only one I'd ever have?

The next morning, Harland was quieter than usual, which made me walk as if I was on a slippery surface. When he left for work, he held me a little tighter and kissed me a little longer, but a voice inside me told me a storm was brewing.

That evening, when Harland entered the kitchen from the garage, I was putting the finishing touches on our dinner. "Hi, honey," I called without turning around. If I had, I might have seen the angry look on his face and possibly have been able to escape. He spun me around and gripped both my shoulders in a vice-like hold. Then I saw the terrifying look on his face, but it was too late.

"What'd I do, Harland? What did I do this time?" Anger stiffened every muscle in my body.

"I'm going to ask you one question, and I want a truthful answer." He bared his teeth in a feral snarl. "Are you doing something to keep from getting pregnant?"

How ludicrous for him to even think such a thing, let alone ask the question out loud. I was dealing with an irrational person who didn't deserve an answer. Panic rioted within me. I jerked free of his grasp and backed away from him.

Unfortunately for me, I backed into a corner. I was trapped. Harland came at me, his hands balled into fists. Putting my hands up to protect my face, I didn't see the blow coming. Harland hit me in the stomach. I doubled over, the pain so severe I couldn't breathe.

With one hand holding my stomach, and the other held out against him, I yelled, "Stop it, Harland." I could barely get the words out for the sobs shuddering in my throat.

Again, he lifted me by my shoulders. "Answer my question. Are you doing something to keep from getting pregnant?"

"No! I'm not doing anything, I swear." I cried so hard a deluge of tears rolled down my cheeks. Shoving past Harland, I ran to the bathroom to throw up. Weak from the whole ordeal, it took everything I had in me to make it to the bed, where I collapsed and cried until I fell asleep.

Several hours later, Harland awoke me. "I fixed you a plate, and I've cleaned the kitchen."

With my mind clouded by sleep, it took a few moments before the dam of reality broke and the misery of Harland's wrath flooded in. He sat next to me on the bed and gently moved my hair out of my eyes.

"Come on, sweetheart, get up or you won't be able to sleep tonight."

I scrambled to my feet. "That was the last time you will ever hurt me. I'm leaving." I didn't even have time to turn around. Harland jumped to his feet and wrapped his arm around my throat. The more I struggled, the tighter he held me. Finally, I gave up and stilled. He released his choke hold, but still held me around my throat. I gasped for air.

"Let's get one thing straight," he said, his voice heavy with authority. "The only way you'll ever leave me is if you're dead. Is that what you want? Would you rather be dead than to be with me and have my baby?"

The delusional, frightening, and just plain crazy man with his arm strangling me was my husband. For God's sake, why didn't I know the man I'd married? How was I going to survive?

He'd released me enough that I was able to get free. This time he didn't come after me. He sat on the bed and looked up at me.

"Montana, if you do something wrong, you must be punished. You are going to have to learn to take your punishment like a man. Do you understand?"

"No, Harland, I don't understand any of this. I'm not doing anything to keep from getting pregnant. When or if we ever have a child is for God to decide. But that isn't even relevant after the way you've treated me. I can't stay here and allow it to happen again."

He went to the dresser and unlocked the top drawer where he kept the gun. I didn't wait to see if that was what he was after. I raced from the room and out the sliding doors to the patio. In the darkness, with only a path of light from inside the house, I ran to the back of the yard, through the gate, and down the path that led past the workshop and into the woods.

Branches scratched against my bare arms and face and snagged my hair. I glanced over my shoulder, but I couldn't see Harland, and I didn't hear his footfalls behind me. He wasn't following. I could stop running, but I didn't. I wanted as much distance between us as possible.

At last a light appeared through the trees. I walked in its direction and came out in the backyard of a house. A large dog charged from a porch, but stopped a short distance from me. He barked.

"Good boy," I consoled the animal who stopped yapping and edged his way toward me. A door opened and someone whistled for him. The dog took one last look at me and ran into the house. I stayed in the shadows, afraid to speak.

Behind me a twig snapped. I prayed it was a nocturnal critter and not Harland. After making my way through the yard to the front of the house, I followed the sidewalk. Soon I came to a small, all-night grocery store. Beside the store, I slipped into a phone booth and called the operator for help.

While I waited for the police to arrive, I stayed out of the bright lights in front of the store and scanned the area for Harland. Fifteen minutes later a squad car arrived. I explained the situation to the operator and told him I didn't know what to do.

"What's your name?" Officer Myers asked.

"Montana Jeffers."

"You're Harland's wife?" That the officer knew him shouldn't have surprised me, but it did.

"Yes. You have to arrest him. He's crazy."

He chewed thoughtfully on his bottom lip. "Well, get in the car, and I'll take you to the station. You'll have to fill out a complaint."

He opened the door, and I got into the backseat. Officer Myers got into the driver's seat, started the car, and we drove to the Jefferses' Memorial Library parking lot. The officer got out and opened my door.

"Let's talk." He took my hand and pulled me from the vehicle. Resisting wasn't an option.

"You see the name on this library? It's named after Harland's father. He put up the money for it to be built back in 1950. The Jeffers have left their mark everywhere on this town. Harland is continuing in their footsteps.

"Just yesterday he wrote a check to the Police Benevolent League to help an officer who was hurt and has fallen on hard times. Citizens of our town would not take kindly to waking up in the morning and finding that one of our most generous citizens had been arrested because he'd gotten into an argument with his wife."

"It wasn't just an argument. He threatened to kill me," I cried.

"My wife threatens to kill me on a daily basis, but I'd never have her arrested for it."

The officer shined his light in my face. "Did he put those scratches there?"

"No, I got them when I ran through the woods."

"And those on your arms, what about them?"

"They came from the woods, too." Exasperation tightened my last nerve. Why did *I* feel like the criminal?

"Do you have any marks on you put there by Harland?"

Harland had hurt me in places that didn't show. I didn't know if my stomach had bruised or not, but I didn't feel comfortable pulling up my blouse right there in the middle of a parking lot.

"I'm sure you can see it would be detrimental for you to report this misunderstanding to my captain." He smiled a Cheshire grin.

"I want to go to the station right now." I climbed back into the squad car.

He got back in the front. "No, you don't, Mrs. Jeffers. I can assure you of that." He started the car and drove me back to Serenity Drive, back to Harland.

The policeman walked up to the gate and rang the bell. I tried to open the door, but found I was locked in the car. Shortly, Harland came out. He shook hands with his buddy and after a short conversation, the officer opened my door, and Harland took my hand and pulled to my feet. At this point, it was two against one. I went without a struggle.

As we watched the car pull away, Harland wrapped his arm around my waist and led me through the rose garden to the front door.

"I guess you're learning I have friends in high places. I think you'd better remember that. It's very late, and I have to be at the office early in the morning. Let's go to bed."

I thought of Vesta, but quickly pushed it aside. How could I expect her to help when the police wouldn't?

After I'd showered all the dirt and blood from my body and cleaned my scratches, I went to bed. Harland kissed me good night. Hugging my pillow against my chest, I prayed for sleep. My body teetered on the edge of physical and mental exhaustion and sleep came quickly.

For the next six months, things went well for me and Harland. Slowly, he divulged more about the abuse his father had inflicted on him. He told me that for punishment, his father would tie him to the bed with rope and leave him for hours to think about what he'd done. That explained the worn places on his old bed, but it didn't explain why Harland had insisted on our bed having the same type of head and footboards.

I'd learned from Harland his father would also make him stand at attention like a good soldier and demand his son not cry, but take it like a man. It was the same thing Harland had said to me.

Any time he talked of his father, Harland's demeanor became that of a young boy. My heart broke with each tale he told. How a father could treat his own flesh and blood like that was beyond me. Of course, Joe was my flesh and blood, and he'd done unthinkable things to me. As a person who understood only too well what betrayal felt like, I felt sorry for Harland and feared him. And part of me still loved the Harland I'd married.

Vesta and I didn't get to visit much. During the past year she had given birth to her second child, was running her own beauty salon, and, of course, was taking care of her own home and husband.

The few times the four of us had been together, Harland became moody. It was as if he resented my relationship with Vesta. I found it easier all the way around to keep her and Harland separated. About once a week, she and I talked on the phone, but with her demanding life and my demanding husband, we seldom saw each other. I missed her.

Clara, the housekeeper who had been with the Jefferses for over twenty years, had gone from cleaning the house five days a week to only once a week. Harland didn't want that to happen, but I insisted. After all, I was home all day with nothing to do but watch Clara do the work I was perfectly capable of and more than willing to do.

The elderly woman jumped at the chance to semi-retire. Since Harland accepted nothing short of an immaculate home, I stayed busy every day making sure our house was impeccably clean. On the days Clara came, I ran errands like grocery shopping and going to the dry cleaner. Between Clara and me, Harland found nothing to complain about as far as his castle went.

Late one afternoon, Clara had put dinner in the oven and given me instructions for finishing the meal. She left shortly before four. The afternoon temperatures had cooled with a pleasant breeze. I sat on the patio enjoying a glass of iced tea and felt thankful for the happiness I'd found during the past few months.

In the wooded area at the back of our property, I heard a dog barking. I figured it was the dog whose backyard I'd wandered into when I was escaping Harland's wrath a few months earlier. The barking persisted, and I decided to check it out.

Following the path from our back gate past Harland's workshop, I walked halfway through the stand of trees. There I found the large black dog, digging frantically under a tree.

"What is it, boy?" I called to him. He looked my way, then went back to digging. Curious, I edged closer. I could see a few bones unearthed by the dog. They appeared to belong to an animal.

My first thought was, since Harland's family had owned the land for many years, that maybe he'd lost a pet at some time and had buried it there. If so, the remains shouldn't be dug up.

I chased the dog away and started kicking dirt back into the hole. Beside the bones lay a collar with a dog tag attached.

"Oh, no." My voice trembled. I reached into the hole and

pulled out the worn piece of leather. The tag read *Scratch.*

I didn't have a moment's doubt how Scratch had ended up buried there. "Damn you, Harland." My hands shook and tears blurred my eyes. I thought back to the last time I'd seen Scratch. I'd let him out before I left for work the day after Harland had been at my apartment. He'd spoken loudly to me, and Scratch went after him. Harland had become indignant over the encounter. Supposedly, he had left for an out-of-town trip that morning.

To the very depths of my soul, I knew Harland had killed Scratch and buried him in the woods. At one time I had felt sorry for Harland. He'd had a sad childhood, and sometimes his way of thinking frightened me, but I never thought he'd kill a defenseless dog just because the animal had tried to protect me.

A year ago, I'd privately mourned the loss of Scratch. Harland had caused that hurt by deliberately taking away something that meant so much to me. Painful sadness vibrated through me, signaling the beginning of another death—my love for Harland.

The hole containing Scratch's remains was too deep for me to fill in by hand. I walked back to Harland's workshop to get a shovel. I'd been inside the building a few times with him while he lifted weights or worked on a wood project. He'd opened the lock with a key hidden behind a shutter.

He wouldn't like me going in there without him, but he'd killed Scratch, and I was angry. I didn't care what he thought.

Once inside, I took a shovel from its proper place hanging on a wall and glanced around at the neatly kept space. *A place for everything and everything in its place.* My mother had always said that, but Harland took the saying to a new plateau. Because of his meticulous placement of things, a terry-cloth towel hanging askew, partially hiding a small television caught my attention.

A horrible feeling sank deep in my stomach and forced me to climb up a step stool and take a closer look. The shock was so great I thought I might faint. As quickly as I could, I got down. Heavy waves of nausea assaulted me. I faced another horrifying truth about Harland. He was the one who'd broken into my apartment and stolen my television.

He'd killed my dog. He'd led me to believe my home was unsafe because someone had come in and robbed me. But it wasn't just anyone; it was the one person who claimed to love me, the man I had loved and married.

It didn't take me long to figure out he'd done it to make me fearful of living there, and to nudge me into moving in with him and speeding up our wedding plans.

With the bitterness of reality slapping me in the face, I looked up. *God forgive me. I despised Harland Jeffers, and I wanted him as dead as Scratch.*

Chapter 13

THE AIR IN HARLAND'S WORKSHOP THICKENED. I GAGGED on the hatred spiking through my body. He had manipulated me into marrying him. Entranced by the sound of my hammering heart, I couldn't trust myself to make a rational decision about what my next move should be. Every one I'd made so far had been disastrous and landed me in a life I couldn't even fathom.

Dread closed in around me and threatened to steal my last thread of sanity. Did I even want to cling to it any longer?

"What are you doing in here, sweetheart?" Harland's voice snatched me from my stupor.

Filled with overwhelming anger, I lunged at him. "You bastard," I screamed and would have pummeled with all my might, but my might was no match for Harland Jeffers.

He captured my wrist inches before I connected with his body. I tried to pull away, but he held tight with no regard to the force he was using. My bones could snap at any second, and by the grin on his face, I knew he would have enjoyed it.

"Calm down, Montana, and listen to me." He pulled

me closer. "You found out my little secret. I broke into your apartment and took back the television I'd given you in the first place. I loved you so much I figured I could speed things up a bit if you moved in here with me. And it worked. You were going to marry me anyway; it just happened sooner than you thought it should."

Flabbergasted that Harland had again made excuses for something terrible he'd done, I stopped struggling. He fully expected me to say I understood and forgave him. I jerked free and glared my hatred at him.

"You have an answer for everything, don't you, Harland? Well, what possible reason did you have for killing Scratch?"

Up to that point, my being upset had amused him. Instantly, his pleasure dissipated.

"I don't have to defend myself to you. You're the one who thought more of that mutt than me. He had to disappear, and I made it happen. Let's go back to the house. When I got home, the oven timer was going off. I take it that means dinner is ready."

"You have got to be kidding!" I yelled. "What kind of idiot would I have to be to just ignore something like this?"

A caustic grin hardened his face. "What are you going to do, Montana? Call the police? Haven't you already learned they're my friends? What's your next step, Mrs. Jeffers?"

"I haven't had time to make a life plan, but for now, I'm going to Vesta's to stay until I figure it all out."

Harland stepped aside, allowing me to leave. I hurried past him only to be stopped by the trademark yank of my hair. With his other arm he locked me in a choke hold.

"You still don't understand that dead is the only way you'll leave me. Maybe I can make it clearer for you." With his free hand, he grasped the back of my neck and tightened his arm over my throat. Darkness came so quickly I had no time to think of anything other than never seeing Berryanne again.

I'm not sure how long I was out, but when I came to I was on the floor of the workshop, Harland standing over me. He nudged me with the toe of his shoe. It was leather, brown, and shiny, and topped by an expensive, perfectly creased, brown pant leg. How could that picture of perfection belong to such an evil person?

His clothes and shoes were never dusty, yet he could dirty his hands killing a defenseless animal or hitting his wife. His house was a showcase, but it wasn't a home. Harland was a married man, but he wasn't a husband.

"I know you're awake, Montana." He kicked me again.

I pushed myself to a sitting position. "I can't do this anymore. You have to let me go."

He held out his hand to help me up. Reluctantly, I took it. My head throbbed. The only clear thought I could form in my addled brain was that I had to get away from Harland.

"Come here, sweetheart." Harland's voice sounded as sweet as a choirboy's.

He led me outside and around the building. I followed like a zombie, too numb to resist. Behind the workshop stood a piece of machinery. I'd never seen anything like it, and I couldn't imagine why he insisted on showing it to me.

"How do you like it?" Harland asked as if he'd shown me a brand-new car.

"What is it?" I really couldn't have cared less. All I wanted was to go into the house, pack my few belongings, and go to Vesta's.

"This is a wood chipper. You put a big tree with limbs right into this hopper." He pointed into a hole in one end of the green monstrosity. And it grinds it into tiny chips and shoots it out back here."

He stared at me in anticipation.

"I don't understand." Weak and exhausted from the whole ordeal, I just wanted to be dismissed.

In a calm, menacing voice, he said, "If you try to leave me, I'll run you through this wood chipper and tell everyone you ran off with a salesman." He laughed. "That would be pretty funny, wouldn't it? While your remains are scattered out here for the varmints to eat, people will be feeling sorry for me and lavishing attention on the man who'd been betrayed by a woman he'd pulled from nothing and had given everything. What a miserable, selfish bitch poor Harland married. That's what the whole town will say. I might just put you in here anyway if it means I'll get that much attention. That's something to think about, isn't it?"

The ferocity of his madness exploded painfully in my head. "Harland, you're sick. Let me go to Vesta's, and I promise I'll find a doctor who can help you."

At a normal pace, he came up beside me. I didn't try to get away. He was faster and stronger, and I was just too tired. He seized a handful of hair at the back of my head and forced me to look up into his reddened face. The pain from my already battered scalp was excruciating.

"You . . . are . . . not . . . leaving." He ground his words through clenched teeth. "As a matter of fact, I strongly suggest you not get your friend involved in any of our affairs."

"Let go of my hair. You're hurting me." I tried to pry his fingers loose to no avail.

"Have you told Vesta anything?"

"No, nothing. Let go of me." I struggled against his grip.

Harland released my hair and pushed me forward at the same

time. "I'm hungry. How long before dinner will be ready?"

"Your dinner is in the oven. I'm going to pack." Finally, my anger kicked in and shoved my fear aside. "I'm not spending another night under your roof. I'm going to Vesta's and nothing you do will keep me from it." I marched past him and started the short trek to the house with Harland dogging my every step.

Once we were inside, I went directly to the bedroom to start packing. He came to the doorway. "I'm only going to say this one more time, Montana. You aren't going anywhere. And let me add this; if you even try, I'll bring Vesta here and run you both through the wood chipper. Tell me, do you want to be responsible for making her two children motherless? You know how I handle things that come between us."

A poor dog was one thing, but Harland killing a person would be something different. "You wouldn't do that. How would you get her here without anyone knowing? Her car would be here. You'd have to get rid of it. No, you wouldn't do it."

"Are you sure, Montana? Do you want to take the chance? Let's just put this nonsense behind us and sit down and enjoy a pleasant dinner. Or how about we skip dinner, get naked, and rub our bodies together? All this fighting gets my blood pumping."

"You really are crazy if you think we're having sex. I'm through, Harland. I'm leaving."

That was the last time I ever said those words aloud and the first time Harland raped me.

Leaving Harland that night was not an option, but it didn't mean I couldn't bide my time and form a plan of action. I couldn't go to Vesta's. That would be the first place he'd look. I hadn't taken his threat of killing her seriously. Vesta had grown into a strong woman. With Mitch at her side, she could hold her own. But still, I didn't want to make my problems hers.

The next morning, after Harland left for work, I tried to comb my hair, but my scalp was too tender. With the way he yanked me around, it's a wonder I had any hair left. When I worked as a waitress, many customers commented on how pretty my hair was. It had been long and shiny.

Since I'd gotten married, it had lost some of its healthy shine and I blamed it on the stress imposed by my husband. What had once been my crowning glory was now a weapon Harland used frequently.

If I didn't have it, what would he use? I needed a change anyway. Pulling the scissors from the bathroom drawer, I randomly chopped away hanks of hair until I could barely grasp a section anywhere on my head. Looking into the mirror I saw a pitiful mess of a young woman with sallow skin, darkly circled eyes, and butchered hair. I'd aged almost overnight into someone I barely recognized. Yet inside of me lurked a child who longed to be protected and loved in a different way than the world had shown me so far.

As the day went on, I roamed around the house trying not to think about Scratch's remains, the wood chipper standing ready behind the workshop, and what Harland's reaction would be when he saw my hair.

By the time he arrived home, my anxiety level was off the chart. When I heard him enter from the garage, I pressed my balled fist against my stomach to relieve some of the queasiness.

"For Christ's sake, what did you do to your hair?" Harland chuckled out loud. "Did Vesta do that for you?"

"No, I cut it myself."

"Did you happen to look in a mirror? Do you know how ridiculous you look?"

I didn't bother to answer. I was minutes away from putting beef stew on the table, when suddenly a thought flashed through my mind—what could I put in the stew to make him sick enough to die?

It was the first time I considered murdering Harland, but it wouldn't be the last.

Having nothing readily available, I served him the stew *sans* poison. Surprisingly, he didn't mention my hair again.

At lunchtime the next day, the front door opened, startling me.

"Montana," Harland called from the foyer. He usually came through the garage, but that day he had parked out front. He had probably forgotten something and was just passing by to get it. By the time I got to the front of the house, he was in the foyer, and Vesta, who was carrying her four-month-old baby, entered behind him.

"Surprise," he said.

Immediately I broke into a sweat. My whole body strummed with fear.

"What—what are you doing here?" I stammered.

"Harland told me you'd cut your hair off. Of course, I didn't think he meant *all* your hair. Why did you do it?" Vesta handed Harland her baby and then, like a true beautician, she examined the state of my locks—or lack thereof.

I glanced at Harland, who was smiling widely. "I explained to Vesta we had a slight disagreement that you'd blown out of proportion and to spite me you cut off all your beautiful hair. She wanted me to take you right over to her salon, but I thought it was best she come to you.

"I'll play with this little fellow." He nodded at the baby cradled in his arms. "As soon as you finish straightening out Montana's hair, I'll run you back to your house."

Vesta pulled a comb and scissors from her bag and hustled me out to the patio. In short order she was clipping away at what was left of my hair.

"What in the world were you two arguing about?" she asked.

I almost told her the truth. I almost spilled my guts at her feet and begged for help. Almost, but then I saw Harland standing at the sliding glass door and remembered his threat about the wood chipper. I realized that *almost* was as close as I would ever come to getting away.

"It was nothing. Just something stupid."

In less than fifteen minutes, Vesta had made my hair presentable. I held her baby all of thirty seconds before Harland announced he was going to be late for a deposition, and he needed to get Vesta home.

She'd gone on to the car, and Harland lingered just long enough to whisper, "See how easy that was? I got her and her baby, and no one knows where she is. There's no car for me to get rid of. Be sure you keep that in mind, sweetheart." He closed the door, and I collapsed onto the nearest chair.

My body trembled with such force I expected it to fly apart. I wanted to cry all the sadness out of me, but no tears came. I had loved Harland and even felt sorry for him because of the abuse his father had inflicted on him. I had lived under the delusion I might even be able to help him.

But the love, the sympathy, and the delusions were gone,

and all that was left was stark, paralyzing fear.

After that day, I avoided Vesta as much as possible. I knew for sure that when she realized my situation and my state of mind, she would try to rescue me. In the process, we could both lose our lives. There wasn't the slightest doubt in my mind that Harland's threats were not empty. If I didn't do what he expected of me, he would kill me and anyone who tried to intervene.

Thankfully, Vesta's life was brimful with her family and her business. I'm not sure she even noticed when I slipped away from her.

The next year and the year after that were filled with more of the same from Harland. I'd long ago faced the fact I had nowhere to go. So I didn't threaten to leave anymore. I simply went through the motions of being a loving wife. Along with Clara's help, I kept the house perfect, I fixed his meals, and I escorted him to charity functions or parties put on by his friends and associates.

In the beginning, when we returned home from one of the affairs I would almost always be punished because I'd chosen the wrong dress to wear, or I'd laughed too loud at something I'd found funny. At the next party, I'd concentrate hard on not doing what I'd done wrong the last time, but there was always another infraction of the rules I didn't know about until I got home.

At one of the firm's Christmas parties, I'd inadvertently smiled a little too much at a young man who was interning with

Harland and his partner. Trying to be nice earned me more than the usual hair pulling, punches to the stomach, or being lifted into the air and thrown to the floor.

That particular time, as I lay on the floor trying to recover the breath that had been knocked out of me, he kicked me. I felt my rib crack. Pain radiated violently through my midsection. While I was in the most excruciating pain I'd ever known, Harland dragged me to the bed and climbed on top of me. He raped me. The pain of him pushing against my rib was so great that my only hope of survival was to leave the agony behind and escape inside my brain.

When it was over, I asked him to take me to the hospital. My rib needed medical attention, but he refused. He gave me a bottle of prescription pain pills. I stared at them and wondered two things: Why did he have a prescription for pain pills? And how many should I take; one or all of them?

I opted for one and wrapped my chest with strips of material and wide tape to hopefully hold my ribs in place until they healed. The pain stayed with me for several weeks. So did Harland. He and his warped mind clung to me like a boa constrictor. He crushed me a little more each day.

The biggest strife between Harland and me was that in almost four years I still hadn't gotten pregnant. He badgered me on a regular basis and half the time it turned into an argument followed by a beating. All I could do was assure him I wasn't doing anything to keep from getting pregnant. Whether he believed it or not was his problem. I was pretty sure the reason was because of the stress my body was under. That, and possibly, it was the one and only prayer God had ever answered. I didn't want to bring a child into the world I lived in. Not the world Harland had built for us.

On the days Clara cleaned, I was usually gone from the house so I wouldn't be in her way, but with a broken rib and the lethargic feeling the pain pills brought on, I didn't want to go out. Shortly before time for Clara to leave, I fixed her a cup of coffee and invited her to sit with me for a few minutes. Just to hear someone other than Harland speak would possibly make a difference in my mood.

"I appreciate all you do for me here, especially on days like this when I'm not feeling my best," I said.

Her warm smile did take away some of the loneliness I'd been feeling.

"I've been with the Jefferses since before Mr. Jeffers passed away, God rest his soul."

Her having the slightest respect for the horrible man who had made Harland what he was today, took me by surprise. "You sound as if you actually liked the man."

It was her turn to look surprised. "I did like Mr. Jeffers. He was one of the kindest men I've ever met."

"To hear Harland tell it, his father was mean and abusive to his son and his wife."

Clara studied my face for an immeasurable amount of time. "No, honey." She touched my hands. "Wesley Jeffers never raised his hand to his wife or to Harland. His mother, however, was a completely different story."

"I don't understand," I told Clara. "But then again, why should I? I haven't been able to comprehend anything since the day I married Harland." Instantly, I wished I could take back those words. Harland would be furious if Clara told him what

I'd said.

"What did he tell you that made you think his father was cruel to him?"

"I'm not sure I should be discussing this with anyone. He'd be awfully mad if he knew."

"You can trust me."

How did I know that for sure? Talking to her about Harland could get me killed.

"Tell me," she urged. "You need to know the truth, but he can never know I told you. He and his mother have more than paid for my silence over the years."

Paid her? Paid her how? Silence about what? What was Clara talking about? The pills must have really screwed with my mind, because even the kind elderly lady in front of me was talking gibberish. I started to get up from the breakfast booth, but she stopped me.

"What did Harland say that made you think his father had beaten him? We have to talk about this, Mrs. Jeffers."

"Please don't call me that. My name is Montana. I hate being Mrs. Jeffers." If I could cry, I'd feel better, but I couldn't make the tears appear. They were gone, along with my hope for a different life.

"Montana, please talk to me, sweetheart." Her compassionate gaze told me I could trust her.

"Harland said his father beat him, and tied him to the bed with ropes until he'd learned his lesson. He said then his dad would start in on his mother and beat her."

"If it wasn't all so tragic, I could laugh. Wesley never raised a hand to Marna Jeffers unless it was to grab hers to keep her from striking him. It was she who hit him with whatever object she could get her hands on. It didn't matter if it was a crowbar, or a fireplace poker. I know we're not to speak badly of the dead, but Harland's mother was the most evil woman who ever walked the face of the earth. She used her money to benefit the needy, but here at home her house was nothing short of a torture chamber." Clara's explanation was filled with pain obviously heavy in her heart.

"His mother would beat him for no apparent reason. I know because I was here five days a week. I saw everything that happened in this house. She tied Harland to the bed. Sometimes he'd be left there all night. I'd untie him when I came to work in the morning so he could go to the bathroom; then I'd tie him back up so she wouldn't know."

"What about the scar on his back? Harland said he caught his father out in his workshop having sex with someone who wasn't his wife. And then his father threw him on a saw and cut his back. The evil man wouldn't even let his wife take Harland to the hospital to be stitched up. She closed the wound herself."

Clara shook her head the whole time I was talking. "To stay out of her sight as much as possible, Harland practically lived outside in the yard or in his dad's workshop. One afternoon, I had gone home, but I realized I'd forgotten my purse. So about an hour after I'd left, I returned right in the middle of Harland walking into his mother's bedroom, where he found Mr. Simpson, from next door, in bed with Marna. When she realized Harland had seen her, she chased after him in nothing but her slip.

"God only knew what she'd do when she caught him. To have a reason to follow and hopefully defuse the situation, I grabbed her robe and ran after her.

"I made it to the building just as she shoved him backward onto a saw that came up through the table. I guess it jabbed into his flesh because he had to wiggle to get off it. Sometimes at night, I can still hear him screaming." Clara hesitated a moment. Chills ran the length of my spine.

"There was blood everywhere. I used the robe to try to stop the bleeding. It was awful. I told her we had to get him to the doctor as soon as possible, but she wouldn't take him. Instead, she insisted I sew him up with a needle and thread, which I did."

"Why didn't you call an ambulance and the police?"

"I couldn't. I needed this job more than you can imagine. My late husband worked seasonal work, so my paycheck was very important to us. We had two little girls. One had asthma really bad, and Mrs. Jeffers saw to it my little girl got the best treatment available. My other daughter needed braces, and she had them. Both my girls got to go to college and have good jobs so they don't have to clean other people's houses." She wiped away her tears.

"You see, my silence was bought and paid for. I had to think of my family. Even now that she's dead and gone, Harland would never say a bad word against her. Back then, if I had called the police, he would have never told them what was going on, and I would have been out of a job that I needed real bad. Also, if I hadn't been here, I wasn't sure what more Marna would have done to Harland."

"So Harland was abused, but not by his father. It was his mother who did those unspeakable things to him and turned an intelligent young boy into the devil."

Clara nodded.

His mother had been the one who taught him how to treat a lady. And I was on the receiving end of that treatment.

He'd lied to me about his father and probably lied to himself.

Evidently, in Harland's demented mind, he could accept being a child and being abused by this father, but he couldn't accept being a teenager and a young man being abused by his mother.

No matter how we'd arrived at that point in our lives, I could add one more thing to my feelings for Harland. Along with fear came undiluted hatred, and I had no remorse for feeling that way. His being abused was not an open invitation for him to brutalize me.

I had other questions for Clara, but before I could ask them, the garage door opened and the son of Satan stepped into the kitchen.

Chapter 14

"ARE YOU TWO HAVING A HEN PARTY?" HARLAND ASKED when he saw Clara and me sitting at the kitchen table. He wasn't expected home for another two hours, but then, Harland never did what was expected of him.

"I wasn't feeling well," Clara lied. "Mrs. Jeffers was kind enough to fix me a cup of coffee."

I opened my mouth to remind her to call me Montana, but her warning gaze and the instant quiver in my stomach told me Harland wouldn't like me being so informal with the maid, especially one who knew so much about him.

"Would you like some more?" I asked.

"No, thank you. I'm feeling much better. I'd better get on home." As quickly as she could without looking obvious, Clara left.

"You're home early." It was a statement because I would never question him.

"There's a reception for the library board. We need to make an appearance. Before the party starts, we're going to meet Mike and Evelyn at Nino's for dinner. Wear that navy blue dress I bought you a couple of weeks ago." He spewed his orders and was off to the bedroom to shower.

Mike and Evelyn Christensen were the total opposites of Harland and me. She wore the Armani pants in that family. Mike was her yes-man. She had been a member of the library board for less than a year. Evelyn and Harland had like minds about every subject that came up. Mike and I spoke only when spoken to. He drank straight scotch, which was probably what got him through the day. Normally, when we dined out, I had one glass of wine, but I was afraid to mix alcohol with the pain pills I'd taken a little earlier. That night, I had to face dinner with the Christensens totally sober.

"Montana, it's good to see you, dear. How have you been?" Evelyn air kissed both of my cheeks. Mike nodded in my direction and saluted with his scotch glass.

Slowly, I took my seat at a round table in the center of Nino's and tried my best not to wince from the pain radiating around my ribs. "I'm fine, Evelyn. That's a very pretty dress."

"This?" She looked down and dusted away imaginary particles from boobs that looked ready to burst out of her bodice. "I found it in a boutique on our last trip to Vegas. Have you two ever been there?"

Harland answered for me. "Not yet, but we are going there to celebrate our fifth anniversary in two weeks."

Slack-jawed, my gaze snapped to him. That was the first I'd heard about a trip. I didn't even think he realized we had an anniversary coming up. A glimmer of excitement rippled through me. Finally something to look forward to. I touched my lips and found I actually had a sincere smile as opposed to the one I always sported in case someone took my picture.

The conversation turned to the new budget for the library. The only thing Mike said for the entire evening was, "I'll have another scotch, please." I said even less.

While waiting for the waiter to return with our tab, Evelyn and Harland discussed the type of books needed for the library. They assumed that romances and mysteries were the most sought-after stories, but, to be sure, they would ask the head of the library for statistics.

Evelyn looked at me. "What do you like to read, Montana?" She smiled and her thin lips disappeared.

"*Modern Romance.*" I was proud to contribute to the conversation.

Evelyn nearly spit out her wine. She threw her head back and brayed like the ass she was. When she realized no one else was laughing, she looked at Harland. "She's kidding, isn't she?" Evelyn acted like I was invisible.

As Harland shook his head, his cheeks colored to bright pink. I'd embarrassed him in front of important people. That was not a good thing.

That night, I never made it to the reception. Harland told the Christensens that I hadn't been feeling well. He was going to run me home, and he'd join them in a little while. I forced a smile, and then said good-bye to the couple.

Inside the car, the air hung heavy, making it hard for me to breathe. Harland's ominous silence was the worst. The longer he went without speaking, the more the fury built inside him, the harder my punishment would be.

We were almost home when he finally started his tirade.

"Do you have to let everyone know exactly how stupid you are? It's as if you look for the best way to embarrass me. Why is that, Montana? Do you have a death wish?"

Something inside me snapped. Before I could stop myself, words I would later regret poured out of me.

"If reading a magazine makes me stupid, then I am with a capital *S*. But to my way of thinking, the most stupid thing I've done in my life is to marry you! And if that makes you kill me and send me through that damnable wood chipper you are always threatening me with, then do it. Just do it. Get it over with." I was screaming at the top of my lungs, expecting to receive the back of his hand across my face.

Harland didn't hit me. Instead, he told me something that carried more punch than he could have ever done physically.

"There was something else you did that was stupid." From his tone I could tell he was delighted to tell me what that thing was.

"What is that, pray tell?" Where had I found the nerve to talk back to him? My voice didn't even shake, but inside, I shuddered with fear and hatred.

"Since you're doing something to yourself so you don't have to give me a son——"

"That's not true. I've done nothing to keep from getting pregnant."

"I don't believe you. Besides being stupid, you're a liar, too. In spite of that, I decided to search for the baby you gave away."

Harland had looked for Berryanne. My chest pinched tight. "Did you find her? Where is my baby?"

He pulled to the front of the house and stopped by the entrance gate.

"Maybe it's a good thing we haven't had any kids. You're too ignorant to raise a child."

I stared at him. His mouth pulled to a sickening grin.

"You took that newborn baby out into the cold night air. She came down with pneumonia. She's dead."

Berryanne was dead. I had killed my baby. The agony crawling around inside me was far worse than anything Harland could have physically done to me. He knew that, too, and it brought him pleasure.

"Go into the house. Put on your red, sexy nightgown. I'll be home before midnight."

I couldn't find the strength to open the door, let alone walk into the house. Harland shoved me and shouted, "Get out, you stupid bitch!"

Somehow I managed to climb out of the car and to collapse against the wall surrounding the rose garden and the path to the elegant house. I sat there on the grass for a long time before I could make my legs hold me up. Digging in my purse, I found the key to the gate.

Entering from the front door, the first room I passed was the guest room, which had belonged to Harland's mother. I turned on the light and entered the pale blue room with plush carpeting and a crystal chandelier. She'd lived in elegance, and appeared to be a model mother and a generous human being, when in fact nothing could have been farther from the truth.

She'd molded her son in her likeness, and he'd mastered the art of control and torture very well. I could vouch for that, because I was a victim of her teachings.

An eight-by-ten black-and-white picture sat on the table by the bed. I picked it up and stared past the gloss on the photo, past the smiles on their faces, and into the empty eyes of a fourteen-year-old Harland and his mother. Even at that young age, his gaze held the seeds of wickedness, and they'd grown into a deadly plant.

A fact that I lived with daily was that eventually Harland would kill me. To this point, I didn't want to die because I thought that somewhere out there Berryanne was waiting for me. But now I knew she was gone, and I had not one shred of desire to live another day.

Inside our bedroom, I tried to force open the locked top drawer of the dresser where Harland kept his gun. The drawer wasn't going to come open without some type of key. I got a hairpin from the bathroom and jimmied the lock just as Vesta had taught me to do a lifetime ago.

It opened. I pulled out the revolver Harland had used to strike terror in my soul whenever he felt the need.

It was loaded and ready for use. With the night-light illuminating some of the bedroom, I readied myself on the bed, leaned back against the headboard, and laid the gun beside me. Across from the bed, on the wall next to the dresser, was a picture Harland had taken, framed, and hung there as a daily reminder for me. The bathroom light lit the photo of the wood chipper. It made my skin crawl.

If the slightest thought of putting the gun back came to mind, I'd feel my broken rib and look at the mocking picture of the device that would grind me into tiny pieces. Those things made me willing to do what had to be done. With all hope gone for ever seeing Berryanne again, I calmly accepted the fact that ending my life was the only option I had left. Yet, I lacked the actual nerve it would take to pull the trigger. I tried hard to make myself do it.

I waited so long to make my move, exhaustion overcame me. I fell asleep. When I woke up, Harland was undressing on his side of the bed. I reached for the gun. Panic gripped me.

"I put it back in the drawer," he said in a normal tone. "I'm too tired and too drunk to deal with this tonight. Go to sleep, Montana."

His voice held no emotion, and that frightened me more than his wrath. In the morning, what would happen when he was rested and clearheaded? Because my mind couldn't fathom what lay ahead, it closed down completely. Until the sun came up, I stayed in that same spot, not allowing any thoughts or decisions or fear to penetrate my brain. Through the long night hours, I stared straight ahead at the framed photo on the wall, paralyzed by the image of the wood chipper.

The next morning, while Harland showered and dressed for work, I fixed breakfast. He never spoke a word and neither did I. When he finished, he took me by the hand and led me into the bedroom. There were four ropes tied around each bed knob.

"Lie down on the bed, Montana."

"What are you going to do?" My body filled with fear as chilling as the ice water that surged through Harland's veins. I shuddered.

"I'm going to tie you to the bed so you can't run away or be lying in wait to shoot me when I get home. We can do this the easy way, or we can do it the hard way. Your choice."

I was stunned. He hadn't realized I'd planned to take my own life. He thought I was waiting to kill him. My interpretation of the whole situation was as crazy as Harland's. Instead of him thinking I was too weak to kill myself, he thought that, had I not fallen asleep, I would have been brave enough to kill him.

That knowledge brought a certain surge of power, which quickly dissipated when I realized no amount of begging was going to keep him from tying me up. I lay down and closed my eyes. I didn't want to see the joy on his face as he tied each of my limbs to a bedpost.

"I'll be back at lunchtime. We'll see if you've learned your lesson and can be set free in the afternoon."

I bit my tongue to keep from begging. I seethed privately inside my brain where I retreated when times were unbearable. I stayed inside that world until I heard Harland close the door. Only then did I begin to cry.

For the next four hours, I lay there, painfully uncomfortable, trying to keep my sanity in check. I stared at my favorite rose, three down, four across.

At lunchtime, he came home.

"Are you going to try to run away anymore?" he asked.

"No."

"Are you going to try to kill me again?"

"No."

That was the end of our exchange on the matter. He untied me and then left to return to work. Instantly our lives were back to the same routine. I walked on eggshells. He exploded with no warning.

Harland was taking me to Las Vegas for our fifth anniversary. For the trip he insisted I buy a new wardrobe of stunning clothes and all the accessories. The one good thing I could say about him was he spared no expense for me to look my best whether at home, running errands, or out for the citizens of Pinehurst to see. My closets overflowed with beautiful and expensive clothing.

I would have rather had love.

I learned early on what looked good on me and what things offended Harland's sense of style. No plunging necklines, but bare shoulders were acceptable. Nothing too short or too tight, but full, flared skirts that swayed as I entered a room delighted him immensely.

As long as the house was in perfect shape and dinner was ready when he came home, I had the freedom and the money to go shopping whenever I wanted. And, yes, at times I thought about getting in my car and driving so far away no one would ever see me again, but Harland's voice played over and over in my head.

"You can't hide from me. I'll find you, and if I don't kill you with a slow, torturous death, I'll make you wish you were dead."

I knew he meant every word, and with his connections, I knew he could find me.

Strangely enough, I was more afraid of running because the unknown was scarier than living in Harland's world. In his world, I didn't know when it would happen, but I knew for sure that one day he would kill me. Knowing I was responsible for Berryanne dying, my death couldn't come quick enough. Until then, I'd walk around like a robot, responding to commands and never allowing myself to feel anything other than dread that I'd have to endure more of Harland's persecution before I would be allowed to die.

On the day I'd gone shopping for my trip to Las Vegas, an unfamiliar sensation buzzed through me. As I walked down Tyder Avenue, I glanced at my reflection in the window of the Pinehurst Bank. A huge smile brightened my face, but that wasn't anything new. I always smiled just like Harland demanded because I didn't know when someone would take my picture.

No, it wasn't the smile that lightened my heart. It was

something else. Something so foreign I couldn't quite put my finger on it. Out of nowhere it came to me. I was excited about going to Las Vegas. During the five years Harland and I had been married, we had never gone anywhere farther than a quick business trip to Raleigh.

There was a little more pep in my stride, and I hadn't had to remind myself to straighten my shoulders. My smile wasn't forced, and I was humming my way along the street. From an entrance to a jewelry store, a woman rushed out and bumped into me, knocking me back a step.

"I'm sorry," I muttered although she had plainly run into me.

The woman looked at me and scowled. "I should hope so," she mumbled and pushed past me.

I recognized her as Patricia Simpson, the woman who lived next door to Harland and me. It was her mother I'd originally thought Harland had caught his father with out in the workshop, but Clara had told me it was Patricia's father who'd been caught with Harland's mother. The only thing more confusing about all that was Patricia's attitude toward me.

During the five years I'd lived next door to her, I'd spoken to her on three occasions when we both had trekked to the mailbox at the exact same time. With an indignant huff, she'd ignored me all three times. The fierce glare she'd just given me spoke volumes. She did not like me and wanted nothing to do with me. Why? I didn't have a clue, and on that particular day, my spirits were too high to let her shadow my thoughts.

That night, since Harland was in a good mood, too, I brought up the subject of Patricia and asked him if he had any idea why she so obviously disliked me when I'd never even met her.

"I told you before that she is the woman my mother had wanted me to marry," Harland answered.

"Did Patricia want that, too? Is that why she's so mad at me?"

"Exactly."

"What about you? Why didn't you marry her?"

"Because I was waiting for you." Harland took the last drink of his dinner wine.

"You and I never met until after your mother passed away. How could you have been waiting for me?" I expected him to say he was waiting for someone like me, but the awkward silence that followed made me wish I'd not brought up the subject at all. It wasn't as if I cared about other women in his life, but he'd made that statement many times since we'd met, and I was curious.

"Let's just say, I always get what I want and I wanted you."

That was the end of the discussion, and I knew it. It wasn't the first time he'd made a statement that made me think he'd somehow singled me out and made me his quest. Yet I couldn't image how that could be. It was probably just part of my short-circuited thinking caused by years of mental, emotional, and physical abuse.

Besides, I was going to Las Vegas, and nothing was going to steal my excitement. Not even jealous Patricia Simpson next door whom I would have traded places with in the blink of an eye.

A few days later, as per Harland's best-laid plans, we flew into Las Vegas and took a rental car to the Mystic Hotel and Casino. After we checked in, Harland sifted through my clothes and picked out a black evening dress with spaghetti straps for me to wear.

I put on the dress, and then fixed my makeup and hair. Harland insisted I model for him, which I did. He nodded his approval, and we were off for a night on the town.

I'd never seen such beautiful lights, all colors, flashing,

beckoning everyone to follow them into casino after casino. I stared like a country girl on her first trip to the big city. In a way it was. The clanging of coins falling to the metal trays of the slot machines, the yelps of lucky winners scattered here and there, and the music from the live band next to the Keno area sent exciting shivers through my entire body.

Watching Harland play a few hands of blackjack, a crazy thought came to me. I could possibly just disappear into the crowd, never to be heard from again. I fantasized about being on my own in such a magnificent place. I could work as a waitress. I'd done that before and was quite good at it. I was good with money. I could be a teller like the ones in the cage across the casino from where I stood. Lost in my own, wonderful world, until he touched my arm, I didn't realize Harland had stepped next to me.

"Are you okay?" he asked.

I jumped slightly. "Of course."

"Are you ready to get something to eat?"

I nodded. He put his arm around my waist and led me through the crowd. In front of us, another couple was also making their way out of the casino. His arm was around her shoulder and hers was around his waist. He whispered something in her ear and she giggled. It was obvious they loved each other and made each other happy.

Did Harland and I look like we were in love? Did we fool those around us? His arm held me close to him. We both smiled widely, yet there was no love in my heart and by his actions he couldn't have any love for me. Did we deceive those around us, or did everyone see the loathing surrounding us as easily as I saw love from the couple in front of me? Evidently not. Harland would not allow that.

After getting our rental car from the valet, we drove to a restaurant just beyond the twinkling lights of the Vegas strip. If I lived to be a million, I will never forget the dinner we had that night—huge chunks of Maine lobster dipped in hot, lemon butter followed by crème brûlée. It was the most magnificent meal I'd ever tasted. I washed it all down with a glass of wine and started on my second.

Harland winked and then tapped my glass with his. "To my beautiful wife. The future is ours."

Butterflies fluttering in my stomach wouldn't allow me to think of my future. It was when I allowed myself that pleasure that the reality of my powerless life was usually driven home by one of Harland's tirades.

I acknowledged his toast with a vibrant smile. Evidently, the waiter had heard what Harland said. "I agree, sir. You have a beautiful wife."

Flushed from the gentleman's statement and the effects of my second glass of wine, I giggled like a schoolgirl. Suddenly, I couldn't stop. Even Harland's warning glares couldn't temper my out-of-control laughter. I dabbed the white cloth napkin tightly to my lips, hoping to stop it, but a hiccup loudly escaped. I was back at it again.

"Our tab, please," Harland said to the waiter, who hurried away.

My *loving* husband gripped my forearm. "Stop it, Montana. You're making a fool of yourself and me in the process."

That quickly robbed me of the happiness of the evening. "I'm sorry. I don't know what got into me." Hoping to appease his anger, I reached for his hand, but he pulled it away.

The waiter returned. Harland paid the bill, and we quickly left the restaurant.

Once in the car, he turned in his seat to face me. "I know you came from a poor, uneducated background, but I thought you at least had common sense. How dare you laugh like a hyena just because some common waiter flirted with you?"

"I said I was sorry. What else do you want from me?" The wine had erased just enough of my fear to loosen my tongue.

The back of his hand connected so quickly and so hard with the side of my face, causing my neck to snap, that I couldn't put logical thoughts together to figure out what had happened. Pain shot through my jaw, and bright lights flashed behind one of my eyes. I put my cold hand over the throbbing heat on my cheek.

"What did you do that for?" I screamed at Harland. "Are you totally crazy?"

Of course he was. Why had I asked such a dim-witted question? Harland Jeffers was an A-class, certifiable psychopath, and I had been the lucky one he'd waited a lifetime to capture . . . and torture. Patricia Simpson should be on her knees daily thanking me for saving her from Harland Jeffers.

He slammed the gearshift into drive, stomped on the gas, and spun tires out of the restaurant parking lot. When we were back on the main street of Vegas, we raced along at top speed.

"Stop this car. You're going to kill us both. Let me out." I'm not sure where the nerve came from to take that stand, but it did nothing more than to incite him further.

We'd left the main drag and were driving erratically though a housing development. Fear filled every part of my brain. It surely would explode.

"Do you hear me, Harland?" I spoke through clenched teeth as much from the pain as for emphasis. "This is not right. You can't treat me this way. Slow down or let me out of this car."

The next few minutes were a blur. He delivered two devastating blows to my face, one with a backhand to my nose and a final closed fist to my uninjured jaw. My head smashed against the passenger door window. I lost consciousness.

When I came to, Harland had ripped my dress straps off my shoulders, bursting the side zipper and was in the process of shoving me out of the car. I was already in a forward motion with no hope of stopping myself. As my battered body fell from the vehicle, Harland tore my dress the rest of the way off. I hit the sidewalk in nothing more than my underclothes.

"You don't want me, then you don't want the clothes I bought you, either." Harland slammed the door. The taillights disappeared out of sight. All I could do was thank God he was gone.

I'm not sure how long I'd lain there, but an angelic figure dressed in white hovered over me. "Do you need help, lady?" the angel asked.

"I think so." I looked up into a sweet, but concerned face.

She helped me to my feet. My head spun. Leaning against her was all that kept me from falling onto my battered face. She led me up the concrete walk, but before I went inside, I stepped to her shrubbery and threw up my lobster and crème brûlée.

Once inside, the lady pointed to a chair in a neat den with avocado carpeting and gold brocade furniture wrapped tightly in plastic. "You sit right there." She handed me a towel. "Hold this tight against your cheek. I'll get my first-aid kit."

"No, wait. I don't want to put you to any trouble. I'll be fine."

Surely I wasn't hurt as badly as the pounding in my head indicated. I removed the towel from my cheek and started in alarm at the amount of blood soaking the terry cloth. I felt blood running down my face, and I replaced the towel. I'd never had to deal with face injuries. Harland always hit me where it wouldn't show, my stomach, the back of my head, or anyplace a garment would cover, but never my face. His violence escalated more each time he punished me.

Even though I was fearful of what would happen to me from this point on, at least I wouldn't have to contend with Harland any longer.

"You are hurt pretty bad, honey. Now just sit still." She wasn't gone but a few moments. When she returned, she held a roll of cotton and alcohol. She swabbed a place on my cheekbone. I cried out. The burning added to the pain shooting through the side of my face.

"My name is Betty, honey. What's yours?"

"Montana. Parsons." I didn't want to be Montana Jeffers anymore.

Betty wore a long, white chenille robe. Her skin flushed rosy red against rounded pale cheeks. A pink ribbon secured her gray curls in a pile on top of her head. Her halo. She not only looked like an angel, but to me she was one.

"I've called the police. They'll be here right away," she said.

My heart jumped to my throat. "No, I don't want the police to come." They were of no use to me. They were Harland's friends. Or were they? Would the Las Vegas police care about what Harland could do for them? We were a long way from Pinehurst, North Carolina, but uncertainty warned me to proceed with caution.

"Honey, whoever did this to you will have to pay. Do you know who did it?" Betty asked.

I made a conscious decision to tell the truth to only those

who could protect me from Harland, should he decide to come back. Since he'd tossed me to the curb, I took that as a sign he wouldn't be back. At least that's what I hoped it meant.

"Who did it?" Her pleading was interrupted by pounding on the door. I jumped and sank deeper into the chair.

Betty took off her robe revealing a long flannel gown underneath. She handed it to me. "Here, let me help you put this on before I let the police in."

That was the first time I remembered my clothes had been torn off. My white brassiere was marred with grass stains and blood. Thankfully, my half slip, although soiled with more blood, covered my panties and allowed me some modesty.

Slowly, I rose, and she wrapped the robe around my hurting body. A strong knock sounded again.

"Police," a man shouted.

As she opened the door, Betty hollered, "Hold your pistol. I had to get the poor thing decent first." She stepped aside, and two officers came in.

They took one look at me and determined I needed an ambulance, which they assured me had been dispatched and would be there any second. My face was numb, and I could barely see out of my rapidly swelling eyes.

The officers bombarded me with questions. What's your name? Where are you from? Where do you hurt? Were you raped?

I answered as quickly as they fired them at me. Just in case they did have a connection with Harland, I told them my name was Montana Parsons.

"Do you know who did this?" one of the officers asked.

That stopped me cold. My tongue stuck to the roof of my dry mouth. Pain exploded in my head, and my body shook violently. What if I told them the truth and they arrested Harland? He might have been able to throw me away, but he'd never ignore my having him arrested. I'd always be looking over my shoulder.

"It's okay, sweetheart," Betty said and then turned to the officer who towered over her. "Hey, buster, can't you see she's hurting? Let the ambulance attendants do their job first and then you can ask all your questions."

After the paramedics finished looking me over and I'd assured them I hadn't been raped, they said I would need stitches, but I didn't appear to have any broken bones. I should be transported to the hospital for X-rays to be sure.

I didn't know what to do. The wretched pain of my screwed-up life far outweighed the physical pain. It bore deeply into my chest. I expected my heart to quit beating at any minute. But it didn't. It kept shoving blood through my body, forcing me to stay alive and face whatever came my way. I didn't want to do that. I begged for it all to stop. I wanted to go to sleep and never open my eyes on earth again.

"Let's get you to the hospital," an officer said. "I'll follow and finish my report there."

"I need to go to the bathroom," I said to Betty.

"Sure, honey." She led me down a hallway lined with family pictures. How lucky she must be. I had no pictures of any of my family. Only a mental image of my mother's beautiful face. At times, when it threatened to fade, I forced it back and burned it deeper into my memory.

Sometimes, when I looked into a mirror, I saw my mother's face looking back at me. I would smile, but then realize it was me. I always thought of my mother as beautiful, but except for the few fleeting moments when I saw the resemblance, I never felt that I was. Especially right then. I'd never seen anything as hideous as the face that stared back at me in Betty's bathroom mirror. My legs grew weak. I held on to the sink to keep upright. Betty, who was getting a towel and washcloth from the closet, put her arm around my waist.

"Here, sit down for a minute." She closed the lid on the toilet and eased me down onto it. After she wet the cloth, she handed it to me. "Put this cool rag on your face."

I did, but it hurt too much to wipe it.

"Are you still dizzy?" Betty asked.

"No, it's passed."

"If you need me, I'll be right outside the door." She left me alone, dreading to look back in the mirror.

I used the toilet and then took a good look at myself again. I gently wiped away the dried blood from my nose and lip. The paramedics had cleaned the section on my cheek where they'd applied a large, square piece of gauze attached with tape. I lifted one side to take a peek at my wound and found a huge gash caused by Harland's square diamond ring. Quickly, I sealed it back before the blood could start to run again.

What should I do next? My clothes were all back at the hotel, and I certainly couldn't march through the lobby in my underwear. I had no money to call a cab. Harland had my purse and my checkbook with him. God only knew where he was, and I didn't intend to track him down for money.

I clung tightly to the edge of sanity, with all hope of getting past the misery crumbling beneath me. I wasn't sure I wanted to survive. For what reason?

A light tap on the door shook me from my reverie. Betty eased the door open.

"You okay, honey?"

I nodded.

"They're waiting to take you to the hospital. Are you ready?"

Maybe there I could talk to one of the nurses or doctors and get advice on what I should do. In the meantime, I'd answer only questions I had to.

"I'm ready." I moved to the door, but Betty blocked my way.

"How long have you been married, honey?"

"Five years." Five nightmarish years. "Why?"

"Is this your first time?" she asked, but I didn't understand. Confusion must have played across my face.

"I've noticed you haven't said if you know who did this." Betty looked at me with kind and knowing eyes. "I recognize that disparaging look on your face. I saw it many times on my own before my husband died." She paused, and I suspected she was looking for my reaction. I tried hard not to give her one. "Your husband did this to you, didn't he?"

The truthful words stung hard. I didn't answer.

"Take the word of a woman who's been through it. No matter what he says, he'll never change. You will, but he won't. You'll change everything about yourself to try to make him happy, but it won't matter. He's unhappy with himself, and he has to have someone else to blame. It couldn't possibly be his own shortcomings, his own mental state, or his own actions. No, honey, none of it will ever be his fault. It will always be yours. He'll tell you that for so long, you'll eventually believe it."

Everything Betty said was true, but when you are neck-deep in quicksand, it's hard to think about anything other than surviving. That's where I'd been for five years, but with Harland gone, maybe I could get my strength back, and ultimately my life.

"You must tell the police who did this, press charges against him, and not back down for any reason. While he's serving the few pitiful weeks the judge will give him, you run like hell and make a new life for yourself. Don't believe any of his lies." My head pounded too loudly to absorb all that Betty said.

It appeared to be the ramblings of an older woman, none of which fit my situation. Harland had thrown me out. He wouldn't be back to tell me lies or for any other reason.

At the hospital, after the X-rays were taken and the cut on my cheek closed, the doctor allowed a police officer to talk to me. Betty had insisted I wear her white robe to the hospital. I hugged it tightly around me to fight off the terrible chill that persisted.

The lapse in time between my first encounter with the police and their appearance in the emergency room had given me time to figure out what I wanted to do about charging Harland with battery. The medication used to numb my face for the stitches, as well as the strong pain pills, all mixed together and helped me with my decision.

"Who did this to you, Miss Parsons?" the officer asked.

Instinctively, I looked around to see who would hear my confession. A nurse who bandaged and taped my freshly sewn stitches was the only other person present.

"It was my husband. He beat me, ripped off my clothes, and threw me out of the car." The words rasped painfully from my throat.

"Where is he now?" The policeman dug further.

"I don't know, and I don't want to know. I just want the nightmare to be over."

"Has he done this before?"

"Yes."

"Would you like to press charges?"

I swallowed hard, stalling for a moment before I spoke the words that would initiate my husband's arrest. Those words were on the tip of my tongue ready to break the thick silence.

The curtains parted and Harland stepped in.

Chapter 15

IN THE JAIL CONFERENCE ROOM, PHILLIP KANE READ THE latest pages I'd written so he could understand how I'd come to murder my husband. During the past two weeks, I'd seen little of Phillip. He had been busy researching, preparing, and investigating every minute detail of my pathetic existence.

He seemed convinced that if a jury heard my story they'd understand how I was driven to take Harland's life. When I tried to look at it through the eyes of someone who had never suffered abuse, all I could see was a weak and stupid human being who didn't deserve to live, especially after that day in Las Vegas.

There, I'd had a policeman with a gun on his hip, who had never even heard of Harland Jeffers or his money. The officer stood to protect me from my evil husband and to cart him off to jail for beating me.

"You didn't press charges against Harland, did you?" Phillip laid my notebook back on the table. By his accusatory yet warm gaze, it was obvious he already knew the answer.

"Sitting here where Harland can never lay another hand on

me, it's easy to see what I should have done, but back then I'd already lived with five years of abuse. My mind was like a cement mixer filled with a ton of fear, a handful of inexperience, and several handfuls of brainwashing. It all tumbled together until I was buried in that mix." My head hammered with the onset of another migraine. As if on cue, Harland's voice beat at my aching brain. *Stupid. Stupid. Stupid.*

As Phillip had done so many times during our visits, he waited patiently for me to gather my thoughts.

"No, I didn't press charges against Harland." Heavy remorse colored my voice. "When he entered that hospital cubicle, his presence loomed like a powerful steam engine about to blow its top. He cast a dark, frightening shadow over my shaking body. His presence sucked the oxygen right out of the room. The fear Harland had beaten into me over the years had taken over and was greater than any strength I could ever muster." My body shook with the same violent shudders I'd felt that day.

"It's okay, Montana. Harland can't ever hurt you again," Phillip whispered.

"Why wasn't I strong enough to have him arrested and then do like that lady Betty said, run for my life? Why didn't the police just take him away? I never understood why they put it all on my shoulders. I was the person Harland would blame for his having a record, maybe jail time, and possibly causing him to be disbarred."

"And you thought that putting it on paper would have made Harland's brutality all your fault," Phillip summarized.

"That's what *he* would have thought. I would have always been running scared, looking in closets, behind doors to see if Harland was there. At least, going home with him, I'd know where he was, and most of the time, when he was coming after me."

"That's pretty sound reasoning, I'd say." Phillip came around the table and took a seat next to me. "But, you see, since I've been on the inside looking out, I see it all as clear as the crystal chandeliers that hang throughout your house."

I paused to reflect not so much on what Phillip had just said, but how he said it. It wasn't a comparison he'd pulled from thin air, but something he knew for sure.

"How do you know about what's in my house?"

"I went there a few days ago."

"Why did you go to my house?" I asked.

"Sometimes vital information comes from seeing the crime scene and, in this case, where you and Harland lived as husband and wife. I needed to make a decision as to whether I wanted the jury to actually visit the scene or just show them pictures."

"What did you decide?" I was curious to know what Phillip thought about where I'd lived. It somehow instilled a closer connection between him and me. Yet, I wasn't sure why.

"Truthfully, I'm afraid the grandeur of the house, except for your bedroom, would bias the jury."

"I don't understand."

"I feel they will see your beautiful home, furnishings, your closets of fine clothes, your pool, and they'll think—"

"That I'm a selfish bitch whose generous husband worked hard to give her everything and in the end, she killed him because he'd expected her to act a certain way. In their opinion, since I didn't conform to the things he wanted in exchange for all he gave me, I deserved to be slapped around. Is that it?"

"Well, I was going to try a more diplomatic approach to explaining it, but you summed it up pretty well. It would make them turn a blind eye to the torture chamber in which you were basically held as a prisoner.

"I was having a hard time convincing the district attorney that we didn't need to take the jury on a field trip to the crime scene. He was all for the idea, because he knew that human nature would dictate that the jury would feel as you and I were just discussing."

I'd met District Attorney Martin Donovan at various functions I'd attended with Harland. He and the prosecutor appeared to be friends even though they often faced off in the courtroom. I'd also seen him at my arraignment. I'd imagined he'd regard me with disgust and hatred, but the few times he looked my way, his gaze was kinder than I'd expected.

"Were you able to talk him out of it?"

"I didn't have to. He made a trip to your house, too. Once he saw your bedroom and the points where your body and your head had knocked holes in the walls, and he saw the wear signs on the bedposts where you'd been tied and tortured, I believe he thought he might lose the jury at that point. We both decided that pictures of the bedroom as the crime scene would work better all the way around."

Who saw this, and who didn't see that, and what anyone thought of me for living there didn't even faze me.

All I knew was I wouldn't have to go back to that house.

That was all that mattered to me.

"Why didn't the Las Vegas police arrest Harland whether I pressed charges or not?" I asked.

"Domestic abuse is a strange thing. A husband and wife fight, she has him arrested. The next day they kiss and make up and she drops the charges. The officers involved have been pulled away from more serious crimes, and usually, in a week or two, they'll be right back at the same house separating the fighting couple again. That makes it tough on a woman who really needs rescuing. Like you.

"And," he sighed, "like my mother. That's why I'm working hard to get a house set up where an abused woman can hide out, get her thoughts together before she has to confront her abuser. She needs to be made aware of her options, know that she's not alone. Every town needs a shelter for battered women, and I'm doing everything I can for that cause."

With the depth of Phillip's compassion, I was sure he'd continue until he succeeded. And if I miraculously managed to win my fight through the judicial system, I'd devote the rest of my life to helping women who suffered at the hands of an abuser.

I glanced in Phillip's direction. Devote my life to helping battered women? I had just been given a mission. A reason to live.

"You're one of a kind, Phillip Kane. You're doing right by your mother, and I'm sure she's watching over you and feeling pretty darn proud of what her little boy has grown into."

He smiled widely, and so did I, all the way back to my cell.

My trial date was growing closer, and Phillip still had a mountain of work to do. I wouldn't be seeing him for a while, but in the meantime, he insisted I keep writing.

Alone in my cell, I mulled over his words about a place for women to go to escape an abusive husband. Would a place to hide have made a difference to me? Would I have found the nerve to leave if I had a secret place to go? It was too late for me to even try to put logical thought to those questions. I didn't leave. I made Harland disappear instead.

For the first time since his death, I felt a pang of remorse. There were so many other ways to handle the problems that I'd faced. At one point, I truly thought I'd found a solution. I had hoarded money away, had obtained false identification documents, and was nearly ready to fade away into an unknown horizon. Each of my steps had been meticulously laid out.

But then the letter came. It was addressed to me and simply stated: *Harland knows where your daughter is.*

Those words shook the solid foundation I'd been building. If Berryanne was alive, that meant he'd not only lied to me, but had tortured my heart and soul for the past five years, making me believe I'd killed my baby.

The letter said he knew where my daughter was. Frantically, I tried to imagine how I could learn that information, too. There was only one place in our house where Harland would hide any written information he might have. That one place would be in the locked drawer of the dresser. I had to see if there was any evidence of Berryanne's whereabouts.

Without thinking of the repercussions, I broke into Harland's locked drawer. I was so lost in my quest for information about Berryanne and so shocked at the one document I did find that I hadn't heard Harland enter the house. I didn't know he was behind me until he slammed my body against the dresser, painfully jabbing the corner into my shoulder and my face into the drawer.

"Do you see what you're looking for?" he snarled and pressed my face hard against the bottom of the drawer. I put my hand next to my head and tried to find leverage to lift away from the hard wood before my nose broke. Suddenly, my hand connected with the cold, hard metal.

Harland's gun.

I felt his hold on me slacken just a bit. That was my chance. Adrenaline rushed through me. Without warning, I forced my head upward and smashed against Harland's nose. He lost his balance and fell to the floor.

I turned and shot him three times.

As I sat in my jail cell writing about the moment Harland took his last breath, only then did I realize that the remorse I felt for Harland's death was not that he was gone, but that he'd taken with him information about where I could find Berryanne.

From the beginning, Phillip had promised to try to get to the truth of Berryanne. Was she dead? Was she alive? If so, where was she?

After weeks and months of searching, Phillip had not been able to find answers. It appeared Harland had taken that information with him to his grave. For that I would never forgive him or myself.

For another two weeks, I continued to document as much as I could of the last five years of my life with Harland. So much of it was a repeat of the days and weeks and years before that I couldn't bring myself to write it down.

From the day Vesta straightened my hacked hair, and I saw that Harland could possibly follow through with his threats against her, I steered clear of any interaction with her. After many attempts on her part to find out why I didn't want to have anything to do with her, she finally gave up and dropped completely out of my life. Hundreds of times during the years we were estranged, I had picked up the phone to call her, to tell her I loved her and missed her. But I'd always hung up.

The year before I was arrested for murder, I answered my front door and found Vesta standing there. Stuck between an overwhelming desire to pull her into my arms and tell her how much I'd missed her and the unmitigated terror that Harland would find her there, I opened the gate, took her hand, and dragged her down the garden path and into the house.

"What are you doing here?" A mixture of happiness and fear battled inside my stomach.

"It's time we had a talk," she said.

"Vesta, Harland can't find you here. He'll—"

"He'll what? Beat me up?" Her I-don't-give-a-damn attitude made me shiver. When that reared its head, she really didn't care what happened to her, but I knew she didn't have a clue what evil she was up against with Harland.

"You don't understand," I said.

"This is what I do understand. You and I were too close and shared too much to not still be the best friends ever. For years now, I thought that you rose to a higher power and were too good to have anything to do with me. I've mourned the loss of your friendship like I would have if you'd died, but I don't want that any longer. I know you better than that, and I'm sorry it's taken me so long to come to my senses. Right here and right now, you and I are going to lay all our cards on the table."

Tears stung my eyes. I'd missed Vesta so much, I ached inside.

"You have to leave." I tried to turn her and shove her back outside. She resisted.

"Here's what I think: Harland refuses to let you have a relationship with me for one reason or another. I might be able to understand that, but what I can't figure out is why you go along with it."

She stared at me, urging me to give her the answers she'd come there to get and evidently had waited years to ask. I thought about it for a short time, but before I could speak, she continued.

"I was watching a television show the other day where a woman was talking about being abused by her husband. She told graphic details about things he did to her. The one thing that struck dread in my heart was that he alienated her from her friends so they couldn't give her sympathy or help her get away from the bastard. It was like someone dropped a ton of bricks on my head. That's why you have chosen to end our friendship. That would be the only reason, and how had I been so stupid to not figure it out?"

"Listen, Vesta, you don't know what he's like. Cutting my ties with you was as much for your own good as it was for mine. Please, you have to accept it. We can't be friends ever again. It's too dangerous for both of us."

I knew the exact moment when the weight of my fear registered in her brain. She grew pale.

"Oh, Montana, I've put you in danger by just showing up like this, haven't I?"

Reminding Vesta of what I'd just said, that she, too, was at risk, wouldn't matter to her as much as realizing she was putting me in peril. "He wouldn't be happy if he knew."

"Does he hit you?" Vesta appeared horrified.

"Please, Vesta, know that I love you with all my heart, but you have to leave." I grabbed her arm and tried to drag her to the door.

She stood firm. "How can I go and leave you here when I know how you're being treated?"

I drew back the curtain and looked out front to see if Harland was there. Thankfully, he wasn't, but panic still rifled through me. "It's because of the way I've allowed myself to be treated that you must go. It's my decision, but you can make it easier for me by not contacting me again."

"No, I can't go any longer without you in my life. Let me help you, Montana."

I shook my head. "You can't. No one can."

She hugged me to her, holding on for dear life. "You have to promise to call me and let me know how you are doing."

Frantically, I racked my brain to find a way to appease her, to get her out of there. "All right, I'll call you once a week when I go to the grocery store. That way Harland won't know. You see, he has the phone tapped." At least that was what he'd told me over and over again. With his compulsion to always know where I went and what I did, I had no reason not to believe him.

"Oh my God, Montana. You have to come with me right now."

"No, I can't. Just go. I'll call you next week when I go shopping."

"You call me every week, because if I don't hear from you, I'll be back with the police."

During that last year of Harland's life, I never failed to call Vesta on my weekly shopping trip. She continuously begged me to leave Harland and go to her house. I always refused, assuring her I was okay.

Little did she or anyone else, for that matter, know what life was like inside Harland's twisted world. For the last five years of our marriage, he'd continued to *punish* me on a weekly basis. Except for the time in Las Vegas, he stayed in control enough to make sure damage to my body could be hidden by clothing. As for those visible injuries I received while we were in Las Vegas, Harland explained them away by saying we were in an automobile accident.

A few weeks later, in a moment of rage, he flew at me. I shielded my face with my hands expecting to be slapped. All the while, chills ran rampant through my body.

Harland began to laugh. I cautiously peeked through my fingers and found him staring at me. "My dear Montana," his voice had carried a sharp edge of ridicule. "I promise on my mother's grave that you never need to worry about my hitting your face again.

"That was stupid of me to put marks of discontent out there for the entire world to see. We made our excuses that time, but never again will I allow you to force me to lose total control of my senses. I do have more restraint than that, and I will use it. My mother would be very angry with my lack of control. So, you can rest assured it will never happen again."

Somehow I'd never found that reassuring. It only meant he'd never have to make excuses for my condition. It didn't mean he wouldn't hurt me again.

His *punishments*, as he referred to them, ranged from shoving, to punching, raping, and tying me to the bedposts. By the end of our ten years together, our bed knobs showed the same wear as the one Harland's had as a child. The scratches and the picture of the wood chipper still hanging on our bedroom wall were daily reminders of what would happen if I tried to escape. And, as Harland insisted, I took my punishment like a man.

Along with the physical abuse, Harland never relinquished his command over my head, heart, or soul. He constantly bombarded me with accusations that either I was doing something to keep from giving him a baby, or because I had been so stupid when Berryanne was born, I had somehow damaged myself, making it impossible for me to ever get pregnant. Either way, it was my fault we never had any children.

And, of course, until the day he died, he continued to torture me with what he touted as the truth—I had taken

Berryanne into the cold night air, and she had died. That, too, was all my fault.

After years of having all that jammed down my throat, and suffering the anguish that accompanied it, I'd finally found something that truly was my fault—Harland's reign of terror was over.

I took the blame for that, and I would take my punishment like a man.

Chapter 16

FIVE MONTHS TO THE DAY AFTER I'D SHOT HARLAND, MY murder trial began. Since Phillip Kane was a tax attorney, he had to learn as he went how to represent someone accused of murder. As he gained knowledge, he also made sure *I* understood the process of preparing for trial. During that time, I learned more about the legal system than I did married to an attorney for ten years.

According to Harland, I was too stupid to discuss his day at the office with him. It was usually at parties or dinners where I would gain any information about a trial in which he was involved. If I didn't understand or if I became curious about the details, I learned very early in our relationship not to ask. I looked ignorant in the eyes of Harland's associates, or at least that was what he would say. Yet I was never allowed to ask questions. Therefore, I remained clueless about the inner workings of the justice system, which was what Harland truly wanted.

Otherwise, I might have learned enough about the law to get away from him and his brutality. Ironically, what Harland hadn't taught me while he was alive, I learned because of his death.

At 8:30 a.m., on March 14, 1978, I sat at a defense table in a courtroom in Bradley County, North Carolina. Phillip had gotten Vesta to bring me a nice suit. Since I'd lost weight, the navy blue skirt topped with a white blouse was a little big, but it still looked and felt better than the jailhouse-issue I'd been wearing for months. Vesta had been allowed to fix my hair and makeup. I had a date with a judge, and I needed to look my best.

Near the end of the time Phillip had been preparing for the trial, I saw very little of him. When we did meet, he would fill me in on as much of what he'd discovered and who the witnesses were he'd be bringing in. I was nervous for some of those people who were being forced to testify either for me or against me.

While the throng of court officials, attorneys, and spectators swarmed near me, I sat quietly, never making eye contact with anyone. I just stared at the paper clip I'd been straightening and reshaping for the past thirty minutes. Finally I dared to take a look around. The wood throughout the room had been recently polished to an even higher luster than it had been on my previous trips there. The tile floor looked slick as glass.

The courtroom and I both were decked out to impress all who would lay eyes on us. If the shine from the wood faded and the floors were scuffed, it could all be cleaned up and the courtroom would have another opportunity to do it again. I, on the other hand, had this one chance to get it right.

Just as I looked at Phillip and tried to gather my confidence that he and I would succeed, the bailiff loudly announced the arrival of the Honorable Davidson Kent. The bang of the gavel rang out.

My murder trial began.

I looked at the serious faces of the members of the jury.

The DA and Phillip had chosen them a few days before, and I had to be confident that they would render a fair verdict for me. But by the lack of expression on their faces, I could tell there was no guarantee.

The judge asked the district attorney to make his opening statement.

"Ladies and gentlemen of the jury, I am District Attorney Martin Donovan. I want to thank you for being here and giving so willingly of your time to listen to the details in the matter of the People versus Montana Parsons-Jeffers.

"I believe that after you hear the facts you will have no choice but to find Mrs. Jeffers guilty of first-degree murder. I intend to prove that self-defense was not the real reason the defendant did willfully kill her husband of ten years. Because of something Harland Jeffers had done years ago, revenge was Montana Jeffers's only motive for taking her husband's life."

I didn't hear the last few words Martin Donovan spoke because I was trying to comprehend the revenge motive I supposedly had. Each time Harland viciously attacked me, I thought I was going to die. Many times, if I'd had a gun, I would have killed him. The only difference between the hundreds of other beatings and the one that happened five months ago was that I had access to a gun, and I used it. I didn't quite understand how that was revenge.

Yes, I was angry over what I'd discovered, but I also knew that because of my discovery, Harland would not let me walk away. That would be the end of the line for me.

Mr. Donovan finished, and then Phillip walked to the jury box to give his opening statement. The paper he held shook, and so did his pants legs right around his knees. I'd only seen confidence from Phillip, so it took me by surprise to realize he was nervous. But as he spoke all telltale signs of apprehension disappeared.

He eased his way down the full length of the banister separating him from the jury members and looked at each one as if that person was the only one in the room. Some sat stone-faced, others nodded, while some smiled at Phillip. When he finished, I sensed that regardless of what they thought of me, they could plainly tell that my defense attorney was passionate about saving his client. Lately, because of his commitment to give me back my life, even I'd begun thinking it might be possible.

The prosecution called their first witness, the police officer who had actually arrested me and read me my rights.

"Officer Winston, can you tell us what you found when you arrived at the Jefferses' home last year on October 14, 1977?" Mr. Donovan started his questioning.

I couldn't recall much about that night after the shooting. I was interested to hear what the officer had to say.

"My partner, Officer Myers, and I arrived at the Jefferses' house. The front gate was locked. A woman who lived next door said she'd heard shots and called the police and then led me to the back of her property. Myers waited by the car in case someone came out the front door. The woman then pointed out a gate at the back of the Jefferses' property." Officer Winston spoke in staid calmness.

"The back door was unlocked. After identifying myself, I entered the house and found Mrs. Jeffers sitting on the edge of the bed. The victim was lying on his back with three shots to his chest. A .38 caliber pistol lay beside the body."

His brief description brought a vivid picture to my mind. I swallowed hard.

"What was Mrs. Jeffers's demeanor?" Mr. Donovan asked.

"I would say stoic. No emotion whatsoever."

"Did she say anything to you?"

Winston looked at me, challenging me to look away. "She said, 'He's dead as a doornail.'"

He won. My gaze dropped back to my paper clip.

"Did you find that odd?" the DA asked.

"Yes, sir."

"Why was that?"

"I'm used to a suspect using stronger terms about the victim they have just killed. Mrs. Jeffers sounded more like a child who'd just discovered her pet was dead."

A sharp jab to my heart jolted me. I didn't remember saying that about Harland, but I vividly remembered my pet goat, Ally, from so many years ago. God help me, I had more remorse for my goat than I did for my husband.

Mr. Donovan shook his head in disbelief. "How long was it before other officers arrived and the scene was secured?"

"It was pretty quick. While I handcuffed Mrs. Jeffers and read her rights to her, my partner began securing the scene. The evidence techs arrived approximately ten minutes later."

"During that time, it is your opinion the defendant showed no emotion or remorse for taking a gun and ending her husband's life. Is that correct?"

"Yes."

"Through the whole process of her arrest, her demeanor never changed?"

"She did display one spark of emotion."

Mr. Donovan turned on his heel to face the witness. "What was that?"

"Just as I started to lead her out of the bedroom to take her to the car, she stopped, looked down at the victim, and then spat on him."

Until I was reminded of that, I had forgotten about spitting on Harland. Of course, that had taken a backseat to so many other disturbing thoughts. Brought to the forefront of my tired brain, I almost laughed. Surely, no one would ask me if I felt remorse for doing that, because I'd have to say yes, but only because, at that moment, my mouth was so dry, I could have used that wasted spit.

While my thoughts had gone in a different direction than listening to the officer on the stand, Mr. Donovan had finished his questioning, and Phillip had stepped up to cross-examine him.

"Patricia Simpson had pointed the way for you to enter the Jefferses' house. Did you allow her to remain in the backyard?" Phillip asked.

Winston shook his head. "No, I told her to go home and wait until someone came to question her."

"Did she?"

"She left, but I believe she went out front and joined the crowd of people that had started gathering on the yard."

"In addition to Mrs. Jeffers calling the police, you stated that Patricia Simpson also called. Is that correct?"

"Yes."

"You testified as to Mrs. Jeffers's demeanor during the time before you took her to the station to be booked. I believe you said she was stoic, and you took that as having no remorse."

"That's correct."

A low hum buzzed through the courtroom. It was very noticeable, but not enough for the judge to demand quiet.

"Is it at all possible that the stoic look, as you called it, was in fact shock?"

"I—I," Winston stuttered.

"What did the rescue squad say about her *stoic* look? Did they think she just lacked remorse?"

"They never examined her."

"Why not?" Phillip demanded.

"She didn't say anything about needing medical help."

"Did she indicate that she'd had a physical confrontation with her husband prior to shooting him?"

The officer's face changed from red to pale white. "Well, yes. She did tell me that he had shoved her head into a dresser drawer and that's when she shot him. I figured there couldn't have been much damage done to her in that short amount of time."

"Well, you were wrong, Officer Winston."

The DA objected, and the judge immediately sustained it.

Phillip returned to his seat. "That's all, Your Honor."

Next up, Mr. Donovan called the jailor who had booked me at the facility in downtown Pinehurst. After being sworn in and stating her name and address, Officer Heller smiled at me. Without thinking, I smiled back.

During my booking process, she had been very kind. In great detail, she explained everything that was going to happen and continuously told me to relax; everything was going to be fine. At the time, no matter what happened to me, I just wanted the nightmare to end.

Five months later, I would look at things so differently. I did care how it all turned out. As I listened to Heller answer the first few questions, I remembered something she said to me while she was taking pictures of the fresh bruises and old scars on my naked body.

We were alone in the room, and she shook her head and said, "You should have shot the bastard six times." At that time, I was too numb to even understand the words. In a bizarre way, her words now comforted me.

On that first day of my trial, I had a different outlook. Whatever the outcome, this was where my life began.

The DA introduced a photograph into evidence. Immediately, the nude pictures Heller had taken came to mind. I prayed that wasn't what they were getting ready to show the crowd. It wasn't. The prosecutor held up my mug shot. Confused, I listened to what he had to say about it.

"Is this the photo you took at the time Mrs. Jeffers was being booked for murder?" he asked Heller.

"Yes."

"Officer Winston said that when Mrs. Jeffers was arrested, she appeared stoic. Is that how you would describe her at the time this picture was taken?"

"No, sir."

"Then, how?"

"I would say she was severely despondent."

"But she is smiling." Martin Donovan was almost indignant. "She's smiling widely, I might add. How does that say 'despondent' to you?" He poked my picture with his forefinger.

Heller chewed thoughtfully on her bottom lip. "Mrs. Jeffers was very solemn. Her expression never changed until I put her up in front of the camera. It was then that she said, 'You never know when someone will take your picture.' Then she smiled."

"So you are saying she was sober-faced until you put a camera in front of her?"

"That's what I'm saying. I also said she was despondent."

"Thank you, Officer Heller." His sarcasm abounded.

Phillip had no questions for her. As she walked past me, she winked.

Patricia Simpson was called up next. She was sworn in and

immediately began to stare me down. One thing I wanted from the trial was for her to see how lucky she had been to have not ended up with Harland.

She appeared to be about thirty-five, tall, thin, and her long blond hair bounced in a pageboy just above her shoulders. She was dressed to the nines, just like Harland insisted I dress. If not for the dour look she wore, I would have considered her beautiful.

Since we'd had no interaction, I couldn't imagine what she could bring to my trial that would help the prosecution.

"Ms. Simpson, how long have you lived next door to the Jefferses?"

"My parents and I moved in there when I was ten."

"How old are you now?" the prosecutor asked.

She gave a little huff of disgust, which garnered snickers from the peanut gallery. She looked at the judge. "I object," Patricia said. "Do I have to tell him that?"

Again, the spectators and some of the jury members laughed.

"You can't object, Ms. Simpson. Just tell us how many years you lived in your present house on Serenity Drive," the judge said.

"That's better." Patricia sat a little straighter. "I've lived there for twenty-six years."

Before they could erupt into laughter, the judge swept the whole room with an admonishing glare. I doubt that it ever dawned on Patricia that she'd just told us she was thirty-six.

"Tell us, Ms. Simpson, since you lived right next door, were you and Harland and Montana Jeffers friends?"

Her glare was back at me. "I stopped going over there shortly after Harland's mother, Marna Jeffers, died. He and I were more or less promised to each other, but somehow that woman had gotten her hooks into him, and then he didn't want to marry me."

Martin Donovan looked at the stenographer. "Let the record show that Ms. Simpson pointed to the defendant. Now, what do you mean you were more or less promised to each other?"

"His mother, Marna, had always said that Harland and I would make a perfect couple and that she would see to it that he married me—"

"Your Honor," Phillip interrupted. "I don't see the relevance of any of this. If it doesn't pertain to the case at hand, then why bring it up?"

"I assure you it is pertinent to this case, Your Honor," Mr. Donovan declared.

"Okay, but get to the point quickly," the judge advised.

"Ms. Simpson, why didn't Harland Jeffers marry you?"

"He told me he'd met a woman about three years earlier. He'd fallen madly in love, and he was going to marry her."

That was strange. I'd never heard of any other woman in Harland's life, but then again, there was much I didn't know about him.

The prosecutor furrowed his brow. "Did he say who the woman was?"

"He said he didn't want to talk about her because she didn't know he was in love with her. He had to wait until the time was right for him to make his move."

"So you never knew the woman's name?"

"Well, eventually I found out her name." She crossed her legs and leaned back in the chair.

Donovan looked at his witness for a short time and then finally said, "Would you mind telling the court who she was?"

"Oh, it was her." She pointed directly at me. "Montana Jeffers."

"How did you come to find out this information?"

"One day, I asked Harland why he wouldn't marry me like his mother wanted. He became very indignant and told me it was because he was waiting for Montana."

"Did he tell you who she was or why he had to wait for her?"

"From bits and pieces I'd gathered during that time, I learned that Montana was eleven years younger than him, and his mother would be mad if she knew who he was planning to marry. Evidently, Marna didn't like Montana."

Phillip objected and the judge explained to Patricia she could only state what she knew, not what she suspected to be the truth.

"Did he say what he intended to do about having things turn out as he wanted?"

"Yes, he said he would wait until she became of legal age and until his mother died."

That was another shock Phillip had uncovered in his pre-trial preparation. Harland had stalked me for years and singled me out to be his possession. When the time was right for him, he threw out the bait, and I took it.

"How long after his mother died did Montana come into the picture?"

"It was less than a year."

"When did you become aware that Montana was, in fact, in Harland's life?"

"First she hung out at his house and then she moved in with him. Before they were actually married, they lived . . . in sin for a couple of months." Patricia Simpson's face grew bright red.

I was amazed at how much she knew about me and Harland and our lives. Did she also know about the abuse? If she did, it appeared she wasn't going to mention that.

Suddenly, Patricia appeared to be ready to burst into flames. "Harland wouldn't marry Montana until his mother was dead. She killed Harland, and I wouldn't be surprised if she had killed Marna, too, to get her out of the way."

Collective gasps and whispers rumbled through the courtroom. Phillip and I rose in unison, but I beat him to the draw.

"That's a lie! I didn't even meet Harland until months after his mother died."

"Montana, please." Phillip grabbed my arm and eased me back into my seat.

"Order!" The judge banged his gavel and then pointed it at me. "Mr. Kane, control your client."

"I'm sorry, Your Honor. It won't happen again." Phillip glanced at me.

Embarrassed by my outburst, I looked back at the judge.

He spoke to Patricia. "I'll have no more of that kind of crap, Ms. Simpson. You answer the questions and keep your commentary to yourself. Do you understand me?"

Patricia nodded.

The judge warned the court to be quiet or he'd clear them out.

My heart pounded ninety miles an hour. I'd never even met Harland until the day he came to the insurance company to file for his mother's death benefits, and I'm sure that was about six months after she'd died. I thought it was strange to have waited that long to get his money from her policies.

It was my turn to glare at Patricia Simpson. The woman had to be totally crazy to think I had pursued Harland. It was completely the other way around.

Until Phillip approached the witness, I was lost in blind fury. "Ms. Simpson, I'm a little confused. During the talks you had with the deceased about his plans for Montana, did he indicate what he might do if the subject of his affection became interested in someone else while he was waiting for his mother to die?"

"Objection, defense is asking the witness to speculate about what the deceased *might* have done."

"Sustained."

Phillip thought for a minute, then asked the question in a different way. "Did Harland Jeffers ever come right out and say what he would do if Montana started dating someone else before his mother was dead?" Phillip stared at the DA.

Mr. Donovan shrugged his approval.

"Harland said something to the effect that he would just have to get rid of the person standing in his way." Patricia laughed. "But he was just kidding."

Donovan shook his head.

Phillip continued. "You testified that Harland and Montana were living in sin. If you didn't visit, how do you know that? She may have been sleeping on the sofa or in a guest room."

"Oh, I know for sure they were having sex," she boasted.

"And how do you know?" Phillip asked with open amusement.

"I saw them in . . . let's just say they were in a delicate position out by the pool."

"And this was before they were married?" Phillip asked.

"Yes."

"Where were you when you saw them?"

"I was at home in my bedroom."

"Tell the court where that is in relation to the Jefferses' pool, and how you managed to see them."

"Harland's parents and mine were good friends. Mr. Jeffers

bought a large piece of property and built his house in the front center section. A year or so later, he sold some of the property to my dad. By cutting the land in half, the property line was moved very close to both houses.

"Mr. Jeffers built a brick wall around his place, but with our house having two stories, I can see into their backyard from my bedroom window."

"You saw the couple making love by the pool, is that right?"

"Yes, but they weren't really a couple then. As a matter of fact, that night after they went skinny-dipping for about an hour, she got dressed and left. There were other nights that this happened until finally she just moved in with him."

Good heavens, did Patricia watch our house constantly? What right did she have to do that, and wasn't there a Peeping Tom law she could be charged with? The thought of her watching us made my skin crawl.

"Officer Winston testified that you were waiting in the yard when he arrived at the Jefferses' house the night Mr. Jeffers died. Since there was no real commotion outside the house until the police showed up, how did you happen to be out there?"

"I heard shots, and I figured she had done something. Their front gate is always locked, but I can go around the brick fence that separates our homes and then come through the back gate, which is never locked. I didn't see anything around the pool, so I went back out front."

Patricia was roaming around my backyard. Why would she do that? How could she have heard shots from inside her house? I didn't believe her for a minute. I took a piece of paper from Phillip's legal pad and jotted those thoughts down.

"Officer Winston said you had called the police, also. Is that right?" Phillip asked.

"Yes." She smiled smugly.

"You called before you went into the backyard?"

"Yes."

"Let me see if I understand this. You heard shots. You called the law and then you went in the back gate to see what was going on. Is that correct?"

"Yes."

"Were you not concerned that whoever had done the shooting might shoot you, too?"

Her expression hardened. "I didn't think about that."

He looked at me and sighed deeply. "When you called the police, what did you say to them?"

"I don't remember. I probably told them I heard shots." She shrugged as if it weren't important.

Phillip picked up a stack of papers and walked back to the judge's bench. "I'd like to enter this transcript of the call that came in to the police department, made by Patricia Simpson."

The papers were duly marked and then given back to Phillip. He handed them to Patricia and asked her to read the highlighted text, which was exactly what she had said when she called to report the shots fired.

She gave Phillip a disgusted look and then read, "She shot him. I knew no good would come of her being over there. Get someone here quick. She shot him three times." Patricia lowered the pages.

"Out of the clear blue sky, you came to the conclusion that because you heard shots, it had to be Montana shooting her husband, and you knew for sure it was with three shots?"

Patricia paused. "Well, yes, I did. Well, I was nervous. I didn't know what I was saying."

Phillip turned away from her and moved back to our table.

"I'm through with this witness for now, but I'd like to recall her at a later time."

There was a confrontation between Phillip and the DA, but in the end it was decided Patricia Simpson could be recalled when the defense presented its case.

Mr. Donovan's next witness was Rob Meloy, the chief investigator on a case that had come to light shortly after I was arrested. Part of the evidence collected from my bedroom was the papers I'd found when I jimmied open Harland's drawer. Because of a letter I'd received through the United States mail telling me Harland knew where Berryanne was, I was searching for any evidence he might have hidden in his locked dresser drawer. I wanted proof that the letter was right.

I had found far more than I bargained for. Inside the secret place, Harland had stashed papers that looked like invoices for the sale of something. As I read, my soul withered, and I couldn't stop the mournful cries escaping my constricting throat. I couldn't steady my hands enough to read the papers. I laid them down on top of the dresser and then, through tears, I grasped the full meaning of the words.

A baby girl born October 5, 1962, the same day as my Berryanne, had been sold for twenty-five thousand dollars to James and Grace Cullen of Tulsa, Oklahoma. The papers were executed by Marna Jeffers and witnessed by Harland Jeffers, attorney at law. In my heart, I knew that the baby girl was my Berryanne.

No words could ever describe the anguish I felt that night. Nor could anyone ever understand the anger that hammered my adrenaline into action. Or the blind fury that gave me the strength to rid my world of Harland.

In the courtroom, listening to the swearing in of Detective Rob Meloy, I knew Pinehurst was about to learn what kind of person their town hero truly was, and how he'd gotten the money he and his mother so graciously donated to charities. As I listened to Detective Meloy, a small amount of satisfaction crept through me.

Because of the ongoing investigation into the baby-selling ring that had been run by Harland and his mother, Judge Kent advised the detective to only talk about items specific to my case. They covered the basics of gathering the evidence, which I'd laid out in plain sight. The detective read the pages aloud and, through Donovan's questioning, explained to the jury that it was more than possible that the baby sold with those papers could have been my own.

Chapter 17

Three weeks before the trial, rumors of an organization running illegal baby sales circulated through the media. Phillip explained to me that there was almost no doubt that Berryanne had been sold through the black market. As if the emotional stress of the trial wasn't bad enough, the devastating news of a black market selling my baby crushed my heart and left me weak.

Hearing Detective Meloy put credence to the rumors, I had to bite my tongue to keep my anguished cries from disrupting the court proceedings.

District Attorney Donovan continued questioning the detective. He asked one particular question several different ways, but he was never able to get Meloy to say that I had actually said I had killed Harland because he'd sold my baby. Finally, after it was determined Phillip didn't intend to cross-examine, Donovan gave up and dismissed the witness.

Ina Carver, the midwife who had attended to me during my pregnancy and ultimately was the one who took Berryanne from my arms, would be testifying. That wasn't a surprise to me, but the fact that she was going on the stand for the prosecution did take me back a little.

Ina had come to the Spade's home six weeks after Berry-anne was born to do a routine postnatal checkup. That was the last time I laid eyes on her until she was wheeled into the courtroom in a wheelchair. Time had not been kind to Ina. Her face and withered body showed it.

After she was situated in front of the witness stand, the judge spoke to her. "Mrs. Carver, I'd like to remind you that you must confine your answers to only that information that relates to this particular trial. No other information in connection with any other case may be talked about at this time. Please think about your answers before you give them."

Ina nodded. "Okay, I will."

The judge signaled the DA to carry on.

"Mrs. Carver, what is your occupation?"

"I'm a retired midwife."

"And just exactly what did you do as a midwife?" Donovan asked.

"I assisted women in childbirth."

"Did you work in a hospital?"

Ina shook her head and said, "No."

"Why not?"

"Midwifery is usually done in the expectant mother's home."

"Thank you for that explanation." The DA glanced through his notes. "Do you know the defendant, Montana Jeffers?"

"Yes, but she was Montana Parsons when I knew her."

"Will you tell the court how you came to meet her?"

"When she was in the child welfare system, Montana became pregnant, and I was asked to look after her and assist her during her delivery."

"Were you an employee of the state's foster care program?

"No, I wasn't."

"Then how did you come to be associated with Mrs. Jeffers?"

"A friend of mine worked for the child welfare department, and if anyone in their system became pregnant, I would attend to them before, during, and after childbirth."

"How did you get paid for your services?"

"I was paid by Marna Jeffers."

Just hearing my mother-in-law's name filled me with rage. I must have made a sound, because Phillip reached over and took my hand. He'd explained the workings of the baby black market and Harland's involvement, but the steel barbs of those details still painfully pierced every part of me.

"Can you tell us about your association with Mrs. Jeffers?"

The judge halted the questioning. "I remind you to only answer as it pertains to this case."

"Yes, sir, I understand. The best way I can tell it without bringing other people into my testimony is to say that I was hired by Mrs. Jeffers to deliver Montana's illegitimate baby."

There was a slight murmur through the courtroom. I suspected it was brought on by Patricia Simpson and her holier-than-thou attitude.

Ina continued, "I was then to fill out a birth certificate using the names of the people who were buying the baby through an agency run by Marna Jeffers."

"Did the foster care agency know this was going on? Surely, they didn't condone something like this."

"The whole agency wasn't involved. Just my friend from child welfare, who was in charge of that area of the county, knew about it. She kept that information out of the files."

"So just to recap and to make sure I have it all right—your friend, who worked for child services, ignored the fact that Montana was pregnant. The person then sent you to be the midwife. When the baby was born, it was sold to a couple who had paid Marna Jeffers for that infant. As the midwife, you falsified papers so that the birth certificate would reflect the names of the couple who had in fact purchased the baby. Do I understand that correctly?"

"Yes, sir, you do." Ina's gaze dropped to her lap.

"How old was Montana at the time she got pregnant?" Donovan asked.

"Fifteen."

"Who was the father?"

I cringed.

"Dirk Spade."

"Can you tell the court who Dirk Spade is?"

"He and his wife, Joyce Spade, were the foster care parents who were supposed to be taking care of Montana until she was of legal age to be on her own."

I cringed even more. If I never heard that man's name again, that would be too soon.

"Was he charged with statutory rape?" the DA asked.

"Not then."

"Wait a minute, Mrs. Carver," the judge interrupted. "Strike that last remark," he said to the stenographer and then he looked at the jury. "You must ignore that last remark. It cannot be taken into consideration. And you, Mr. Donovan, please be careful of the direction you take your questions."

I had recently learned that Dirk had not heeded Ina's demand that he stay away from other girls put in his custody. He had raped the next foster child, and that girl told the principal of her school. Dirk was arrested and was locked away from society. Luckily, for the other girl, she didn't get pregnant. She had the courage to tell someone. If only I had. That wish and thirty cents would get me a cup of coffee.

"Yes, Your Honor," Mr. Donovan said. "Okay, Mrs. Carver, let's go in a different direction. Take us from the time Montana went into labor up to the time the baby was handed over to the . . . for lack of a better way of putting it, the adoptive parents."

Ina told the jury about Berryanne's delivery, the deception carried out at the hospital, and my running away. I was watching her, listening carefully to every painful word and feeling the agony and torture to my heart for the millionth time in my life. Gradually, I became aware that Ina had stopped speaking. Her chin was shaking, and tears were streaming down her face.

The judge handed her a box of tissues. Ina took them and tried to dry her tears, but they came faster and harder until she was reduced to body-shaking sobs. The judge declared a ten-minute recess for her to gain her composure. He left the bench. Phillip joined Mr. Donovan and Ina at the witness stand.

I knew why she was crying. She remembered how hard I'd begged her not to take my baby away, but she did it anyway. In my stomach, I still carried a hard knot of hatred for her. I'd never been able to forgive her.

When court was brought back into session, Ina had pulled herself together. Mr. Donovan quickly resumed his line of questioning.

"Before the recess you told us that Montana was found hiding out in the Spade's barn. She was weak and hemorrhaging. What happened after that?"

"I took her baby from her." Ina drew in a ragged breath. After a brief pause, she was able to continue. "I had to literally pry the infant from her arms. Montana's scream came from so deep in her soul that it almost sounded nonhuman. I never forgot that sound. It haunts me still."

Her teary gaze looked my way. "I'm sorry, Montana. I'm so sorry." Again, she cried aloud. "I knew Harland had lied about your daughter being alive. That's why I wrote you the letter."

Phillip had already learned Ina had written the letter, and he'd passed the information on to me. I assumed it was her way of trying to make up for what she'd done, but it was too little, too late.

While the judge reprimanded Ina and the DA tried to console her, I felt my hatred for her loosen its tight grip around my throat. Not completely, but enough to allow me to take in a little empathy for the tortured woman.

"I only have one more question, Mrs. Carver," the prosecutor started again. "I'd like you to put yourself in Montana's position. Imagine you had a baby wrenched from your arms fourteen or fifteen years ago, then you find out that the man you'd been married to for ten years was responsible for that baby being taken away. And, to make the nightmare even worse, the baby was sold through the black market, would that be a reason for you to kill the person responsible?"

Ina took only a second to think about her answer, and then she said, "Yes."

The witness was turned over to Phillip, who asked, "During Montana's pregnancy, did you have occasion to get to know her as a person, more than just an unwed mother?"

"Yes."

"Would you say you got to know her pretty well?" Phillip had a slow manner of speaking that made a person want to listen.

"I believe so."

"In your opinion, and this is strictly your opinion, even

with the heartache Montana suffered with your help, did you ever feel she was capable of killing you?"

"No."

"Do you feel she would be capable of killing someone in self-defense?"

"Maybe."

"Do you feel that if she came face to face with someone responsible for taking her baby away, would she have killed that someone for revenge?"

"No."

The DA objected, vehemently. And the judge ordered it stricken, but her answer couldn't be stricken from my mind. She had spoken up for me. Not many people had ever done that. I wouldn't forget it.

Judge Kent adjourned until the next morning.

Court reconvened at 8:30 the next morning. A few more witnesses for the prosecution were called by District Attorney Martin Donovan. The coroner told in detail how the bullets entered Harland's body and which bullet ultimately killed him, intimating that the last two bullets were useless in killing Harland. Therefore, he contended, my actions were nothing short of overkill. The coroner also stated that Harland's nose had been broken, and yes, it could have been done by a head smashing into it.

There was a fingerprint expert who verified I had handled the gun. And another technician explained the pattern of blood spatter on the wall.

I wanted to scream to the rooftops that Harland was dead, and I did it. That should be all that mattered, but the proceedings went on for the whole morning.

Just before lunch, the prosecution finally rested. After a two-hour recess, we all filed back into the courtroom ready for the defense to present their case.

I was exhausted and suffering from a damnable headache.

First to the stand was Patricia Simpson. She'd already been sworn in the day before, so Phillip started right in.

"This morning, Officer Winston and I were at the Jefferses' house, which, as we all know, is right next door to you. Did you happen to see us over there?"

"You know I saw you. You even waved to me when I was looking out my bedroom window."

"Yes, I did. While Officer Winston and I were next door this morning, did you hear any noise of any kind?"

Patricia chewed her bottom lip. "No."

"You didn't hear any out-of-the-ordinary commotion?"

She shook her head. "Should I have heard something?"

"I'd like you to watch this little movie I made this morning." Phillip motioned to a bailiff.

The court officer rolled a television into position where the jury, judge, and witness could watch a video. On the screen, Phillip set a wooden box with a pillow stuffed into it on the floor where Harland's body had fallen. Phillip then disappeared from the frame.

Officer Winston stood approximately where I had stood when I fired the gun. Winston aimed a pistol at the target and pulled the trigger three times. The microphone picked up the loud pops. I jumped with each.

"Ms. Simpson, I looked at the distance from the Jefferses' house to yours. I really didn't think you could hear shots being fired all the way over there. Even if you were standing by a window, I just couldn't convince myself that you could have heard the shots fired that night. So, while I was out on the back patio of the Jefferses' house waving to you as you stood right next to your bedroom window, Officer Winston was in the house conducting this little experiment."

The DA objected. "The defense is doing his summation a little early," Donovan snickered.

Judge Kent thought for a moment and then said, "I'll allow it. I want to hear Ms. Simpson's explanation."

Excellent, Phillip, excellent. His mother would be so proud. I was proud of him, too.

Patricia went pale. "Well—"

Phillip held up his hand. "You are under oath, and you've already lied about where you were when you heard the shots. Having said that, I'd like to add that I believe you did hear them, but not from inside your house. Why don't you just tell the court where you were when the shots rang out?"

Her gaze swept the whole place and then came to rest on me. A smug smile pulled at the corners of her mouth. "I was waiting for Harland in his workshop."

The whole room gasped in unison, but I believe mine was the loudest. Harland spent at least one or two evenings a week in his precious workshop. I didn't know what he was doing and I didn't think I really cared, but Patricia had dropped a whole new layer onto my hatred for Harland.

It took me several minutes to regroup.

"Were you and Jeffers having an affair?" Phillip asked.

"Yes, and he had finally decided to leave his crazy wife."

Lively whispers echoed from the audience behind me. My gaze met Phillip's. I could see his concern for me cross his face.

"It's okay," I mouthed.

"How long had this been going on?" he asked Patricia.

"For about a year."

Phillip stared at me for several seconds. When the puzzle fell into place for him, his eyes went from a dark, troubled brown, to a soft gentle gaze.

"How often did you two get together?"

Patricia appeared to be mulling over his words. After a short pause, she shrugged. "Once or twice a week. He'd call before he left his office and set a time that he would be out in the workshop."

"Was this usually after dark?"

"Sometimes."

"What about the night Mr. Jeffers died? It was still daylight and earlier than he usually got home from work. Yet you were out there waiting for him?"

"I called him at his office and told him I was tired of being the other woman. I thought it was time he told her he wanted a divorce. He said he was going home right then, and he'd meet me in about thirty minutes. So, I went out there and waited."

"Ms. Simpson, during any of your visits to the building behind the Jefferses' house, did you ever hear any arguing between Harland and Montana?"

"A couple of times."

"Can you tell us about those times?" Phillip stepped in front of me, blocking my sight from the witness. I sensed he did it deliberately.

"I heard a crash near the back of the house. I edged closer to see what was going on. Montana was screaming at Harland."

"What was she saying?"

"She was telling him he was crazy and telling him there was something wrong with him."

"During those times you were privy to their disagreements, did you hear anything that would lead you to believe that Mr.

Jeffers had hit his wife?"

"Never, but by the way she'd yell at him, I wouldn't have blamed him if he did."

I couldn't even feel any emotion at the statements the delusional woman was making. I just shook my head and stared in amazement.

"What about you, Ms. Simpson, did Harland ever raise a hand to you?"

"Of course not." She answered so quickly and so defensively, there was no doubt in my mind that she had just lied on the witness stand again.

Phillip finished with Patricia. Mr. Donovan cross-examined.

"Do you happen to remember the first time you overheard an argument between the defendant and the deceased?"

"I don't know the date, but it was a few months after they were married. It was almost dark, and my dog wouldn't come in the house when I called her. I chased her to the back of my property and was in back of Harland's workshop when I heard yelling. Montana came running out the door. She went through the gate and ran as hard as she could into the section of woods that separates our two houses from the housing development that was built several years ago."

I remembered that night, running through the dark woods, scraping against trees and branches. While my heart was pounding from sheer terror, Patricia Simpson was hiding at my back gate believing that if Harland hit me, I deserved it. My nerves were strung tight and the overbearing woman was strumming them.

"Did Harland follow her?" Phillip asked and finally moved over so I could look at her cruel and spiteful face.

"No," she said.

"Did you see Harland?"

"Yes, my dog ran through the open gate, and I had to chase her into his backyard. He was standing on his patio. I asked him what was wrong with her."

"What did he say?"

"He said she was crazy."

Phillip objected, stating that the witness's integrity was already in question. It was ludicrous to allow her to make such defaming statements about his client. Donovan told the judge that the witness's testimony was important to show the mental stability of the defendant, which, of course, was me.

I was abused for years, and I killed my abuser. How much mental stability could I possibly have? The judge allowed the DA to continue with his line of questioning.

Mr. Donovan asked, "What else did Mr. Jeffers say to you that night?"

"He said they had been arguing about the fact that Montana didn't want to have a baby. He said she was taking birth control pills and lying to him about it." Patricia looked directly at the jury. "Harland would have made a good father. He had a lot to offer—"

Phillip objected and asked that the last statement be stricken from the record. Judge Kent agreed and admonished Patricia.

"Did Mr. Jeffers go after his wife?"

"No, he said he hoped she didn't come back. He didn't want her if she didn't want to have his children."

"Evidently, she did come back. Do you happen to know when she returned to their home?"

"It was an hour or so later. I saw a police car pull into the circle drive in front of their house. Harland met the police at the front gate, and after they talked for a few minutes, the policeman let Montana out of the backseat of the squad car."

"No further questions, Your Honor," Mr. Donovan said.

The judge called an hour-long recess. I was moved to a holding room, and Phillip joined me there.

"How are you doing?" he asked. I was sure he was referring to me finding out that Harland had been cheating on me.

"When it comes to Harland, nothing can surprise me. Did you get the feeling she was lying about him hitting her?"

"I did, but I'm not going to go after that. In my heart I had suspected she might be stalking Harland or you or both. I really thought that's what I would prove with my experiment, but she stole my thunder when she told the real reason she was outside your house." He paused and gave me a gentle smile. "I'm really sorry about that."

"It's not like she knocked Harland off his pedestal for me. As far as I'm concerned, it was just another nail in his coffin." I instantly regretted being so harsh. "I guess I should show more respect for the dead, but I knew him so well while he was alive, it's hard to shut that off just because he is gone."

When we returned to the courtroom, Vesta was seated in the gallery. We exchanged smiles and waves. Just knowing she was nearby meant a lot to me.

Officer Myers, the policeman who had politely returned me to Harland when I'd called for help, took the stand.

"I know you were one of the first responders the night Harland Jeffers died, but did you ever have an occasion to meet Mrs. Jeffers before that night?"

"Yes."

"When was that exactly?"

"I can't say for sure, but it was around nine years ago." The officer looked at me, but quickly glanced away.

"And how did you come into contact with her?"

"I was dispatched by NCIC to a convenience store at the corner of Madison and Briarcliff. Mrs. Jeffers was hiding behind the building. She came out to meet me."

"What did she have to say?" Phillip asked.

"She said her husband had threatened to kill her, and she wanted him arrested. I asked her if she had any bruises or marks on her body put there by her husband."

"Did she?"

"She was scratched on her face and arms, but she said she had gotten them in the woods, and she didn't have any from her husband."

"Did she file a complaint against her husband?"

"No."

"Why not?" Phillip's voice was edged with steel.

"Because I took her home instead."

"Why didn't you take her to the police station like she asked?"

"I couldn't believe Harland had done the things she said. I thought it would save her some embarrassment for having someone as well thought of as Harland arrested just because they'd had an argument." There was sadness in his voice, and I wondered if he was sorry that he hadn't helped me that night. Possibly he even felt responsible for Harland's ultimate death.

I couldn't blame him or anyone, for that matter. The blame for what happened could only be laid on two people's shoulders—Harland's, for what he did to me, and mine, for allowing it to happen.

Next, several easels were brought into the courtroom and blown-up pictures of the bedroom Harland and I had shared for ten years were placed where everyone could see. I cringed when I saw the panoramic images of nothing short of a torture chamber.

Phillip resumed questioning Officer Myers. "We have established that you were one of the first officers on the scene, is that correct?"

"Yes. Officer Winston and I were the first."

"It is my understanding that you were part of the team that gathered evidence from the crime scene, is that correct?"

"Yes."

"So it is fair to say that you spent a great deal of time in that room and can possibly answer a few questions about what you saw there."

"I should be able to."

"Let's take a look at this first photo." Phillip pointed to one of the pictures. "Tell me what I'm looking at here."

"That is the knob on the right side of the headboard of the bed that was in their bedroom."

"What is significant about that particular knob?"

"Nothing about that one in particular. There are four on the bed, two on the headboard, two on the footboard, and they were all worn and scratched from something being tied around them."

"Do you know what was tied around the knobs?"

"Yes, we found lengths of rope under the bed, and there were fibers imbedded in the worn wood where it appears they had been tied and subjected to force."

"Do you know what kind of force would cause those marks?" Phillip knew and so did I, but he had to ask the question. I rubbed my wrist, and as much as possible, I tried not to remember.

"If someone was restrained and was struggling to get free, that would make those marks."

"So the defendant's claim that her husband, on numerous occasions, tied her to the bed and left her there while he went to work, could possibly be true?"

"Yes."

"How many times would you estimate that she would have had to be tied to that bed in order for it to show that much wear?"

"Innumerable times."

"Thank you. Now in the next picture we see a wall with two holes knocked in the Sheetrock. Were you able to determine what caused those holes?"

"According to Mrs. Jeffers's statement, her head."

"Right above those two holes is a picture of a piece of equipment. What is it a picture of?"

I found it impossible to believe that my stomach could tie itself into any more knots, but it did.

"It's a commercial wood chipper used by road crews to chop tree limbs into tiny pieces."

"Did you think that was a strange picture to have hanging on the wall of a bedroom?"

"Again, according to Mrs. Jeffers's statement, it was hung there by her husband as a constant reminder that if she tried to leave him, he would use it to dispose of her body."

"When she told you this, did she appear to put any credence in his threat?"

"As she talked about the wood chipper, her whole body shook like a leaf in a gale."

Mere words could never express exactly how I felt each time I looked at that picture. It was just a picture, for God's sake, but I fell to pieces each time I saw it. There in the courtroom, I chose not to look up. I sat with my head bowed and listened to the witness relate my story.

The policeman went on, "She was visibly terrified just looking at a picture of the machine."

Phillip turned the witness over to the DA.

"Officer Myers, where was this horrific piece of equipment

that Mrs. Jeffers was so terrified of?"

The policeman seemed hesitant to speak. "She said he kept it out behind his workshop."

"Did you find a commercial wood chipper behind Mr. Jeffers's workshop?"

"No," the officer said, his voice nothing more than a whisper.

"Did you find any evidence, like dead grass or tire marks, to prove there had been a commercial wood chipper there?"

"No."

"Did you find any evidence that Mr. Jeffers had ever purchased, owned, operated, or ever had a need for a commercial wood chipper?"

"No."

After Mr. Donovan turned to the jury and smiled, he dropped his notes on his table. "No further questions."

At one time, there had been a wood chipper right where I had said it was. I saw it, and I had nightmares about it for many years. Where it had come from, how long it was there, or what happened to it, I didn't have a clue. I had reasons to believe my mind had slipped into a dark place, but that wasn't part of my imagination. Harland had shown me a wood chipper and had threatened to kill me and dispose of my body with the wretched machine.

A man by the name of Josh Gilmore was sworn in. He stated his occupation was the owner and operator of Gilmore Commercial Landscaping.

"Did you know Harland Jeffers?" Phillip inquired.

"Yes."

"In what capacity?"

"Many years ago, he handled a legal matter for me."

"So, he was your attorney?"

"Yes."

"Did you ever have an opportunity to go to Mr. Jeffers's home?"

"Yes."

"And why was that?"

"My business partner and I had come to odds. Mr. Jeffers advised me to hide some of the equipment I had bought with my own money until after the judgment was set down so that my partner wouldn't be able to take what belonged to me."

Phillip rolled his notes into a tube and bounced them in his palm. "What kind of equipment did you hide and where?"

"There was a trailer, and a riding lawn mower, and a wood chipper. I hid all three pieces at Mr. Jeffers's house behind a building just outside the gate that led to his backyard."

Relief flooded through me. I knew I wasn't crazy, and perhaps now others would know that, too. At least where the wood chipper was concerned.

"How long did you leave the equipment there?" Phillip continued.

"About three weeks."

"Mr. Gilmore, the picture hanging on the wall of the Jefferses' bedroom—is that the same type, size, and color of the wood chipper you left on the Jefferses' property?"

"Yes, sir, if you look closely, there is a tarp covering something just to the right of the machine." Phillip handed him a pointer, and the man indicated some writing on the tarp. "It says *Property of Gilmore Commercial Landscaping*. My lawn mower was parked on my utility trailer and covered with that tarp. It is parked right next to my wood chipper."

"So, is it safe to say that Harland very well could have walked Mrs. Jeffers around his workshop and shown her a piece of equipment, explained how it worked, and scared the living daylights out of her? Is that correct?"

"Yes, sir, it is."

"Your Honor, I'm sure Mr. Gilmore is a fine landscaper, but I fail to believe he is qualified to testify to the defendant's mental state," Donovan said.

"Sustained," the judge said and then nodded for Phillip to continue, but Mr. Gilmore spoke up.

"My wood chipper was parked on Jefferses' property for three weeks. What went on while it was there, I couldn't say, but I can say for sure that it was there."

Chapter 18

BRIGHT AND EARLY ON THE THIRD DAY OF MY TRIAL, I FELT like I'd been thrown back in time onto an old television show. I expected Ralph Edwards to walk through the door at any moment and say, "Montana Inez Parsons-Jeffers, this is your life."

The first witness was my old boss from the diner. Cal testified that I was a loyal, trustworthy, and dependable employee who worked long and hard hours, but never complained. I wasn't used to hearing good things about myself. With every compliment, my face warmed more and more. My smile for Cal was the only way I had of thanking him.

The district attorney had a couple of questions for Cal. "You said that Mrs. Jeffers was a model employee, but something made her fall out of your good graces."

Cal gave the DA a quizzical look. "I don't know what you mean."

"Well, is it not true that you eventually had to fire her?"

He tilted his head to the side like he always did when he found something humorous. "As a matter of fact, I did fire her."

The DA looked pleased.

"And why was that?" he asked.

"Because she had been offered a job at an insurance company making twice what she did working for me. She would be a secretary, work nine to five. She'd never have to show up at six in the morning and then stand on her feet slinging hash for the next eight to ten hours. It was an opportunity I couldn't let her pass up, and she would have out of loyalty to me. That's the way Montana was."

He was dismissed. While the shuffling and rearranging of chairs and papers were taking place, Phillip leaned close to me and whispered, "I'm not sure what your reaction will be to our next witness, but I've held off telling you he was coming because I didn't want to cause you any more angst than you already have." He squeezed my hand. "You will be just fine."

Phillip stood and glanced to the back of the courtroom. Without even looking, I knew who was back there. I felt his gaze on me, and my body hummed with the uncertainty of why he had come.

Phillip announced, "The defense calls Edward Shannon to the stand."

Gradually, I turned and watched him walk down the aisle. Until he was seated, his gaze was locked with mine.

"Mr. Shannon, will you please tell us how you know the defendant." Phillip stood near the jury.

"I met Montana at Shirley's Café. I was in town working on the new bridge that was put in about ten years ago. I'd eat breakfast there most mornings."

"What kind of relationship did you have with the defendant?"

Martin Donovan rose. "I object. The outcome of this trial should not depend on how wonderful an old boyfriend thought the defendant was ten years ago. Unless this witness has some connection to the matter at hand, I suggest he be dismissed, and let's move forward with this trial."

"Judge Kent," Phillip walked to the bench, "I assure you this witness is very much connected to both of the Jefferses, living and dead."

"Very well," the judge said, "but get to it quickly."

Phillip asked his question again. "What was your relationship with the defendant?"

"We were going to be married."

"Then you would say you had a very good relationship?"

Eddie looked at me and nodded. "Yes."

"On the last night you saw Montana, did she divulge a secret to you?"

I certainly had done that. A secret I had ripped from my gut. Eddie had been so disgusted by it, he had left and never returned.

"She told me about being raped by Dirk, having her baby, and then being forced to give it away."

Simple words for so much heartache.

"Did this repulse you or change your mind about her in any way?"

"Of course not. She was perfect, and I loved Montana with all my heart."

"Your Honor, relevance?" Donovan croaked.

Phillip held his hand up to the judge. "I promise it will be just one more minute," he said.

"Quickly, Mr. Kane."

"Okay, you've told the Court that Montana was the love of your life, she was going to marry you, and you were not disgusted by the things she told you. But can you tell us why you disappeared from her life without an explanation or even a word of good-bye?"

Eddie's face turned a light shade of purple, he twisted his hands, his bottom lip quivered, and I thought he might break into tears at any moment.

"Mr. Shannon?" Phillip edged him on.

"Harland Jeffers paid my mother's medical bills. She was very sick at the time. It was more money than I would have made in two or three years."

And the money would have been just a drop in the bucket to Harland.

Phillip moved closer to the witness. "How did you come to know him?"

"Out of nowhere, he appeared at my job site and told me he had an offer for me. He said he knew my mother needed surgery, and he was in a position to pick up the tab for all of it. All I had to do was disappear out of Montana's life and never come back."

"What did you say to that?"

"I told him he was crazy. I could never leave her. I told him I was working on getting the money for my mother by myself and for him to go away and not bother me or Montana again."

"Well, of course, we all know that didn't happen. So why did you leave?"

"A few hours later, my boss called me into his work trailer and told me I was fired. He was real vague on why, but nothing was going to change his mind. As I went out the door, Jeffers was waiting for me."

"And?" Phillip prodded.

"He said there was more misery where that came from, and it would be a shame if something happened to my pretty little sister. He handed me a business card and told me to send him the hospital bills for my mom's surgery.

"I got into my car, and I went home. Until I was subpoenaed a few days ago, I never came back to Pinehurst."

If I didn't know anything else, I know that at one time, Eddie loved me very much. His mother meant the world to him. I also know that Harland could be very persuasive when it came to having his way. When I laid those stumbling blocks side by side, I realized what a difficult decision Eddie had been forced to make. Suddenly, it didn't hurt so much that he hadn't picked me.

Donovan cross-examined Eddie. It was obvious he just wanted to shadow Eddie's testimony by making him appear weak for letting Harland bully him. Whether the DA succeeded in the eyes of the jury, I wasn't sure, but I knew what it was like to run into that brick wall known as Harland Jeffers. He was a master of demonstrating backlash that could come from crossing him. Not only didn't I blame Eddie any longer, I actually sympathized with him. Sadly, I thought of Scratch. Eddie was lucky to have escaped with his life.

After Casper Lockwood was sworn in, he took his seat, and Phillip approached the witness box.

"Mr. Lockwood, at one time did Montana work for you?"

"Yes, she was my secretary."

"Did she do a good job?"

"Yes."

"How did she get the job at your insurance company? Did you run a want ad, and she applied for the job?"

"No."

"Then how?"

"Harland Jeffers told me to hire her."

"Did you do everything Jeffers told you to do?"

"Apparently, I did. He was my biggest customer. A fourth of my business relied on him and entities we insured in Jeffers's name. I stood to lose a lot of money if I lost him and all the pies he had his fingers in."

"So, how did it all happen?"

"I went to the café where she worked, asked her boss about her, if she stole, if she was lazy, that kind of thing. I asked how much money she made. He told me, and I told him I wanted to give her a job with great benefits. Montana wasn't at the café that day. She was off taking the test to get her GED. I gave the man my card and told him to have Montana call me.

"She did, and I had her come in for an interview. When she asked how I'd even heard of her, I told her I worked with the school where she'd been studying for her GED exam and that they had recommended her. That wasn't the truth. Harland had strongly recommended her, and that was enough for me."

I frantically scribbled a note to Phillip. He glanced at it and then asked Mr. Lockwood, "Did you feel that Montana knew Harland during the time he'd coerced you into hiring her?"

"According to Jeffers, she didn't know him at all. He said he'd been admiring her from afar since she was sixteen years old, and he wanted to make sure she was taken care of until she was old enough to appreciate a man."

"Did he give any indication when he thought Montana might be ready for that?"

"No, but the first time she ever met Harland was several months after she started working for me, and I officially introduced them."

"While their relationship was developing, she continued to work for you?"

"Yes."

"What happened to make her leave her job at your insurance company?"

"Harland happened, that's what."

"What do you mean?"

"He wanted Montana to quit work, marry him, and be a stay-at-home wife. According to Harland, that wasn't in Montana's plans. In true Harland fashion, he made it her plan."

Phillip nodded for him to continue. "He forced me to fire her. Again, with the threat of pulling his business completely away from me. That would have been devastating."

"You hired Montana and fired Montana because of threats issued to you by Harland Jeffers. Do I understand that right?"

"Yes. Since this all happened, I've been really sorry I did that." He looked my way and then, after being dismissed, he left the stand, never looking at me again.

At lunch recess, Phillip brought food from the cafeteria for him and me. He came through the door, hands filled with a loaded tray. When he stepped aside, Eddie entered the room.

I didn't know what to say. My feelings for him had exploded into so many pieces it was impossible for me to pick one out. And, at this stage of the game, what difference did it make how I felt about him?

"Hello, Montana. I'm so glad they said I could see you for a few minutes." Eddie edged his way to the table, then hesitated.

I pulled the chair next to me away from the table and patted the seat. "Here. Sit down."

Phillip set our food down at the other end. "I'm going to step into the hall. You only have five minutes."

I watched him leave and wished he had stayed. I'm not sure what I saw in Eddie's eyes, but I knew what I felt in my heart.

313

He'd been young when he had been bullied out of town by Harland, and knowing what I knew now, if he hadn't left, he would have died.

"You look good, Eddie." I rubbed the back of his hand, which trembled under my touch. "Are you happy with your life?"

He nodded, and appeared very uncomfortable. "Yes, I have two beautiful girls and a very sweet wife."

"I'm glad to hear that," I said and honestly meant it.

"I feel so guilty. If I'd been man enough back then, I might have saved you from the horrible life you had during those years."

"But then you wouldn't have your wife and girls, Eddie. That should be more important than anything. Take care of them and cherish them."

"I'll always love you, Montana." He squeezed my hand.

"And you've always been in my heart."

We stared deeply into each other's eyes. At that moment, I blessed him and set him free, and it felt good.

Phillip opened the door. Eddie kissed my cheek and left.

For the rest of the afternoon, pictures of my battered and naked body were put on display for everyone in the courtroom to look at and examine at length. They had placed strips of black tape strategically to help save some of my dignity. What dignity? I'd lost that when I'd lost my virginity. My body was never my own. It belonged to someone else to do with as they pleased.

Shortly after Phillip took over my case, I had received a complete physical. The doctor who had performed the exam was called to the stand. He used X-rays and the photographs to match up old injuries, like my broken rib, which had never knitted back together as it should have. For what seemed an eternity, I listened to him describe in technical terms what he could see. He speculated how the injuries could have been sustained.

I didn't have to speculate. I knew for sure and as each one was pointed out, I remembered the raw pain, the primal fear, and the prayers that God would just let me die.

But I was still alive, if you could call what I was going through being alive.

The doctor finally finished. The judge said it was too late to call another witness, so we were excused for another day.

As Phillip gathered his papers into his briefcase, and I waited for the guards to escort me from the courtroom, I asked, "Who's next? Any more surprises?"

"I don't think so. I was just concerned the expectation of seeing Eddie again might be too much for you. The element of surprise might work better."

"You're probably right. It was good to see him. I was able to clear a few of the ghosts away."

"I'm glad. Tomorrow, we'll bring to the stand the doctor who treated you when you were in Las Vegas. Also, the officer who did the report will testify about the shape you were in."

"What about the woman? Betty? Will she be here, too?"

"I'm afraid not. She died a couple of years ago, but I think the doctor and the officer will be able to show the brutality Harland was capable of."

Chapter 19

THE DOCTOR FROM LAS VEGAS READ FROM THE NOTES HE'D made in my chart. He stated I had been brought into the hospital with multiple injuries including a five-centimeter cut under my right eye, which he had sewn shut. I had two black eyes and a bruise on my jaw. I had multiple scrapes to my arms and legs that could have been caused by being pushed to a concrete sidewalk from a car, which is what the patient said happened to her.

And the patient, that would be me, had a sprained wrist from trying to catch herself as she landed on the hard cement. He talked as if I wasn't in the room or had anything to do with any of the proceedings.

"Do you know what Mrs. Jeffers was wearing when she came into the hospital?"

"No, by the time I first saw her she was in a hospital gown."

Phillip finished and when Donovan didn't cross-examine, the Las Vegas policeman was called.

From his report, he read most of what he'd written that

night. His story of what he found when he arrived and when he followed me to the hospital was pretty cut-and-dried.

"Do you remember what Montana was wearing?"

"When I arrived at the house of the woman who had found her and who had taken her into her home, Mrs. Jeffers had on a . . ." he looked at his notes, "heavy, white robe, which I was told was given to her by the house owner. Under the robe she wore a bra, panties, and a half slip. All white and all blood- and grass-stained."

"Did she tell you who had inflicted the horrible injuries to her face and had thrown her out of the car, leaving her lying there on the sidewalk?"

"She said it was her husband."

"Thanks. That's all the questions I have for this witness."

Mr. Donovan rose and hurried to the railing in front of the jury. A boastful smile lurked on his face. "Officer Hasan, did Mrs. Jeffers press charges for assault and battery against her husband that night?"

"No."

"Why not?"

"My answer would only be speculation."

"I'd still be interested in hearing your thoughts," the DA edged him on.

"I think it was because she was scared out of her mind."

"Scared of what?"

"She was scared that, even if I took him away at gunpoint, her husband would hunt her down and kill her."

"But it was my understanding that her husband allegedly dropped her off, left, and hadn't come back."

"According to my report, he came to get her just as she was ready to swear out a warrant for his arrest."

"Was it a tearful reunion, all kisses and hugs and a lot of 'I'm sorry we quarreled'?" Donovan asked.

The policeman shrugged. "It's been five years—"

"Yes, I understand that, but does your report say anything about what happened when he came to get her?"

"What I started to say was that it's been five years, but I still remember the look on that woman's face," he pointed to me, "when Jeffers stepped into the cubicle where she was being treated for injuries he'd given her."

"Supposedly given her."

"Well, Mr. Donovan, that's your speculation. Mine is that he did it."

"Very well, do your notes contain anything else that might shed any light on the temperament of the Jefferses as they left the hospital, you know, like was he apologetic? Did she seem to forgive him?"

As the officer studied the DA, his jaw quivered like he was struggling for control. "Are you asking if I made any notes as to my thoughts on the situation?"

"Yes, I guess I am."

"The last line I wrote in my report reads, *Dead woman walking.*"

The witness was quickly dismissed.

Clara, our housekeeper, was up next. This was the first time I'd seen her since two days before Harland died, when she'd spent the day cleaning our house. She'd been awfully close to Harland for the biggest part of his life, and I wasn't sure how she would feel about me. I couldn't blame her if she hated me.

Immediately, Clara alleviated all my doubts. She smiled at me and crossed her arms over her chest as if to send me an imaginary hug. I cherished the dear woman and felt sorry she had to say things against one of the Jefferses who had done so much for her.

Phillip took Clara through the paces of establishing her connection to the Jefferses. Mr. Donovan and the judge decided early on that the abuse Harland had suffered at the hands of his mother should not be discussed. The contention was that a person can only blame their actions on their parents for so long, and then they must take responsibility for themselves. Phillip agreed with them because he thought that kind of knowledge would only garner sympathy for Harland.

Phillip began his questioning. "Mrs. Griffin, the Jefferses' next-door neighbor, Patricia Simpson, stated that Mr. Jeffers had once told her that he thought Montana was doing something to herself to keep from giving him a child. Were you present in the courtroom when Ms. Simpson made that statement?"

"Yes, I was."

"Did you have any personal knowledge of this?"

"Only what Montana told me about Harland accusing her of doing something to herself."

"When did she tell you this?"

"On a couple of occasions after I'd finished my work, she and I would sit for a few minutes and talk. I could tell she was lonely."

"Objection," Donovan said, but didn't even bother to rise.

"Answer the question only, Mrs. Griffin," the judge advised.

"Yes, sir. I'm just nervous."

Phillip smiled at her. "You're doing fine. Did Montana give you any indication she was taking birth control pills or using any other kind of contraceptive to keep from getting pregnant?"

"No, not at all. Actually, she denied doing anything."

"Did she tell you he was very upset with her because she wasn't pregnant yet?"

"Yes."

"Do you have any personal knowledge as to why Harland and Montana never had any children?"

Mr. Donovan objected. "Why would a housekeeper have knowledge about something so personal about her boss?"

"I knew Harland very well," Clara said, glaring at the DA. "I worked for the Jefferses for years."

The judge overruled the objection and then signaled Phillip to continue.

"Would you tell us, please, what you know about why they never had any children?"

"Harland couldn't make babies." Straight and to the point.

"And how do you know that, Mrs. Griffin?"

"He was injured playing football when he was sixteen."

"I know you're not a doctor, but can you tell us how that injury kept him from . . . making babies?"

"He was hit in his private parts really hard and had to have surgery to have a testicle removed."

Donovan flew to his feet. "I object, Your Honor. This is strictly hearsay."

"The doctor who told me this isn't here to say because he's dead, but I know the truth," Clara said.

Phillip pleaded, "Your Honor, I assure you this is very important to the case."

"Go on," the judge said.

The DA threw his pencil a little ways into the air and then collapsed back into his chair.

"How did it come about that you know this personal information about Harland Jeffers?"

"He spent a week in the hospital, and his mother was too busy to be with him. I was there practically night and day. He was only sixteen, and he was scared to death."

"So you got the diagnosis and reports directly from the doctor, correct?"

"Yes."

"What did he tell you, Mrs. Griffin?"

"He said that both of Harland's testicles were injured, and the doctor would have to remove the right one. He also said that even though he wouldn't have to remove the left one, it was very unlikely he would ever have any children."

"Was all of this explained to Harland?"

"Yes."

"Do you feel he understood the complications he was faced with?"

"Definitely."

"During your talks with Montana, did you ever discuss this with her?"

"No."

"Is there a specific reason why not, especially since she told you he was hassling her about not getting pregnant?"

"That wasn't my place to tell her. Harland went to great lengths to make sure she never knew he'd lost a testicle."

Spectators whispered among themselves.

"Montana and Harland were married for ten years. How did he keep that fact from her?" Phillip asked.

"Six months before they were married, Harland had an artificial testicle implanted. When Montana was talking about her problem with Harland, she never mentioned knowing about his injury. And I never mentioned it to her, either."

"Mrs. Griffin, you have taken an oath to tell the truth. Am I correct?"

"Yes, and I have told the honest-to-God truth."

"You are telling the Court that Harland Jeffers knew before he and Montana were ever married that he could never have children."

"Yes."

"And we know from previous testimony given in this trial that Harland Jeffers harassed his wife, blaming her for not having children. Yet, he knew all along he would never be able to get her pregnant.

"We have also learned from previous testimony that Harland had singled Montana out to be his wife years before she even met him. He manipulated her life to make sure she married him. And now you are telling us that he even went so far as to have reconstructive surgery to hide the fact that he'd lost a testicle in an unfortunate accident, then spent the next ten years belittling and punishing her because she couldn't get pregnant."

Clara casually nodded her head to the rhythm of Phillip's recounting each fraction of Harland's whole plan. When Phillip had finished, she said, "That's right."

"Tell me, Mrs. Griffin, why?" Phillip asked. "Why would he do that?"

"Because if he admitted it, that would have made him inferior or damaged, and Harland couldn't handle that."

The courtroom grew quiet and the air thickened. Phillip looked my way, and I was sure he sensed how Clara's testimony caught me in an avalanche of realization of how deep the madness was I'd been living in. I'd been suspended on the outside of reality, looking deep into a realm of insanity. And the hard truth was, I had to be crazy to have stayed there.

I buried my head in my folded arms on the table and cried as if I'd never cried before. This all had to end soon because my fingertips were bloody and tired of holding on to the ledge.

It would be so easy to just let go and spiral downward into the black hole where the voices had been calling my name. It all had to end soon.

When both sides agreed that they had no more questions for Clara, we were dismissed for the day. Phillip helped me to my feet, and he and the guard helped me to the room where we had eaten lunch.

The guard left us alone. Phillip took me in his arms and held me tightly. "I'm so sorry, Montana," he whispered. "If I could shield you from all this, I would do it."

"How long have you known Harland was sterile?"

"I didn't know for sure. It was when I deposed Clara that I got the feeling there were things she wanted to say, but was afraid to."

We separated and took a seat next to each other on a bench. "I read her deposition over and over again until I figured out the right questions to ask without stepping over the line or leading the witness. In there on the stand, I watched her eyes the whole time. There was a light inside her that burned brighter as she revealed another layer of the truth.

"I had a strong feeling Harland couldn't have kids, but I never dreamed the explanation would be so drastic or traumatic for you." He put his arm around me and drew me to his side. "I'm really sorry about that. Will you forgive me?"

"How could I not? You've done so much to bring light to lonely, dark places in my soul. And it's like I've said all along, no matter what happens from here, I'll never forget what you've done and are still trying to do for me." I stared up into his moist warm eyes and realized his lips were moving closer to mine.

There should have been too many things swimming in my brain to even think about what it would be like for Phillip Kane to kiss me. Somehow, the black gunk from the day separated in my mind and made way for an eagerness I'd never known. I wanted to taste his lips and nothing was going to stop me.

The surprising softness of his lips on mine melted away the hard shell surrounding my heart and, for the first time since Eddie, I felt I was where I belonged.

When we separated, there was no awkwardness, no shyness. We stared into each other's eyes and months of unspoken words were silently transmitted in our gazes.

"Come on, you have to go back, and I have to get to work on my summation. I only have one more witness, and unless Donovan has something up his sleeve, which I don't think he does, we'll be ready to enter our closing argument and put it all into the hands of the jury."

"You've done an amazing job, Phillip."

"You are the one who is amazing. Let's get out of here before we both end up in trouble," he chuckled and opened the door for the guard to take me back.

Phillip's last witness was Vesta. She testified that she and I had become instant friends while living at the Spade's. And that we had a few years of estrangement until she decided there had to be something terribly wrong for me to cut off our friendship. She explained how she confronted me and after I'd admitted the truth but wouldn't leave with her, Vesta had been keeping close tabs on me.

She recounted the time she was worried about me and came to the house. She'd jimmied the back door and found me tied naked to the bed. She untied me and then tied me back exactly as Harland had left me, so when he came home at lunchtime, he wouldn't know.

She was turned over to Mr. Donovan, who approached the witness stand. "Mrs. Connor, you stated that Montana Jeffers is your best friend, and you'd do anything for her."

"That's right."

"You went to her house and tried to rescue her, but she wouldn't leave with you?"

"That's right."

"But still you continued to try to help her?"

"Of course, there isn't anything I wouldn't do for Montana."

"Would you lie for her?"

"Objection," Phillip said.

"Withdrawn. That will be all, Mrs. Connor."

Phillip had made the point that Vesta was a good friend and would do anything for me. The district attorney had also made the same point. If anyone were keeping score, those two would have offset each other.

There were no more witnesses to be called, and Mr. Donovan was more than ready to deliver his closing argument.

"Ladies and gentlemen of the jury, we certainly have had an interesting week. We've learned all about the sad life of Montana Jeffers." Mr. Donovan shook his head to emphasize the poor, dejected tone of his statement. "But you know, I'll bet each and every one of you could tell stories to compare or even surpass those you've heard in this courtroom this past week.

"Yes, it's sad that Montana was mistreated by her husband. Most women would have turned tail and run at the first sign of the deep-seated problems Harland Jeffers has been alleged to have. But for some unknown reason Montana Jeffers stayed. She stayed in spite of the horrendous treatment she'd received." Mr. Donovan moved closer to the jury.

"Why do you think that was? Could it be that it wasn't as bad as she'd like everyone to believe? Or is it possible it never happened in the first place? What would Harland have to say about those allegations if he were still alive? We can only go by the evidence presented by the defense. So let's say that Montana Jeffers was abused by her husband, and she did refuse to leave their home. The fact remains that during any of the other times she didn't take a gun and shoot him.

"So we have to ask ourselves what was different about this time. Harland Jeffers had been a player in an illegal baby market, one responsible for Montana Parsons losing her baby girl. She had been told that because of something she did, the child was dead. After years of anguishing over this, out of the clear blue sky, she receives a mysterious letter telling her that Jeffers knows where the daughter is. This leads Mrs. Jeffers to look for evidence that her daughter might still be alive and any evidence her husband might have, which we all know she found.

"Put yourself in her shoes. If a similar thing happened to you, what would you want to do? I'd probably want to take a gun and shoot him. And that's exactly what I contend happened in that bedroom on Serenity Drive the night Montana Jeffers pulled a gun and fired three shots into her husband. It was not in self-defense, as she has said, but nothing more than pure, unmitigated revenge.

"There can only be one finding in the matter. Montana Jeffers did kill Harland Jeffers in cold blood and must be found guilty of first-degree murder.

"The prosecution rests, Your Honor."

Phillip walked to the middle of the floor.

"Mr. Donovan put himself in a hypothetical situation in which none of us can picture him or ourselves living in. And why can't we fathom it? Because most of us have families we could have turned to in our time of need. Montana Jeffers had no family to turn to, and throughout the trial we heard testimony that shows Harland Jeffers singled her out probably because she was alone and had no one to turn to. Harland Jeffers stalked the woman who would eventually become his wife. He manipulated her life in ways most of us find hard to believe. But believe it or not, that's exactly what he did." Phillip looked the jurors in the eyes.

"And once he'd captured his prize, he took her home, caged her, and exacted torture in ways that would have caused a lesser woman to crack years ago. Harland beat her, told her horrible lies, degraded her, and basically made her live in fear for her life every day they were married.

"Why did he do that? I believe it was because it was his way of restoring his manhood. A manhood, which, to his way of thinking, had been taken away when he was a teenager playing football. He even went so far as to have reconstructive surgery to help give him back what he had lost.

"Harland Jeffers was incapable of accepting the fact that he could not produce children, because to do so would have meant, at least in his eyes, that he was imperfect. So drastic was his need to be virile that he blamed his wife for not giving him children. Blamed her continuously. Eventually, he told her he was glad she had not gotten pregnant because she had been responsible for her only baby's death.

"With statements like these, Harland battered Montana's heart and soul. He also went out of his way to break her mentally in order to keep her under his control."

Phillip pointed at me. "When she would try to get away, it would result in painful blows to her body. She had no one to turn to for help. Even the local police turned their back on her.

"So after ten years of unthinkable physical, mental, and emotional abuse, and with no end in sight, Montana took her life back. Did she plan to shoot Harland? Of course not. She had been abused hundreds of time. But on the night of October 14, 1977, Harland slammed her body against a hard wooden dresser and shoved her face into a drawer, all the while screaming brutal, degrading things at her. But she became stronger than Harland because she held a gun. She didn't stop to think about what would happen to her after she shot him. Because she'd broken into Harland's private drawer and discovered a dark secret, Montana Jeffers knew exactly what would happen to her if she didn't shoot him. With all probability, what awaited Montana was her death.

"Self-defense is the only verdict that fits this unfortunate incident. Montana has been in Harland's prison for ten years, and it's time she is given her freedom.

Evidently, the prosecution and the defense presented tough facts for the jury to consider. They were released for deliberation shortly after lunch on Friday afternoon. By five o'clock, they reported to the judge they had not reached a decision. Phillip seemed to think that was a good sign for us. I just wanted it to be over.

The jury was sent home for the weekend and was admonished not to discuss the trial with anyone, or watch the news, or read the newspaper if there was any coverage of the trial. With the media swarming around as they had been, a person would have had to have been living on an island not to have heard details of my trial.

In the beginning, I thought Phillip would ask for a change of venue, but when I asked him about that, he said he believed the facts of what led up to Harland's killing would speak volumes, and Phillip trusted that human nature would intervene.

I spent the weekend in my cell, updating my journal with details of the trial. I wrote about the surprises I'd gotten, like seeing Eddie, finding out Harland was sterile, and the wonderful kiss I'd shared with Phillip. I knew I was acting like a giddy schoolgirl, but it felt good to think about something other than the fate that awaited me. And that fate covered a wide spectrum.

The prosecutor had asked for a conviction of first-degree murder. Of course, Phillip had faith that I'd be found not guilty because of self-defense. I'd had five months to concentrate on nothing but what had brought me to that point in my life. In just a few more days, it would be over. Surprisingly, I wasn't nervous or apprehensive. I was amazingly calm and ready for whatever the verdict would be.

Around noon on Monday, I was taken to the courthouse. The jury was ready and waiting for me to arrive. Once we were all in our places and the formalities were out of the way, Phillip and I stood facing the forewoman. The judge asked her to read the verdict.

A guard moved into position next to me.

"We, the jury, find the defendant, Montana Inez Parsons-Jeffers, guilty of voluntary manslaughter."

I had heard the guilty verdict and immediately lost control of my legs. I dropped into the chair. That brave front I'd imagined I had all weekend deserted me and left me weak and confused. Too shaken to make my legs move, I was carried by two guards back to my cell, where I would wait four more days before sentencing.

Phillip came to see me that evening. I was allowed to visit with him for thirty minutes.

"I thought if I was found guilty it would be for first-degree murder. Voluntary manslaughter is something completely different, isn't it?" I asked Phillip.

"I had an opportunity to talk with a couple of the jurors. Their feelings were that because you took control of the situation so quickly, only sustaining the one visible bruise to your shoulder, you could have held him at gunpoint while you called for help. He had no weapon with which to fight back."

"They had no choice but to find me guilty, but why voluntary manslaughter?"

"Because they didn't feel you had time to think about the murder or to plan it out. It was an opportunity that presented itself, and you took it. Manslaughter is a lesser charge with less jail time. And," he smiled at me, "the jury has asked for leniency in the sentencing."

"What does that mean?"

"You could get six to ten years. And they are asking that you get the least amount of time. Six years, Montana."

"Six years compared to a life sentence isn't very long, is it? It's not even as long as I was married to Harland."

"It won't be a maximum security facility, either. Actually, you'll be with women a lot like yourself. And, if it's okay with you, I'd like to come visit you every chance I get."

I looked up into Phillip's face and felt honored that I had someone like him in my life.

Epilogue

March 24, 1984

THAT WAS SIX YEARS AGO TODAY, AND PHILLIP DID MORE THAN visit me *once in a while*. He drove two hours every Sunday to visit me since the day I'd been transported to my present home.

I glance at my watch for the tenth time in so many minutes and hols out my hand to look at the finger where Phillip will be placing a wedding ring later in the afternoon.

Vesta had taken care of all the plans for a small, intimate wedding at her house. Somehow she'd come up with quite a guest list. I had never realized how many people cared about me.

I don't think much about Harland anymore. I don't wake up shaking from nightmares that he'd somehow escaped his grave and come back to get me. Those bad dreams had gradually faded and were replaced with good ones about the life that lay ahead of me with Phillip Kane. During the past six years, he'd managed to have two battered women's shelters erected. One was named Virginia's House, and the other Montana's House.

Once I am breathing free air, I will be running the houses while he continues with his law practice. I'm not sure I am capable of running a facility like that, but, as usual, Phillip has more faith in me than I do. He assured me on every one of his weekly visits that I would be a natural when it comes to understanding and guiding the women who would come to our shelters. God, how I want to do that, and with Phillip's guidance, I will.

My world is perfect, except for finding Berryanne. Recently, I'd decided I had to let her memory go. If she could have been found, Phillip would have done that. Through Ina we learned that James Cullen had been killed in a car accident when Berryanne was three years old. Grace Cullen had remarried, and her husband had adopted Berryanne. The trail to finding her ended when James Cullen died. And even though Phillip tried everything he could, he never found her.

At long last, the guards have come to escort me from the prison compound. Through the chain-link fence I see Phillip waiting with his big, beautiful smile that always warms my heart. In a motion that surprises me, the two guards each hug me and wish me luck. They'd both been with me for several years, and their actions bring tears to my eyes.

I take that first step beyond the gate, and then I run into Phillip's arms. He lifts me off the ground and holds me to him. Those first moments with him are etched into my heart forever.

"I love you, Montana. I've waited so long for this day. I'm not sure if it's real or just one of the dreams I have every night of you."

"I couldn't have made it to this point if you hadn't been here waiting for me. I love you, Phillip. I always will. You are my soul mate. The one I'd searched for in all the wrong places. This time, my dear Phillip, I got it right."

Our first long, passionate kiss covers me like a warm summer wave that comes in and then rolls back out, flooding me with exhilaration and longing for more.

Just as Phillip lowers me down so my feet will once more touch the ground, a taxi cab pulls to a stop next to us. A beautiful young woman gets out of the backseat. While Phillip pays the driver, the woman lifts a baby from the cab.

She has long, shiny brown hair and eyes that make me think of a time long ago. While I stand silently staring at every inch of the young woman's face, Phillip takes the baby from her arms. Bewildered, I glance at Phillip, who still has that beautiful smile brightening his face.

"Montana, I'd like you to meet Sherry Fiennes. She's your daughter."

Phillip's words jar me in a way that keeps me from understanding them.

"I'm sorry," I say. "I didn't understand you."

"I found your daughter. Her name is Sherry now."

For several breathless moments the earth stopped turning. I can't believe I'm awake. I fear reaching for my daughter. In all the nightly dreams I've had of her, she disappeared before I could wrap my arms around her. I didn't want this to be just another dream.

"Hi," Sherry says, and puts her arms around me.

The warmth of her embrace relieves my fear. "You're real. You're not a dream." I can barely speak.

It takes a moment before I can move, but when it all sinks in, and I realize I have my baby right there with me, I pull her into my embrace and hold on for dear life.

"I can't believe you're really here." I lean back to look at her again. Those eyes I'd recognized were just like my mother's. "You're beautiful," I cry.

"So are you," she says.

I look at Phillip, who also has tears streaming down his cheeks. "Thank you," I whisper to him. "Thank you with all my heart." I still cling tightly to my daughter.

When we separate, Phillip hands me the baby. "Here."

"Oh my God, do I have a grandbaby, too?"

The little bundle wiggles. I clutch it close to me.

Sherry nods. "A granddaughter, to be more exact."

My heart pounded so loudly surely it will wake my wonderful granddaughter. I ease back the blanket and, for a moment, I am twenty years younger, looking down at my own daughter's tiny face.

"She's perfect, just like you were." I look up at Sherry. I can't believe she is right there with me.

"Let's go home where we can have a long visit." Phillip opens his car door, and Sherry gets into the backseat.

Home. A real home with the family I've always dreamed of. "This is the happiest day I've ever known. I'm so glad you're all here for the beginning of my new life." I take one more peek at the precious child sleeping in my arms.

I ask Sherry, "What's her name?"

She looks up at me with more tears streaming down her face. "When Phillip found me a couple of months ago, I was very sick and couldn't travel. I was so sick I hadn't even picked out a name for my baby. He told me the story of my birth, and how much you love me. As soon as they handed me my little girl, I knew what I wanted to name her."

A sob jabs hard in my chest. I had prayed for years to hold Berryanne again, and I know even before Sherry speaks the name that my prayers have been answered. I look at the baby again and say, "I love you, Berryanne."

photo by Studio 16

D.J. Wilson

Dolores was born in Morgantown, West Virginia. At age eleven, she was transplanted to Tampa, Florida. She and her husband, Richard, love traveling in their motor home, where Dolores enjoys one of her favorite pastimes, visiting and researching historical sites, but she says it's always nice to come back home, where she can spend time with her grown children and grandchildren. She is an avid reader, but also enjoys bluegrass music and a multitude of crafts.

Dolores lives in Jacksonville, Florida, with her husband and beagle, Buster.

www.doloresjwilson.com

First, there is a River

Kathy Steffen

A family conceals a cruel secret.

Emma Perkins' life appears idyllic. Her husband, Jared, is a hardworking farmer and a dependable neighbor. But Emma knows intimately the brutality prowling beneath her husband's façade. When he sends their children away, Emma's life unravels.

A woman seeks her spirit.

Deep in despair, Emma seeks refuge aboard her uncle's riverboat, the Spirit of the River. She travels through a new world filled with colorful characters: captains, mates, the rich, the working class, moonshiners, prostitutes, and Gage-the Spirit's reclusive engineer. Scarred for life from a riverboat explosion, Gage's insight into heartache draws him to Emma, and as they heal together, they form a deep and unbreakable bond. Emma learns to trust that anything is possible, including reclaiming her children and facing her husband.

A man seeks revenge.

Jared Perkins makes a journey of his own. Determined to bring his wife home and teach her the lesson of her life, Jared secretly follows the Spirit. His rage burns cold as he plans his revenge for everyone on board.

Against the immense power of the river, the journey of the Spirit will change the course of their lives forever.

ISBN# 9781932815931
Trade Paperback
US $14.95 / CDN $18.95
Available Now
www.kathysteffen.com

IN STEREO WHERE AVAILABLE

BECKY ANDERSON

Phoebe Kassner didn't set out to be a 29-year-old virgin, but that's how it's worked out. And, having just been dumped by her boyfriend, she doesn't see that situation changing anytime soon.

Meanwhile, her twin sister Madison—aspiring actress, small-time model, and queen of the short attention span—has just been eliminated on the first round of Singing Sensation.

Things aren't looking so great for either of them. But when Phoebe receives a surprise voice mail from some guy named Jerry, victim of a fake phone number written on a cocktail napkin, she takes pity on him and calls, setting in motion a serendipitous love story neither of them ever saw coming.

And suddenly Madison's got a romance of her own going, as one of twelve women competing for two men on a ruthless, over-the-top reality show. As Phoebe falls in love with the jilted high school English teacher who never intended to call her in the first place, Madison's falling in love, too—after a fashion—clawing and fighting her way through a tide of adorable blondes. Could it get any crazier?

Stay tuned . . .

ISBN# 9781933836201
US $15.95 / CDN $19.95
Trade Paperback
Available Now

CHASTISED FOR NOT COOPERATING with the oil company giant New World Petroleum, zoologist Cassidy Lowell is reassigned from the jungles of the Niger Delta to Yellowstone National Park, where wolves are disappearing. Jake Anderson, Special Forces operative, is working within the shadows of Cassidy's organization, Zoological Ecological Biological Research Agency. His mission? To determine the threatening connection between ZEBRA and NWP.

An alarming genetic mutation of the parvovirus is discovered: CPV-19: human parvovirus merged with canine. And the virus is loose in Yellowstone. Murder, execution, and deadly helicopter rides lead Jake and Cassidy down a road rife with double-crossing and an underlying plot that forces them back to the Niger Delta and into the heart of NWP.

This is the twenty-first-century gold rush— welcome to the dark side!

ISBN# 9781934755556
Hardcover Fiction
US $24.95 / CDN $27.95
MARCH 2009
www.juliekorzenko.com

Julie Korzenko

From the author of *First, there is a River*

Jasper Mountain

Kathy Steffen

**Two lost souls struggle to find their way in
the unforgiving West of 1873 . . .**

Jack Buchanan, a worker at the Jasper Mining Company, is sure of his place in the outside world, but has lost his faith, hope, and heart to the tragedy of a fire.

Foreign born and raised, Milena Shabanov flees from a home she loves to the strange and barbaric America. A Romani blessed with "the sight," she is content in the company of visions and spirit oracles, but finds herself lost and alone in a brutal mining town with little use for women.

Surrounded by inhumane working conditions at the mine, senseless death, and overwhelming greed, miners begin disappearing and the officers of the mine don't care.

Tempers flare and Jack must decide where he stands: with the officers and mining president—Victor Creely—to whom Jack owes his life, or with the miners, whose lives are worth less to the company than pack animals. Milena, sensing deep despair and death in a mining town infested with restless spirits, searches for answers to the workers' disappearances. But she can't trust anyone, especially not Jack Buchanan, a man haunted by his own past.

ISBN# 9781933836584
Trade Paperback / Historical Fiction
US $15.95 / CDN $17.95
NOVEMBER 2008
www.kathysteffen.com

THE
FRONT PORCH
PROPHET

RAYMOND L. ATKINS

What do a trigger-happy bootlegger with pancreatic cancer, an alcoholic helicopter pilot who is afraid to fly, and a dead guy with his feet in a camp stove have in common?

What are the similarities between a fire department that cannot put out fires, a policeman who has a historic cabin fall on him from out of the sky, and an entire family dedicated to a variety of deceased authors?

Where can you find a war hero named Termite with a long knife stuck in his liver, a cook named Hoghead who makes the world's worst coffee, and a supervisor named Pillsbury who nearly gets hung by his employees?

Sequoyah, Georgia is the answer to all three questions. They arise from the relationship between A. J. Longstreet and his best friend since childhood, Eugene Purdue. After a parting of ways due to Eugene's inability to accept the constraints of adulthood, he reenters A.J.'s life with terminal cancer and the dilemma of executing a mercy killing when the time arrives.

Take this gripping journey to Sequoyah, Georgia and witness A.J.'s battle with mortality, euthanasia, and his adventure back to the past and people who made him what he is—and helps him make the decision that will alter his life forever.

ISBN# 9781933836386
Hardcover Fiction
US $25.95 / CDN $28.95
JULY 2008

For more information
about other great titles from
Medallion Press, visit
www.medallionpress.com